What Readers Are S~~aying about~~
The Other W~~ay Home series.~~

A Journey by Chance

"*A Journey by Chance* is a wonderfully moving book about Dr. Gina Philips, a veterinarian afraid to practice again after being injured by an elephant under her care, and Brady Olafsson, a bestselling Christian author. Gina visits Valley Oaks, Brady's hometown, for her cousin's wedding and is determined to leave as soon as it is over. Brady is to be her escort during the wedding ceremony, and they have to spend much time together. Even though both fight the growing attraction each feels for the other, God's plan for their futures prevails in the end."

—*Christian Library Journal*

"This is the first book by Sally John I have read. I loved it so much I couldn't stop reading! I learned so much about forgiveness and love. I can't wait to read the rest of her books."

—*Amanda Davis*

After All These Years

"Well done!!! It was a great book...I enjoyed it and read it in a 24-hour period. Thanks so much for writing a story filled with so much love and grace. It sure showed me that I need to take the blinders off. That Christians aren't perfect, just SOOOOOOOO forgiven."

—*Denice Leavitt*

Just to See You Smile

"These books are truly inspiring and I felt drawn closer to God myself after reading them. All of the books in Sally John's The Other Way Home series are filled with the wonderful story of God's love for us and also let us know that no matter how bad things may seem, life is full of second chances and many surprises as we walk along the paths of our life's journey. When we have faith in God's wisdom and trust Him to direct our paths, there is no limit to what can be achieved in our lives."

—*Christian Library Journal*

The Winding Road Home

"I couldn't put this book down because I wanted to know how it would end. It was a touching story of forgiveness and healing. It touched me personally and I know it will touch others personally who have encountered similar situations. Kate was Tanner's personal cheerleader, and she reminded me that God is our personal cheerleader, always encouraging us to continue on. I would give Sally's books a 10. I think that she shows the way to salvation in a simple way for all to see. I think it would bring any nonbeliever to question why they aren't believing in Jesus Christ as their personal Lord and Savior."

—*Patty Blake*

"As usual, Sally's story is captivating. I had tears in my eyes! The characters were so colorful, especially Adele and Kate. I could visualize everything about them. I truly wish this series would never end. I'd like to get to know everyone who lives in Valley Oaks!"

—*Deborah Piccurelli*

In a Heartbeat series:

In a Heartbeat
"GREAT book. I don't normally read fiction but won this book from a local Christian radio station. My daughter read it first, as I was in the middle of another book, and finished it in two days. It's a 'can't put it down' book. It's my turn now, and I have stayed up way into the late hours reading. I can't wait for follow-up books in this series. Great work, Sally!!"

—*Lisa Cunningham*

Flash Point
"Sally John does such a tremendous job creating believable settings and genuine characters. Gabe and Terri are delightful, and you find yourself rooting for them as they attempt to make sense of their world while following their faith and facing tragedy. I laughed and cried right along with them."

—*The Romance Readers Connection*

"Sally John's characters show us how to live God-honoring, fruitful lives in this broken, less-than-ideal world. They falter and stumble, but along the path they show us the freedom of trusting God and of a healthy emotional life, and drop these truths lightly into our hearts. I may begin her books anticipating another take-me-away story, but soon into the journey, gentle truth seeps into my soul and I find nourishment for my real-world living."

—*Margo Balsis*

MOMENT OF *Truth*

SALLY JOHN

HARVEST HOUSE PUBLISHERS

EUGENE, OREGON

This novel is a work of fiction. Names, characters, places, and incidents are either the product of the author's imagination or are used fictitiously. It is the intent of the author and publisher that all events, locales, organizations, and persons portrayed herein be viewed as fictitious.

MOMENT OF TRUTH
Copyright © 2005 by Sally John
Published by Harvest House Publishers
Eugene, Oregon 97402
www.harvesthousepublishers.com

Library of Congress Cataloging-in-Publication Data

John, Sally, 1951-
  Moment of truth / Sally John.
      p. cm— (In a heartbeat; bk. 3)
  ISBN 0-7369-1315-7 (pbk.)
  1. Policewomen—Fiction. 2. Police—Illinois—Chicago—Fiction. 3. Undercover operations—Fiction. 4 Chicago (Ill.)—Fiction. 5. Soup kitchens—Fiction. 6. Clergy—Fiction. I. Title. II. Series.
  PS3560.O323M66 2005
  813'.6—dc22   2004021025

For Norma,
in search of a home

In memory of
Arlene John (1926–1997) and
Wayne Carlson (1926–2001),
already there

Acknowledgments

As always, my stories are the result of a group effort. I am grateful for those who so willingly offered their expertise. Many thanks to:

Sue Laue, dear friend and Chicago connection.

Deborah Piccurelli and Rebecca Groff, fellow writers with inside tracks to police work.

Rhonda Roush, Rev. Steven McClaskey, and Trinity Episcopal Parish, Rock Island, Illinois, who provided material details for my fictional church.

Trisha Owens, motorcycle enthusiast.

Elizabeth John, number one daughter and research expert on any subject.

Everyone at Harvest House Publishers, who all encourage me with a smile each step of the way as well as superbly edit, design, market, sell, and distribute this work.

Also my thanks to those who assisted in other ways:

Tracy John, number one daughter-in-law, brainstorming expert, and helpful reviewer.

Dave Buzzell, giver of music.

Marilee Proulx, giver of timely story suggestions.

My readers, givers of great encouragement.

Kim Moore of Harvest House, editor and friend, giver of trustworthy editorial advice.

Tim, giver of everything else I need.

And where we love is home,
Home that our feet may leave, but not our hearts.
The chain may lengthen, but it never parts.

—Oliver Wendell Holmes

There's no place like home. There's no place like home.

—Dorothy, *The Wizard of Oz*

Then they called to Yahweh in their trouble
and he rescued them...
bringing them...safe to the port
they were bound for.

PSALM 107:28,30

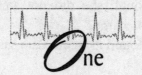

One

"Granny." Cara Fleming uttered the name through clenched teeth. She heard a distinctly edgy tone, evidence of the furious words that stomped impatiently in her chest. They crashed about, scuffling for release like a rodeo horse against fence boards at the starting gate.

Not exactly a good situation for a police detective at the scene of a crime.

She closed her eyes. It didn't help. The sight remained: Tiny Rubyann Calloway, the 77-year-old friend she called Granny, sat in an upholstered chair, her head against a crocheted doily. An oxygen mask cruelly marred the peaceful repose. It mashed tight, snow white curls and pinched skin the color of mocha and soft as a downy feather.

Kneeling alongside the chair, Cara clutched the woman's hand and tried to pray. The horse only kicked again.

"Cara." The steady voice belonged to Terri Schuman.

It cut through her agitated thoughts. She opened her eyes and looked over at her friend. The navy blue-clad paramedic knelt on the other side of the chair, her gloved hands on Rubyann's arm.

No. It was the *victim's* arm. If Cara couldn't divorce herself from the personal side of the situation, she might as well turn in her badge.

She unclenched her jaw. "What?" The restive tone was still there.

"You look a little flushed. Why don't I check your blood pressure too?" Though she did not smile, her dark eyes sparkled. "No extra charge."

The subtle hint found its mark. Cara sat back on her heels. "I'm okay."

Terri's eyebrows disappeared beneath her bangs. She wasn't buying that answer, but she turned her attention back to Rubyann.

The other medic, a 20-something guy of slight build, stood behind the chair. He blinked rapidly in Cara's direction, his Adam's apple bobbing conspicuously.

She wondered exactly how new he was to the profession.

With a conscious effort, she inhaled a deep breath and let it out slowly. The warmth in her face receded. She felt strands of hair tickle at her cheek and smoothed them back into the bun at the nape of her neck, repositioning bobby pins. It was a nervous motion she would not have noticed except for the sharp poke of a hairpin. Most days, Cara did not make nervous motions.

Behind her Marcus Calloway breathed fire. She knew it for a fact without turning, and she wasn't about to turn. A glance at her partner would only reignite her own smoldering heat. Rubyann was *his* grandmother, not hers. He had dibs on spouting while she was tagged with the duty of remaining calm and sedate.

"Granny." His growling voice, usually a melodious tenor, shot over the back of Cara's head. "Tell me again why you didn't call 911?"

Cara should have told him to relax, but calm and sedate hadn't quite taken hold of her own demeanor yet.

Rubyann appeared the least ruffled of them all. When not weighted down in her armchair by emergency medical equipment and the looming presence of two medics and two cops, she was as spry as a robin. She pulled aside the mask and glared, her maple syrup-colored eyes devoid of their usual sweetness. "Now, Marcus, why would I bother that nice dispatch lady when my grandson and his partner are detectives with the Chicago Police Department?" Her weakened voice hadn't lost its matter-of-fact delivery. "And I know both their cell phone numbers like the back of my hand?"

He grumbled something about how they had to call 911 anyway for the ambulance.

Cara rolled forward onto her knees again. "Granny, can you tell us what happened?"

Now Terri glared in her direction.

She ignored her friend. Though Rubyann had given an account when she and Marcus arrived on the scene, they heard it with distraught ears and totally missed the details. The woman probably should have called 911 instead of them.

"Rubyann." Terri patted her arm. "Hon, you don't have to talk."

"Oh, I'm fine now that you're all here. I was a little upset after that young man barged his way in when I opened the door."

A little upset? The guy had knocked her to the floor and torn apart the bungalow. Cara glanced around the small living room. End tables were overturned. Sofa cushions and a broken lamp lay on the carpet. She noted the wrought iron bars across the windows. They had offered no protection from an intruder who arrived in broad daylight and rang the doorbell. "A little upset" hardly seemed an appropriate response.

Rubyann went on, her tone no different than if she were explaining a cookie recipe. "He just lives down the street."

"You recognized him?" Cara's voice hit squeak level.

"Yes. I told you that, honey-child. He was wearing a ski mask, but—"

"Gran!" Marcus sputtered. "It's September! It's eighty degrees! Why would you open—"

"Hold it!" Terri raised a hand. "We're outta here. She's going to the hospital right now."

Rubyann sighed. "He's going to bust a gut if I don't finish."

Terri locked eyes with Cara, in essence telling her to get a grip and intervene.

Cara highly respected the medic. They had met about a year ago when their paths crossed during a police investigation. A friendship sprang naturally between them, founded in a common faith as well as a down-to-earth, practical attitude. The ensuing months had thrown Terri's life into a major upheaval. As Cara helped her through it, their bond of trust deepened. Terri would listen to her opinion. As long as her voice didn't sound like a monkey's.

Cara spread the fingers of one hand, a silent plea for five minutes. They needed more information, and the sooner they gathered it, the sooner they could go after the bad guy. Surely a few more moments was not too much to ask of Rubyann. After all, the woman had picked herself up from the floor and calmly phoned her grandson.

Terri made an obvious show of checking her watch and gave a half nod.

That meant they had exactly five minutes and not a second more. If push came to shove, Cara knew she and Marcus were no match for Terri Schuman.

Late that afternoon, Cara sat in the passenger seat of the parked car and stared through the windshield at a rundown, two-story duplex. Located a few blocks from Rubyann's house, the narrow street was lined with vehicles, tenements, and more duplexes.

"Marcus, we've got to get Granny out of this neighborhood." She glanced at her partner behind the wheel.

He nodded. "Maybe she'll listen to us now, after this incident." A steely tone had replaced his overwrought one, lowering his voice to what Cara considered threat level.

She looked at him again.

Oh yes. He was definitely at threat level.

What Marcus lacked in height, he more than made up for in physical strength and—when he chose to—in attitude. A lightweight olive green sport coat easily concealed his gun, but not his muscular shoulders and chest. His face, the skin a medium brown color like his grandmother's, had grown taut and lost its boyish hint of roundness. He kept his hair so short it was a mere shadow on his scalp, a style that further hid any trace of gentleness. In profile she saw no light shining through his deep brown eyes. His long, curved lashes did nothing to soften the chilling effect. He sat still as a rock, but the air around him vibrated like the ticking of a time bomb.

She resumed her observation of the house and murmured casually, "You're not going fanatic on me, are you, Calloway?"

He didn't reply. After a long moment he shifted in his seat and the tension eased. "I'm fine."

"I don't want you shooting the guy the second he opens the door."

"I promise to wait until his eyes are on my star." He referred to his police badge.

"Glad to hear that."

"How about you, Cucumber? You up for this?"

The nickname struck its mark. Cara's mellow demeanor had earned her the reputation of being cool and composed. That translated into "Ice Lady" or "Cool as a Cucumber" Fleming. Obviously she wasn't exhibiting her habitual traits. She felt his eyes on her and turned.

He said, "You mess with your hair one more time and I'm going in alone."

She lowered her hands and smoothed her khaki slacks. The blend of cotton and linen did not live up to its wrinkle-free promise. Not that she cared. Comfort and practicality won out over appearance. Only two things mattered when it came to clothing. She needed a breathable fabric in the Chicago heat and a jacket large enough to make the gun holster and bulletproof vest somewhat inconspicuous.

"Marcus." She swallowed the unglued, whiny tone and tried again. "It's Granny."

"Yeah." He gazed at the street again. Their eye contact seldom lasted beyond a split second. A combination of training, habit, and experience kept them vigilant to the environment no matter where they were. "Tell me something I don't know."

"I may shoot him before you do."

Marcus grunted.

Okay, so they were both too personally involved with the situation. At least they were waiting for backup to arrive before charging into the house, guns ablaze at the kid who had terrorized Rubyann.

Cara prayed, mouth closed and eyes open. For as long as she could remember, she often prayed in silence, eyes wide. Too many dreadful things happened when she shut them. Going into police work had been a natural choice for her. She suspected she had developed the art of quiet watchfulness while still a babe looking through the bars of her crib.

Now, focused on the job at hand, she addressed at some deep level the reality she called Jesus. *Lord, hide me in the shadow of Your wings. Let Your peace reign in me. Keep us from taking vengeance into our own hands.*

Marcus swore loudly.

His exclamation was not an unusual close to her prayers. She trusted God understood when she couldn't quite get off an "Amen."

"What?" She heard the sound of approaching sirens and groaned. "Oh no."

They had requested backup to arrive without fanfare. In that particular neighborhood it was bad enough to just sit in their car. The boxy dark gray vehicle had neither a rack of red, white, and blue lights on its roof nor the blue "Chicago Police" lettering along its sides, but unmarked did not mean unrecognizable. It reeked of official business. Even if the telltale license plate prefix weren't in view, no one would mistake the car as belonging to Mr. Joe Average. She felt like a deer with a bull's-eye painted on its flank, surrounded by a pack of camouflaged, trigger-happy hunters.

The siren noise increased. It was too late to remedy the situation.

Marcus was on the radio. "We're going in," he informed dispatch and opened his door.

A rush of adrenaline tore through Cara, at once heightening her senses and dulling the image of Rubyann strapped to a gurney.

～

Gaining entry into the house was not a problem. They knocked on the front door and Lathan Miller opened it.

Marcus stormed inside and had the teenager cuffed before completing, "You're under arrest."

A shouting match ensued. Patting him down, Marcus recited rights as the boy yelled denials. They hadn't even accused him of anything yet.

The hair on the back of Cara's neck prickled. She sensed someone else in the house.

They stood in a living room that resembled Rubyann's in neatness and cleanliness. Evidently the boy lived with parents who respected property, a trait that had bypassed their son.

Lathan was a slight, short person. Rubyann said she identified him by his size, a missing front tooth, and a pierced nostril from which protruded a topaz stud, visible even through the stretchy knit of the ski mask. The only thing she couldn't describe was the gun he pointed at her.

Marcus now pointed his at Lathan and ordered him to be quiet. The kid was high on something and uncooperative. The need to support his drug habit would have driven him to an easy target like Rubyann to steal money and goods. Depending on his drug of choice and how attached he was to it, her fifty dollars in cash and VCR could have paid his way through a few days, maybe more.

Her own weapon raised, Cara moved quickly into the adjoining kitchen. She knew Marcus had an eye on the staircase in the living room, but she was nowhere near a level of comfort. There were too many variables: nooks and crannies, a basement, an upstairs, and a wild kid. Relief filled her as she saw a uniformed officer hurry past a back window.

She opened the kitchen door and motioned for him to accompany her downstairs. They made fast work of searching a tidy laundry room and a game room with a Ping-Pong table.

He followed her up the steps. "Hey, sorry about the sirens. We hit a traffic jam about three blocks away."

She nodded. "Turned out all right." So far. She scratched the back of her neck.

In the living room another officer hauled Lathan, still shouting, out the door. The house instantly quieted. Marcus held a piece of paper, the search warrant that probably meant as much to the boy as the recitation of his rights. No matter. They played by the rules.

She and her partner went upstairs and systematically took turns searching rooms while the other officer stood guard in the hallway. One room obviously belonged to Lathan; it wasn't tidy. The third and last bedroom door was half open. Cara pushed it with her foot.

And there, across the room, was the source of her tingling sensation. A little girl, about eight or nine, sat in the center of a full-sized bed atop a frilly pink-and-white comforter.

Like Cara, her arms were outstretched and between her hands she held a gun.

It was pointed directly at Cara's chest.

Two

"Whoa, sweetheart!" Cara said gently with a smile and spread her arms wide, letting her finger slip away from the trigger. "I thought you were a bad guy." She locked eyes with large, frightened ones barely visible behind the pewter cylinder of a handgun. "I'm just going to put my gun away, all right?"

The girl only blinked in response. Given the circumstances, her hands were incredibly steady.

Cara chatted in a nonchalant tone and slowly lowered her arms until her gun pointed at the floor. "I'm switching on the safety here. Don't want to accidentally shoot myself in the foot. Here's where I keep my gun." Not once shifting her eyes from the girl's, she lifted aside her jacket and slid the weapon into its holster on her waist. "See? It's put away."

Marcus stood off to the side, in her peripheral vision but hidden from the girl. Cara sensed his anxiety. He didn't know what she was facing, but he knew her well enough to decipher that she needed to gain control of the situation without him intervening.

Barely giving herself time to breathe in between sentences, she kept up a steady stream of words. "That's a pretty big gun you've got there."

Marcus inhaled sharply.

"You can lay it down on the bed if you want, hon. I don't want you to get hurt. Sometimes those things go off when we don't want them to. I'll just stand right here. I won't come in your room."

Thoughts flashed through Cara's mind. Between terror and the heavy weapon, the girl would not be able to hold her position much longer. If she managed to shoot, the recoil would throw her flat on her back...but not before the bullet's impact rammed Cara against the wall. Of course, if the gun rose a few centimeters, the bullet would miss her safety vest and hitting the wall would be the least of Cara's worries.

"Are you Lathan's sister?"

A slight nod. Her tiny build resembled the boy's.

"I bet he's a good big brother. He probably gave you that gun so you could protect yourself. My name's Cara. What's yours, sweetheart?"

Her lips parted, but no sound came. She tried again. "Denesha," she whispered hoarsely.

"Well, hi, Denesha. It's nice to meet you. I like your braids with those beads. Does your mama fix your hair?"

Another half nod.

"Let me guess how old you are. I bet you're eleven." She guessed high, hoping the flattery would encourage the girl to open up.

Denesha shook her head.

"Twelve?"

"Nine."

"Really? You're such a pretty young lady. Hey, I have an older brother too. He used to tease me all the time. Does Lathan tease you?"

She nodded and the gun wobbled.

"Sometimes he would tease so bad I'd cry. But he was nice too. He even drew pictures with me and I love to draw. He got sick, though. He talked crazy and he would sleep a lot. Maybe Lathan does that?"

Another blink.

"My brother had to go to the hospital. He didn't want to, so the police had to help us. I think Lathan is sick in the same way. We need to take him to the hospital. I know the police car out there is scary, but I ride in it all the time." The window faced the front yard. Denesha probably saw her brother placed in the squad car, hands cuffed behind his back.

One large tear slid down the girl's cheek.

"I promise you, we won't hurt him. Can I sit by you?" She inched her way forward until she reached the bedside. "How about I take this, sweetheart? You don't need it now."

Denesha let go of the gun as Cara wrapped her hand around it. A glance told her the safety catch was off. She sat and enfolded the girl into a one-armed hug, holding the weapon out behind herself. When she felt Marcus take it, she hugged with both arms, grateful that her vest was absorbing tears instead of bullets.

~⁓~

In spite of the ice water she sometimes thought ran through her veins, Cara could hug a hurting child or distraught victim at the drop of a hat. With Marcus it was a different story. The most physically demonstrative she ever became with her partner was to touch his forearm. In turn he—now and then—patted her head. Four years of working together and of practically sharing a grandmother had not tumbled the professional wall between them nor changed either of their reserved natures.

Which was one reason Cara especially appreciated Renae Bishop. Marcus's girlfriend was a psychology professor, former model, 5'10", and so beautiful it didn't matter she wore her black curls nearly as short as an Army recruit's. Her most endearing quality was her ability to sense the need for hugs and then to freely dispense them. She had walked into the hospital waiting room and flung her arms around Cara.

They sat now on orange vinyl chairs, drinking coffee-machine gunk out of paper cups while Marcus paced. Rubyann had suffered a broken wrist in the fall and was in recovery, not yet ready for visitors.

Renae turned to Cara. "I assume you stayed with the little girl until her mother arrived?" The psychologist knew her well.

"Of course."

Renae shook her head. "How do you do that? Look down the barrel of a gun and not totally lose control?"

The woman's low, well-modulated voice always captivated Cara. "You're fishing for class material."

Renae laughed. "I never have to go far, what with you two always providing some new slant on warped personalities."

"You owe us for that textbook I know you're writing." She smiled. "But I should pay you for these counseling sessions."

"That makes us even. Seriously, how did you handle it?"

Marcus slowed and patted Cara's head. "Miss Cucumber."

Cara raised a brow. "Or queen of warped personalities."

He chuckled and continued his nervous pacing.

Renae said, "No, Cara, you're not warped. You're just different. It's people like these children with guns who are warped before they have a chance not to be. That confounds me."

"Denesha was just a scared little girl. I'm the police. I'm it. Who else am I going to send in? Marcus? Ha. I don't think so. And I'm certainly not going to shoot her. So I put my gun away and we talk."

Marcus grunted. "And make up stories. You don't have a brother."

"So I took a little editorial license."

He stopped again and stared at her from across the room. Comprehension dawned on his face. "He was one of your mother's boyfriends."

She shrugged. "There were two I liked. He was one of them."

"What was his drug of choice?"

"Heroin." She turned back to Renae. "Anyway, they'll all get help. The mother suspected Lathan was involved with a gang, but she didn't want to admit it. Dad's not in the picture. She has a good job and provides well."

Marcus said, "According to her, she never stepped foot in the kid's room. Had no idea of the drugs and guns stashed under his bed. Just easier to ignore. Granny never ignored anything about me." There was bitterness in his voice, and he shook his head. "The DA will make a deal. If Lathan turns stool pigeon, he gets off and we might, *might*, get a small piece of the puzzle, like the name of the dealer half a step above him."

"You didn't think life was fair, did you?" Cara addressed herself as well as him. Rubyann's attacker would not get his just desserts. The thought of forgiving him turned her stomach.

～

Late that night, pager and phones turned off, Cara soaked in a bubble bath. By the light of a dozen candles, she read from the biography of a missionary. Winnie the Pooh would call it a "sustaining" book, the kind that comforted and encouraged. Like the bear stuck in a rabbit hole, she felt squeezed from all sides. Her emotions were too big to fit within herself.

A mug of herbal tea sat on the edge of the tub, its scents of cinnamon, chamomile, and licorice mingling with the bath oil's lavender. Strands of Mozart floated from the radio, compliments of the Chicago Symphony.

The therapy was cheaper and far healthier than strong drink or narcotics. Other familiar words interrupted the ones she read, and a tune took shape, pushing aside the Mozart. The song came from a favorite CD. *Never let me grow so strong my heart cannot perceive Your hand at work, spilling forth the mercy You've placed within so others might receive.*

She closed her eyes.

It was part of the therapy.

Never let me grow so strong. Never.

Dear Lord, melt the ice water in these veins. Soften my heart.

She had already thanked God Rubyann wasn't hurt more seriously, Lathan was taken into custody without major incident, the gun did not go off in Denesha's hand. She thanked Him yet again for her own childhood, fodder for that story which spoke to the little girl's heart and defused the situation. She even thanked Him for the ice water. Without it, she would not survive a day on the street as a police detective.

The fact she loved her work puzzled Cara to no end. Yes, it came easily and naturally, fitting her personality and convictions like Cinderella's foot in the glass slipper. But that necessary ice water threatened to obliterate her heart at times. A heart required warm blood to function. How could a follower of Jesus serve others with an automatic ice maker in place of a viable, beating organ?

And so she fed her soul. She read the Bible and *The Book of Common Prayer* and true stories of faithful people. She made time to be still, and she soothed her senses with water, candles, and quiet music. She regularly helped out in soup kitchens and shelters for the homeless. She conscientiously cared for others and hoped the giving would defrost the freezer and melt all those ice cubes.

May I never grow so strong my heart cannot perceive Your hand.

Her strength did not lie in any innate ability to be as cool as a cucumber. Rather, it was in the One who had the power to still move her heart.

Tears seeped through her eyelashes.

It was part of the therapy.

~

"Granny, I'm serious." Cara sat on the hospital bed, holding Rubyann's right hand, the one not encased in plaster. "You can live with me until we find you an apartment."

"Honey-child, I appreciate the offer." Her deep brown eyes twinkled. "But the last thing you or Marcus or Renae need is this crippled old woman disrupting your lives. It's been settled. I can move into Essie's this afternoon."

"But she's your least favorite sibling."

"She's the only one who doesn't live in a nursing home. She's the only one who can take in a roommate."

"But she's way out in the suburbs, so far from your church and friends."

"Cara." She pressed her hand. "Into every life a little rain must fall. The sun will shine again. You know that as well as anyone."

Rubyann Calloway always entered through the back door of Cara's heart. Rather than knock, she simply appeared. In the early days, when they first met, Cara would jump and feel annoyed at the intrusion. But that was four years ago. Now Rubyann slipped in like a favorite neighbor bearing home-made cinnamon rolls.

"Oh, Granny. Haven't you seen enough rain for one life-time?"

"Long as I'm on this earth, it's going to rain. Now don't you go feeling sorry for me. God's walking right beside me. That is, if He's not carrying me. And you know that too as well as anyone. Right?"

Her friend's words brought to mind the circuitous route Cara had followed over the past 38 years. She appreciated the advantage of being able to look backward and see how God indeed had carried her through storms. She had weath-ered a drug-addicted mother, being stalked, living on the streets, and moving from Seattle to Los Angeles to Chicago with various stops in between. The sun had indeed dispelled the clouds. Against all odds she became a functioning member of society, graduating from college and serving as a police officer.

"Yes, Granny, I know that."

The woman's lips bunched together, and she nodded in satisfaction, the epitome of an old sage.

Cara knew the look. This was when the neighbor removed the foil cover from that pan of hot rolls, releasing the lus-ciously combined scents of yeast, sugar, cinnamon, and caramel which promised a taste of heaven...soon...right after the knife cut one roll away from the batch.

From the moment Marcus introduced them, Rubyann showered Cara with love. She called her "honey-child" and, little by little, taught her how to see that winding route through God's eyes. Even as a child Cara had recognized His presence in her life, but Rubyann revealed the boundless expanse of His compassion and power. Cara's faith soared.

And so, when her mentor spoke, she listened and trusted that if the knife caused pain, there was a reason.

"Honey-child, talk to me. There's something going on behind those hazel eyes of yours. They're gray. Lost all their color."

Only Rubyann would notice her eyes. Their changing color was the one physical aspect Cara could not bring under control. With that observation, Rubyann cut to the heart of a matter Cara would rather ignore for the time being.

But she knew better. "Lathan Miller."

"Now why is he on your mind? Pshaw! I'm fine. He's just a hapless little gnat who served one good purpose. His shenanigans made me see I've got to move to a safer place."

Her vocal cords felt gummed together. At last she croaked, "Me too."

"You too what?"

"He made me see I've got to move to a safer place."

Rubyann frowned, waiting for an explanation.

Decisions didn't hurt as much buried in the comforts of Mozart, candlelight, and bubbles. Holding them up to the light of the sage's loving scrutiny was altogether different.

"Granny, I knew it long before this incident. I just wasn't ready to admit it. The thing is…it's time for me to move on. I've been in Chicago for over six years." She paused. "Long enough for…him to find me."

"That's fear, straight from the pit!" Rubyann's voice was harsh.

"No, it's self-preservation."

"Cara! I said it's fear, just out-and-out fear. After all this time, that man is not coming."

"He did once before. Waited years and years and then—"
She bit her lip.

"The Lord says to fear not. That's His command, not a suggestion to follow if you feel like it."

"I know, I know." Cara shook her shoulders as if the physical motion could release the cloud that had steadily moved from her horizon to where it hung now directly overhead. How could she explain its blackness was made up of more than the memory of an ugly relationship?

Rubyann knitted her lips together again, giving her time to search for the words.

"Granny, I rent a cozy apartment with a full bathtub. A wonderful, big bathtub."

Her lips straightened briefly into a tiny smile. "You rented that place because of the bathtub?"

"Yes, I did. And you know I love my job. I love catching bad guys. Marcus is the best I could ask for in a partner. I have a few friends. Most especially I have you. You're everything I never had: a caring mom, a grandma, a mentor, all rolled into one spunky little woman. Life has become incredibly comfortable."

"God's against *incredibly* comfortable?"

"Evidently He is for some of us."

"You think because as soon as you got all comfortable those other times and things fell apart, it'll happen again."

She nodded. Rubyann was the only person on earth who knew her entire history, who knew that since the age of three she was forced time and again from situations she called home, from relationships she called family.

"You think if you bail out before things fall apart, you won't get hurt."

The thought of not being near Rubyann cut her to the quick. "I'll hurt, but not as much. I mean, the more time I spend here, the more attached I get. The further down my roots go—"

"You called it self-preservation."

"Right."

"And where does our Lord teach we need that? On the cross? I don't think so, Cara Fleming." Her springy curls blurred as she swung her head side to side. "I don't think so."

Cara held her hands out in a helpless gesture. "It is not fear. It's just being practical! I am not made for being settled in one place! God has always moved me on—"

"Shh. Come here, honey-child." Rubyann pulled Cara's head onto her shoulder and patted her back awkwardly with the cast-covered hand. She murmured soothing words. "Just come here. God is not going to pull the rug out from under you. He is your rug. He is your rug."

Cara shed tears of frustration. She had made up her mind last night! Life was so much easier without the entanglements of relationships, without the attachment to temporal things! She knew that for a fact because, more often than not, she had been without either. How had she become so stinking involved?

At last she voiced what she dreaded most. "Oh, Granny, I don't know what I'd do if I lost you!"

"If?" She chuckled softly. "Given my age, you will lose me. But our God will take care of you, same as He's always done. No reason to run away this time."

"But I know how to start over. What I don't know is how to stay."

"Sure you do. It's called faith." She stroked Cara's cheek, tears brimming in her own eyes. "And besides, six years ago you didn't have me praying for you, right?"

"Right."

"Honey-child, it's okay for you to enjoy the gifts the Lord has given you. Friends. A job. A nice apartment with that big bathtub. You're safe here. Stay in Chicago and just let Him love on you. All right?"

The woman's love for her flowed into yet another dark corner she hadn't known existed. This was when she tasted the cinnamon roll. It fed her with a courage not her own. Stay in Chicago? Live under the cloud? Believe God's plan was not one of doom and gloom when that was what her life had always been?

Rubyann smiled. "Just let Him love on you."

Her faith was contagious.

"I'll try, Granny. I'll try."

Three

The Reverend Bryan D. O'Shaugnessy, rector of St. James Episcopal Church on Ashland, was tired. Tired beyond measure.

He sat in his study, his large chair turned away from the desk and toward a pair of windows. Framed in oak, they were tall and mullioned, like a set of French doors that he could unlatch and push open in pleasant weather. When the custodian wondered at the unusual swarms of wasps in the building, Bryan feigned ignorance. He had begun to think of it as a game between the two of them. The loyal Roger Smithson knew the cause but would not suggest installing screens because he understood the rector did not want them. They'd obscure his view.

It wasn't the type of view to increase real estate value, but it always soothed Bryan. About a tennis court's length away sat the rectory, his home for the past 15 years. A miniature version of the church, it had gray stone walls and mullioned windows too. At the moment, the upstairs bedroom window reflected the late afternoon sun and shone in brilliant gold. The yard below consisted of a small patch of grass, two maple trees, a birdbath, and a magnificent profusion of leafy green plants and September blossoms. Created and maintained by parishioners, the perennial garden lined the sidewalk between house and church and was, he thought, a work of art.

He heard a rap on the door and the simultaneous click of its opening. Without turning he knew Meagan had entered. His sister as well as his secretary, she was the only one who did not wait for him to respond to a knock.

"Bry!"

The lilting sound of her voice made him smile. He swiveled in the chair. "Hi, Meagan."

Except for the fact that he was a bulky 6'3" and she only a snip of a woman in blue jeans, Bryan could have been gazing into a mirror. Meagan's green eyes, slender nose, and somewhat thin lips duplicated his own. Unlike him, she kept her wild red curls trimmed to layers of mere waves which often stuck out in every direction. He wished he possessed a fraction of the joy and energy always spilling from her like water from the birdbath during a heavy rain.

"Hi, yourself." She crossed her arms. "Tell me, *please* tell me, you're not hiding in here."

"That would be lying."

"Bryan! This whole thing was your idea!"

He made a patting motion in the air, a request she lower her voice. Sometimes all that energy tended to throw her into a coloratura.

"Do you have a headache?"

"No, Meagan, I'm just exhausted."

"Did you play racquetball today?"

"No."

"It's Saturday! You're supposed to take the day off and get some exercise. And your diet does not help matters, you know. I bet Mrs. G made pancakes and bacon for you right before a ham sandwich and cookies."

She referred to Lillian Gregory, his housekeeper, as dear a woman as Meagan. Despite his affection for both, he felt he had more than enough women looking after him. Evidently single priests emitted SOS signals that ignited the nurturing bent of every female within a 100-mile radius. He was rather glad his mother lived in Florida.

He shrugged. "What's going on out there?"

"Wanda's having a snit fit." Meagan walked around his desk and began kneading his neck muscles.

Wanda Koski. Another self-appointed matriarchal figure in his life. The mother of his boyhood friend, she had known him since he was very young. She was appalled when his parents moved south permanently.

Meagan worked on a knot near his shoulder blade. "At least it's a quiet snit fit, not like the kind she used to have."

"She is mellowing with age." He shut his eyes. "Mmm. That feels good. So what's the problem?"

"Just opening-night jitters." Although Meagan could unleash a string of negative reactions, she usually followed it up with a quick positive spin on things. "But you need to get out there." She swatted his shoulder. "And I need to get home. Jed and I have a dinner party to attend, and the kids are not invited!"

"A real date. Have fun." He watched her scurry back around the desk and cross the study. Five years his junior, she enjoyed her role as a minivan driving wife and mom of two in middle America. "Thanks for helping."

Halfway out the door, she turned to him. "Bry, you don't have to thank me. This is my church too. It's not your responsibility alone."

Of course it was. The perpetual buck kept stopping at his desk. His sister had just left one there herself.

Lately he had forgotten how to pass them on to his heavenly Father. Which probably explained why he was so very, very tired.

⟋

Bryan locked the study door behind him and turned to gaze down the long hallway lined with photos of former rectors and bishops, 175 years' worth of them. At the far end the set of double doors that led into the back of the church were shut. In between were the parish hall on the left, the chapel and main front entrance on the right.

A column of people stretched from the entry to the parish hall. With a quick prayer, he walked toward them.

They were the "thing" Meagan had referred to, the "thing" which was his idea. Some parishioners backed him, of course, else it would have come to naught, but he had pressed heavily. Perhaps too much so?

Yet how could reaching out to others ever be too much so?

The crowd was a scraggly bunch, though not rowdy in the least. One glance confirmed that the men, women, and children were in dire need of food, clothing, and shelter. One glance seared into his heart a determination to see the first two met through his parish. It flamed the idea he hadn't yet presented to the board, that providing shelter was next on his list.

Right after defusing Wanda Koski.

⟋

Unless he was walking through a team of uniformed football players, Bryan towered over most groups. He knew, though, that his physical size was not what drew people's attention to him. It was instead the clerical collar he wore. Flashing like the beacon of a lighthouse on a starless, moonless night, the collar got noticed. Some people glanced at him and then hastily shied away. Some accused him of being responsible for every ill known to mankind, from dull hymns to genocide. And some—God bless 'em—some glommed onto him. They were the ones who struck a resonant chord because in their glomming they acknowledged a painful, humbling truth: Navigating life's stormy waters wasn't meant to be done without some help. The collar suggested he could point the way.

He himself had been a wallflower as a child, an accuser as a teen, and at last a "glommer" at age 22 when an Army buddy died in his arms. A pointless death. If he hadn't glommed onto the chaplain, his own death would have been just as pointless and taken place in a gutter long before now.

Bryan reached the line of people. The aroma of fried chicken disintegrated, overpowered by an odor of humans who had spent many warm summer days outside without the benefit of soap and water.

"Welcome." He smiled, shook hands, and touched shoulders. *Lord, have mercy.* "Welcome. How are you?"

Cautious stares met him. A man without any front teeth grinned and thanked him. A woman wearing a wool sweater three times too large for her bony frame murmured that the line went faster at St. Bart's.

Bryan apologized. "It's our first time. If you have any ideas of how we can change things, let me know."

A scrawny young man smiled shyly. He held a child, probably less than a year old, against his shoulder. Bryan guessed from the grubby blue T-shirt that he was a boy. A short woman, just as thin as he with the same hollow eyes, stood beside him.

The man said, "Thank you, Father. I've been a little down on my luck lately. And my wife's been sick. We appreciate getting supper here."

"You're welcome." *Christ, have mercy.* He patted the youngster's back and was rewarded with a tiny smile. He asked their names and chatted.

Bryan repeated the scene and slowly made his way along the line of unfortunates that wound into the parish hall, where rectangular tables were set up in long rows. About a fourth of the 200 chairs were occupied. His congregation had invited the neighborhood hungry for Saturday night dinner. Evidently there were many.

Against the far wall was the kitchen with its cafeteria-like serving window. Wanda appeared from its vicinity and made a beeline toward him.

Lord, have mercy.

~

They met off to one side of the room, away from most of the crowd, near the row of stained-glass windows that faced an enclosed courtyard. With the air conditioning running, the windows were shut against the heat. Bryan thought he might open them after dark to air out the odors of people and chicken. The donut-bearing, coffee-making, cologne-doused folks who would arrive before Sunday services tomorrow were not the same volunteers now serving in the kitchen. They might take offense.

He looked down at Wanda, a short woman of 71 with gray curls and dark eyes. Her appearance was borderline emaciated, though he couldn't recall her ever being ill. Neither had she appeared an ounce heavier.

Like many of his congregants, she had known him since the day he was born. In his early years as rector, that situation preoccupied him. How could he be the shepherd when so many still regarded him as a bumbling lamb?

"Father Bryan." Though Wanda's cantankerous temperament was legendary, she had publicly addressed him in gracious formal terms since the day he was ordained. Through her respect for the office, she encouraged him to grow into his priestly shoes. He was indebted.

"Good evening, Wanda. You've done a fantastic job coordinating this outreach."

She smiled, an expression probably lost on strangers, but Bryan recognized the almost imperceptible lift at the corners of her mouth. "After forty years of waitressing, I could organize a soup kitchen in my sleep. But we are in a pickle."

"What's wrong?" He glanced around the hall, genuinely pleased at the orderliness.

"There's a woman here from the Lazarus Outreach." She referred to the organization with whom they had joined forces.

"They told me they'd send some volunteers with food who would stay to help this first time."

"Yes, well, the one I'm talking about is not exactly a help. We're going to run out of mashed potatoes and gravy if she keeps filling plates to the brim. I raised five sons. I know how to figure mashed potatoes and gravy. We are running out."

"Did you mention your concern to her?" As if he didn't know the answer to that question.

"She told me not to worry. That if God could make a few fish feed thousands, He's not going to have a problem replenishing mashed potatoes for a hundred."

He laughed. "She's got a point."

"Maybe you won't be embarrassed when that last family in line there misses out, but I will."

"I would feel bad. Do you want me to chat with her or run to Chicken Delight?"

She wagged a finger in his face. "We are not spending a nickel more on tonight's supper."

"No, ma'am. I'll chat with her."

"Only two of the volunteers don't belong to St. James. You want Cara Fleming. She's dressed like a hippie, like something straight out of the sixties." She pressed her lips together in apparent disapproval.

Was it at the hippie clothes or the fact she didn't belong to the church? Something was bubbling beneath the surface. Perhaps a territorial kitchen struggle? No matter. It was time to disarm Wanda. "Hey, how's that great-granddaughter of yours?"

Her eyes danced. "Victoria is just fine. We talked on the phone yesterday. Well, I talked and she breathed except when she said 'Gamma.'" Her unmistakable grin now stretched from ear to ear. "Rachel's bringing her next weekend! Just the two of them."

"Rachel's coming?" It was his turn to smile. His best friend's widow had moved to Iowa more than a year ago. Her visits were too infrequent.

Wanda nodded. "So we expect you for Sunday dinner. I'll cook a ham."

"I'll mark my calendar."

"Good." She turned her attention to someone behind him. "Sir, would you like some more coffee? I'll get it for you."

With that she was off and serving, a natural for the task at hand. He was grateful she had volunteered to run this dream of his. If Wanda quit, he'd be delegating kitchen chores and serving food. That thought gave him nightmares. He'd better deal with the hippie who somehow made her feel threatened.

Bryan approached the kitchen window, curious for a glimpse of the stranger. As the line moved, she came into view. And he stopped abruptly, dead in his tracks.

When Bryan gave his life over to Christ at the age of 22, his family thought he had gone off the deep end. What was this "born again" business? He'd grown up in the church. What else was there?

His was not a casual decision. If he was going to serve God, he was going to do it one hundred percent. He considered joining a strict monastic order that would dictate he hide away from the world and spend long, uninterrupted hours in prayer. Everyone heaved a sigh of relief when he chose instead to become a priest. In that capacity his life was steeped in prayer and yet at the same time—as his dad said—he made himself somewhat useful in the "real" world, at least to women and children.

Still, Bryan balked at embracing too much of the "real." He limited his social life to family affairs and racquetball. Since his ordination 17 years ago, he had felt absolutely no interest in pursuing a relationship with a woman. It was as if God had entirely canceled that aspect of his manhood. He accepted it as a gift.

Though he had seen God answer countless prayers over the years and though he knew what it was to lose himself in prayer, he was not personally acquainted with visions. He trusted in the mysterious presence of the Christ and did not worry about what some might consider proof.

Now, standing in his parish hall surrounded by the homeless and indigent, he felt a major shift within his being. For one fractured second he sensed God hand him a pair of bifocals and say, "Here, try mine."

The woman stood perhaps 20 feet from him. As the curtain of people in front of her parted, Bryan saw a flash of dazzling white and silver light. From its center she smiled at him. Her hair hung about her shoulders and, like her clothes and skin, it reflected that ethereal brightness.

Before he even had time to blink, the scene before him returned to normal. The woman was not looking at him but rather at a man accepting a plate of food from her.

Bryan blinked several times. He felt lightheaded, unsteady. His heart pounded. What had just happened? A vision? He didn't really believe they occurred anymore. Besides, what would have been the point? No, it was his overactive imagination coupled with exhaustion and anxiety. He'd better take some time off. He'd better get some exercise. He'd better—

An emotion flooded through him then, as odd as the dazzling light. He felt a yearning and deep compassion. His body literally ached because he could neither contain nor express it.

He looked at the woman. What did she have to do with this onslaught of a nervous breakdown?

She chatted and laughed, clearly at ease with strangers. Her hair was not loose to her shoulders, but pulled untidily back into a ponytail. The "hippie" clothes consisted of a yellow T-shirt, something white tied around her waist, and what appeared to be a print skirt. No beads, no dangling earrings.

Then he noticed details. Unclear at 20 feet, they came to him heightened as if by a knowledge he didn't possess.

Her mouth was wide, balancing the wide-set eyes. They were a hazel and would be dotted with gold flecks tonight, taking on the color of her shirt. Her narrow nose was centered between high cheekbones and above a square chin. All in all it was an ordinary face.

Except for that intangible glow that shimmered every time she stretched forth her hand across the counter to a needy person.

Bryan's throat closed. If memory served him correctly, the emotion resembled what hit him when, at the age of 17, he gazed at Annie Cahill in U.S. history class.

Overwhelming attraction at first sight?

He nearly choked. That was the most preposterous thought he'd ever had in his entire life. No. A nervous breakdown made sense.

Like God had ever made sense to him.

He turned and strode toward the back door. Wanda would have to fight her own battle tonight. He needed some air.

Four

"I met…" Cara patted her jacket pockets. Where was her calendar? "No, I almost met your— Ah, here it is." She pulled a small three-by-four notebook from the blazer's inside breast pocket. Her personal memos did not require much space compared to the endless notes she compiled on a daily basis for work. "Tell me the date— Wait." Where was her pen?

Across the table, Terri Schuman laughed. They sat in a booth at a delicatessen during the lunch rush, eating pastrami on rye. "You're doing your Columbo routine."

Cara cocked an eyebrow and stuck both hands into her blazer pockets. "The old TV detective? Hmm." She checked the pockets of her slacks now. "How am I— Ah!" Her fingers touched the pen.

"It's when you don't complete a sentence because your mind is going ten different directions. Anyone who doesn't know you might think you're addled."

"I am frequently addled."

Terri grinned. "No, you're not. Your brain actually has ten tracks capable of working simultaneously, and sooner or later, everything gets connected."

"They better connect sooner today. If things go as scheduled, I'm testifying in court this afternoon. My 'routine' would

41

not go over well with the district attorney. Anyway." She opened her tiny notebook. "When is the wedding?"

"October twelfth. Two o'clock."

Cara wrote in the information. "I will be there unless it's the only time available to arrest some major bad guy."

"Arrest some major bad guy," Terri repeated, shaking her head. "I can't believe how casually you mention what has got to be unbelievably horrible. To face a murderer or whatever, point a gun, and slap on handcuffs."

"Somebody's got to do it. Just like somebody's got to patch up all the sick and hurt people."

"Do you think we'll ever stop trying to save the world?"

She shrugged. "What else would I do? Now you, on the other hand, might have to take some time off to have a baby or two."

Terri rolled her eyes. "I don't think so. I've reached my peak getting engaged and accepting two half-grown stepkids. Pregnancy is out of the question. Remember when you and I first met? Neither one of us trusted men."

"And then you met Gabe and fell head over heels."

"Yeah." She smiled, glanced at the diamond ring on her finger, and then grew somber. "Cara, tell me if I'm getting too personal, but—"

"You want to ask about...him." His name was Nick Davis. She never said it aloud. "There isn't much to the story. I was eighteen when my mom died of a drug overdose. I don't know who my dad is or was; I don't think she did either. I fell in love with him at nineteen. Thought the abuse was part of the package." She smiled wryly, thinking of how her situation hadn't been all that different from her mother's. "History does indeed repeat itself. Except I turned to God instead of drugs. The last beating— It doesn't matter. I told you he stalked me?"

Terri nodded.

"So eventually I left town and became a police officer."

"And moved thousands of miles away."

"Right." She never said the city names aloud either.

"I'm sorry."

She saw Terri's dark eyes turn to liquid. "Oh, Ter, don't go soft on me. We'll both end up sitting here bawling. Our reputations will go straight down the tubes."

Terri sniffed. "You cry?"

"In the bathtub by candlelight."

"I never used to cry. My hormones have been haywire since Gabe came along." She blew her nose. "Do you date?"

"Your average male does not want to date a policewoman."

"I suppose his masculinity would be threatened."

"Just a tad. First he'd be fascinated, then reality would sink in. 'She carries a gun. She could arrest me!' That tends to mess with a guy's head. Superman might be able to overcome it, but— Excuse me." She looked down at the vibrating beeper attached to her waist band. It was Marcus. "But Superman is not real. Anyway, my life is full between work and volunteer— Speaking of which." She dug her cell phone from a pocket. "I was at your church Saturday night."

"Really? For the supper?"

"Yeah. I think I told you I help out with the Lazarus Outreach. They needed someone to deliver food and help your folks through their first serving."

"I heard things went well."

"Extremely so."

"Did you meet Bryan?"

"He's your rector?"

"The redheaded lumberjack."

She pressed the "2" and "enter" on her phone. Marcus's number was programmed, second only to Rubyann's. "That's

what I started to tell you. I almost met him. Only saw him
from a distance." She heard her partner's voice answer on the
other end of the phone. "Excuse me, Ter—Calloway, it's
lunchtime! Leave me alone."

"I am," he said. "Instead of calling, I paged. Get down here
by one. They nabbed Rossi, and we've got first dibs on him."

Rossi. The name had been provided by the teen who
attacked Rubyann. The guy was a minor cog, but a cog
nonetheless. In her mind's eye she thrust an arm into the air
and shouted *Thank You, Lord!* She would never verbalize
such a reaction. Her trademark lack of expression could not
be attributed to police training. The discipline had been
instilled long before she joined the academy. "Got it."

"Don't get too excited now, Fleming." There was a rare
softness in his own voice.

She smiled. "See you." She closed up the phone. "Sorry,
Terri."

"No problem. I was wondering if you'd like to come to St.
James next Sunday. I know you grew up going to church, but
now your schedule interferes…" Her voice trailed off,
eclipsing her usual take-charge demeanor.

They had discussed church in the past. Terri was new to
it. Although Cara's childhood church played a significant role
up until the age of 23, she had not attended in years. Following a suspect into a service once did not count. With Terri
she blamed her crazy work schedule and avoided difficult
explanations. The truth was, seven years ago in Los Angeles
her brief involvement in a church allowed Nick Davis to find
her. Sufficiently frightened, she hadn't even considered one
since moving to Chicago.

Terri went on, "But it sure would be great to have a friend
go with me. I mean, everyone's nice and all, but the women
aren't exactly…" She shrugged. "I don't know."

As on other occasions, Cara intuitively knew what Terri meant. "Let me guess. Either the women are older or they're career-oriented—as in they wear business suits and heels—or they have young kids and spend the majority of their time cooking and driving car pools. In any case, none of them in their wildest imagination can comprehend why anyone would want to look at a gunshot wound, let alone touch it."

Terri grinned. "Something like that. Actually, Rachel will be in town, so she'll be there." She mentioned her good friend, whom Cara had met. "But she'll be preoccupied with her in-laws and showing off their great-granddaughter. And Gabe's working—"

"Hold it, Terri. You're not asking me to go to church. You're asking me to hang out with you at the coffee hour."

"Well." She wrinkled her nose. "Yeah, I am. Come on, I promise we can be inconspicuous together."

"Hmm." She shifted in her seat. Terri's request yanked on a long-buried ache and pulled it clear on out into the light of day, making it impossible to ignore even right there in the deli after eating a huge pastrami on rye. She felt like a desert hiker in desperate need of a source of water. The craving for a return to formal worship with fellow believers created actual physical pain. Now Rubyann's voice jumped into the frantic process of divorcing emotion from level-headed practicality. *Go for it, honey-child. Welcome this simple gift of friendship she's offering.*

Simple, my eye.

"Cara, it's a big church. We really won't stand out."

Oh Lord. "Hmm," she hummed again and took a breath. What could one time hurt? She would simply not sign the guest registry. No personal information need be recorded. She refocused on Terri. "But do you have glommers?"

"Glommers?"

"People on the lookout for new attendees to glom onto and coerce into joining all the guilds and committees."

"Oh, those people. No. They won't come near. I scared them away months ago."

Cara smiled, a cover-up to her growing sense of unease. Terri's gift added yet another layer of comfort to life in Chicago.

Cara wished with all her might she did not feel it.

Five minutes inside St. James Episcopal Church on Ashland, Cara knew she was in trouble. She knelt in the pew Sunday morning alongside Terri, trying to combat an attack of nerves. The distant, somber peal of bells clanged like a warning alarm to her ears, and she forgot all about turning her thoughts toward worship.

St. James exuded a distinct ambience that she had failed to absorb that evening in the kitchen. Today it bombarded her senses the very moment she stepped into the church proper.

In a glance she perceived the age-old gleaming wood of floor, pews, and altar. Bright stained-glass rainbows filled the row of windows along each side wall and, in the rear, three more behind the baptismal font. Interspersed with the aroma of rich wood were wispy fragrances of incense and candles, as if the vaulted beams exhaled them. There was a hushed sound of gathering: gentle murmurs and footfalls, echoes of what had filled the place for more than a century.

Cara closed her eyes and stopped fighting anxiety. She let the ambience do its work. Within moments she felt awash in comfort.

Small wonder the origin of that sensation. She first experienced such tranquility and joy as a four-year-old.

All-Saints in Seattle filled an entire city block. Like St. James, it was huge and built of gray stone. Its double front doors were painted a vivid red. Cara lived three streets east of it in a public housing development. Railroad tracks ran between the neighborhoods. "The other side of the tracks" was never a simple figure of speech to her. The phrase still brought to mind rattling windows, ear-splitting whistles, and a foreboding sense of caution.

The old colossal-sized church sat midway between home and Taylor Elementary. As a four-year-old she already knew the route to the school because her sister, older by five years, often walked her to its playground. One day when life became unbearable, Cara's little legs transported her to All-Saints. She had no recollection of deciding to go there, only of pulling open its big red door and finding immediate respite within its walls.

There was wood, stained glass, a hint of incense, and a kindly priest who seemed at least as old as the stones. Over the next 20 years the effect was the same every single time she entered that church. Now, 14 years after she'd left Seattle and half a continent away in an unfamiliar place called St. James on Ashland, that same effect enveloped her. She felt, instantaneously, *at home*.

Above all, Cara Fleming did not want to feel *at home*.

Cara Fleming did not want to attend coffee hour either. Yet there she stood in the crowded parish hall, politely listening to

Terri's introduction and shaking the Reverend Bryan O'Shaugnessy's lumberjack hand.

The acts of worshiping and receiving communion failed to
restore Cara's equilibrium. They should have, shouldn't they?
She hadn't even seen it coming. She could not handle emotional surprises. Give her a knife-wielding man jumping from
the shadows any day. She instinctively knew how to respond.
This deluge of comfort unnerved her. As Rubyann said, whenever Cara had grown comfortable in the past, life fell apart.
Relationships blossomed beyond her control and people got
hurt. Why on earth would she ever want to feel at home? It
only led to trouble. Except for the quiet time alone in her
apartment, she avoided the sensation.

And now there she was in a church. A church! She knew
church was off limits. She knew it would inundate her with
that sweet, mysterious comfort and lull her into thinking she
was safe. At least she had not signed anything or given out
any business cards.

The breaking of her self-imposed cardinal rule sent her
mind reeling. She felt like a fish lying along the lake's edge,
thrashing about, incoherent, and in a foul mood. Not the best
frame of mind with which to socialize.

What was Terri saying to the priest? Scrambling to apply
her last ounce of courtesy, she listened.

"Cara and I met on the job— Oh." Terri gazed somewhere
behind Cara's shoulder. "Excuse me a minute." She strode
away.

Well, there went Cara's sole reason for being at coffee
hour. She glanced around the room. Where was the nearest
exit?

"Are you a paramedic too?"

"Hmm?" She turned her attention back to the tall rector.

His brows, raised in question, were the same paprika red as his curly hair. "Terri said you met on the job."

"Oh. No. I mean, yes we met on the job, but I'm not a medic." Her mind, like the fish, flopped onto its other side. What to say to the stranger who had led the worship and served the sacrament to her and thus triggered this tidal wave of hominess? "Memorable sermon."

"I hope not." He smiled, and fine crow's feet seamed eyes the color of peridot, a pale, almost transparent green. "It was basically a rerun. If anyone remembers it, I'll have some explaining to do."

His candid remark threw her off guard and she chuckled. "Well, it gave me new insight into John 15. I guess God can use reruns."

"With visitors, at any rate." He tugged on his right earlobe. "Would you like some coffee?"

"No, thank you. Actually, I have to get going—"

"I'm sorry we didn't meet the other night. When you helped in the kitchen. Thank you for doing that, by the way."

"You're welcome. If you'll excuse—"

"So what do you do when you're not serving soup?"

"Uh, I'm a detective. With the police department." She saw the slight shift in his brows and knew what was coming.

"You don't look like one." His quick smile appeared again. "I bet you hear that all the time."

"Yeah. I always apologize for not being big and Irish."

Her description of him was not lost. He laughed. "The cop gene missed me. Not so my grandfather, father, uncle, and brother. But I think cops and priests have a lot in common with our front row seat on the underside of life. And we have a propensity for trying to help."

"That's true. Though I'd like to hear more confessions myself."

"So would I." He laughed again.

His laugh, like his voice, was deep, though not foghorn deep. Soft on her ears, the sounds were mellifluous, easy to listen to. His animated face was gentle on her eyes as well, effortless to watch. Though etched with life, a youthfulness beamed from it. Wide yet not flabby, it suited the shock of longish hair and broad shoulders. He had shed his white outer vestment and wore the black cassock with its head-to-toe line of buttons. Overall, he was a large man. She guessed him to be at least a few years older than herself.

Physically he did not in the least resemble Father Palmer, the grandfatherly priest from her childhood. Still...there was something...some vibration emanating from him, adding yet another layer of comfort, pushing aside her defenses to maintain a distance—

"Cara, forgive me. I'm monopolizing your time. It was a pleasure to meet you."

"Thank you." She reverted to courtesy and shook his outstretched hand, but she did not go so far as to parrot empty phrases. Meeting Bryan O'Shaugnessy had not been a pleasure. As a matter of fact, meeting him was like worshiping in his church.

Both were downright disconcerting.

Courtesy detoured Cara, guiding her steps to Terri. She touched her friend's elbow. "Excuse me."

Terri turned from a circle of gabbing women. "Hey. Let me introduce—"

"I-I need to go."

"Sure. Are you all right? You look a little strange. I thought I left you in capable hands."

"You did. I'm fine. And you seem fine at your coffee hour *on your own.*"

Terri smiled and whispered, "We're talking medication."

"Great. Look, I...I'm glad I came. I'll be back next week."

Surprise registered on Terri's face.

Cara gave her a crooked smile and walked away.

At-home comfort worked like a drug. Oh, the folly of dabbling in it! Of accepting Terri's invitation, staying for the service, receiving communion. Of shaking Father O'Shaugnessy's hand! All recognizable, progressive steps that could only lead to one possible outcome: succumbing to the sweet sensation of letting go, of giving up the fight.

She would need another fix by next Sunday...if not before.

Five

Bryan watched Cara Fleming walk across the parish hall. She moved in the manner of a woman comfortable in her own skin, shoulders back, limbs loose. Her straight hair hung to her shoulders. She wore a long print skirt and casual top the color of the ferns growing outside his study window.

He had seen no more visions, but the actual sight of the stranger sitting in a pew was like having a wild pitch thrown at him. No time to duck before the ball smacked him. He stumbled three times over liturgical words as familiar to him as his own name. During the sermon he lost his train of thought and very nearly did not recover it. His hand trembled when he placed the wafer in her upraised palm.

Lord, have mercy.

The best thing he could do was get back into the batter's box as soon as possible. Instead, he avoided eye contact with Terri. She didn't pick up on his hint and made her way through the crowd, her friend in tow.

Christ, have mercy.

Face-to-face with Cara Fleming, he felt torn as his mind galloped off in disparate directions. Ever the responsible priest, he engaged her in polite conversation all the while noting a thousand and one things.

Her eyes were a combination of colors, meshing into the green of her top.

She could raise one brow at a time. The left one.

She was anxious to leave.

She was a cop? A *cop?*

Typical cop. Her expression was bland, her manner aloof. She gave nothing away.

But he sensed it anyway...deep below the surface...a fragility.

And all that was just for starters.

His heart ba-boomed. If he didn't end the conversation soon, he would announce his fascination with crazy words like "join me for dinner, a walk, bookstore browsing, a ride on my Harley, cleaning out the garage?"

Fascination?

Oh Lord! Have mercy.

∽

"Father Bryan."

Wanda's voice dislodged his reverie and jerked him into the present. She stood before him, her great-granddaughter propped on her hip.

"Did you talk to that Cara woman about the mashed potatoes?"

"Now Wanda, you didn't run out, did you?" He held his forefinger in front of the toddler. "Hey, Victoria. How's my favorite little girl?"

The cherub giggled and grasped his finger in her chubby hand. "Bine."

Wanda laughed. "She said your name!"

His throat constricted. Victoria was the spitting image of her late grandfather, Vic Koski, Bryan's best friend since childhood. She had a head full of espresso brown curls and dark blue eyes that promised mischief.

"And look at that!" Wanda continued. "Holding your hand. Not the least bit afraid. Grandpa Stan doesn't get that kind of treatment, and she's spent plenty more time with him than you."

Rachel Koski appeared at his side. "It's Bryan's Jesus vibes." She squeezed his arm. "Everybody feels at home, and all he has to do is stand there."

Vic's widow had always exaggerated about him in that way. Her face radiated now with a somewhat toothy grin beneath a strong nose and wavy reddish brown hair.

She said, "Wanda, will you keep an eye on Victoria? I want to steal Bry for a few minutes."

Wanda grinned, and her face crinkled into a dried prune. "You have to ask?"

Rachel turned to him.

He saw the question in her eyes. Could he slip away? She must want to talk to him alone. Though they had greeted each other before the service, there had been no opportunity to converse. Dinner at the Koskis' would be a crowded affair.

"No problem." He said. "Let's go to my study."

With minimal delay he managed to exit the parish hall. He ushered Rachel into his office where they sat in what Meagan called the casual conversation corner. His sister had placed two armchairs, an end table, and potted plants in an arrangement beside a wall of built-in bookcases. It fit the bill when he wanted to dispense with the formality of sitting behind his desk.

"Bryan, you look like something the cat dragged in after a long fight."

He smiled. "You're looking beautiful."

"Don't change the subject."

"You are, though."

She frowned at him.

More than two years ago now, when they lost Vic, Bryan had stepped alongside Rachel. He became her confidant and the most constant friend when so many others seemed to let her down. And she became his comfort.

There had been a time when he wished he could love her as Vic had. How he wished he could fill the ugly void that defined her life! But the truth was that he had never been attracted to her in that way. Though she was fiercely independent and fiercely devoted to God—exactly the traits he would want in a wife—he always saw her as an extension of his best friend. He loved her like he loved his sister. There was no changing that. Marriage was not a possibility.

But he knew her like he knew his sister too. Rachel did not think herself pretty, let alone beautiful. Only Vic had been allowed to get away with calling her that. Bryan gave in now to her objection to his compliment.

"Rache, you're looking healthy."

"Thank you. I'm feeling— Well, I'm feeling great. And that makes me feel guilty."

He smiled. "It's okay to feel great. Life goes on or we turn into bumps on logs."

She studied his face. "And where are you on the scale between greatness and log bump? You're as pale as a sheet and you stumbled over words during the service."

"I'm tired." *And there was this odd occurrence with a stranger named Cara.* "Exhausted."

"Will you take time off? Go on a retreat?"

He nodded. Just as soon as this and that were taken care of...

"Bryan."

He heard the hesitant note in her firm teacher voice and looked at her.

"Aren't you over it?" she asked.

His chest felt suddenly heavy. So full he could scarcely take a breath.

Rachel's eyes filled with unshed tears. "You've carried me through more than two years. You prayed for me when I couldn't, when I doubted God even cared. You never stopped saying 'Life goes on.' That in time everything will be—not exactly like it was—but it will be okay because God is the God of restoration."

He nodded.

"Then why are you still in mourning?"

His breath came then, a barely contained sob.

"Oh, Bryan. You carry this entire congregation, not to mention a battalion of firefighters and me. Who carries you?"

"Vic did." He gazed toward the window.

They sat in stillness broken only by the quiet brush of a handkerchief across Rachel's face. At last his composure returned.

He pressed fingertips against his forehead and then looked at her. "I'm sorry. That sounded horrendously childish, as if God is incapable of carrying me directly. I know He carries me—when I allow Him to. It's my priestly bad habit, thinking I have to do it all."

"You're still angry." Only Rachel would dare confront him with that fact.

"Yes." He gave her a tiny smile. "But not as much as yesterday. The thing I keep searching for is a real answer to give hurting people who lose a loved one. I don't want to say *in time* everything will be all right. I want to say this is how I did it. Follow steps one, two, three, and—poof—you'll come out the other side."

"Sounds like a bestseller."

"Except there's no such formula. However, that doesn't stop me from demanding one."

"What can I do for you besides pray?"

"Be happy."

Now Rachel's shoulders heaved. "I am."

He studied her face and suddenly knew why she looked beautiful, healthier, and more refreshed than he'd seen her in years. This was why she wanted to talk to him.

"Phil asked me to marry him."

Phil Rockwell. A neighbor of hers in Iowa, a farmer. A new friend she had told him about months ago. They went together to church, dinner, auctions, movies. She rode in his combine last autumn, his tractor this spring. When she talked of him, Bryan envisioned a Norman Rockwell, the lean man as well as his homey paintings.

In January during a phone conversation, she had laughed in that old carefree way of hers, an unfamiliar sound after such a long absence. He remembered his decision not to comment. He had only smiled to himself while an ice storm raged outside his window. Life went on.

"Bryan, you've been a spiritual father to me. I'm asking for your blessing."

Joy sliced off a chunk of his anger. Not exactly a poof, but Rachel had come out the other side and was trying to drag him along with her.

He stood, pulled her to her feet, and wrapped his arms around her. Vic would be pleased.

Another wild pitch.

Cara Fleming showed up for Wednesday night Eucharist. A Wednesday night! What kind of newcomer attended mid-week services?

After his two previous encounters with her, Bryan was still unprepared for the impact she made on him. The liturgy did not go smoothly. The serving of the Sacrament almost ended in disaster when he saw tears streaming down her face as she knelt at the altar rail.

Though a rare occurrence, tears happened now and then at the altar. But the sight of Cara Fleming weeping made him want to place his hand on her cheek, sit down, and talk awhile. Resisting that urge, he stepped backward instead of sideways and bumped into the deacon holding the goblet. Only Edward's nifty balancing act and the grace of God prevented an impromptu baptismal spraying of wine.

With the arrival of summer's end, more people attended the midweek service again, and the cozy chapel with its single aisle was crammed wall-to-wall. At least there was only one exit. After the service he planted himself in it. Like some lovesick adolescent on a street corner, he waited for her to walk by.

Ridiculous. His intention was to conquer the nerves by stepping right back into the batter's box.

People filed out, most in a hurry to get to choir practice, a guild meeting, or dinner. Evidently Cara was not in a hurry. She remained seated after everyone had left.

Bryan studied the back of her head. She wore a suit tonight, a beige color with white blouse. Her hair was in a low bun. She appeared to be staring straight ahead.

Maybe she wanted to be alone.

He shook off the attack of cold feet. *Batter's box. Get in it.* He went to the pew where she sat. "Cara?"

She turned to him, a dazed expression in her eyes as if her thoughts were miles away. "Father O'Shaugnessy." She glanced around the empty chapel. "Oh, I'm sorry. It's time to go."

"You're welcome to stay as long as you like."

"You don't mind?" Her cheeks were dry, but her face glowed like one who had found a wellspring of sustenance in a crusty wafer and sip of wine.

He felt absolute fascination. No question about it. "Of course I don't mind. That's what the church is for."

She smiled. "I know. I've missed it something awful."

"Missed it?" He slid onto the pew in front of hers and turned, crooking his elbow atop the back of it to face her. "You've been away then?"

"Only for about fifteen years, give or take a few months." The left brow went up. It matched her wry tone. "There was a brief stint of attending about six years ago."

"Fifteen years is a long time. Even six years is a long time."

"And a long story." She obviously didn't want to talk about it.

He did. "Was it Episcopalian?" He knew it was. She was obviously well acquainted with the traditions. Never missing a beat, she acknowledged the name of Jesus with a slight bowing of her head. She genuflected when leaving the pew to come forward to receive the Eucharist, and she crossed herself on cue. She spoke and sang the liturgy without cracking open *The Book of Common Prayer*.

Not that he'd been watching her.

"Yes," she said, "it was Episcopalian. And an old building like this one. With a hundred-year-old priest who—I am convinced—was a human replica of our heavenly Father."

He caught a fleeting glimpse of that fragility again and assumed she talked of her childhood. "Amazing. I grew up here with that very same priest."

She smiled. "The guy sure got around, didn't he?"

He returned the smile. "He made all the difference in my life."

"Mine too. What an opportunity you have as a priest to impact lives, especially young ones, for the good, like ours were."

"It's also an opportunity to ruin them. Too much power for a measly human being. The thought keeps me on my knees."

"Father O'Shaugnessy, if you're on your knees, you are not going to ruin the kids."

Fascination snapped and crackled like a growing flame. "Call me Bryan."

She looked down, touching a pager at her waistband. "Hmm." Her mind was on the pager.

"Have you had dinner?" Out of the blue.

"Excuse me?"

He plucked at his earlobe. "Have you had dinner?" No, not out of the blue. He wanted to spend time with her. Pure and simple. That required an invitation. Dinner sounded more plausible than cleaning out the garage.

She glanced at him and stood. "Uh, no, I haven't."

"Would you like to get something to eat?" He stood too.

She flashed a smile. "Does the last one to leave always get dinner?"

Only when accompanied by a vision. He shook his head, trying to rephrase the invitation and not use words like *vision* or *You fascinate the socks off me.*

They walked down the aisle toward the door.

He said, "No. I just like to meet with newcomers outside of church. I hoped now might work for you."

"I wish I could, but my partner left three messages to call him. Marcus does not leave three messages within a forty-five minute period unless he needs to see me right now if not sooner."

They left the chapel and headed down the hallway.

"Father Bryan."

Father Bryan. He meant for her to call him *Bryan.* Just *Bryan.* Forget the formality. It was the first barrier between them he wanted to tear asunder. He pressed his lips together. Would she think him even more odd than she must already if he insisted she drop the title? They'd only just met. What was the protocol here? He was atrociously out of practice. Out of practice? He'd never been "here" before!

She stopped beside the front doors. "My hours are crazy. I don't know how much I can volunteer at the church."

"No problem. You're welcome no matter what. Even if you do give away all the mashed potatoes."

She laughed, a burst of unrestrained delight. "Wanda."

"Yes, Wanda." He smiled. "She told me what you said to her, about God multiplying fish and potatoes."

Her eyes watered and she sobered. "I've seen it happen."

"I wish I could see it happen."

"Keep feeding the poor, Father, and you will." She pushed open the door. "Bye." And then she was gone.

He laid his hand on the door's exit bar and hesitated. *I just like to meet with newcomers outside of church.* Was that lame? No, it was the truth. As far as it went. Dinner was never part of an initial get-acquainted time. But...why couldn't it be? Why shouldn't he open the door and call out another dinner invitation? They were two grown adults. She wore no wedding band. Surely she would have mentioned a husband by now. All the married women who attended without their spouse did so, usually in complaint of his absence. Surely she would have sent out the "unavailable" signal if she suspected the motive behind his request.

He gripped the bar more tightly and imagined a headline: Forty-five-year-old behaves like an idiotic 16-year-old and scares away new parishioner, who happens to be a cop and will probably think he's a weirdo and begin an investigation into his past.

He sighed.

Man, he was so out of practice.

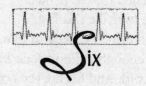

Six

An expert at compartmentalizing, Cara shut a mental door on everything related to St. James Church and Father Bryan the moment she'd turned her back on him and raised the cell phone to her ear. Marcus was on the other end with news of a major player's arrest at O'Hare Airport.

Organized crime eclipsed any faint residue of warm fuzzies left over from the service.

Twenty minutes later she greeted Marcus at the station with a slap on his raised palm. "Got him."

Marcus allowed himself a rare grin. "Got him. From Lathan Miller to James Rossi to Ian Stafford."

"And you didn't think it could be done," she teased. "What's the charge?" They walked down the hallway toward an interrogation room.

"Possession. Airport security found it in—get this—in his briefcase, in a fancy jar marked 'bubble bath.'"

"Well, why not?" She shrugged, resigned to the fact that criminals were cheeky. "Security is too busy looking for explosives and sharp objects. So why didn't he get away with it?"

Marcus winked. "You. If you hadn't pushed to red flag his name, nobody would have opened the briefcase. Of course it helped that a topnotch security woman knew the difference between bubble bath granules and cocaine."

"Send her a dozen roses." They stopped before a closed door, and she reached for the handle.

"Cara, we have to make this fast."

She paused and turned to look at him.

"There wasn't enough coke to lock him up for long. He doesn't have a record. And his lawyer's on the way."

"Okay. Let's do it then."

~

When Cara opened the door, Ian Stafford swiveled on his heel to face her. He must have been pacing, though the expression on his handsome face hinted at no distress.

"Mr. Stafford, I'm Detective Fleming and this is Detective Calloway. Have a seat, please."

"I have nothing to say until my attorney gets here." He slid onto a chair across the rectangular table from them and yanked impatiently at the crisp white cuffs of his shirt. Gold links appeared below charcoal gray suit coat sleeves. A diamond glittered on his right pinkie; a wedding band shone from his left hand.

Cara studied him. Compared to his photos, he was even better-looking in person, no doubt a heartthrob to Chicago women. Six-two, broad shouldered, wavy, deep brown hair, full mouth, and blue eyes. Lake Michigan on a bright sunny day.

Slime.

"Mr. Stafford," she said, "cocaine was found in your briefcase."

"I didn't purchase cocaine. I purchased bubble bath." He'd vowed not to talk. Evidently he wasn't as calm as he appeared.

"Do you often carry bubble bath in your briefcase?"

He sighed dramatically. "I'm on my way to a meeting in New York. I often take a gift to my business associate's assistant." His voice was refined, appropriate for the thousand-plus dollars he wore on his back.

Cara was already tired of listening to it. "Let's talk about Melanie Lareau."

He narrowed his eyes. "My cousin died in a car accident over a year ago. What—"

"She left a few unregistered, untraceable guns in her closet. Know anything about them?"

"Why would I?"

"She was an alderman on the City Council, somewhat controversial. Maybe she had political enemies who threatened her. Maybe she didn't want to go through legal channels and so she asked you for a gun. You're general manager of the Park-Mont Inn with wealthy connections who enabled you to make huge contributions to her campaign. Maybe those connections know where to get guns."

Park-Mont was an international conglomeration which in recent years had taken over several hotel chains. As a general manager of the downtown Chicago property, Ian Stafford was, to put it mildly, a bigwig. Cara noted the flicker in his eyes, the almost imperceptible perspiration bead on his upper lip.

Marcus leaned across the table. "Stafford, I'm gonna cut to the chase. We know you're involved with the Outfit." He referred to Chicago-based organized crime, a world unto itself, one he and Cara spent most of their time investigating.

Marcus went on. "They funnel money and arms through you. Do you honestly believe they're going to need the services of an idiot who carries cocaine through airport security? And gets caught? I suggest you think again."

"I have nothing to say."

"Give us a name, and this all goes away."

Ian Stafford crossed his arms.

But Cara saw the flush on his neck. The guy owed his life to the Outfit. At some time in the past he had needed a favor; they stepped in and provided it. Now he would be willing to pay fines or go to prison for the rest of his life before giving up a name. At least he'd still be alive, something he wouldn't be if he snitched. She and Marcus didn't even have proof of the rumors, just a lot of hearsay and the shaky word of a schizophrenic addict named Rossi.

Still, they had to try.

"Ian," she said, employing a low, intimate tone. "Give us a name and we'll give you a new life."

His eyes met hers. He knew she was talking about the witness protection program. A sneer marred his handsome features.

The door burst open and a silver-haired man strode into the room. He was as elegantly dressed as Mr. Stafford.

Cara knew the party was over. At least they had gotten their foot in the door.

⁓

Standing in the middle aisle at St. James on Sunday morning, Cara and Rubyann waited in line to greet Father Bryan at the back of the church.

"Granny, you are a trooper to keep up with all the motions like you did." The woman's arthritic joints must surely be hurting.

The old woman grinned. "That was a powerful lot of going up and down for these old bones, but I liked it, honey-child. Liked it a lot. Now I know what you mean about your church when you were a little girl. It was beautiful. Just beautiful. I almost shouted 'Amen' a few times."

Cara noticed the smiles of those in line beside them. Her friend's personality always drew out the best in others.

An older gentleman no bigger than Rubyann sidled up to her. "That's the only thing missing here, a little hand-clapping and foot-stomping and amen-shouting."

Rubyann peered at him over her glasses. "What do you think the red-haired one would do?" The two of them laughed like children and launched into an animated conversation.

With a gregarious Rubyann on her arm, Cara met more people standing there than she had last week at the coffee hour. Of course, seven days later she was feeling more sociable herself.

The change in attitude came as she knelt at the altar Wednesday night, struck by the audacity of her ability to snub God. How dare she turn her back on the respite He offered at St. James? If He poured at-home comfort upon her, who was she to refuse it?

As always Rubyann had been right. Concern for self-preservation only fed fear and starved faith. To leave Chicago was to ignore the church's role in her life and the friendships which had been growing, some now for six years. It was time to stop running. Snippets of a new peace had entered her thoughts since Wednesday night's revelation. Only snippets, but real nonetheless.

Father Bryan came into view at the end of the line. She found him extremely likable. He had the makings of a Father Palmer in him, the man who influenced her as a youngster. Even at 40-something, the younger priest exuded an intangible quality of wisdom and goodness that must surely affect his parishioners.

He smiled at her now and stretched out his hand. "Good morning, Cara. You're back."

She shook his hand. "Yes, I'm back. The bad guys called in sick for the day. I'd like you to meet Rubyann Calloway. Granny, this is Father O'Shaugnessy."

"Bryan," he corrected. "How do you do, Rubyann?"

Still grinning, she pumped his hand. "Young man, that was a wonderful service. Hallelujah and amen! My granddaughter tells me you do this four or five times a week."

"Uh...not always with the choir, but yes."

Cara saw the confusion on his face and chuckled. "Unofficially adopted granddaughter," she explained. "Her grandson is my partner."

Rubyann added, "But they snap at each other like brother and sister. Well, I might visit again if I move close enough to the church."

"Please do," he said. "Are you looking for a place to live? I just heard of an opening two blocks from here." He proceeded to describe an ideal situation for seniors.

Rubyann grew even more excited, and the two of them were off and running in a conversation that promised not to end until the sun set. Cara missed the segues, but somehow the topic came up of his parents' living quarters in Florida. Cara mentioned the line of people waiting to greet Father Bryan and eventually pried her friend away.

In the parking lot, Rubyann rocked on stiff legs. "I wish I could skip! Cara! Just think. Two blocks from a church is better than two blocks from your apartment! You have your own life to live. Such long hours working. I don't see all that much of you now. But a church's doors are always open, especially one that's got black *and* white folk like this one does."

"The neighborhood isn't the best."

"But look around." She waved a hand.

The church was located in what had once been a middle-class region with pockets of upper-middle-class. As cultures clashed and populations shifted west toward the suburbs, much of the area fell into disrepair. However, Cara had to admit there were signs of new life in the old houses. Only every other one appeared rundown.

Rubyann said, "Look at those majestic shade trees. This is far better than my neighborhood, but close enough I could still get over to my church when I need to do a little stomping and shouting."

Cara laughed and opened the car door. "Okay, okay. We'll go take a look." She guided Rubyann onto the seat, went around, and climbed in. "I think Father Bryan said it was east of here."

"Bryan."

"What?" She started the engine.

"He said 'Bryan,' like that's what you're supposed to call him. Without the 'Father' business."

"Granny, I couldn't do that. I mean, he's a priest. He's in a category by himself."

"Pshaw. He's in the man category, and he looked at you like you're in the woman category. If you get my drift."

"Huh?"

"They don't *neuter* your priests, do they?"

She took her hand off the gearshift and turned to Rubyann. "What are you talking about?"

"You know, for a cop you sure can miss some obvious signals. Bryan thinks you're the cat's meow."

Cara shook her head. "I was standing there the whole time. When was it you had this conversation with him?"

"Honey-child, he didn't need no *conversation* to get his message across. It was right there in his eyes, plain as day. And the way he didn't want to stop talking to you. Flirting. Kind of awkward about it, like he was out of practice or something, but he was flirting. Mark my words. Those green eyes were all a-sparkle. Is he married?"

"I have no clue. What difference does it make?"

"You think there's no room in your life for flirting, don't you?" The sage's lips bunched together. "There you go again. Telling God what you will and won't do."

"Church is one thing, but—"

"Hush. God's in control."

Halfway through their tour of the senior complex near St. James, Rubyann wanted to sign on the dotted line. By the end, Cara thought she might have to tackle the woman. Instead she convinced the manager to hold the apartment while she contacted Marcus.

"Granny, you know he'll want to see it."

Her face scrunched into disapproval. "It's heck to get old. Can't even make my own decisions about where I'm gonna live."

Cara didn't bother to mention that Marcus signed the checks. No reason to rub in that loss of independence. She steered Rubyann through a courtyard and onto a bench bathed in sunshine. Five minutes later she'd explained everything to Marcus over the cell phone. He and Renae would be there shortly.

She kissed Rubyann's cheek, puffed out from her sulky expression. "He still asks how high when you say jump. Don't fret now. I'm sure he'll approve. It's a great place."

The woman pouted.

Cara closed her eyes and soaked up the sun's warmth. The moment was a rare one of sheer contentment. She sorted through the threads of her life, wondering what triggered the emotion. There was church, a definite enhancement to her spiritual side, which, of course, affected every other side. Work had gone well that week, so well she hadn't consciously thought of an investigation now for hours. Friday night she'd met with friends for a barbecue and laughed. Heartily laughed. She was trying to take Rubyann's advice and accept the gifts God had given her, to consciously settle into a place...call it home.

Perhaps she need not leave Chicago. Perhaps the curse had been broken.

"He was flirting."

Cara opened her eyes. "Granny, why do you want him to flirt?"

"Because you need a man, honey-child. It's time you got Nick out of your system." Only Rubyann knew his name. Only Rubyann said it aloud.

"He is not in my system."

"'Course he is. Nineteen years is long enough for the likes of him."

Cara shut her eyes again and tried to imagine Nick Davis, the man she'd fallen in love with 19 years ago. The thought of him sent a chill through her even yet. Nothing, though, like the paralyzing fear of the past. *Thank You.* Her image of him had faded to a grainy shadow. *Praise God.*

She remembered thinking he was cute, that he was strong, that he would fill all those empty spaces within her, all the holes dug into her psyche by the hands of an absent dad, a sick mother, and a string of live-in "uncles." Nick had his own baggage and looked to her for the same fulfillment.

Immature reasoning. Neither of them were even remotely capable of accepting themselves, let alone of truly loving another. Figuratively and literally he beat out of her the desire to have a relationship with a man. Evidently it was a permanent condition because in the 15 years since she left Seattle, though she had male friends, she'd had no romantic association. Not a one. If a guy showed tendencies in that direction, she managed to disconnect, sometimes unconsciously. Something in her sent up a red flare that translated into a negative response. Distancing herself was as reflexive as blinking at a hand swung toward one's face.

"Cara."

What happened to "honey-child?" She looked at Rubyann.

Sunlight reflected off the lenses of her clip-on sunglasses. Her mouth was relaxed, no bunched-up sage lips. "The Lord says to keep on knocking. You know I've been pounding on the gates of heaven a long time about this. Pleading with the Lord to get that poor excuse for a human being out of your life once and for all."

"I know."

"He is not going to show up. I'm convinced of that. I got the Lord's peace on that matter."

Not that she doubted Rubyann's peace, but she herself didn't have it. Had the trail really grown cold? When she was overly tired, she remembered too many statistics about stalkers. Miles and years meant nothing to them. Most days, though, she trusted in the meandering path God had provided. Her tracks were covered. Not even the smartest detective could follow.

Rubyann said, "The Lord says to keep on asking. I been asking for your heart to get set free. Now that I've met your Father Bryan, I got a feeling it just might happen. 'Course, that's my own thinking, not the Lord's. That's how He does it sometimes, though. Gets me to thinking one way. Then I see it work out 'zactly so."

Cara stared at her for a long moment, and then she snickered.

"Don't you go disbelieving! I know when God's making His move."

She laughed outright. "Oh, Granny, sometimes I'm really, really glad you belong to Marcus and not me."

Rubyann went back to pouting.

〜

Priests flirted?

No way.

Cara raised her foot through the bubbles, wrapped her toes around the hot water faucet, and pressed down to turn off the rushing stream. Not only was the tub oversized, it had great slender faucet handles. She rested her head against the bath pillow and looked at the shadows on the tile cast by candlelight. A Bach concerto floated from the radio.

Old Father Palmer had been ancient when she met him, and he remained ancient for the next 20 years. After all, where did one go after ancient? His wife had been ancient as well. Had they flirted before they'd grown old? Before they married?

In Cara's mind, wives of priests were of the same ilk as the clergy, which meant they were set apart from regular society. Not that they were perfect—she wasn't naïve—but they were different somehow It was hard to put a finger to it, but she knew Mrs. Palmer was as holy as Father Palmer. If there'd been any flirting going on, it would have been holy flirting.

She smiled, wondering what that would look like.

If Father Bryan flirted, it was in teasing Rubyann, the holy spark in him reaching out to the holy spark in her. They were of the same ilk. Cara was not of the same, neither of theirs nor of the Palmers. And besides...

She slid lower in the bathtub until the bubbles tickled her chin.

There was Nick.

No, Granny, he is not in my system. There are remnants, though, that touch everything...

Nick had very nearly beat out of her the desire to survive. But not quite. At the age of 23, as at the age of four, she found her way to All-Saints and Father and Mrs. Palmer's arms. And then Nick found her.

The police came, thanks to a watchful custodian. The Palmers were taken to the hospital, Nick to jail. Cara let a medic treat her at the scene and only went to the hospital to see Father. His wife was fine, but she had been sedated. He too would be all right. Her last sight of him was as he laid in bed, his head bandaged, his arm in a sling, his good hand tracing the sign of the cross over her. With his forgiveness and blessing, that night she left Seattle, the city she'd always called home, never to return.

Priests flirting?

No way.

Priests were for taking care of all the rest of them.

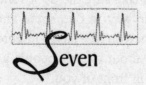

$\mathcal{S}$even

In the end Cara succumbed to curiosity, reminding herself that it killed the cat, not the cop. After all, to investigate was her stock-in-trade. Why shouldn't she try to learn what went on behind those "all a-sparkle" green eyes of the Reverend Bryan O'Shaugnessy? Though she hadn't picked up on any weirdo emanations from him, she had on occasion in the past been fooled. The smart thing to do was get to know him.

And besides, there was that question of flirting.

When he invited her yet again to dinner after the short Wednesday evening service, she debated only briefly with herself. Because, of course, the question of whether or not he would repeat the invitation had already crossed her mind. She blamed Rubyann and her infernal power of suggestion for planting the question.

Curiosity had the final say and although she had plans, she invited him to accompany her in them. He accepted. She couldn't detect any particular sparkle, just a hint of curiosity on his own part.

They drove separately and met in a business district. He stood outside a freshly painted robin's egg blue door, waiting for her.

He smiled as she approached. "What's in the bag?"

"Dinner."

"You must be feeding an army."

"Nope." She handed him two six-packs of soda to carry and pushed open the door. "Just you and me and whoever else is hungry. Make sure the door's shut?" Inside she crossed the narrow entryway in one stride and began climbing the staircase. "I hope you like tacos. I figure since you're a priest, you're out and about visiting people a lot. You probably eat whatever's put in front of you."

He chuckled. "I also have a housekeeper who more or less expects me to eat what she puts in front of me, just like a mother."

"Well, feel free not to eat." She smiled over her shoulder at him. "You've probably got some delicious homemade concoction waiting at home."

"Wednesdays are leftover nights. Mrs. G leaves early."

"Aww, you poor thing."

"It's a rough life."

They reached the second floor and Cara opened another door. "Welcome to Miriam House."

Inside was a big, open area furnished only with a long rectangular table placed under a recessed ceiling light. Most of the room stretched toward the right, its green-and-white checkered linoleum hidden in shadow. To the left a door stood ajar, revealing a kitchen. Four women sat at the table.

Cara walked over. "Hey, ladies."

"Cara! Hi!" They returned her greeting. "Smells like Mexican."

"Good guess." She set the bag on the table and began pulling out food. "Tacos. Burritos. Salsa. Rice. Beans. Plates. And Father O'Shaugnessy."

The women took turns shaking his hand and implored him to sit.

"This is Polly, Helen, Lana, and Ruthie." They were a motley group, two white, one black, one mulatto, aged 32 to 65, slender to obese, Pendleton suit to threadbare blue jeans.

Lana smiled. She was the elegant one, mid-forties, of African descent, and wearing the suit. No one would guess she was homeless. "Father, would you say a blessing for the food?"

"Yes, of course."

He was the priestly prototype, ever gracious. Cara wondered if the demeanor would hold once the women started talking.

He bowed his head. "Blessed are you, O Lord God, King of the Universe, for you give us food to sustain our lives and make our hearts glad; through Jesus Christ our Lord. Amen."

"Amen," the others echoed.

Polly smiled in her shy way. Two teeth were missing from the top side of her mouth, compliments of a boyfriend. She was 32, slender to the point of scrawny, and wore the threadbare jeans. Cara guessed that her large blue eyes came from her mother, her coarse wavy black hair from her father. "We don't get preachers at supper too often. God took good care of me today. He helped me finish cleaning the ladies' room on time."

Father Bryan returned her smile, a hint of sadness in his eyes. He held back on helping himself to what a normal serving of food must be to a man his size.

Cara had invited him to attend a meeting about a homeless shelter. Because his church sponsored a soup kitchen, she knew he was interested. She hadn't mentioned they were meeting *with* homeless people. That fact was probably beginning to sink in right about now. His real test would begin when Ruthie, the oldest of the group, spouted her opinion. Or when Helen Rafferty, the director, repeated like some talking parrot the phrase "we can't."

Cara turned to the abnormally subdued Ruthie. "You okay?"

The heavyset woman shook her head of sparse iron gray hair. "Those gangbangers came in the store again today. Intimidating us. Scares me to leave work. What if they follow? What am I supposed to do then?"

"Call the cops."

"Right. On my cell phone." Thick sarcasm laced her tone.

The others laughed.

Cara smiled. "Call from the store. Did anyone call them today?"

"Won't do no good."

"Ruthie." She exhaled, pushing aside the frustrated tone. They'd had the conversation once or twice. Cara suspected Ruthie was looking for an excuse to quit her job. "I'll come. I'll bring four uniforms with me and we'll scare those kids away."

Polly asked eagerly, "Will you pull out your gun?"

"Only if they don't do what I say." She saw a familiar fear in the young woman's eyes and touched her arm. "Polly, did you see him?" No need to say his name either. They all knew the boyfriend.

She shook her head. "Well, yeah. One time. Yesterday. Before work."

"Want me to take you to work tomorrow?"

She nodded.

"Okay. And Ruthie, I'll come by your store."

Helen sighed. Disapproval filtered through the sound. In her mid-fifties and quite knowledgeable in the field of social work, she at times presented herself as an overachieving executive complete with stony expression and bossy attitude.

The clothes emphasized her mannerisms. She wore nothing but dark tailored suits which slenderized her slightly plump figure. Gray streaked her short brown hair, which was curled to perfection. "We better get to our discussion. All right with everybody?"

Cara gave her a thumbs-up. There was much to discuss.

About an hour and a half later, Cara sat alone with Father Bryan at the table drinking coffee from Styrofoam cups. Helen had just shut the door after reminding Cara to lock up. As if a police officer would not think to lock up. That was the annoying thing about Helen. Though efficient at her job, she majored on the big picture, which made her prone to missing details. People existed in the details.

"Cara." Father Bryan's voice was hushed.

She had watched a host of emotions march across his face during the meeting. He wouldn't make a good cop. She hoped his brother was better at it.

"Where are they going?"

She waited a beat. Surely he knew the answer. "To the streets. To a car. To a public building with an understanding security guard who looks the other way from eleven to five."

"They have to leave because this shelter, like others, is only open from November to April. Even though it's sitting here empty with lights and gas. Right?"

"Right."

He rubbed the back of his curly hair. His face said he struggled to comprehend.

"This place isn't quite ready for occupancy. For one thing, the cots haven't been moved over yet from the old place."

He nodded. "They all have jobs?"

"Yes. Ruthie stocks shelves at a discount store. Lana is an office worker. She finds her elegant clothes at secondhand stores. Polly cleans an office building part-time. None make enough money to live on. None have helpful families. Except for a little financial help from the state, they have no other viable means of support."

"They don't choose to be homeless."

"No. They also sometimes don't choose to pull on their bootstraps with all their might."

"They're beautiful women."

His words struck Cara like a surprise tackle that nearly toppled her composure. He wasn't talking of physical beauty. He'd seen beneath the surface.

"You seem to be their negotiator with Helen."

"They've known me for a while and have grown to trust me. They don't trust Helen or some of the others who say they want input from the homeless, but then don't consider a thing they say. It seems the people who need this place are the ones who best understand how to run it."

"I want to do this." He waved an arm, encompassing the room. "At the church."

Cara stared at him. "Open a shelter?"

"Yeah. Just like this. A place to eat dinner, sleep, do laundry, have breakfast. Maybe I'd even keep it open during the day. For sure it'd be open year round."

"Have you got space?"

"The basement. It needs some work, but it could be as nice as this."

"Would you offer it to men or women?"

"I don't know."

"It would take a lot of money."

"God has a knack for filling that need."

"You're serious."

He blinked. His eyes seemed to refocus on her. "I can't get my mind off of it. It's as if God put it there and seared it in with a branding iron."

"It's a worthy cause."

"Why are you so involved?"

Now he is getting personal. She stood and gathered their cups. "I lived on the streets for a time."

She walked into the kitchen, bringing an end to the conversation. *Sorry, Father. Not even a clerical collar holds the key to that door.*

~

"I'll walk you to your car."

Her back to Father Bryan, Cara grinned at the robin's egg blue door as she locked it.

He chuckled as though catching her thoughts. "Or you can walk me to mine, since you're the one with a gun."

She looked up at his face nearly hidden in shadow. "Is this what is called chivalry?"

"I don't know. My dad just always said it's what a guy does with a girl."

"Hmm. That's sweet. I can't quite see us as a guy and a girl though."

"Your gun and my collar distort the image."

"Yeah."

"But we are, professions aside."

"Hmm," she repeated, lamenting again Rubyann's power of suggestion. What was it she had said? Something about a man and woman category. No way. She buttoned her coat against a chilly breeze. "How about we walk each other, Mr. Knight in Shining Armor? I parked across the street from you."

They strolled down the sidewalk.

"So, Cara, did I pass your litmus test for creeps?"

She grinned. "You're a little too familiar with the way a cop thinks."

"I've had some exposure to it. My dad didn't trust the grocery store clerk, mail carrier, or my sister's kindergarten teacher. Understandable. It comes with the territory. He'd nail them with this look that would make Jack the Ripper run the other way—his hair's flaming red and he's broad as a barn and looks strong enough to lift one—then he'd ask for their life's history. I must say, you're a bit more subtle."

"What makes you think I was doing it?"

"You listen more than you talk. And you've got this little smile that says 'I have a computer at the station with access to all kinds of information which will tell me whether or not to believe you.'"

She burst into laughter.

"Were you able to get into the juvenile records?"

They walked under a streetlight and she glanced at him. He smiled in a gentle way, removing any hint of condemnation in his question. If she'd had to entrust her family to a clerk, mailman, or teacher, she would have behaved in much the same manner as his dad with the help of the latest in technology. Of course she had punched Reverend Bryan O'Shaugnessy's name into the computer and searched for any arrest information. "No. No juvie records."

"But that's where the good stuff is."

"Father, you passed my litmus with flying colors. I don't need to read the good stuff."

"If you know the sordid details, then maybe you can call me Bryan. Like a woman would call a guy."

"You're not a guy. You're a priest. And I can't call a priest by his first name."

"Sure you can. It's just two syllables. Say *Bry*, then *an*. That's all there is to it. Go ahead. Give it a try."

"Fa-ther." She exaggerated the syllables.

He groaned. "What is it, against the law?"

"In a way. A higher law established by Father Palmer."

"The priest you told me about, from your childhood?"

"Yes. I met him when I was four. He made this indelible impression of such pure, absolute goodness. It's never gone away. From that moment on I knew priests were not common riffraff and therefore should be treated differently. Like not being called by their first names by common riffraff such as myself."

"Even though by now you must have outgrown such naïveté and know we are in fact common riffraff? No different beyond this calling to be ordained and wear a collar—"

"You are not common riffraff. You are not a regular guy. You handle the Blessed Sacrament, the body and blood of Christ. That sets you apart."

"I appreciate your respect for the position."

She stopped beside his car parked parallel to the sidewalk.

He went on. "And I respect your position. Take this right here for example. You know which car is mine, though you haven't seen me in it."

"That was an easy one. I saw it tonight parked next to the sign that says 'Reserved for Rector.'"

"But you've probably even memorized my license plate number."

She shrugged. "Habit."

"Are you offended I don't call you Detective Fleming?"

"No. I'm used to being addressed by all sorts of names. But then, mine is not a holy calling."

"It is, Cara, it is. They're all holy callings. The only difference is yours requires a gun and badge while mine requires a collar and vestments."

Though his voice wasn't raised, the tone had taken on an impassioned plea. What was he really talking about? "Why is this first name basis so important to you?"

He held out his hands and then dropped them at his sides, as if at a loss for words. "Because…" Now he yanked on his earlobe. Perhaps that would shake loose words. "Because I've never done this before. At least not for twenty-some years. So forgive my bluntness, but I don't remember how to ask a woman out on a date. And if she keeps calling me 'Father,' I will never get there."

Now Cara was at a loss for words. Rubyann had been right on target. As usual.

"Did I scare you away yet?"

"Um, you're coming pretty close."

"You got a rule against dating clergy?"

"Not that I know of."

"Will you have dinner with me Friday night?" Once he got rolling, he didn't mince his words.

Her mind raced through a host of reasons why she should say no. Nothing stuck. Maybe it was the way he had conversed with Polly and the others. Referring to them as beautiful. Or his admission to wanting to build a shelter in his church. Or the fact that because of his dad's career in law enforcement, he would not invite her simply to satisfy a peculiar infatuation with police.

Actually, he had a few things going for him. Except for the collar.

"Cara, you have my permission to unseal those records or whatever needs—"

"All right. Yes."

He cocked his head. "Yes? To dinner?"

"Yes." *Father. Bryan.* She'd work on the name later.

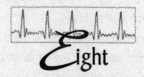

Eight

Her hair tucked under a long black curly wig, Cara flattened the bubble gum with her tongue against the back of her teeth and blew a bubble. It popped. She slurped the wad back into her mouth and resumed chewing. "No kidding."

The hotel maid sitting across the table smiled. "No kidding. But you didn't hear it from me."

Cara gave her a thumbs-up. "My lips are sealed, Evie."

The friendly young woman nodded and flicked the tab off a soda can. Like Cara, she wore an aqua dress, the standard uniform for the Park-Mont Inn housekeeping staff. It consisted of short sleeves, a fitted waist, and a straight knee-length skirt. Cara felt as though she'd stepped into a 1950s photograph. At least athletic shoes and bobby socks completed the outfit rather than heels and a string of pearls.

Though no one else shared the break room with them, Evie glanced over her shoulder and lowered her voice. "They say Ian Stafford is with the mob."

The gossipy employee of the large hotel referred to the general manager, the man Cara had recently interviewed. Evie had just described his mistress who "everyone knew" lived in a penthouse on the twenty-fifth floor overlooking Lake Michigan.

Cara snapped her bubble gum and pushed the yellow-shaded eyeglasses further up the bridge of her nose. "The mob. No kidding."

"Oh yeah. It's like the whole world knows except the cops. I mean, where is the law?"

Cara chewed harder. *Well, in the first place, hon, it's not against the law to manage a hotel or keep a mistress on the top floor. Secondly, defense attorneys on retainer wearing shark-skin suits remind us how insignificant possession of a little coke can be. Thirdly—* She stuffed the gum against the inside of her cheek. "So how did you actually get assigned to work in the penthouse?"

"I met Jasmine Wakefield when I was cleaning her elevator."

The mistress she had named.

"We hit it right off. She's gorgeous. Typical blonde bombshell." Evie patted her own bleached platinum blonde bouffant hair. "She's got these almost yellow eyes, kind of tigerlike, and dark skin like she's from Egypt or somewhere over there. Anyways, she teased me about my hair because it looks just like hers, big and pouffy. The whole world knows this color is not from mother nature. Then we just got to talking. She's real friendly, you know. Common as dirt. Next thing I know, the super sends me upstairs."

"Good for you. What does Jasmine do all day?"

Evie shrugged and drained her soda. "Sit around and eat bonbons and wait for the hunk to show up, I guess. She says she does bookkeeping for him, but he's come in a few times and the look on his face says no way is he going to talk about numbers. She tells me to come back in a couple hours. Just imagine not having to work. A hotel staff at your beck and call. Fantastic view. A wardrobe to kill for. And the most handsome guy in Chicago, who also happens to be filthy rich, has the hots for you."

Cara shuddered inwardly. "Isn't he married?"

"Yeah. Guess that doesn't matter to some folks." She shrugged. "Who am I to judge? Anyway, Miss Wakefield is always extra made up on Thursdays. Dressy outfit and fancy hairdo. I seen her get in a limo two or three times. Maybe they go out. Everybody knows they're a couple, but they're— What's the word I want? They're not that obvious about it."

"They're discreet?"

"Yeah, that's the word. Discreet. Maybe his wife doesn't know."

The door behind Evie opened and an older woman entered the room. An authoritative air accompanied her, plainly announcing itself without words. Her bold voice emphasized the impression.

Crossing her arms, she fixed a glare on Cara. "Who are you?"

Evie replied, "This is Missy. She's a temp. Missy, this is Ardath, the supervisor."

"Well, Missy, how come I haven't met you?"

Cara shrugged. "Just started today. Marilyn told me to follow Jenny around and take my break down here."

"Marilyn? Who's Marilyn?"

"The woman who sent me with Jenny." Jenny she had met on the tenth floor. Marilyn, on the other hand, was a fabricated name referring to some sort of manager, as much a mystery to her as to Ardath. "I probably got her name wrong. Marilyn, Shirley, Eileen? Something like that. Gray hair. She's…" Cara waved her arms in a vague way, as if outlining a figure. "You know."

Evie chimed in. "You mean Betty."

"Yeah, that's it. Betty." Not exactly close.

Ardath breathed a derogatory word. "Always trying to take over. You better lose the gum. And what's with the sunglasses?"

Cara stopped chewing, touched the rimless lenses, and pushed back her chair. "My eyes can't take these hotel lights. Well, I'd better get back to work."

Evie stood also. "Me too."

They left Ardath shaking her head in front of the snack dispenser, muttering to herself about Betty.

A few minutes later, as Evie prepared to exit the slowing service elevator, Cara said, "Hey, would you want to maybe go out sometime?"

"Yeah, sure."

"I've got a pen here." She pulled a tiny pad and pen from her pocket. "What's your number?" After Evie had provided her last name and phone number, she said, "Be careful up there. The mob's a serious thing."

Evie flicked her hand, dismissing the caution. "If the rumors are true that you-know-who is part of it, I'm just an innocent fly on the wall. No big deal. I know how to keep my mouth shut."

The doors swooshed open. Cara grabbed her new friend's arm. "If I worked for them, you'd be in deep yogurt right now."

Color drained from Evie's face.

"Not that I do." She let go of her arm. "Just be careful."

Evie held the door open and stared at Cara for a long moment. "Your lips are sealed?"

Cara pressed them together. *As far as your name goes. Lord, keep her safe.*

Three blocks from the Park-Mont, Cara stood on a sidewalk outside an upscale grocery store. She huddled in a windbreaker, small protection in a short skirt against a sharp breeze. The late afternoon sun shone in fractured rays that glinted between skyscrapers. Her mind raced, quickly compartmentalizing a myriad of details she had accumulated during her four-hour stint posing as a maid.

One item was to send Evie an anonymous gift. Like the security guard at the airport, she had unwittingly added a yellow brick to the road that would eventually lead to Ian Stafford's downfall. She deserved a thank-you that could never be made public. Though Cara had jokingly told Marcus to send a dozen roses to that other woman, she herself had taken care of the act, wearing dark glasses and paying the florist in cash. She would do something similar for the maid.

A sporty black car with darkly tinted windows approached. It belonged to Marcus, but he didn't even slow as he drove past her.

Cara sighed in exasperation. Not wanting to draw attention, she didn't flag him down, even though it was his third time around the block.

Marcus had spent the first two of their four years together watching her closely. Eventually he came to trust in her ability to shoot straight, cuff a 200-pound drunken male, interrogate, spot a tail, and watch his back. He knew she would not be standing there at the appointed spot if she'd been followed. He might swing by twice to double-check, but not three times.

No, the reason he didn't stop was because of the black wig. The wig was a new addition to her incognito wardrobe. Marcus hadn't seen her in it because another detective had driven her to the area.

His fourth time by she stepped off the curb and stuck out a thumb. He braked.

She jerked open the back door and climbed in. "Calloway, either you're blind or this window tint job is illegal."

He stared over his shoulder at her as she slammed the door shut. "Whew! You are good. You are really good. It's not the wig or the glasses. Man, your whole—I don't know—your whole person changes. Demeanor. The way you stand. You're not even the same height! Are you? You look six inches taller in Reebocks—*Reebocks?*"

"Just drive, will you?" She pulled off the wig, yanked at the barrette holding her hair up, and finger-brushed her scalp, glad to spot her gym bag next to her on the backseat.

He chuckled and eased the car into traffic. "'Course it's not every day I see your legs in a short skirt and bobby socks. Cute touch."

Cara blew out a breath and unzipped the duffel bag. "I look like 'Hazel.'"

"No way Hazel ever looked like you, Fleming. Not by a long shot."

"Keep your eyes on the road." She began unbuttoning the front of the uniform.

He laughed and flipped the rearview mirror away from his line of vision. "Like you're going to show something. You're wearing a T-shirt under the dress, for pete's sake. So how'd it go?"

"Not bad." She paused for effect. "I learned he has a girl-friend who lives at the Park-Mont."

"Do tell."

She leaned between the front bucket seats and whispered in his ear, "And...she keeps his books."

Marcus howled like a lion declaring his kingship in the jungle.

She slapped the palm he raised toward her and laughed. Their case against Ian Stafford had just exploded with possibilities. She told Marcus to drive back to the hotel where they could watch for a platinum blonde named Jasmine Wakefield. If Evie the maid was right about Thursdays, a limousine would soon arrive.

Cara proceeded to pull on slacks and a sweater and then wriggle out of the dress. Privacy had been a rare luxury throughout much of her life. It simply did not exist in shantytowns or shelters. Out of necessity she developed a knack for quickly and modestly changing clothes.

She described her afternoon of chatting with employees, learning about the penthouse maid, and tracking her down. After their visit in the break room, she had slipped aboard the private elevator, rode it up and down, to and from private floors, polishing the brass for a good hour and a half before someone noticed. Jasmine hadn't appeared and, without a key, Cara was unable to get any closer to her.

Now she shrugged into her black blazer, which her meticulous partner had draped over the passenger seat. She found her pager, gun holster, and cell phone in the gym bag, squeezed between the front seats, and plopped down beside Marcus. "So," she finished the story while she clipped the trappings of her trade onto her waistband, "keep your eyes open for a blonde bombshell."

"Looks like three limos lined up." He slowed near the drive that looped past the busy hotel entrance and parked on the street behind a line of taxis.

Two cab drivers on the sidewalk glared in their direction.

"Yeah, yeah," Marcus muttered. "I dare you to come over here. Come on. Make my day."

"Calloway, you derive way too much pleasure out of scaring people." She found a tissue in her pocket and rubbed it across her lips.

He grinned at her. "Hey, you look good in lipstick. Why are you wiping it off?"

"It's called war paint, and I look like a clown."

"Maybe red's not your color— Head's up. Is that her?"

Cara watched a shapely blonde slide into the back of a limousine. "It's got to be. How many women look like that, come out of this hotel, and get into a limo on a Thursday night?"

He shifted into drive. "Probably at least half a dozen. But let's follow this one."

～

Less than 15 minutes later, Cara stood inside the Venetian Palace, a popular restaurant located minutes from the hotel. While Marcus parked his car, she watched the blonde bypass the elegant dining room and ascend a narrow staircase to the more intimate one on the second floor. As she neared the top, Cara started the climb.

Marcus joined her three-fourths of the way up.

"That was fast," she said.

"Found a spot a block away."

Though he probably wouldn't have entrusted his precious car to a valet anyway, it wasn't a choice. They might have to leave quickly.

She murmured, "This place always gives me the creeps."

"Food's worth it, though."

In her opinion, it wasn't. She would rather eat takeout in a shelter with a group of homeless women. The landmark, four-star eatery oozed with history, much of it related to organized crime. *Al Capone sat there* kind of history. *Big Jake Esposito was shot here* kind of history. *See the bullet holes there* kind of history. *They say he died on the floor right here* kind of history.

No thanks.

At the top of the stairs, she pressed through the crowded entry, her eyes glued to the back of a platinum blonde head, the hair pinned with rhinestone-studded clippies. Rhinestones or diamonds?

One of the three hosts led Jasmine Wakefield into the dining room. Cara noted where he seated her.

Cara considered the place a dive, but it attracted tourists and Chicagoans by the hoards with its history and décor and—when she felt like admitting it—the food. Framed black-and-white signed photos of famous people filled the entryway walls. Strings of tiny white lights crisscrossed the dining area. Other tableside lamps shone dimly, creating a grainy cast over the whole place. Scenes of hills, grapevines, and villas had been painted on the walls, their colors muted in the low light.

Marcus nudged her. "How about dinner?"

Like she had a choice.

Interrupting the maitre d' in the middle of a sentence he was directing to someone else, Marcus said. "Excuse me."

As when E.F. Hutton spoke, conversation halted when her partner used The Voice. Neither threatening nor loud, it reminded her of a mourning dove's coo, gentle with a decidedly eerie undertone.

The tuxedoed man with slicked-back dark hair turned.

"We need a table," Marcus said.

"It's a thirty-minute wait, sir. I'll get your name right after…"

The detective straightened his sport coat, exposing the gun holster and badge attached to his waistband. It was a subtle movement, but understood by someone Cara suspected was an expert at things like money laundering.

"Please," Marcus added superfluously.

"Excuse me," the maitre d' now said to the other man and then turned again to Marcus. "Right this way, sir. Do you have a preference in tables?"

Cara pointed across the busy restaurant. Jasmine Wakefield was not in sight, but Cara knew where she was. Scattered about the odd-shaped room were enclosed areas. They jutted out between tables, creating a maze effect. The woman had entered one of the closetlike spaces. At right angles with its door-width entry, along a side wall, was a vacant table for two.

The maitre d' led them to it without hesitation, his smooth features not in the least perturbed at their commandeering a spot he'd obviously been saving for someone. As they sat he handed them oversized menus. "Madam. Sir. *Buon appetito.*"

Cara faced the enclosure. Its opening was only wide enough to reveal a table. Booth seats off to its sides were blocked from view. She caught a glimpse of Ian Stafford when he leaned briefly over the table to lift a piece of bread from a basket. Jeweled rings flashed from a feminine hand as it refolded the linen napkin atop the container.

"Brazen fellow," Cara said. "Granted they arrived separately, and they're not downstairs in plain sight, but the man is married and not exactly an unknown figure about town."

Marcus closed his menu. "Lighten up, Fleming. It's dinnertime. Wouldn't it be satisfying to finish a meal? Let's order." He held up a hand and bent his fingers, signaling a waiter. It worked like The Voice.

"Yes, sir?"

"We're in a bit of a hurry." He used his special tone again. Half the customers might be in a hurry, but the phrase took on an altogether different nuance when Marcus said it. He looked at her. "Honey?"

She only raised a brow.

He turned his attention back to the waiter. "She'll have the linguini in clam sauce. I'd like the lasagna. Two salads, house dressing. And bottled water. One of those large ones."

Evidently Marcus had eaten there a few more times than she had.

The waiter rushed off, replaced by a server who delivered a bread basket and scurried away.

Marcus stopped scanning the room long enough to glance at her again. "You'll enjoy it."

Cara smiled. "Tell me you don't order like that for Renae."

"I give her thirty more seconds to decide. What's going on?"

She shifted her eyes again to the enclosure behind him. "He's drumming his fingertips. She's wringing her hands. Hmm. Hints of trouble in paradise. Can you hear anything?"

Marcus leaned back in his chair. Another three feet and he could have rested his shoulders against their table. Tilting his head, he listened for a moment. "Nah."

She wasn't surprised. The restaurant was packed, and the din of voices bounced back from a lofty ceiling.

Marcus poured olive oil from a tall bottle into a little dish and helped himself to bread. "You did good today."

"Thanks. And to think it all started with Granny."

He raised his water glass. "To Granny."

From Rubyann to her attacker Lathan to the druggie Rossi to the mob front man Ian to the maid Evie to the girlfriend Jasmine. The puzzle pieces were revealing themselves. Now all she and Marcus had to do was piece them together.

Trouble was, they didn't know what the final picture was supposed to look like.

⌁

Although they did not mind if Stafford recognized them, Marcus predicted the self-absorbed man would not. It happened as he said. Jasmine Wakefield emerged first and strode past them in four-inch heels with the sway of a runway model. Stafford followed, his hand lightly touching the small of her back. They walked right on by without a glance in their direction.

"Do you think he'd recognize us in a lineup?" Cara asked.

"He might think you looked familiar because he is a ladies' man." He chuckled. "He probably wouldn't remember where he'd seen you, though."

They had already decided to drop the surveillance for the night. Tomorrow they would share information with the FBI. They would pour over databases and learn what they could about the woman. After that the waiting game began. Someone would make a mistake that would give shape to the final puzzle.

"How about dessert, Fleming?"

"And give these goons another chance to poison us?"

He laughed. "The linguini was fine, wasn't it?"

She'd been reluctant to eat food prepared by someone who worked for the maitre d'. The guy could have ordered the chef to alter it. Marcus coaxed her into tasting it. One bite was all it took. She nearly inhaled the plateful of scrumptious pasta. "It wasn't bad."

"You're going to love their tiramisu. Trust me."

$\mathcal{N}$ine

Bryan shut his car door and noticed Cara emerge from hers across the parking lot. She raised a hand in greeting. Nearer the restaurant entrance than she, he waited for her.

To meet there rather than ride together had been her suggestion. She had no idea where she might be at 6:30 Friday night, but she did know it would not be at home. He embraced the plan wholeheartedly. Watching her come toward him, he chose not to think about his weird emotions, the ones interfering with his ability to recall liturgy and nimbly distribute communion wafers.

Or the fact that when personally welcoming single female newcomers, he always invited them to his study for tea and he always—but always—included Meagan or his housekeeper, Mrs. G.

Lord, have mercy. What am I doing here?

He watched her approach. She wore black slacks and blazer with a white blouse. Her hair was pulled back in a bun. Very professional-looking. A lower corner of the jacket flapped in the breeze and silver flashed from her waist. Like his dad and brother, she would never be totally off duty. She served the citizens of Chicago 24/7. The badge let others know she was there for them. He did not see her gun, but it would be in her possession along with pager and cell phone.

Probably handcuffs too. Perhaps she carried them in the shoulder bag hanging at her side.

"Hey." She smiled. "You're incognito."

He touched the mock turtleneck shirt at his throat. It was a brown color, a gift last Christmas from his sister along with the herringbone wool blazer. He'd worn it in an effort to remove the ecclesiastical barrier Cara saw between them.

The choice had nothing to do with those weird emotions. Nothing whatsoever.

Yeah, right.

He shook her outstretched hand. "You made it on time."

"You too. I bet that doesn't happen every day with you either."

"No."

As they headed toward the restaurant, she asked, "Is that another commonality between priests and cops?"

"Mm-hmm. The nature of our work puts the schedule at the mercy of someone else's needs."

"You're right. It sounds like a miracle we actually made it here tonight."

You have no idea.

"But," she went on, "the real trick will be to make it through dinner before someone else's need calls."

He reached around her and pulled open the door. "I left my pager and phone in the car."

She looked up at him as she walked by. "Me too, Father. Bryan."

⌒

The restaurant had been Bryan's suggestion. Neither too fancy nor too down-home, its middle ground appealed to him as a setting for their dinner that fell short of a date and into the category of get-acquainted time. The casual ambience encouraged lingering but did not promote romance—in spite of the candles and linen tablecloths. After all, businessmen frequented the place.

Again like his dad and brother, Cara exhibited the ingrained habits of an officer who never went off duty. She asked the hostess, who led them to a center table, for another spot in the room. Then, at a corner table, she sat in the chair against the wall, the one offering the best view of the restaurant's main room and entrances. Though she focused on their conversation, her eyes hadn't immediately settled on him. He knew she was memorizing faces of waitstaff and other patrons and noting their behavior.

"How was your day?" he asked after they'd ordered.

"Fine. How was yours?"

"Fine."

She grinned. "How about those Cubs?"

He returned the smile. "Priests and cops again. We spent the day doing stuff we shouldn't discuss with someone we hardly know."

"Whatever shall we talk about, Father? Bryan?"

Pillow talk with the woman would be fascinating. Maybe she could get beyond the formal title. He could ask her opinion of Mrs.—

Bryan broke out in a cold sweat. *Pillow talk! Pillow talk?* He slipped a finger behind the mock turtleneck and pulled.

Cara was still speaking. "Of course we're both adept at getting others to open up. There's always the weather. And the Cubs. And da Bears. Or Rubyann. We have her in common. I'm sure you'll see her again at church. She is so grateful to you for mentioning that place— But I know she called you to say thanks."

He gulped a mouthful of ice water.

"Then there are the old standby questions, like why was it you pulled the trigger? But I don't imagine you use that one too often. Are you all right?"

He nodded and almost choked on the swallow.

"It is hot in here. Which brings us to the weather. Rather warm for early October, don't you think?"

He placed the napkin over his mouth and coughed as discreetly as possible with water trickling down his windpipe.

She waited for him to find his voice, that left brow of hers cocked.

At last he cleared his throat and lowered the napkin. "Five minutes ago I was comparing you to my dad and brother, cops through and through, but all of a sudden...uh" *All of a sudden I'm thinking about pillow talk.* "I see a-a feminine side."

She shook her head and sighed dramatically, sarcasm plain in her expression. "Try as I might, I cannot get rid of that side of me. I guess it's in the genes."

"I don't mean to sound prejudiced." He saw forgiveness in her smile and tried again. "I've never met a female cop."

"You think it's an oxymoron."

"Not exactly. You're like my dad and brother, and yet you're nothing at all like them. They've seen such— How does one sum it up? Unspeakable horror. It's gnawed at their souls until there's nothing left. You've seen that same unspeakable horror. You've had to. But still you're...human. How is that possible?"

"You've seen me in church, not on the street. Some of the guys call me Ice Lady. Marcus calls me Cucumber, as in cool as."

"That's a gift for your survival. Cara, my dad and brother have no emotions. Absolutely none."

She blinked. "But for the grace of God, there go I."

"Still, what..." He closed his mouth before blurting out *Whatever in the world possessed you to become a police officer?* An incredulous tone punched his mental voice up a notch. He took a breath and rephrased the question in a normal pitch. "Why did you go into police work?"

"You skipped right over the weather and the Cubs."

"I'm forty-five. Life is short."

She gave him a small smile, the enigmatic one he had seen on other occasions. "You are a priest, through and through. Even without the collar."

"Sorry."

"You should be. It's unfair. You make it too easy to talk, which may not be a good idea. In the past, talking has always...complicated my life."

He remembered how she told him at the shelter that she had been homeless. Afterward she abruptly left the room and dropped the subject. He sensed—again as with his dad and brother—that she did not easily trust people. Given a background that included living on the street, she very likely possessed a double dose of the malady.

He asked, "I don't imagine you talk to many people?"

"Rubyann." She shrugged a shoulder.

"Maybe she's enough."

"She would say it's not healthy. How about you?"

"Vic Koski. You've met Rachel?"

She nodded, and then the implication of what he said dawned in her eyes. "I'm sorry."

"Thank you. Guess you and I are just a couple of lonely ships passing in the night."

That one brow of hers crept upward.

"Too esoteric?" he asked.

"Too final. I'd hoped to be in church on Sunday."

He smiled. "That analogy won't do then. How about new friends getting to know each other?"

Something slipped away from her face. In the split second before she looked down, he glimpsed behind the hint of aloofness that hung about her. Despite her friendly demeanor, a part of her always remained closed off, hidden from view. Until now.

Anticipation filled him, the type he felt whenever he'd sit on his motorcycle, rev the engine, and think about the map sitting on the kitchen counter back inside the house. With no destination in mind, he needed no map to show him the way. Once he took his hand off the brake, the adventure began.

Time to release the brakes and let the adventure begin. "So, why did you go into police work?"

Cara's story took shape through the salad course.

"When I was a kid there were only two situations that made me feel safe. One was in church. The other was whenever the police showed up on our doorstep. When I grew up, I didn't think I was holy enough to be a preacher, so I became a cop."

Bryan stopped eating.

"Yeah, that about sums it up." The little smile played about her mouth. "But it opens a can of worms, doesn't it? Now you'll want to ask why police came to my doorstep on a semi-regular basis."

He gave a half nod.

"How about the CliffsNotes version?" she said. "My mom was an alcoholic and drug addict. She never married, but neither was she ever without a man. Of course, she was drawn to guys who were similarly addicted, which made for wild and crazy times. One of my earliest memories was of being hugged by a uniform. I was probably three, my sister eight. She knew how to call the cops and taught me. We were never afraid of them. After they arrived, the result was always instant relief and comfort."

"I'm sorry."

She brushed a hand in the air as if shooing off a fly. "It's all right. I mean, the whole scene gave me survival skills. And more or less threw me on God's mercy." She smiled. "And He is merciful. I have moved on to an unbelievably better life."

"How did you ever move on in the first place?"

"My sister Cheri-Lynn—actually my half sister; neither of us knew our dads—ran away when I was ten. She came back now and then, but when our mom died, I couldn't find her. We've never reconnected."

"How old were you then?"

"Eighteen. I was out of high school, working as a clerk in a discount store, still going to church when I could, and dreaming about being a cop but totally confused. I fell in love with the first guy who looked at me twice." She pushed aside her half-eaten Caesar salad. "From there the story gets too ugly to talk about over dinner."

Despite her hint, he barged ahead. "He was probably like all those boyfriends of your mother's."

"A clone. Pretty predictable, huh? I didn't leave because I didn't know how I could survive without him. Typical mental state of the battered woman. Eventually I realized I wouldn't survive *with* him. So I…disappeared."

"You lived on the streets?"

She nodded.

"In Chicago?"

"No." She paused. "Seattle."

"You're a long way from home."

"Well, if home is where the heart is, that's not my home. Interesting thing about being homeless for a while. It taught me how to hold things loosely, even life. I mean, this earthly phase is a temporary condition. Why get settled in? Jesus promised our real home is elsewhere." Her crooked smile was self-deprecating. "There I go, expositing Scripture to a priest."

He flashed a grin. "That preacher still lurks within you."

"Let me out! Let me out!"

The waiter appeared and delivered their entrees. Small talk disrupted the flow of their conversation. After the young man left them, Bryan surreptitiously eyed Cara as he cut into his steak. Either she hadn't cared for the salad or the discussion had squelched her appetite.

She picked up her fork, prodded at the salmon on her plate, and set the fork back down. "Bryan."

The knife slipped from his fingers and clattered against his plate.

Her eyes remained downcast. "How do you think the Bears will do this season?" Then she looked at him, her gaze steady.

Something was changed in her face. The aloofness was back in place, the door shut to that vulnerability within.

But apparently the porch light still burned. After all, she had called him by his first name.

～

Bryan sat in his car parked in the restaurant's lot. He tapped the steering wheel and ignored the periodic beep of the cell phone on the seat beside him, alerting him that urgent

messages awaited. Every fiber of his being locked his attention onto Cara Fleming.

Cara Fleming.

A cop. A *cop.*

An attractive woman not many years younger than himself.

Whose vulnerability made him long to hold her.

Whose compassion made him want to unburden his own
soul to her.

Whose faith exhorted him to love and good deeds.

Whose baggage could sink a ship.

He felt as though he sat on the Harley again, only now he
raced like the wind, catapulted by a stranger's smile down an
unknown highway.

Was it that smile or her intriguing mind that prompted him
to imagine the pillow talk scenario?

Pillow talk. *Lord, have mercy! What am I supposed to do
now? The usual when faced with a murky future? Take one
step at a time? Which is about next to impossible when the old
bike's doing ninety miles an hour.*

The phone rang and he jumped in surprise. Rubbing a
hand across his face, he exhaled noisily. A glance at the cell
showed his sister's number displayed in the window. Life
went on.

"Hi, Meagan."

"Where have you been? Never mind. You're here now.
Harry Franklin's had a heart attack." In her succinct manner,
she answered his questions and filled in the details.

"I'm on my way."

"That's what I told them. Bry, have you been playing racquetball? You sound all out of breath."

"No, I just, uh, I just had quite a stimulating conversation."

"Well, whatever, keep doing it. Your voice is upbeat.
Which is—need I say the obvious?—a refreshing change of
attitude. Call me!" She disconnected.

Upbeat? Chuckling, he started the car. Why wouldn't he sound upbeat? Ten minutes ago over dinner he had discovered a priceless treasure. Like the man who unearthed a fortune, reburied it, and then went off to sell all he owned in order to buy the field, Bryan wanted to tuck away Cara Fleming for the time being.

At least until he figured out the cost of loving her.

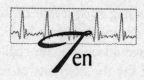

Ten

Cara sat in the passenger seat as Marcus drove them quickly through the empty Sunday morning streets, emergency lights flashing. Six blocks away from her place he had to remind her to put on the seat belt.

Thirty-six hours after the *date* and Bryan still impaired Cara's ability to compartmentalize. Focusing on mundane details like seat belts was out of the question.

Bryan. Make that *Father* Bryan O'Shaugnessy.

Too late. The distance between them had been bridged. He was Bryan.

If not for helping Rubyann on Saturday, Cara might well have packed her own belongings in a bag and bought a train ticket for anywhere east or south of the Midwest. She had never lived in the South. That area might be nice. Chicago winters would not be missed.

Marcus intruded upon her musings. "Thoughtful of the Coast Guard not to find the boat yesterday. Granny might not have gotten moved into her new place."

The day before, they'd helped Rubyann get settled into the apartment. Busyness and hordes of people prevented Cara from telling Rubyann about the dinner...about the...flirting.

Yes indeed, there had been flirting. Or something. Something that she willingly—oh, so willingly—responded to. That trustworthy sixth unconscious sense of hers did not even send up a warning flare! To her chagrin, Bryan's goodbye hand-shake jolted her heart into a double-time beat. The extra thumps ricocheted into her throat.

Verbally expressing such a line of thinking gave it more credence than it deserved. It was best not to tell Rubyann. The old woman would only again challenge her not to run away. She would say the comforts of relationships and that big bathtub were God's gifts, His way of loving Cara. They were to be accepted with a grateful heart.

But Nick...

Rubyann would have said *Pshaw*. But nothing. That excuse no longer remained valid.

She shook her head. The ice water in her veins felt luke-warm.

"Fleming, you okay?"

"Hmm?"

"You're ticked, aren't you? You wanted to go to church with Gran."

"Uh, no. Well, yeah, I did— I'm fine. She'll be fine."

Actually, not being able to attend church was probably an answer to some prayer sniveled from the depths of her being. If she were at church, she might very well choke on the wafer served by the man who had succeeded where all others failed, save for Rubyann. He somehow compelled her to talk about the past.

Not a pretty picture, needing the Heimlich maneuver per-formed at the altar rail.

Marcus said, "Yeah, Granny will understand. She'll figure out that work kept you away. She probably has a dozen new friends there already."

"At least." She punched his arm lightly. "And she'll tell them we had to do some dangerous police work. They will *all* be praying for us." And then she muttered, "Even the priest."

"The priest? Now that sounds like serious stuff."

"Yes, Marcus, it is very serious stuff."

～

Pulling on a pair of latex gloves, Cara ducked beneath the yellow crime scene tape stretched across an area of a dock at Lake Michigan. She nodded at a member of the Coast Guard and walked toward a 200-foot yacht. It was a beautiful boat, with royal blue awnings and a white hull that gleamed in the October sun. Its mast soared to the sky. Hot pink script proclaimed its name: *All That Jazz.*

Marcus caught up with her as she stepped onto its wooden deck. He had paused to talk to a Coast Guard official. "ATF has been notified." He referred to the Department of Alcohol, Tobacco, and Firearms, a federal organization they often worked alongside. "Nobody's been on board except two of the guards who found it and two cops."

"Three too many."

"At least it got sent through appropriate channels fairly quickly. The Coast Guard towed it in a short while ago."

He and Cara were at the end of those appropriate channels. When illegal firearms were found in or near their district, they were notified.

She asked, "Where was the vessel?"

He didn't reply immediately, and she heard a silent reprimand in his hesitation. He had probably already given the answer to that question on the drive over. "Fleming, is there something we need to discuss?"

His gruff tone reminded her that incomplete focus on her part endangered him. Closing her eyes, she willed the thought of Bryan with all its accompanying emotions into a mental cupboard and clicked shut the door. She met her partner's gaze. "No."

"The yacht was drifting about six miles out. Some eagle-eyed guardsman spotted an assault rifle lying on the bow."

The details sounded vaguely familiar. "They searched the water?"

"Nobody bobbing around."

Over 22,000 square miles to search. Needle in a haystack.

He said, "They're canvassing the area now, talking to other boaters."

"How about registration?"

"The boat's registered to a company named Armstrong Limited."

"Armstrong? Hmm. That's cute."

"What do you mean?"

"Arms. Strong. AK-47s are what I'd call pretty strong arms."

"Fleming, your mind is bizarre."

They explored the yacht. Between childhood events and her ten years as a police officer, Cara thought she had seen everything. The world was not a fair place. It was full of discrepancies, and people were evil. Why would anything surprise her? Seldom did she breathe the word "unbelievable." Now and then, though, a scene blindsided her. Odd that it was not the grotesque that affected her so, but rather something like this yacht.

The contrast of her previous night's stint at a shelter with the luxury she now moved through might have been the cause of her amazement. How did one make enough money to pay for such things? More to the point, why would they spend it in that way? Didn't they have anything better to do with it or with their time?

She followed a trail of blood on the deck floor. "It's on the railing here."

"Here too," Marcus said from a few feet away. "What do you think?"

"Deal gone bad. Gun deal." They'd already seen the crate of assault weapons below deck.

"They shoot each other and everybody falls overboard?"

"No. There's got to be another boat involved. But why would they leave guns on this one?"

"They ran out of time or space."

"Why not throw them overboard? Eliminate some evidence at least."

"They're idiots." He pulled his ringing cell from a pocket.

Marcus often concluded their hypothesizing with that summary, "They're idiots." Whenever it proved true, Cara rewarded him with a bag of his favorite candy bars. The man should have been overweight by now.

He shut his phone, a lopsided grin on his face. "Guess who's a major stockholder in the corporation called Armstrong Limited? I'll give you a hint. He's a friend of ours."

A friend. They had plenty of "friends." Ones they'd helped send to prison. Ones who were informants. Others who had gone by the wayside, their files still open but no proof or leads to actively pursue. And then there were the ones whose images haunted their dreams.

Ones like Ian Stafford.

The late Melanie Lareau was his cousin. Unregistered guns were found in her apartment. Now there were guns on a yacht. A yacht called *All That Jazz*. Jazz... Jasmine? The girlfriend?

Cara looked at her partner. "Ian Stafford."

His grin widened.

The following Saturday afternoon Cara fidgeted in a back-row pew along the far-right aisle in St. James. Terri Schuman was about to become Mrs. Gabe Andrews, and Cara's mind was light years away.

She rolled the wedding program into a tube. Unrolled it. Clenched her fist. Unclenched it. Pinched her skirt. Smoothed it. Heard bits and pieces of the organ music. Heard the words in her head drown it out.

The words echoed from that night at Miriam House when Father Bryan asked why she was so involved with the homeless. *Now he is getting personal*, she had thought and avoided an explanation. *Not even a clerical collar holds the key to that door. Nope.*

Flash forward to dinner at the restaurant last week. The guy shows up without the collar and she turns to gelatin. He'd shed his usual black "uniform," those priestly clothes worn as a constant humbling reminder to himself that although he was a front-and-center representative of Jesus, he was human and born of a sinful nature just like everybody else. But to Cara that "uniform" marked him as set apart from regular people. While on one level she acknowledged that did not mean he walked on water, on another level she respected his position to such a degree as to think they had nothing in common beyond their faith, which remained at best an abstract mystery. And that was fine with her. It added order to her world.

Then that separation vanished. Collarless, Bryan O'Shaugnessy was even more formidable as a *regular* person. She no longer reacted to the office but to the man.

A man the likes of which she'd never met in her entire life nor even imagined existed on earth.

If Jesus Christ were of Irish descent with curly red hair and green eyes, people would confuse him with a Chicagoan named Bryan Donahue O'Shaugnessy.

He mesmerized her with his quick smile, gentle manners, guileless conversation. There was no escaping the undisguised compassion that permeated every word, every gesture, every sparkle of peridot.

Of course he held the key to that door which opened into her past. Why wouldn't she want to share the memories with someone who treated them like injured sparrows and promised to fix them if given half a chance?

No two ways about it. She could love such a man.

But that wasn't going to happen.

Lord, I signed up for not leaving Chicago. I signed up for staying close to Granny. I signed up for being Terri's friend. I even signed up for church. But I did not, I repeat, did not sign up for this. And You know why.

She laughed mirthlessly to herself. Had she really been concerned about "glommers," people who might urge her to join church committees and whatnot? She should have worried about the priest! Hands down, his glomming technique won the blue ribbon. It melted the ice water in her veins like the desert sun on a bowl of ice cubes. Pffft. Gone.

The organ music changed, and the crowd rose as one to the tune of the Bridal March. Cara followed suit.

She saw Bryan up front.

Bryan.

Father Bryan.

Today he wore his collar and white gownlike vestment and, over that, elegantly embroidered gold apronlike vestments. Today he was his position.

She breathed more easily.

~

Cara chatted with those around her who waited to greet
Terri and her new husband, Gabe. Though the wedding party
was small, Terri insisted she had used up every ounce of
courage just agreeing to a church ceremony. Still, the line
moved like a caterpillar through the back of the church and
out into the vestibule.

Cara told herself she could do this. Stand, chat, hug Terri,
slip out the side door. Offer a polite "no, thank you" to
anyone reminding her there was a buffet and cake in the
parish hall.

The smiling couple came into view. Terri's tough
demeanor was lost in a sleeveless mid-calf ivory sheath dress
and string of pearls. One side of her short black hair was
pinned back with tiny flowers, revealing a pearl earring. She
looked decidedly feminine.

Beside her Gabe Andrews was handsome in his fireman's
navy blue dress uniform. A firefighter herself, Terri could have
worn her own uniform. She blamed crazy hormones on her
choice of outfit. Cara thought it a good decision; Gabe
couldn't take his eyes off her.

Cara chatted briefly with Rachel Koski, Terri's friend from
Iowa and lone wedding attendant. As in the other times she
had talked with the young widow, she was struck by the
serenity that surrounded her. Surely it was God's grace.

She continued down the line and offered hugs and congratulations to the happy couple. Then, instead of following
others to the right, she turned left. Her hand on the door's exit
bar, she thought, *Home free.*

"Cara!"

She turned and saw Bryan striding down the long hall.
Gone was the gold brocaded outer vestment, but he still wore

the billowy white surplice cinched at the waist with a rope. It suited him, she thought, that ancient dress of men, representative of the timeless quality of Christ's work on earth. A work remembered in the rope's five knots, symbolic of the wounds inflicted upon Jesus on the cross.

He stopped before her, smiling. "Do you have a few minutes?"

The comfort she felt under his gaze steamrolled her reply right on through from heart to vocal cords to tongue. There was no thinking involved whatsoever. "Sure."

"I want to show you what we talked about and get your opinion." He gestured back down the hall. "It's this way."

She fell into step beside him. What was it they had talked about? A shelter. At the church.

"I have to get keys from my study. It was a beautiful wedding, wasn't it?"

"Yes, it was. Terri's so happy." Her eyes strayed to a row of eight-by-ten photographs hanging on the wall. Bryan's stood out naturally, with his curly paprika hair. Even his compassionate demeanor seemed to jump from the glossy paper. The photo must have been taken years ago. Fewer crow's feet lined his eyes; the laugh creases were less well defined. He had aged.

Bryan pushed open a door and stepped back to let her enter. "Do you know Gabe?"

"Not well."

"He's dancing on air. It's a good thing they're headed to Hawaii for two weeks. The shape they're in, I wouldn't want them fighting fires or caring for accident victims."

The rich odor of wood greeted Cara as she stepped into his office. Like Bryan, the room and its furnishings were bulky and solid. Large. Old-fashioned.

He walked around a massive oak desk and pulled open a drawer. "I haven't mentioned this shelter idea to many. Actually, only my sister, Meagan, knows. She's my secretary too. Have you met her?"

"No. What does she think?"

"That I'm crazy." He palmed a key chain and smiled at her. "But that's nothing new."

She imagined he could be a difficult boss to keep up with, or brother, for that matter.

"The soup kitchen is going well," he said. "We've gotten more volunteers since moving it to Fridays."

"That's what I heard." She gestured at the office. "This is a wonderful room."

"Isn't it, though? Except for Meagan's rearranging of the furniture and adding the plants, it hasn't changed since I was a kid. I was in awe of it then and used to peek inside every chance I had. Once my mother dragged me in to meet with the rector. I think I was ten. She demanded he do something with me before my dad killed me. An exaggeration. Dad never laid a hand on us kids. Not that he needed to with that mug of his."

"What happened?"

"Mom left and I sat in that chair." He pointed to a leather winged-back. "I ate ice cream, Father Handley smoked his pipe, and we had a man-to-man talk. The first of many."

Cara inhaled deeply. "That's what it is. You smoke a pipe. Cherry tobacco."

"Ah, the cop nose. No one else notices."

"Or they don't dare mention it."

He grinned. "I lean out the window. Except when the snow flies."

They left the study. He turned down a narrow hall toward the rear of the building. It ended at a small entryway. She noticed the back door she had entered the night she helped with the soup supper. Next to that was the kitchen. Clatter seeped through its shut door. The wedding reception was in full swing.

Bryan unlocked a door, and she followed him into the foyer of what appeared to be a newer wing of the building. She had noticed it before, the two-storied exterior with its less ornate architectural style and grayish brick walls that didn't quite match the 175-year-old stone.

She asked, "What's this used for?"

"The youth. Except for this open area here, the section is all classrooms. We built it a decade ago. A parishioner left us millions of dollars with the stipulation it be used for this construction, for the children. We'd outgrown the old structure." He shrugged. "A neighbor sold property to us, enabling us to expand. We even gained a parking lot. God spoils us."

"I thought people were leaving churches in droves."

"He spoils us *rotten*."

"Or uses you mightily."

He shifted his eyes from hers and turned to unlock yet another door. They went through it and descended a staircase. "Not too mightily. We haven't grown into the basement. It sits empty day in, day out, year in, year out."

In a word the basement was nice. The walls were paneled. The linoleum was shiny. The ceiling was plastered. Windows at the top of the walls were large enough to let in the daylight. The expected musty odor was nonexistent. She heard the subdued hum of air purifiers.

She said, "It doesn't have a basement feel to it."

"Ten years ago we needed the space for the kids. Now, although people aren't leaving in droves, the congregation is aging and the young families are smaller."

He opened a set of double doors. Behind them lay a huge open area, like the upstairs. He walked to the center of it and held out his arms.

"So here's my idea. This is the sleeping room. Restrooms are down that way." He pointed. "Kitchenette through there. Behind that sliding door is an alcove that could be a sitting room. We only need to add showers—the plumbing's all there—and a locker room. The whole place is separate from the main church, with its own outside entrance. That door we came through is kept locked except on Sunday mornings." His arms fell at his sides and he looked at her. "What do you think?"

The man carried his generous heart like a watering can, tipping it indiscriminately. Some dry corner of her spirit leapt as droplets of compassion rained about her. "Oh, Bryan, it's perfect!"

He grinned, a little kid drinking in praise. "Really?"

"Yes!"

His grin faded until only one corner of his mouth remained lifted. "All I need is money, the congregation's support, rules, a director, volunteers, and a plan that addresses who gets to use it and when."

She raised her hands, palms up. "Piece of cake."

"Such faith."

"No. I'm just crazy enough like you to believe it can happen."

"We make a good pair."

Something rearranged itself inside of her, and a sensation of melting flowed through her veins. In the blink of an eye she knew Bryan Donahue O'Shaugnessy was not a man she *could* fall in love with. Nope. She was already there.

Not good. Not good at all.

"Cara." He gave his earlobe a quick tug. "Will you have dinner with me tonight? Tomorrow night? Take a walk this afternoon? Browse through a bookstore? Help me clean out the garage?"

"Your date invitations are starting to flow pretty easily."

"I've been practicing in front of a mirror."

She glanced around the room, the walls, the ceiling, the floor. Anywhere but at him. How had she gotten into this situation? The last she remembered she was sitting in church beside Terri, minding her own business.

He said, "I'm sorry. I thought it went well with the mirror."

She gave him a brief smile. "It's not you."

"All right."

"Which leaves me." She took a deep breath. "Bryan, I had dinner with you as a friend. I don't date per se. I can't date. I can't get involved with..." Her lungs ran out of air.

A long moment passed. "I thought— I assumed you were available. You don't wear a ring and you didn't say— Please forgive me. I'm out of practice. I should have sensed you were involved. Instead I imagined there was...something mutual between us..." His lack of breath echoed her own.

Her heart ached at the confusion on his face. She tried again. "I'm not involved in that way." And it probably wasn't his imagination.

"Then what?"

Just say the words. Two stinking words. Nip it in the bud. You have to nip it in the bud. Chase him away. Finish it. But the words were buried with Nick's name, with the name of those cities—

"Cara?"

She opened her mouth. At first no sound came forth. At last a whisper gave up the two stinking words so long suppressed. "I'm married."

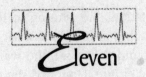

Eleven

"I'm married."

Bryan hadn't felt the wind knocked from him since his Army days. He never would have imagined the possibility of it happening while he stood perfectly still, several feet from another person. But then never would he have imagined himself falling in love with a policewoman at the drop of a hat.

Calm, cool, and collected Detective Fleming stammered, "I mean, I think I am. Still. I-I never talk about him. Or to him. Only Rubyann knows. H-he's not part of my life. But legally...biblically..." Her voice trailed off yet again. "I told you I hold things loosely. Even friendships. All of life is just so temporary."

As he struggled to take a breath, her reserved manner disintegrated. A weight had descended, pressing down her shoulders, crumpling the smooth lines of her face. She needed a hug. He needed a hug.

"I-I didn't mean to deceive you, Bryan. This..." She waved her arms in a helpless gesture. "Whatever *this* is— What is this?"

He found his voice, a hoarse scrape of vocal cords, and whittled the complicated emotions he felt toward her down to one word. "Attraction."

"Too strong. For goodness' sake, we just met! Call it an adolescent crush."

"We're too old for that."

"We just met!" She threw back her shoulders and widened her eyes. Self-control was being restored. "It's early enough to nip this whatever in the bud. I need some air."

He touched her arm before she'd turned completely away. Going upstairs would end the conversation. "Wait, please. Tell me more. At least the CliffsNotes version?"

She pressed her fingertips against her eyes for a few seconds. Then she brushed her hands across her face. The uncharacteristic fragile expression was erased, aloofness reasserted itself. "Does anyone ever refuse you?"

He accepted the muttered question as rhetorical and ignored it. "You told me at dinner you fell in love with the first guy who looked at you twice. I just assumed you didn't marry— He's not the one, is he? The one you ran away from? In Seattle?"

She crossed her arms. Her confidence was faltering again.

"How many eons ago was that?" He couldn't mask his astonishment.

"Several."

"Why not file for divorce? You said it's an ugly story. I'm sure you've got grounds—"

"Bryan, he stalks me. I'm not contacting him in any way, shape, or form. Not even through lawyers or cops."

"Wouldn't he have declared that you've deserted him or something by now? Aren't there divorce laws—"

"Not in Washington." She shook her head, more of a nervous gesture than negative response. "He found me in Portland, San Francisco, and Los Angeles. He'll keep hunting me until the day he dies. I've been in Chicago a long time. Too long. I should leave. I should definitely leave now. But I promised Granny..."

"What's his name?"

Her eyes widened. "The last time I saw him, I shot at him! I only missed because he'd smacked me and I couldn't see straight. Every day I hope and pray that scared him off for good but—" She bit her lip.

Now he understood. Fear engulfed her. She would not breathe his name. If there was any chance anyone would repeat it— "Isn't there some law that says after so long people are just automatically divorced?"

She gazed at him. "I don't think so. Bryan, there's no getting around this fact."

"In all this time you've never been attracted to someone? Fallen in love?"

"No."

His brows rose, giving expression to his incredulity.

"It happens."

Of course it happens. What was he thinking? That he owned the corner on being single and free from distractions along the way? "I know. That's been my experience too. Until now."

Again a little shake of her head. Dismissing his words. "I've dealt with this in the abstract. The conclusion is I'm married. Period. Biblically speaking, I will be married until one of us is dead."

He felt his own eyes grow wide now. "Cara, Jesus described an ideal to strive for. He didn't say if the guy beats you, sit there and take it."

"I didn't sit there and take it. Jesus also did not say if the guy beats you, get a divorce. End of CliffsNotes."

"You are a perfectionist."

She uncrossed her arms, shrugged, and turned on her heel. "I need some air."

He followed her through the basement, thinking of her dinner conversation last week and filling in blanks. Her bent

toward perfectionism meant she'd never been loved uncon-
ditionally. Or it was a lame excuse for not facing old fears.

Baggage.

Lord, have mercy.

They climbed the stairs.

"Cara?"

No response. They went out the back door and into the
crisp, late afternoon October air before she turned to look at
him. "I just don't want to talk anymore right now. Okay?" Her
voice had recovered its normal even tone, but her eyes
squinted as if holding tears at bay.

He swallowed his question about having dinner later. "All
right."

Again she swiveled on her heel and walked away.

He watched her take long determined steps down the
length of the building. Watched her hips sway in that wild-
print skirt, her hair swish, her arms swing. She didn't look
back, not even when she rounded the corner.

I don't want to talk anymore right now. Did that insinuate
they could talk at another time? As far as he was concerned,
it did. After all, bud-nipping required two-bladed clippers. Or
at the least two fingers, a thumb and a finger to pinch off the
bud. In the case of a blossoming relationship, two people
were needed to snip. She couldn't do it on her own. And he
certainly wasn't about to help.

⌒

His lungs still not working to capacity, Bryan entered the
parish hall and hoped no one would ask if he'd been jogging. Had the reception been for almost anyone else, he
might have considered abandoning it. But Gabe was a good

friend, and he'd counseled Terri long before she met Gabe. He owed them the effort of putting in an appearance.

Besides that, Rachel was there. With her friend. Norman Rockwell. The fiancé who hadn't been at the previous night's rehearsal dinner. With no rain in the forecast, he'd had to spend the day in his fields. Imagine structuring life around the weather. Midwest weather at that.

Rachel grabbed Bryan's arm. "There you are! Please come and meet Phil."

Phil Rockwell, not Norman. He submitted to her towing him through the crowd. The guy was easy to spot across the room. Six-four or five. All gangly angles. "Is he related?"

Rachel grinned over her shoulder. "To Norman? No."

"Quite a resemblance."

She made the introductions and excused herself to go help Terri with something or other.

Phil smiled. "It's good to finally meet you, Father Bryan. Rachel has told me so much about you." His voice was that of a man who spent much time alone in a tractor cab and spoke mainly to plants and machines. Soft.

"Call me Bryan. Vic and I were like brothers, so Rachel's practically family. It's good to meet you too." Though he meant the words, he didn't hear much conviction in his own tone. To make up for that, he added, "Congratulations, by the way."

"Thank you." His complexion was ruddy, his eyes light, his hair a medium brown and scarcely long enough to run a comb through. He appeared to be around Rachel's age, late thirties.

They made small talk. The weather. The drive from Iowa. The tollway versus I-80. The season's crop outlook.

Bryan didn't relax. Cara's news hovered at the edge of his awareness. Vic loomed at the forefront of his mind. Phil Rockwell was an intrusion.

"Bryan, I love Rachel."

He jerked to attention.

"I know I can never take Vic's place in her life. I'm not trying to."

Father O'Shaugnessy, the priest with a word for every occasion, was speechless.

"I just wanted you to know that." Phil smiled. His eyes creased nearly shut.

He nodded once. "Appreciate it."

Phil held out his hand and shook Bryan's. "We hope you'll come to the wedding. Valentine's Day. Good meeting you."

Bryan nodded again and watched him lope away.

Like another punch to his stomach, he felt the pain of losing his friend all over again. He blamed Phil Rockwell. He did not want to like Phil Rockwell. And what kind of name was *Rachel Rockwell*? It didn't sound right.

He owed them an apology.

If he could ever catch his breath.

Twelve

A loud shrill rang out, filtering into Cara's dream world. Bryan held her close, his large hands cupped over her ears as a deafening fire alarm clanged.

Were there smoke detectors in his church basement? They would be needed. She must tell him that.

The noise deafened again, and a half-formed thought overtook the dream. She rolled over and dropped her hand onto the radio clock's snooze button. Eyes shut, she fought against the consciousness nibbling at a comfort so real she smelled the fresh scent of soap on his hands.

Again the dissonant piercing.

Another tap on the clock only heightened its *brrrrnng*. She opened her eyes. The room was dark except for green digital numbers displaying 4:11. Why would she set the alarm for 4:11?

The phone rang.

She hadn't set the clock for 4:11.

Closing her eyes again, she moved her hand from the clock to the phone next to it. "H'lo."

"Hey, Sleeping Beauty." Marcus. "Want to get in on a Stafford interview?"

Stafford? Stafford who?

"I followed him home from the hotel. Got here about two. I say we go in and ask him about his boat before he leaves again. The guy keeps strange hours."

Ian Stafford, the hotel guy. Owner of the yacht *All That Jazz*. Jasmine Wakefield, the girlfriend. Guns. Big guns. Militia-type guns.

"Fleming? You with me?"

The coziness of the dream was snuffed out like a candle. "Yeah." She sat up. "Where are you?"

"On his street. Here's the address. It's in Wilmette." He recited a number and street name. "You got thirty minutes. Call me when you hit Sheridan and I'll talk you through the turns."

She hung up the phone and swung her feet to the floor. Thirty minutes wasn't much time. At least she'd taken a bath the night before. At least she'd prepared the coffeemaker. At least she had a clean blouse hanging in the closet.

At least she didn't have to explain to anyone why it was she would race through the predawn hour to a suburb to roust an uncooperative hotshot from bed before she even had her second cup of coffee.

That was her real world, not the dream one.

Shaking off the last vestiges of coziness and soap-scented hands, she headed to the kitchen, a strange new prayer on her lips: *Lord, bring back the Ice Lady so I can think straight again.*

⁓

Cara slid into the warm car beside her partner, handed him a travel mug full of coffee, and shut the door against a predawn mist. "Morning."

He grinned. "Thanks."

"Like knowing you'd get fresh coffee wasn't the reason you called me."

He swallowed his first sip. "Ah, perfect. Just the right amount of milk and sugar. You do take good care of me, Fleming. Renae says I should marry you."

I'm already married. A dream fragment rushed at her. Bryan walking beside her along the lake, saying her marriage status didn't matter. Had she dreamt of him all night long?

Chilled to the bone, she reached down and flipped the heater's fan on high. "Marcus, Stafford will charge us with harassment barging in at this hour. We're out of our jurisdiction. I thought we decided to contact him later today. Why not wait until a reasonable time? Seven at least. Bring in a local investigator. Find some donuts in the meantime. More coffee."

"You know why. We want to catch him off guard. Get his wife in on things. See what she's like."

"But what excuse are you giving to his lawyer?"

"We haven't been able to catch old Ian at the office. He wasn't home last night."

"We haven't tried to reach him at the office. I take it the second reason is valid?"

"Yep. Okay, let's go." He set his mug in the cup holder and shifted into drive. "Backup is across the street."

She hadn't even noticed the cop car. Where was her mind?

Probably with her heart, all wrapped up in that dream world.

~

The mansion was set back quite a distance from the street. Cara marveled at the length of the circular driveway. A parade complete with floats and bands could easily be held on it.

Security lights lit the front and side yards. Huge oak trees filled the parklike area. The house, in shadows, appeared to be three stories of red brick.

Marcus parked under an open-ended carport. Its roof, held aloft by thick white columns, extended out from the front door and over the drive. Motion-sensitive lights burst on, flooding the place with noonday-bright light.

They walked up to the wide set of double doors and Marcus rang the bell three times, pausing briefly between each. Several long moments passed before a voice came through an intercom.

"Who is it?"

Marcus held his shield up to the door's peephole and identified himself and Cara. "We'd like to speak with Mr. Stafford."

The door opened to reveal Ian, his eyes puffy with sleep. He wore a burgundy silk robe.

Marcus said, "Sorry to disturb you at this hour, sir." The man could be absolutely charming.

"We've met before."

"Yes, we have. We'd like to ask you a few questions. It doesn't concern what we discussed at the station."

Well, not yet anyway, Cara thought.

"I want my attorney."

There was movement behind him. A raven-haired, dark-eyed woman came into view. She was quite beautiful with her long hair tumbling about her face. A distinct softness emanated from her. Nothing at all like the girlfriend.

"Darling, what is it?" she asked, the voice as soft as her appearance.

"Cops."

As she stepped around Stafford, her shape came into view. She wore a fluffy white zippered robe. She was quite obviously pregnant. "What's wrong?"

Marcus said quickly, "No cause for alarm, ma'am. We're sorry to disturb you. We just need some information. I'm Detective Calloway and this is Detective Fleming." He reached in and shook her hand.

"I'm Lisa Stafford. Come inside, please. It's cold out there. I'll make some coffee. Ian, let them in." She turned away, clearly ignoring the scowl on her husband's face.

Cara and Marcus followed Stafford through an entryway, a set of French doors, and into a living room. A sense of opulence struck her, but there was something else. Though wood gleamed everywhere—banister, door frames, floors, woodwork—and furnishings appeared in showcase condition with no knickknack nor pillow out of place, the house had a lived-in feel. A distinct *hominess*.

Ian waved a hand toward the couch and sat in an upholstered chair. "I'm not answering any questions without my attorney present."

Marcus chose a chair. "You have that right, of course. Please, feel free to call him. We can wait."

"I'm not calling him at five in the morning!"

"Or we can meet him downtown."

Ian glared.

"Suit yourself."

Cara pulled her notebook from a pocket and sat on the couch. A display of framed photographs covered an end table beside it. They were all of two children, a boy and a girl between the ages of four and seven, both graced with the good-looking genes of their parents.

Ian shifted uneasily in his chair. "Go ahead and ask your questions. Let's get this over with."

"We'll wait for your wife." Marcus smiled, crossed his legs, and flipped through his notepad.

To the average citizen, the situation would feel awkward. Cara and Marcus were accustomed to long silences and skipping over small talk.

The wife would fill in blanks, not so much in her response to questions but in her manner, in how she related to her husband. Cara felt again the distinct hominess, as comforting as Rubyann's place. Never having lived in such an environment, Cara always noticed it. Like a cactus drinking in sporadic rainwater and storing it for long dry spells, she soaked up the ambience.

Odd that it appeared at Ian Stafford's house. The man was a criminal. He dealt in illegal arms. He was probably in the pocket of organized crime. He had a girlfriend as well as a pregnant wife and two children. Why would Lisa Stafford put up with him? She hadn't cowered in his presence. She never would have even come downstairs if their relationship threatened her in any way. Of course, if materialism fed her soul, she could put up with a lot to live in this lap of luxury.

Lisa entered the room, and Ian immediately rose to his feet to take a laden tray from her. He set it on the coffee table. At the sight of the silver pot and basketful of mini muffins, Cara's stomach rumbled.

Lisa chatted amiably as she poured coffee into china cups and placed a muffin on each saucer. While Marcus remained silent, Cara responded to the moment. She stood, passed around the goodies, and joined in the conversation. The gracious hostess talked of their children, when the baby was due, coffee beans, her PTA involvement, and the weather forecast.

After everyone was served, Marcus spoke again. "Mr. Stafford, we'd like to ask you about your yacht."

Lisa chuckled. "Oh my. We don't have a yacht! I don't even like the water."

Marcus said, "I should have said, the Armstrong Limited yacht." He tilted his head at Ian. "What does Armstrong Limited do, by the way?"

"It's an investment corporation." He turned to his wife. "One of the companies, dear."

"Oh."

Marcus asked, "What does it invest in?"

"Different things. It has a website."

"The entire world has a website. You're a stockholder?"

"Yes."

"Do you use the yacht?"

"It's available to me. I've used it for business outings. Lunches. That sort of thing."

"Interesting name."

Cara watched Lisa.

Marcus went on. "*All That Jazz*." He emphasized the last word.

A flicker in the wife's eye.

Marcus went on. "When was the last time you used it?"

"I'd have to check my calendar. It would have been in the summer."

"Not last week?"

"It's a little late in the season."

"Do you know where it is?"

The side of his neck darkened to the color of his silk robe. "It's not personally mine. I don't have a clue."

"I see. Who would report it if it were missing?"

"The people who take care of it. I'll get you a number."

"That won't be necessary. We found the boat, evidently before it was reported missing." He stood. "Thank you for your time."

Cara swallowed her last sip of the delicious coffee and followed suit. "And thank you for the coffee. We are sorry for disturbing you at this hour."

Lisa politely led them from the room. "No problem, Detective. I'm usually awake half the night anyway with the baby kicking up a storm."

A moment later, the door shut behind her, Cara stood still while Marcus continued on to the car. She waited for any unusual noise like a husband fussing at his wife for being kind to the enemy. Nothing reached her ears.

But she knew the Staffords were not as they seemed. Lisa knew the name Jasmine, perhaps suspected the woman's role in her husband's life. Ian hadn't yet heard of the yacht being found.

Marital bliss? A happy home?

Cara felt sorry for them and said a prayer. She wondered why more women didn't choose a different way, even if it meant living on the streets.

Thirteen

"Bry, you sure you don't want a beer?" Flynn O'Shaugnessy untwisted the cap from his own bottle.

Sitting at his brother's kitchen table, Bryan set down a glass of water. "I'm sure." He eyed Flynn closely. Three years his elder, he could have been mistaken for Bryan's twin except for the haggard face and thinning hair. "You look like you just worked three straight shifts."

"You should've been a cop." He grinned. "I had one off in between."

"Why do you do that?"

He shrugged a shoulder. "Ellen's out of town on her annual trek with the women friends, shopping at that whatchamacallit mall in Minneapolis. Like there ain't enough shopping in Chi-Town. No reason for me not to pull in some extra dough while she's gone." He barked a laugh. "Gotta keep her in shopping money."

It was not a fair statement. Ellen worked full-time. "How are the kids?" Besides being uncle to Meagan's little ones, Bryan had two grown nephews, Flynn's sons.

Pride straightened his brother's shoulders. "They're great. Still loving school, paid for out of their own pockets. Law and dentistry. They'll take care of me in my old age."

An old age that might have already arrived. Bryan worried over his brother's deterioration. Like with their dad, police work had worn him down. Unlike their dad, Flynn drank too much and hinted at personally knowing about bribes from certain unmentionable sectors of society.

"So, Bry, to what do I owe the pleasure of your visit?"

The snide tone was not lost on Bryan. They seldom saw each other and when they did, polite conversation usually fell apart unless Ellen or Meagan served as buffers. Adolescent rivalry had not matured into mutual respect. Flynn thought the priesthood a cop-out; Bryan thought Flynn had sold his soul to police work. His sons might be making a success of their lives, but they were doing it in spite of Flynn, not because of his fatherly influence. They too seldom saw him. His loyal wife was staunchly faithful, though. She and Cara would get along well. *Stand by your man.*

Bryan cleared his throat. "I need to find someone. Who's the best private investigator you know?"

"Depends. Who's the someone you're looking for?"

"A guy. I don't know his name. He's not from around here."

"Not much to go on."

"I know his wife's name. His last known address was in Seattle."

"So the wife wants to find him?"

"No. I do."

A small smile curved his thin lips. "Vengeance is mine, saith the Lord."

Bryan took a drink of water. Flynn had heard what he heard, the nuance in his own voice declaring he would take care of this bottom feeder. *No. I do.*

Flynn laughed, reached over and cuffed him on the shoulder. "Cops and priests. We're not all that different underneath, are we?"

"He's a stalker."

"No wonder the woman doesn't want to find him. Sure you don't need to go through police channels?"

He shook his head. "It needs to be done discreetly. The guy must know people. He tracked her across three states, maybe more."

"She belong to your church?" Flynn himself had not set foot inside of it since their parents retired to Florida. He used to show up occasionally to please their mother. His wife went to a different one without him.

"Yeah, she comes to the church."

A smile spread slowly across his brother's face. Bryan used to see that smile on their dad's face. It wasn't a nice one.

Flynn chuckled. "You got the hots for her."

Bryan stood, nearly knocking over his chair.

His brother roared in laughter.

"Look." He felt his face flush. "Do you have some PI's name or not? That's all I need. Just a name."

Flynn wiped a tear from his cheek and rose. "Oh, don't go getting all huffy, little brother. It's good to see you're human after all. I was beginning to worry. Sit down. Sit down. I gotta go dig out the guy's number. He's not in the book."

Fists clutched at his side, Bryan watched his brother saunter down the hall. Yeah, he was human. Yeah, he had the hots for Cara Fleming. Yeah, he wanted to take out the guy who'd hurt her.

And yeah, cops and priests were not all that different.

Bryan thought he was in a bad movie.

He had trudged up five flights rather than ride the elevator of a building the fire department surely must not have inspected during his lifetime. It had condemned written all over it. He sat in an office the size of a walk-in closet. Grime covered its single window. The only light came from a desk lamp nearly hidden beneath a clutter of papers, file folders, and books. A computer caught his eye from some other surface, but he didn't want to inspect the corners of the room too closely. Blue smoke hung in the air.

Behind the desk, his sneaker-covered feet propped on it, Private Investigator Ray Abbott puffed on a cheap cigar. He appeared to be in his mid-fifties. His long-sleeved shirt of indeterminate color hung on his frame as if made for a man twice his size. He wore a blue Cubs ball cap.

"Okay, Padre." Ray studied the legal pad resting against his knees. "Let's go through this one more time. The guy you want me to find is from Seattle. He's married to Cara Fleming, late thirties. Abused her. She left him approximately fifteen years ago."

"That's a wild guess. She grew up going to an Episcopal church and she told me she had been away from church that long."

"Then it's a valid assumption."

"Palmer!"

"Huh?"

"She called him Father Palmer. Her priest. It just came to me. I remembered thinking his name was similar to the priest I grew up with, Father Handley. You know, palm, hand."

"Whatever works." He wrote it down on his pad. "Okay. So she grew up on the wrong side of the tracks, maybe close to the church. Her mother died when she was eighteen. She has a half sister named Shelly or Cheryl or Sherry. Cara has lived in Portland, San Francisco, and Los Angeles." He looked up. "You think Fleming is her maiden name? Good chance she wouldn't keep the name of the guy who abused her. Or even use one he knew."

Bryan's heart sank. He hadn't thought of her need to change names.

"No worries. Happens all the time. There's always a paper trail." He paused. "Mind if I ask what you're going to do once I find this guy?"

That he had considered. "Tell him to leave her alone."

"You don't think that's been done?"

"Not by me."

Ray laughed. "You sound like Flynn."

Cops and priests.

"You know, Padre, it wouldn't take much for me to find out what she does for a living."

Bryan had refused to give him that information. "Like I said, I don't want you talking to her coworkers or friends. She told me that except for one person, no one else around here knows her story. If she gets even a whiff of your investigation, she'll disappear, go to the streets."

"I won't chase her off. Promise. You've got to trust me. It's the only way this business deal here between us works. You trust your brother, don't you?"

Bryan hesitated. The compassion he so freely gave to most anyone who crossed his path dried up when he thought of Flynn. The man did not deserve it. And besides, he would only fling it back in Bryan's face.

Sometimes Bryan confessed his sin; sometimes not.

Still, blood ran thicker than water. Flynn would not deceive him on important matters. He would not have steered him to Ray Abbott unless the PI knew his stuff.

222

He cast aside his discomfort with the situation—the dive of an office, the dirty business it represented, the rough character to whom he'd chosen to display his secret treasure. He studied Ray more closely. His face was smooth. Not like he'd just shaved but like a young boy's hairless jaw line. There was no hair showing below the baseball cap, not even a buzzed trace.

As last he replied, "Yes. I trust my brother."

"Good. Then you can trust me. Our conversation is like you listening to someone's confession. You don't go airing some guy's dirty laundry in front of your church members, do you?"

"No, of course not."

"Same thing. Anything you tell me stays between us, and it might help in ways you can't foresee. Not to mention it'd save me time from figuring it out on my own. Time I'd have to charge you for."

His secret treasure collided with practicality. He listened to his head instead of those churning emotions that threatened to drown out reasonableness. "She's a Chicago police detective. I don't know what division."

"Who's the one person she told her story to?"

"Her partner's grandmother. *I'll* talk to her."

"You got it. Who's her partner?"

Rubyann Calloway's grandson. "Marcus. Calloway might be the last name."

"Okay."

They finished with monetary details. The parish provided for many of Bryan's needs, and his salary, while not large, was more than adequate to help Cara with this matter. If that meant hiring a detective to find the man who still held her in the powerful grip of fear, then that's what he would do.

He stood and shook the PI's hand. "I'll pray for you. For success. And for your health."

Ray gazed at him, his dark eyes nearly hidden beneath the cap's bill. "Doc thinks they licked it this time. Chemo treatments are done. I'm fit as a fiddle. But thanks. I'll leave for Seattle in a day or two."

Bryan walked down the stairs, struck as he was at times with hindsight of God's role. He'd been a priest for 17 years, at times curious that he did not yearn for a woman's companionship. Now he knew it was God's hand protecting him from complications. As a young man he would not have possessed the capability to manage both the priesthood and a woman.

He walked through the seedy lobby of the seedy building in a seedy neighborhood and wondered why he thought he had it now.

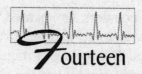

$\mathcal{F}$ourteen

"Granny, don't give me that nonsense!" Cara sat on the edge of Rubyann's couch, tightly gripping her knees.

The old woman's lips bunched together. Her rocker creaked out a regular beat. "It is not nonsense. Our prayers are more powerful when we know a few details to pray about."

"That's just an excuse for spreading gossip."

"Father Bryan will not spread gossip about Nick Davis. He did not ask for his name. I told him because he cares about you. And he's a clergyman, for goodness' sake!"

"What else did you tell him?"

"Honey-child, your attitude is downright sassy and disrespectful."

Cara let go of her knees, scooted further back on the cushion, and lowered her voice. "I'm sorry. But you know how I feel. Marcus doesn't even know details."

"Marcus doesn't have to know details. Your relationship with Bryan is different. You're the one who done told him you're married."

"Well, he wanted to—" She clamped her mouth shut.

"Wanted to what? Get to know you?"

"Date."

"In other words, get to know you. Of course he wants to get to know you. He thinks he's in love with you. How else can he find out if that's true or not unless he spends time with you?"

"That would be pointless. I'm married."

"Pshaw! You're no more married than the man in the moon. And besides. The feeling is mutual. Otherwise you wouldn't have avoided him by missing church two Sundays in a row."

"Marcus and I worked again this week."

"Mm-hmm."

The rocker creaked in rhythm with the clock's ticking pendulum. Cara tried to shut out Rubyann's words, but the truth of them interfered. The feeling between her and Bryan was mutual. There was a connection. An attraction. A desire to linger over the thought *what if...* What if she weren't married? What if they spent time together, getting to know each other? What if she let down her guard and allowed another human being besides Rubyann to move in next to her heart? What if she honestly made long-term plans to remain in Chicago?

That thinking was a slippery slope. She'd better shore it up before sliding on into an emotional abyss. The old woman held necessary information that she wasn't about to release if Cara didn't quit asking questions like a cop. She loosened her shoulders and softened her clear, strong voice.

"Granny, please. I need to know what else you told him. It will help me communicate with him."

The old woman ceased rocking. Tenderness filled the dark eyes she turned upon Cara. "Oh, honey-child. I just gave him a peek into what you've been through. Things you've had to do to keep Nick Davis from finding you."

A hollow feeling edged its way into Cara's chest. "You told him I changed my name?"

"I did. It shows just how awful things were for you. I mean—to give up your own identity! You couldn't even keep the name your mama gave you." She shook her head, a look of pity on her face.

"Did you tell him that name?"

"No. I don't remember it. You only said it to me that one time. Two, three years ago now. You're Cara Fleming to me. Always will be."

Not Cari-Ann Wilson, the little girl. Nor Cari-Ann Davis, the young wife. Would she ever forget the names? Would God ever wipe clean the slate of memories associated with them?

"I did tell him you chose Fleming because it was the name of your mother's one nice boyfriend. And I told him Nick was a small-time dope peddler. The first time you left him, he found you at a shelter for abused women, a so-called safe place he shouldn't have been able to find. Another time he found you at the parsonage. He almost caught up with you in Portland and San Francisco. He did find you in Los Angeles. You've been here six years. Only prayer will keep you here and Nick Davis away."

Cara's stomach ached. Her history wasn't nearly the most wretched she'd ever heard, but she had lived through it one gruesome day at a time. She supposed it made up who she was today. Still, nobody in their right mind would want to sign up for that baggage.

"All right, Granny, I changed my mind. I'm glad you told him. It's enough to send him hightailing the other direction."

Rubyann set her rocker in motion again. A tiny smile played about her lips. "You're right. And there's a milkmaid up there with the man in the moon, busy making green cheese." She laughed and laughed.

Sometimes the woman really did get on Cara's nerves.

Cara walked through the evening dusk. Vehicles lined the curbs on both sides of the street. She'd had to park three blocks away, nearer the church than Rubyann's apartment building.

No one lingered outdoors. Autumn was in the air. Such a sad season in the Midwest. Leaves dressed in bright colors, only to go out in a blaze of glory, fluttering one by one to the ground. Separated from the life-giving tree, they dried up and crackled underfoot. On rare occasions when the sun glowed, it was through stark branches, only a false promise of warmth as night crept in before the afternoon ended. Birds escaped the area, winged clouds soaring southward, hordes of them every day. Rubyann's bones ached in the chill, and the woman who could put a positive spin on just about anything complained.

Cara folded her arms across her chest, holding her jacket more tightly shut. The church steeple loomed ahead. Another half block and she'd be able to see the front door.

"Lord, did you really have to move Granny practically next door to St. James?" she muttered to herself. "No wonder I dream about him." She was beginning to avoid saying Bryan's name as well as Nick's. "He's everywhere I turn." *Sundays, weddings, Granny's conversation, this neighborhood.*

She hadn't had time to attend a Wednesday service, though she hoped to when given a chance. Midweek soul-feeding enhanced life tremendously. Of course, he would be there. She had served again at the church's supper for the needy. Of course, he was there too. And he had shown up at the Lazarus Outreach shelter to help serve the same night she was there.

He had become part of the landscape.

From behind her the roar of a motorcycle broke the neighborhood silence. It passed by, cruising well over the 30-mile-an hour speed limit. Not much she could do about it on foot.

Couldn't they just be friends? Enjoy each other's company. Engage in stimulating conversation. Exchange ideas. Serve at soup kitchens.

And ignore the attraction. Ignore the curious way her heart beat when she saw him. Ignore the longing her dreams stirred up: to be held in his arms.

After a few days away from him and lost once again in her work, she noticed the dreams lessened. Ice returned to her veins and replaced the sensation of melting. That moment in the church basement—when he described his shelter idea and she fancied herself in love with him—that was gone. In love? How silly could she be?

Lord, I promised You I would remain loyal to the marriage vow 'til death do us part. I will not tear asunder what You brought together when Father Palmer married us. I don't want to undo Your sacrament. Isn't that the right thing? Even though it would be suicide to live with my husband.

She shuddered and glanced around. Spontaneous fear. The reaction was typical whenever she thought of Nick Davis. Her steps quickened.

Down the block the motorcycle's brake lights reddened. The driver made a U-turn and the bike roared back in her direction. Within seconds it reached a parked car she neared. The driver braked and cut the engine. He reached up and removed his black helmet. As curly red hair came into view, Cara halted, parallel to him.

Bryan grinned and called out, "You won't give me a ticket if I double-park here, will you?" Not waiting for an answer, he swung his leg over the bike and stepped between two parked cars, the helmet under one arm.

"I should give you a ticket for speeding, Father O'Shaug-nessy." That funny little twitch did its thing in her chest, making her aware momentarily of her heartbeat. "Forty in a thirty. Tsk, tsk."

"Pshaw."

"You've been hanging around Rubyann. But I knew that without you quoting her favorite word." The accusatory tone intensified. Backlash to Rubyann's gabbing or her own heart-beat's betrayal? "You had pie at her place last night."

Laughing, he leaned against the fender of a car and crossed his arms, the helmet dangling from a hand. Even in the dim light she could see that his face was flushed, ruddy from the wind as if he'd been riding for a while. He wore black slacks and a black leather jacket snapped tight at his throat.

"Mm-hmm. Blackberry. She's a fantastic baker."

"She talks too much."

"You sound disturbed."

"That's putting it mildly. She had no right to blab all my business to you."

Always the thoughtful listener, he didn't immediately reply, no doubt structuring his words with care. "She loves you. Maybe the information was getting to be too much for her to carry alone. Maybe she thought since I'm in the priest busi-ness, I know how to keep my mouth shut."

Her righteous indignation fizzled, and she gazed across the darkening front yards. What he said rang true. She had burdened Rubyann, taking advantage of the old woman's compassionate nature.

"Cara, do you want to talk about it?"

She turned her attention back to him. "There's nothing to talk about. You really can't help. It's over and done with. It's not like I'm living in the middle of that horrific situation anymore. I'm thousands of miles away. With friends. With my own home even. My first ever. I attend church and love my work."

"Then let's talk about us."

"*Us?*" She cringed inwardly at her suddenly soprano voice. Its effect blew her in-control demeanor to pieces.

"You took off before we finished the topic the other day. I think we'd gotten to the point where we agreed there may be something to an *us*."

"No, we'd gotten to the point beyond that where I stated there can't be an *us* because I'm married."

"Good heavens, I'm not asking you to marry me."

"But that would be the sole reason to date."

"Huh?"

"Why date unless it's to explore that mutual whatever, to see if there is an *us* which might possibly lead to marriage? Or living together, a situation I doubt either of us would consider."

"All right. Truce. How about a friendship? Friends go out to dinner together. They browse through bookstores together. The activity doesn't have to be referred to as a date when it's between friends. I think we're friends. Can we be friends?" He echoed precisely her own thoughts.

Why couldn't they be friends? The guy had become part of her landscape, a fixture like Rubyann and fellow police officers were. She wasn't likely going to be able to avoid him without abandoning church again. A chill hardened somewhere in the center of her being, that place beneath the ice water, the place that was supposed to stay warm.

No. She would not abandon church again or go through the process of finding another. Only one choice remained.

"It's a possibility," she said. "But no more talk about us?"

He hesitated.

"It has to be that way, Bryan. I think we are friends, but I cannot complicate my life with…whatever."

He cleared his throat. "Well, I don't know that I have the time or energy for complications either. Being a priest pretty much consumes me."

"Same with being a cop." There. They'd both said it straight out. They were friends, period. Old enough and busy enough not to be sidetracked by…whatever. By complications.

She straightened her shoulders. All right. Slippery slope dammed up with words and promises and common sense. Heartbeat? Normal. Okay.

She held out her hand, and he shook it. "Deal?"

"Deal. Are you hungry?"

At the question, she felt ravenous. "Yes, I am. Rubyann didn't offer *me* any blackberry pie."

"That's because she likes me best."

She laughed, and the Midwest autumn didn't seem quite so sad anymore.

ᔆifteen

Cara walked beside Bryan as he pushed his big motorcycle the last block to the church. Her natural curiosity returned and she discounted the suspicion that Bryan harbored ulterior motives with his dinner invitation. Though she didn't trust a soul on earth besides Rubyann, she felt confident he would keep his word and not promote a serious relationship. After all, he was a priest, a shade more trustworthy than the average Joe.

He had suggested they eat at the rectory because his housekeeper was expecting him and she always prepared enough food for unannounced guests. Cara agreed that a home-cooked meal sounded more appealing than any restaurant.

They entered the house through the back door. She followed him across a mudroom and into a brightly lit, high-ceilinged kitchen. Warm air greeted her along with the scent of roasting garlic, herbs, and chicken.

A tall woman turned from the sink and dried her hands on her apron. "Welcome home, Father." Her face, pulled taut by an iron gray bun at the back of her head, was that of a stern schoolteacher, but a tiny smile softened the effect. She was probably in her late sixties.

"Thank you, Mrs. G," he said. "This is Cara Fleming. Cara, Lillian Gregory. Have you two met at church? Everyone calls her Mrs. G."

Cara shook her hand. "We haven't. Nice to meet you, Mrs. G."

"Nice to meet you."

Bryan shrugged out of his coat. He wore the usual black slacks, black shirt, and black standup collar with the white underpiece showing at the base of his throat. In spite of the cooling October temperatures, he hadn't yet exchanged short sleeves with long ones.

"Cara's staying for dinner."

"I'll set another place." No sign of panic in the housekeeper's demeanor.

"Will you join us?"

"No, thank you, Father. I have plans." She walked about the room, gathering dishes. "I'll just clean up the pots and pans. You leave the rest for me to deal with tomorrow."

"Hot date? On a Tuesday?"

The woman gave him a withering glance over her shoulder. "Young man, some days I swear you're still thirteen."

"I've been teasing this poor woman most of my life." Laughing, he held his hand out for Cara's jacket.

She gave it to him and noticed Mrs. G's double take toward her midsection. The paraphernalia must have caught her attention. Before Cara could explain the badge, pager, and gun holster clipped to her waistband, the housekeeper pressed her hip against a swinging door, the impassive expression back in place. Plate, glass, and flatware service in hand, she disappeared into what Cara guessed was the dining room.

The woman was the epitome of a perfect housekeeper, discreet and unobtrusive. She exuded an air of no-nonsense that hinted of a mother bear mentality toward the priest. Though she probably scrutinized all his guests and wouldn't hesitate to protect him from riffraff, her kitchen domain vibrated with homey comfort. Cara suspected it mirrored the entire house. Father O'Shaugnessy was well cared for.

Bryan returned from the direction of the mudroom.

Cara smiled at him and whispered, "God's not the only one who spoils you rotten."

He winked, nodding in agreement.

~

Cara and Bryan sat across from each other in the dining room. The glossy cherry wood table—like its matching hutch, the crystal chandelier, floral wall paper, and china—were from a bygone era but well maintained. A muted symphony drifted through the closed door from the kitchen radio.

Small talk flowed easily between them. Partway through the meal of wild rice, chicken, broccoli, and warm rolls, she set down her fork. "Excuse me while I pinch myself."

He smiled. "What?"

"I'm dreaming, right? I mean this food, this house, this sur-rogate mother." She tilted her head toward the kitchen door behind her. "It's like something out of a fairy tale. And you *live* in it."

He nodded, a sheepish expression on his face. "Yeah. Fully extended, this table seats sixteen. Upstairs are four bed-rooms. One bath down, two up. My study is a thirty-second walk across the backyard to the church, but there's another one here complete with desk and bookshelves. If I don't share more of these material goods with the less fortunate fairly soon, the guilt is going to give me an ulcer."

"Guilt is a prime motivator." She smiled. "But you shouldn't feel it. All this is a history of congregations loving their rectors. The current one just happens to be single with no kids to fill the place. And it doesn't look as if money has been spent on redecorating."

"I draw the line at anything beyond maintenance. Well, except for this cheap set of plates. The crystal and English bone china are over there in that hutch. Like they say, you can take the cop's kid out of the tract house, but you can't take the tract house mentality out of the cop's kid."

She chuckled. "That's what they say, huh?"

"Mm-hmm."

"Was it hard to get used to living here?"

"You could say that. I'm the proverbial bull. Which is why I insisted on keeping the good china in the hutch."

The size of his freckled forearms attested to the possibility of clumsiness. "You seem graceful in church."

"God's dispensation. When I put on those robes, I'm totally His representative. To the point even of not bumping into altars or knocking over goblets. Most of the time, anyway."

"I don't know what I would do in a situation like this. It's as far from my childhood as the moon is from earth."

"You said something earlier about having your own home, your first ever."

And she thought Rubyann talked too much! She'd done some of her own running off at the mouth as they stood in the twilight. "Uh, yeah. My very own apartment with trees outside the window, quiet neighbors, and a big bathtub." She raked her fork through the rice on her plate and shrugged.

"Did you and your husband have your own place?"

"A rented trailer which I thought was heaven for about three weeks. I did have a place for a short while in Los Angeles, a room above my friends' garage. They had picked me up hitchhiking and were the kindest Christians I'd ever met. But something was always missing wherever I lived, and I never felt *at home*— By the way, will you promise not to repeat his name to anyone?"

Bryan halted his fork two inches from his mouth.

"Please?" She twisted the linen napkin on her lap. "I'm sure you think I'm being unreasonable. I guess I am when it comes to— Good grief. He doesn't even know *my* name. There's no way he could find me unless someone told him where—" Her mind was running simultaneously on those ten tracks. "In the other cities I was still going by Cari-Ann Davis. Still doing the only thing I knew how to do: Live at a shelter when one was available and work minimum wage jobs. Of course he found me in those places. Then in Los Angeles my friends helped me go to school. My life was totally different. Until I went to church. That's how he found me that time. Church records and an office woman who talked too much— And now I'm really talking way too much."

He was gazing at her, his hand still aloft. His left hand. He was left-handed. She had noticed before, of course, but the fact struck her anew. It was an odd note to tuck away in her Bryan O'Shaugnessy file. Along with that curious note about how every time they were together her tongue loosened and thoughts poured forth like water gushing through opened floodgates.

She picked up her fork and pointed it at him. "Next time some bad guy won't fess up, I'm bringing you in to get him to talk."

He lowered his hand. "You're not being unreasonable. I won't tell anyone his name or repeat what you just told me."

A long moment passed as his words sank in. She nodded once. "Thank you."

"You're welcome. Did you become a police officer in Los Angeles?"

"Yes. That couple fed me, clothed me, housed me, and loaned me the money to go to community college. I joined the force, got my bachelor's degree." She shrugged and stopped short of the ugly part. Shooting at Nick, telling her friends goodbye, never contacting them again for their own safety as well as hers. "I left town and eventually arrived in Chicago, where I had to do the training academy thing all over again. Chicago is particular about its cops."

The swinging door opened partially and the housekeeper peered around it. "I'm leaving now."

Cara turned. "Mrs. G, this is the best meal I've eaten since I can't remember when."

The woman smiled broadly. "Thank you."

"Thank *you*. I'll clean up after us."

"That's what they pay me to do. You're our guest tonight. Just enjoy. There's apple pie warming in the oven. Ice cream in the freezer. Father, do you need anything else?"

"No, Mrs. G, thanks. Say hello to Roger for me."

"Oh you! Goodbye." The door swished as she ducked away.

Cara watched its little back and forth motion, lost in thoughts of comfort, her emotions overwhelmed in the face of such *pleasantness*. The stuff of fairy tales.

"Roger is the groundskeeper," Bryan whispered.

She looked at him.

"Those two have been flirting for twenty years. I can't imagine why they don't marry." He paused. "Cara." His whisper lost its staginess and grew husky. "I really won't tell anyone."

She blinked. "I know. I was just thinking about—" She twirled her hand in the air. "All this and her surrogate mother personality. She reminds me of Rubyann. Imagine having one of them for a mother! I can't. The attention, the food, the concern. I am surprised she's leaving you alone with me. I must have passed *her* litmus test, and I bet she doesn't even have a database to check."

He grinned. "You were just being yourself." The smile faded. "The one that peeks out from behind the cop persona. She comes and goes."

There he went again, seeing what she didn't think was visible. She explained, "Chances to survive on the street get reduced to zilch if 'she' peeks out more often."

"I understand. Mind if I ask a question before 'she' goes underground again?"

Cara shifted in her chair. Conversing with Bryan O'Shaugnessy had begun to feel like an instant case of peeling sunburn. Her skin itched, and she searched in vain for some mental aloe vera, some thought that would neutralize his effect on her.

He said, "I'm making you uncomfortable."

"No, I'm fine. Go ahead and ask."

"Do you want your apple pie with or without ice cream?"

On the other hand, conversing with him might be a delightful way to spend an evening. Especially if it included Mrs. G's cooking.

She smiled. "With."

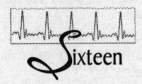

Sixteen

Bryan stood at the open window in his church study and inhaled a whiff of autumn air. It wasn't clean and crisp, but laden with the thick smoke of burning leaves. He chewed on the end of his unlit pipe and pretended he was sitting on a creek bank, his Harley parked nearby, and enjoying a quiet smoke in solitude. There were no jumbled feelings about a female cop. There was no private eye's voice in the telephone at his ear coaxing him like a plaid-coated salesman to change what he knew was a right decision.

He wished he'd never talked to his brother.

He wished he'd never laid eyes on Cara Fleming.

He wished he'd stop thinking about his homeless shelter plans, the vestry members' resistance to it, and the graceful curve of her jaw line.

"Padre, you listening?" Ray's voice broke through his thoughts.

"I won't change my mind. She asked me not to tell anyone her husband's name."

"Then why on earth did you tell me you knew it?"

"Just trying to be up-front with you."

Ray sighed heavily. "Then why won't you tell me what else you learned?"

All night long he had considered telling the investigator what else he'd learned. After all, Cara asked only that he not reveal Nick Davis's name. Technically that did not mean he couldn't tell Ray about *her* name and how she had changed it. Technically he could discuss her going to school in Los Angeles and about her joining the LAPD.

But "technically" crushed the spirit of her request. The past she'd entrusted to him was a secret she felt necessary to hide. And besides, he had given her his word. "She trusts me, Ray. I won't betray that."

"It's going to cost you more for the hours I gotta spend figuring it out on my own."

"Money is not the issue."

"I suppose ethics is." He paused. "Listen, Father, you and me are at opposite ends of the pole. You sure you still want me to proceed?"

No, he wasn't. Cara was his parishioner and friend. Their relationship was based on a mutual trust grounded in a common faith. And despite that strange occurrence the first night he saw her as she stood in the parish hall kitchen serving mashed potatoes, he did not believe in love at first sight. True love developed over a period of time. Time they hadn't yet shared. Time that would never be available if she left Chicago because of a fear that had spurred her halfway across the country.

Perhaps it was a groundless fear or a fear someone else could eliminate for her.

"Padre?"

"Yes, I am sure I want you to proceed."

"My way?"

"As long as that doesn't jeopardize her identity."

"It won't. Okay. Then I'm off to Seattle tomorrow."

"Where will you start?"

A chuckle filled the phone line. "I started this morning. Took her photo at a bagel shop a few blocks from her apartment. Detective Calloway was with her."

"You know where she lives?" Bryan's words sputtered and his stomach turned. "You took her *photo?*"

"This is my way. Maybe I shouldn't tell you details."

"I can't believe—"

"Hey, I won't show it to the husband. But I've got to trace her history in order to figure out who he is. A photo might come in handy."

"It's like you stalked her!"

"Nah. Nothing like it at all. You know, you should be impressed. It's not like she's listed in the phone book, but I found her. And have you ever tried snapping a picture of two of Chicago's finest in a postage-stamp-sized coffee shop without either one of them detecting you?"

"Why wouldn't you take it from outside with a *telephoto?*" His voice remained octaves above normal level.

"Aw, you know my secrets." Ray chuckled again. "Relax, Padre. Talk to you later."

The line went dead.

"Bryan."

He turned to see Meagan standing inside the door he hadn't heard open. Her hands were on her hips.

"You're beet red. What is the problem?"

"Nothing." He fumbled with the phone. His hand shook and the instrument clunked as it missed the cradle. He tried again.

Meagan took the phone from him and set it in place.

He met her stare. "It's nothing. Really. Personal stuff. I'm trying to help someone. It's a frustrating situation."

"I'll get you some water, and then I'm calling TJ."

"Meagan, I'll be fine."

"That's for your doctor to say. If you don't sit down I'll call 911 instead. And don't you dare light that pipe."

She scurried from the room as he sank onto an arm chair. Not because she said so or because he wanted to, but because he really didn't have a choice.

~

"Bryan, it's high." Dr. TJ Carlton pulled the stethoscope from his ears.

"How high?"

"Just this side of sky-high." Bryan's friend knew the numbers meant nothing to him. "The medication's not working." He undid the blood pressure cuff.

"I suppose that might have something to do with me not taking it?"

"Yeah, it might." TJ sat in the other winged-back chair and studied him, his blue eyes unblinking behind horn-rimmed glasses.

Bryan had always thought that except for the glasses, TJ resembled a Ken doll: tall, lean, and handsome. He'd even married a Barbie clone and now had three miniature dolls. Until their sophomore year in high school, Bryan and TJ participated in sports together. By the age of 16 they'd grown apart, TJ choosing the straight and narrow path and advanced science courses while Bryan busied himself rebelling against everything under the sun. They met up again at a class reunion. Bryan needed a doctor, TJ needed a church.

"TJ, I did take it for a few days. It made me woozy. I couldn't think clearly."

"Then we'll try a different kind. I know you don't like taking pills, though, so let's go the other route."

"I can't fire Mrs. G."

"She'd do anything for you. I will talk to her. I will give her a new cookbook. I will give her a list of food that will kill you if you keep eating it."

"She'll take it personally and be totally crushed." He didn't mention how he'd fasted on Sunday, not just his usual fast before the first service but a full 24 hours. No donuts at coffee break. No lunch or supper, meals which Mrs. G prepared for him on Saturdays. Not wanting her feelings to be hurt when she saw the food still in the refrigerator Monday morning, he'd given it to some street people.

"Bryan, this is serious. We're into the deadly serious stage. Do you understand?"

"Okay. We'll do the diet thing."

"And the exercise thing."

He winced.

"You like playing racquetball. Tell Meagan to put it on the calendar. And park the Harley and walk!"

"There's so much to do... There are hundreds of families in this parish who need..." His voice trailed off.

"What? You don't think God can get it all done without you? Listen, if you don't start carving time out for yourself, you won't be doing anything down here on earth." TJ pulled a prescription pad from his pocket and wrote on it. "Here." He ripped off the top sheet and handed it to Bryan.

"'Diagnosis: Messiah complex. Rx: Call in sick. Spend two weeks away beginning immediately.' TJ, I can't—"

"Yes, you can. That's why you have a deacon. That's why you have a retired rector. That's why you have a bishop who offers whatever you need. You've been in that pulpit for at least a year straight, Bryan. Lunatic behavior." He stood, dug into his pants pocket, and retrieved a set of keys. "The condo's empty until Thanksgiving." He twisted a key off the ring and handed it to him. "Here. Go read, golf, and don't use a cart."

"TJ, it's not as simple as—"

The door opened and Flynn walked in unannounced. "He's got woman trouble." Grinning, he crossed the room, hand outstretched. "Hey, TJ. Meagan told me the doctor was in."

Seated in the chair, Bryan saw his brother's black police shirt stretched tightly across his potbelly, buttons near to bursting. Fine specimen of health he was. Funny how all the same cop junk that hung on his midsection sat so neatly at Cara's feminine waist.

TJ stood and shook Flynn's hand. "Woman trouble?"

Flynn nodded his head. "For real."

"No way. Our monk who'd be happiest living alone in a cave in Spain?" He turned to Bryan. "You dog. Why didn't you say something?"

"Because there's nothing to say. I have a female friend who's in trouble. I'm trying to help."

"Well, whatever. All the more reason to take care of yourself." He gathered his things. "I'll get that information to Mrs. G, and I'm calling the bishop. See you. But it had better not be in the pulpit." He strode across the room.

Bryan said, "Thanks, Mom."

TJ waved and shut the door behind himself.

"High blood pressure?" Flynn settled into the chair TJ had vacated, his holster creaking.

"Yeah. What's yours like?"

"High." He shrugged. "Has been for years. An inherited blessing from Dad. One of them. What's a person to do?"

"Take some time off, I guess."

"You could take the chick with you. Cara Fleming."

Bryan clenched his jaw.

"Leave the collar at home. That way you wouldn't have to keep up appearances and pay for two rooms."

"Ray told you her name?" Why had he ever gone to a friend of Flynn's?

"Nah. This may come as a surprise to you, but he's so ethical he wouldn't tell me. I didn't even bother to ask. Meagan, on the other hand, never questions a brother's motives."

His ears felt afire. He was hearing a rerun of Cara's Los Angeles church experience.

"I came by yesterday and asked who's new at church? Meagan pulls up a file on the computer. Impressive. Three new families in three months. Good for you. Only one single lady, though. Rubyann Calloway. Meagan says she's old and black." He shook his head. "That can't be her. I ask if some people don't sign up for the register. Sure, she says. Like Rubyann's friend Cara. Bingo."

"Your point?"

"I was just curious. All right, maybe nosy about who you're hanging with. Meagan hasn't met her, but she knows Rubyann, who brags on Miss Fleming because she's her grandson's partner. Partner. As in cop. You could have told me."

Bryan poured himself another glass of water from the carafe Meagan had left on the end table and drank half of it. He really wasn't feeling well.

"Bry, you don't like cops."

"Maybe God put her in my path to cure me of that prejudice."

"In that case, you can give her a message."

He locked his eyes on his brother's and saw the coldness there. The deadness. "She's not like you."

Flynn barked a laugh. "They're all like me, Bry. Like Dad. Just different degrees. About the message." He paused. "Tell the detective to back off her investigation."

"What are you talking about?" He held up a hand. "No, never mind. I don't want to know. I don't even have a clue what area she works in and—"

"Well, I do, and if you're tangled up with her, it's gonna spill over onto you. No dame detective's gonna pull a number on my brother." He stood. "Just tell her to back off. She'll know which one I'm talking about." Without another glance or word, he left the room.

Bryan had fasted and prayed before considering what to do for Cara. He was clearheaded and confident when he decided to talk with Flynn and Ray. He thought his actions would help her. Now a spotlight had been turned upon her, one she would not need nor want, one that might even endanger her. What had he done?

Lord, have... The prayer died on his lips.

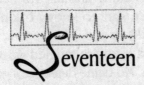

Seventeen

"Renae wants to get married." Marcus stared through the windshield toward the red stoplight. The only display of emotion accompanying his unexpected words was a rapping of his fingers against the steering wheel.

Cara discerned no rhythm in the rat-a-tat-tat. Off hours, her partner played drums with a jazz band. His tapping always included syncopation. She said, "Married to you?"

His sidelong glance at her would have sent shivers through most people.

She said, "No more jokes from her about how you should marry me?"

He shook his head.

"That bothers you."

He smacked the steering wheel. "Of course it bothers me. We've got a good thing going. Why mess it up with a license that says we've got to live together twenty-four/seven and explain our schedules to each other? Talk to me, Fleming. What is going through that woman's mind?"

"I'm sure she told you. Renae is the most articulate person I know. Or maybe you weren't listening."

"She said some nonsense about her biological clock."

"Hmm. That is nonsense. She doesn't need to be married to have kids. What was she thinking?"

Marcus glanced sideways at her, his eyes squinched. "No son of mine is growing up without a dad." A fatherless childhood had left its scar on him.

"So then it's not nonsense."

He growled and drove through the intersection, steering deftly through heavy downtown traffic.

"Marcus, did you ever consider marriage as having a spiritual side? Something vague and yet so real it defines the relationship? You don't even have to believe in God to feel a sense of it."

"Cosmic glue."

"Exactly! Perfect description—"

"Renae's phrase."

"Then that's what she's thinking. She wants to get married because the license puts a handle on something that's bigger than the two of you."

He grumbled, either at the traffic or her opinion. She wasn't sure which.

"You realize you scare people simply by being in their vicinity, don't you?"

He shrugged a shoulder. "You do it too, Cucumber."

"But I usually have to work at it. I think it comes naturally to you."

"Because I'm black or male?"

"Neither."

"Whew. Thought I was going to have to file a discrimination suit against you."

She ignored his joke. "Sometimes I worry I'm dying inside. That all that ice is spreading like a glacier. I'll wake up some day and realize it's taken over the very core of my being."

"You think I've got ice at my core? That I'm dead?"

"No. As a matter of fact, I'm convinced you're not. But I see signs, and there is the tendency in this work for emotions

to die. I just want you to *feel* what Renae's talking—" A movement down an alley they passed caught her eye. "Stop!"

Without hesitation, he braked.

As tires squealed, she plunged her hand into the gym bag
at her feet, pushed aside the black wig, and pulled out her
gun and handcuffs. En route to the Park-Mont Inn to play
housekeeper again, she wore a maid's uniform under her
raincoat and had stashed her things. She bolted from the car.
Her athletic shoes hit the damp pavement running. She
sensed more than saw Marcus flip on emergency lights and
leave the car in the right hand lane of a busy one-way street.
He would be on her heels.

She rounded the corner of the alley they'd just driven past.
Half a block down three teenaged males hurried in the other
direction. She slowed slightly as a young woman slid down
along a wall as if her knees had given way. Even that half a
glance registered the terror written on the victim's face.
Marcus would tend to her.

Cara raced on and came within a few yards of the kids
when one of them turned. He must have heard her feet
pounding the gritty concrete.

"Police!" she yelled. "Stop!"

The other two heads jerked around, and then they all ran.
Evidently the words meant as little as the gun in her hand.

Cara zeroed in on the kid wearing a long duster-type coat.
More than likely the hand in a pocket was going for a
weapon, but the coat would slow him down. She left the guy
holding the woman's purse for Marcus to chase. The third
would get away unless some crazy passerby tackled him.

The three scattered, but she had the momentum and
reached her target, shoving him off balance. He crashed to the
pavement. Before he could twist around and point the switch-
blade he'd flicked open, her knee was between his shoulder

blades and her gun where he could see it from the corner of his eye.

"Drop it!" she yelled. "Drop it now!"

He screamed a string of obscenities about police brutality and about not doing "it." Whatever "it" was. At least he didn't struggle as though he were strung out on drugs, only enough to indicate he'd peaked out on adrenaline.

As had Cara. She cuffed his left hand and shouted above his voice, "Drop it! Drop it!"

He loosened his grip on the knife.

She finished cuffing him and stood, her breath ragged. "Don't move!"

Glancing to her side, she saw Marcus with the other boy against a wall.

Her partner grinned and yelled, "I never have this much fun with Renae!"

⌒

Cara and Marcus resumed their drive to the hotel. She studied her image in the visor mirror and arranged the black wig over her light brown hair. The wig was a good one, its long wavy locks realistic in feel and style.

Marcus picked up the subject of his girlfriend again. "Seriously, Fleming. There's no way Renae can understand why I get a kick out of chasing bad guys, let alone do such a thing with me. Just imagine her running in her heels or trying to hold a gun. I'm always opening a jar for her. And she'd take those guys' death threats seriously and want to analyze them."

"Renae's a tough cookie. She's not a cop, but she'd never back down in an emergency. And she certainly would have been kinder to that victim than you were."

"Hey, that's your department. Besides, we had a Good Samaritan nurse in the crowd. The thing is, Renae lives in a different world."

"It's not exactly an ivory tower, though. You two complement each other. You don't love her because she's like you. You love her because she's different. She doesn't love you because you're a college professor, right? Opposites attract."

"Does that hold for the long haul?"

Cara uncapped a lipstick, twisted up the "Crimson Frenzy" war paint, and smeared it across her lips. Her hand shook. The diversion with the purse snatchers had rattled her more than it should have. Adrenaline still pumped. She bared her teeth at the mirror. Red streaked three of them. She rubbed a fingertip over them. "What would I know about long hauls?"

He shrugged. "Women are supposed to be tuned into this stuff."

Dropping the lipstick back into the gym bag, she noticed grime splattered on her white shoes, kicked up from the rain-soaked alley. Some Park-Mont Inn supervisor would disapprove. She dug again into the bag for a towel and wiped at the dirt.

"Cara."

"Yeah?"

"What makes you think I'm not emotionally dead yet?"

"Huh?" She looked up.

He turned toward her long enough for her to glimpse a rare velvety sheen over his brown eyes. "Earlier you said you worry about the ice taking over, but you're convinced I'm not dead. Why do you say that?"

She went back to cleaning her shoes and hid a smile. In the blink of an eye Marcus had placed himself in an emotionally vulnerable situation, a first as far as she was concerned. She stowed away the towel and sat up. "Because you don't scare me even if you are edgy with victims and make bad guys shake in their boots with that glare of yours."

"But you don't count. Nobody scares you, Cucumber."

He'd never heard her talk about Nick Davis. "Well, that's not exactly true, but it's more than simply not being scared. It's possible to *not* be afraid of someone and still not feel safe with him. With you, I feel safe."

They'd reached the drop-off point a block from the Park-Mont. Marcus stopped the car alongside the curb and turned in his seat to look at her. "That's a good thing."

"It is. And I'm sure Renae feels the same way."

"But why?"

"Because you're not emotionally dead."

"How do you know?"

"I feel safe with you."

"You're talking in circles."

"Mm-hmm." She wriggled out of the raincoat.

"Women." He shook his head. "Way too much emphasis on *feelings*."

"I'd better go." She opened the car door and stuck out one foot. The adrenaline still pounded through her, still cutting short her breaths.

"Don't forget your glasses. Here."

She turned back and took the rimless yellow lenses from him. "Thanks."

"Not like you to forget a detail like that."

She caught his gaze. The usual stoniness had replaced that soft brown velvet, but concern lined his forehead. Unintentional words flew off her tongue. "What do you think about postponing your interview and hanging around the lobby?"

"Sounds like a waste of taxpayers' money."

"No, really, what do you think?"

His brows went up. "What are *you* thinking?"

"It's more like…" She winced. "Feeling."

Clearly vexed, he puffed out a noisy breath and shook his head again.

"Look, Marcus, I just don't feel right about this gig, okay? I need you close by."

"For crying out loud, what's gotten into you?"

"It's crazy, what we do. You know? Chase down kids with switchblades and not enough sense between their ears to fill a tablespoon. Ring the doorbell at five o'clock in the morning of some guy who buys and sells guns for organized crime. It's crazy!"

"This is a new thought?" His voice rose.

Her own voice echoed in her head, fearful words spoken in a whiny tone. Anger at her loss of control flashed through her. She swung her other foot onto the pavement, climbed out, and leaned over to meet his glare with one of her own. "Calloway, I want backup today because the hair on the back of my neck prickles. So get a newspaper and plunk yourself down in the lobby *tout de suite*."

The corners of his mouth lifted, resulting in something between a grim smile and a sneer. "That's more like it, Cucumber."

She slammed the door shut and hurried down the sidewalk. The hair on the back of her neck did *not* prickle. She'd only resorted to that to get Marcus's attention. What prompted her to place him nearby was not intuition nor sixth sense but a *feeling*. A vague abstract thing that set in motion a sudden unreasonable craving for safety.

The feeling occurred now and then, settling about her out of the blue. She figured it was residue left over from earlier years. But she'd never shared it before with Marcus. His unexpected plunge into vulnerability must have given her a sense of permission to open up in return. Typical Marcus, he'd bullied that response right out the door. No matter. She knew he was there for her, and he did make her *feel* safe. Which was, after all, one of the reasons she'd stayed so long in Chicago.

"Thank You, Lord, for my muscular, foreboding angel." Smiling to herself, she unwrapped a piece of bubble gum and pulled open the door marked "Employees Only."

Cara found Evie in the break room, sitting alone at one end of the table reading a magazine. Two other housekeepers stood at the soda machine, whispering in conspiratorial tones.

Cara slid onto a chair kitty-corner from Evie, facing the door and the other two women. "Hi, Evie."

The blonde housekeeper looked up and grinned. "Hi yourself, stranger. Haven't seen you for a while."

"I've been working nights a lot. Seems like they need more temps then."

"Yeah. It'd be the pits to work that shift."

"How you doing?"

"Oh." She glanced over her shoulder at the other two women. "Fine."

And there's a milkmaid on the moon. Cara leaned across the table and said softly, "Still on special assignment?" She tilted her head, indicating Evie's work in the penthouse.

The young woman shook her head.

"That stinks."

She nodded, her lips pressed together. Evidently she was taking Cara's advice about not discussing the job.

The conversation would go nowhere as long as company remained in the room. She lowered her voice even further. "How come? She liked you."

Evie threw another glance over her shoulder. No sound came from her throat, but she mouthed, "She's gone."

The words hit Cara like a cupful of cold water splashed at her face. She jerked. Gone? Without the possibility of somehow getting close to Jasmine Wakefield and the books she kept for Ian Stafford, the case against him could be stuck in the mire.

Coins clinked into the soda machine, and a can slid down the shoot with a chugging noise. Cara realized the other two housekeepers weren't talking. She said in a normal pitch, "So then I told him to pack his bags and take a hike."

Evie's eyes widened.

Cara snapped her gum. "I know. You think I'm crazy. He looks like Tom Cruise. But give me a break. I mean, how many hints do I need? The guy was totally not going to leave his wife. Not in my lifetime."

The door swished shut behind the women.

Cara straightened and smiled.

Evie stared at her. "That was good."

Takes a lot of practice. "I didn't want you getting into trouble."

"Thanks. I'm pretty shook up."

"What happened?"

Her face crumpled, and she looked close to tears. "You're not with them, are you?"

Cara reached over and touched her arm briefly. "I'm not with them. Honest."

"Since you told me to stop talking, I have. But now I've got to tell somebody!"

"You can trust me. It's not like I'm here enough to know somebody to blab it to. I'm just curious." *And I want to nail the creep.*

Evie nodded and took a deep breath. "Monday, I went up like usual. *He* was there. And she wasn't!"

"Was that unusual?"

"Yeah! He's never been there without her. He screamed at me to get out and not to come back. Then he yelled for my keys. He grabbed the key chain from my hand and yanked off the one for the penthouse."

"Did he say why?"

"No. I told my supervisor. She said who knows and told me to keep my mouth shut. Like you did. I'm scared enough. I'm not talking!"

"I think that's smart. What's happened since two days ago?"

"Ardath said just do my other jobs and read a magazine instead of going upstairs until she figures out how to reassign me. Then this morning she said Ms. Wakefield won't need my services anymore. No explanation. And don't ask, she says. At least she didn't blame me. I can't figure out what I did wrong."

"It doesn't sound like it was your fault."

She flipped the magazine shut. "Well, at least I'm caught up on all the stars' lives."

"What'd the penthouse look like?"

"That was the weird thing. You walk in and there's this little entry way. Right off the bat you know a woman lives there. Jasmine leaves clothes and jewelry and purses and shoes all over the place. I loved picking up after her. It was all gorgeous stuff. You know, stuff you see window-shopping on Michigan Avenue. She gave me a purse once. The thing must have cost hundreds of dollars. It was a beaded evening bag. All sparkly golden beads."

"Were her things gone?"

"No! It looked like it always did, especially on a Monday. Stuff everywhere. I got as far as the living room, and I could see into her bedroom. Clothes on the floor, as usual. The other weird thing was her desk. It's in the living room, and it's always as neat as a pin, but nothing was on top of it. I think she really does work. The floor around it was a mess, though, like everything had been pushed off of it. And I think I saw a *drawer* laying in the middle of it all! I got out of there fast as I could with him yelling the whole time."

"Have you heard anything about what might have happened? Any gossip?"

She shook her head. "That's another weird thing. Sometimes when he's in a bad mood, word gets around that his girlfriend must be giving him a hard time. Nothing. I don't think this was your run-of-the-mill fight."

"Weird."

"At least I haven't lost my job. Yet."

"Like I said, it doesn't sound like it's your fault." Cara pushed back her chair. "Guess I'd better get to work."

Evie grabbed her arm. "Do you think she left him?"

"No. Nobody leaves the mob. I'll call you."

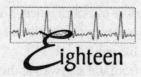

Eighteen

Cara pressed her thumb against the buzzer in her apartment to release the building's main door lock three flights below. Bryan O'Shaugnessy was on his way up.

She wasn't sure how she felt about that. Probably because the time was after 9 P.M. and less than an hour ago she'd let her emotions whirl down the drain with the bathtub water. All the day's highs and lows—the morning office work, the alley chase, the off-the-wall talk with Marcus, her momentary lapse into fear, the news that Jasmine was gone, the scramble to piece together more of the woman's biography—they all flowed away to the Chicago River, replaced with the scent of lavender, music, a "sustaining" book, and a self-promise to get to bed early.

Then Rubyann had called, and Cara had changed out of her pajamas and into sweats.

She opened her door now, stepped into the hall, and leaned against the jamb, crossing her arms.

Bryan didn't have her number or address. They were unlisted. She hadn't signed the church visitor registry. She made donations in cash rather than by check. Her path intersected often enough with his; she figured there wasn't a need to give him the information. After all, he could always call the police.

Or Rubyann.

True to her word, Rubyann did not give out the number but called Cara with the message he wanted to talk. She suggested the man hadn't asked for it because, as she had said before, he was horribly out of practice. There had been a definite smile in the woman's voice. Still, out of deference to her, Cara had returned his call.

Bryan emerged from the stairwell at the end of the hall. His clerical collar showed through the top of his black raincoat. Cheeks flushed, he smiled and waved.

Cara waved back.

He followed her into the apartment, and she shut the door behind him.

"Hi," he huffed and held up a hand. "Yes, I am totally out of shape, but I promised my doctor I will exercise and lose twenty pounds."

"I wasn't going to say anything."

"But you're supposed to."

She smiled. "I am?"

He nodded. "All female parishioners fuss at the rector. At last count I had one hundred thirty-seven mothers. The tendency to treat me like a son is included in their profile."

"Sorry. I tend to ruin all kinds of profiles. I never have fit the norm."

"Probably why I'm here," he murmured and tugged on an earlobe absentmindedly.

"Can I take your coat?"

"Yes, thanks." He shrugged out of it and handed it to her. He wore a black suit coat over his black shirt. "Nice place."

"It's home. Have a seat." She draped his damp coat over a kitchen chair, glancing around her apartment.

Though small and sparsely furnished, it was comfortable and contained all she needed. Square-shaped in a square-shaped brick building with nine other units, it had four corners. Clockwise the front door was in one corner, the kitchen in the next, bedroom and bathroom after that, then the living room. Door between that and the bedroom. No hall needed. Two windows facing the street to the southeast. Gentle morning sun. Clean, fairly new beige carpet. Clean, bare white walls. Rubyann was always after her to decorate. A foreign word in Cara's vocabulary. She'd chosen the place for its bathtub. She'd bought furniture for practical reasons: things upon which to sleep, sit, or place books. Things that would be easy to leave behind at a moment's notice.

He sat on the loveseat, she on the recliner. If one more person came, the living room seats would be taken.

"Would you like some water or coffee? Tea?" she asked.

"No, thank you."

She nodded. Too tired for small talk, all she could think of was the question of why he had come. Too tired to figure out how to ask it politely, she sat quietly.

"Cara, I am sorry for the late hour."

Again she nodded. He'd already apologized on the phone while insisting that he needed to see her. A phone conversation would not do, he had said.

He leaned forward, elbows on knees, and clasped his hands. "I just wanted to let you in on a few things. It won't take long."

"Okay."

"As a friend." Something underscored his last word.

She shifted her weight in the chair, tucked her legs beneath herself. "Shoot."

"I'd like your help with the shelter at the church. I know you don't have time to be personally involved, but..." His shoulders sagged. "Do you really think Miriam House can be duplicated at St. James?"

"Definitely."

"My problem is the vestry. These people look at me like
I've sprouted horns whenever I bring up the subject. I think
if they heard from a fellow parishioner who's experienced
with shelters—and who's a member of the police department
as well—their opinion might change. Once they heard details
about your Miriam House and similar places, they'd listen with
a different ear to my ideas."

"Bryan, I'd be more than happy to talk to them. You know
that, don't you?"

"Well, I had hoped..." Again his voice lost steam.

He should have known. They'd talked much about homelessness, about their identical desire to be involved. About
his baby steps, about her immersion in it. She studied his face.
It was still uncharacteristically flushed. The crow's feet around
his eyes were pronounced.

"What's wrong?"

"I'm tired." He gave her half a smile. "Have been for a long
time. Which brings up another thing."

She watched him rub his forehead, hesitating, as if
searching for words. Intuitively she knew his health wasn't the
best. And then she realized what was there all along, something she should have grasped long before now: Like with
Marcus, she felt safe with Bryan. Physically, emotionally, men-
tally, every which way. Why else would she have invited him
to the Miriam House meeting? Not to mention discuss her
past?

He looked at her again. "I usually go once or twice a year
to a retreat center. A week or two at a time. I stay completely
out of touch with everyone for the duration. Except for urgent
messages from Meagan, who would kill me if I didn't at least
check voice mail. Anyway, the last time I went was a few

months after Vic's death. Which happened two years and three months ago."

"You haven't taken a day off since?"

He shook his head. "Rachel says I'm still in mourning. Still angry. She's probably right. I need to finish sorting through it."

"No, you need to let God finish healing it."

"Right." He smiled. "Maybe you could take the pulpit while I'm gone?"

"You're leaving?" Emotions were building again, a tumbled mixture of loss, denial, relief, despair. She was going to have to start all over and take another long hot bubble bath.

"Doctor's orders. My blood pressure is high. I really dislike taking the medication. Its effect reminds me of the time my Army buddy got hold of a particularly good batch of pot."

"Father Bryan, are you telling me what I think you're telling me?"

"It's the medication talking."

She burst into laughter. "You've come a long way."

"Yes, I have. Thank God." He paused. "So, as I was saying, I will be gone for two weeks. Again, doctor's orders. He even provided a condo. Over in the Galena Territories."

"That sounds like a good idea. When will you go?"

"Tomorrow. Uh, I'd like to give you my cell number."

"It's printed in the bulletin."

"Not this one. Only Meagan has it."

She blinked, letting the implications sink in. "Okay. I suppose you want mine in return?"

He smiled. "I promise not to give it out."

"Well, the department has it. Marcus has it, of course, and Rubyann. Other friends. People who need to talk to me about investigations. It's not exactly a secret."

"Except from me?"

"Did you ask for it?"

"No."

She teased him with a smug smile. "Tell me, how serious is the blood pressure thing?"

He tilted his head side to side. "It needs to be addressed. I haven't done much to combat it except take pills that only made me feel worse. First stop then is the bishop's. Can't hurt to have him pray for me."

"No, I wouldn't think so. I will pray too."

"Thank you."

She stood and walked past him. "I'll get a pen and make some tea. Herbal decaf."

"Careful. You're slipping into that mothering profile."

Turning into the kitchen nook, she caught a smug smile on his face. An adolescent whim to stick out her tongue struck her. She resisted. Curious, though. She couldn't remember the last time she'd wanted to flirt.

Her tiredness vanished somewhere between boiling water and exchanging phone numbers. She served the tea and sat back down.

Mug in hand, Bryan leaned back against the couch and crossed his legs, ankle to knee. His black shoes were shiny. She wondered if Mrs. G polished them, but then thought not. An ex-Army guy would keep his own in tip-top shape.

He said, "I told you about my brother, Flynn."

"He's the cop?"

"Right. Beat cop. Never interested in doing anything different." He gave her his district number. "Do you know it?"

"I'm familiar with the area."

He nodded. "Brothers talk. A sister who has met Rubyann talks even more." He paused. "He found out your name. He found out what you do."

Instantly her guard went up. A church worker again, giving out her name. But this time it was to a brother, not some stranger. It was not her unlisted phone and address. She relaxed.

"I told Meagan never to do that again."

She shrugged. "It would be easy enough for your brother to learn what I do, especially since he's with the department."

"Flynn is—how should I put it? He walks a fine line out there. I think he's spent too much time on the other side. Do you know what I'm saying?"

She suspected that at the very least, Flynn wasn't opposed to accepting bribery. If he were crooked, it would help explain Bryan's obvious disdain for police work. "You're saying more than you should to a cop."

"I want you to understand where he's coming from. He gave me a message for you." Bryan uncrossed his legs, set his mug on the lamp table, and placed his hands on his knees. "He said to tell the detective to back off her investigation."

Cara lived in two worlds. The one where ice water ran in her veins and the other one where she soaked in bubbles and knelt in church and developed a friendship with the priest now sitting on her couch drinking tea. Suddenly the two worlds collided, and her mind felt as if a fuse had been blown.

"He said *what?*"

"He said to tell you to back off. That's it. I don't know what you do. I don't have to know. I just thought…Flynn saying it, I should…tell you."

Her thoughts raced. Organized crime, guns, a neighborhood street cop. What was the common thread tying the three

together? Flynn O'Shaugnessy was in the same category as
the first two? He worked with the mob? Even if he didn't
know details of her current investigations, he could have
learned she was part of the gun team. Was that enough to set
him off? Perhaps. Especially if he was paid to look the other
way when gun deals went down. Maybe he just didn't like
female detectives. Maybe he was a missing link somebody on
her team needed. She'd run it by Marcus tomorrow.

"Cara?"

She saw him staring at her with a concerned expression.
"Bryan, you should know a few things. It's no secret I made
detective in record time. I used to work in organized crime
intelligence. Now I'm part of a fairly new unit that investi-
gates illegal firearms. A cache was found recently. Anybody
could learn that much about me."

"But what he said—"

"Forget it. People warn and threaten me every day. Just
this afternoon some sixteen-year-old promised to slice and
dice me."

He winced.

The guy was extraordinarily sensitive. His rough-and-
tumble appearance was deceptive.

"Cara, I still don't understand how you handle this stuff.
Especially in light of your experience with what's-his-name."

Nick. She smiled briefly, grateful for his avoidance of the
name she hoped he'd forgotten. "Remember, as a kid I felt
safe with the police. Being a policewoman helps me feel safe
in my environment, at least in control. With him—with the
mere thought of him—I'm instantly a victim again. And terrified."

He nodded as if understanding. "Then Flynn's message
won't cause you to look over your shoulder?"

"I'm always doing that. Trade habit. Don't worry, though. The message won't disrupt my life."

"All right. Good. Well, I should be going."

She followed him across the room to the kitchen table near the door. He retrieved his coat from a chair, put it on, and then he looked down at her. She was struck again with his size. If he were to lose those 20 pounds, or even 30 beyond that, he would still be a large man. Big-boned. The width of his shoulders completely blocked the door behind him from her view. His hands, with their freckles that matched his paprika red hair, were nearly as broad as the oversized, gold-covered Bible he used during the church service.

He was focused on her face. Though his eyes were somber, Rubyann would discern a twinkle in their green depths. "The doctor said if this blood pressure thing keeps up, I could count on a heart attack or stroke. Pronouncements like that tend to encourage a person to imagine his death. Which really doesn't disturb me. I figured out long ago that birth is a death sentence. I've tried to deal with things that would cause regrets as soon as I become aware of them. Tonight I realize I missed one."

She felt a subtle tremor, an imperceptible quivering of air.

He gave his earlobe a decided yank. "If I died now, I would have only one regret. Which is that I hadn't kissed you."

His words registered slowly. "Hmm." She scratched her forehead. "Um, we weren't going to talk about—" She twirled her hand in a vague motion. "About anything beyond friendship."

"I'm not *talking* about anything. I'm just wondering if you'd mind if I kissed you. Think of it as a dying man's last wish."

"You're not— What do you think I am? A one-woman Make-a-Wish foundation?"

He grinned. "Sure."

"Bryan! I told you! I'm married!"

He stepped nearer, eliminating the space between them, and touched her cheek. "You don't know that for a fact." His voice grew soft and whispery. "Stop hiding behind ancient history. Stop being afraid."

"But I promised God. I vowed to keep my word!"

"To do what? Love and honor in hiding? Remain a prisoner to fear? Let it go, Cara. Your Abba loves you, and He's given me an outrageous love for you."

As if encircled by a sudden windstorm, she felt her breath whisked away. The whirling filled her, uprooting the tendrils of fear so long rooted within her heart. Then, in the blink of an eye, it was gone. Left in its wake were sunshine and comfort, newness and truth.

Bryan held her face in both his hands now, his thumbs like feathers stroking her skin. "Okay?"

She closed her eyes. When his lips touched hers, the air quivered again…as if angel wings beat from the four corners of her home.

⌒

Cara and Bryan parted without a word.

Ten minutes after shutting the door behind him, still no words came to mind. She turned off the lights, swung the recliner around to face the window, and sat in it, looking out over the darkened neighborhood. The streetlamps were shrouded in foggy halos. Trees looked like hulking shadows.

Her head felt full of emotions. They jostled about like balloon bouquets, gently touching and rebounding. At last one word came, vague at first, swallowed up time and again by the balloons. And then it cut through and revealed itself.

Mystery.

That was the word. Mystery. Nothing explained what had happened. What *was* happening. It made no sense whatsoever.

The tears came then. Falling slowly, almost one at a time. No steady stream. Just an overflow of gratitude released in tiny droplets. Gratitude for the sunshine that still shone within her. For the absence of the black fear. For the home she'd pondered leaving because fear disallowed comfort. And acceptance.

And the totally unfathomable possibility of love.

So now what? Where did things stand between her and Bryan O'Shaugnessy? She didn't know. It was a mystery.

And perhaps, when all was said and done, some mysteries were best left unsolved.

Nineteen

No regrets.

Bryan parked in the driveway of TJ's condominium and climbed from the car. Turning a slow circle, he breathed crisp unpolluted air and feasted his eyes on the magnificent October scenery. Beyond the nicely spaced, contemporary housing units and the lush green fairway of a world-class golf course, far-flung hills rolled endlessly. Trees covered them, and though the peak season had passed, some leaves retained their brilliant hues of red and gold.

No regrets.

He'd kissed Cara Fleming. Several times actually. He'd held her close, a physically strong woman whose arms fit round him like bark on a tree.

No regrets.

She had allowed him to see her fragile self, the mask of fear gone.

He smiled to himself. Nope, no regrets. He could die a happy, fulfilled man.

"But I'd rather not today, if it's all the same to You, Lord."

He opened the trunk of the car. Suitcase and gym bag, packed by Meagan. Box and cooler of food, packed by Mrs. G, each item blessed by TJ. Box of books, packed by himself. Where to start?

A prayer came to mind. "O God, You will keep in perfect peace those whose minds are fixed on You; for in returning and rest we shall be saved; in quietness and trust shall be our strength."

The time had arrived to quit talking, perhaps even to quit thinking. It was time to listen for God's voice, which was sounding an awful lot like the voices of Rachel, Meagan, Mrs. G, and TJ.

Lord, have mercy.

He pulled the gym bag from the trunk. The deserted golf course would make an excellent jogging track.

$\mathcal{T}$wenty

"Jane Waite was born in Milwaukee thirty-two years ago." Marcus read from the computer screen on his desk in the police station. "Graduated from high school there. Cocktail waitress— How can you be a cocktail waitress at age seventeen or eighteen?"

Standing behind him, Cara looked over his shoulder. "She did that later. Look at the years."

"What'd she do until then?"

"Hung out."

He grunted. "That's what it looks like. Well, so much for the bio. Her life ended ten years ago in Milwaukee. No tax returns. No bank accounts. No nothing."

"Except she changed her name and wound up in Chicago." Which was why it had taken so long to trace her.

"Moving and name-changing. She's hiding something."

"Or hiding from someone." Cara touched her stomach. It felt as though a fist pressed against it from the inside. They'd found Jasmine Wakefield because the woman had opened a bank account last month using her real social security number. What mistake had Cara made that would allow someone to pick up her cold trail?

"So what do you think, Fleming? Take a run up to Milwaukee? Her parents are listed at the same address. She's probably got old friends there too."

"How about we call first and see if her parents know anything?"

"A surprise visit would be better. Less of a chance for them to warn her. Maybe she's even there."

"Not if she changed her name." Cara walked around his desk to hers. The two faced each other in a small roomful of detectives' desks. She slid onto the upholstered wheeled chair. "No way is she going back there."

"All right, I'll call and ask for her. But we should go there. On Sunday."

At his tone she looked up from a stack of paper work, in time to notice the corner of his mouth twitch. He had an ulterior motive for heading to Wisconsin on Sunday. "Football game."

He grinned.

"Take Renae. I'm sure she could ask the parents some creative questions. Then the two of you can snuggle in forty-degree temps on the bleachers."

"Renae won't want to—"

"Oh, just ask her, Marcus. Stop predicting what she will and won't do. Let the mystery have its way."

"Mystery?"

"Mm-hmm." Her attention had reverted back to the papers. Another investigation involving stolen guns held more promise than the Stafford-Jasmine-mob triangle.

"Whoa!" Marcus yelled.

"What?"

He passed a paper to her. "Lab report. It was in my stack of mail."

She read and felt her eyes widen. "Rossi." The fingerprints of the man who had led them to Ian Stafford were found on the bloody handrail of the yacht *All That Jazz*. She looked up. "Do you think he's dead?"

"Let's go find out if he's been around." He stood and pulled his jacket from the back of the chair. "Or when he was last seen."

Cara stood, grabbing her suit jacket and ringing cell phone. The caller ID didn't show up, but that seldom stopped her from answering. "Hello." She followed Marcus to the staircase, one arm in the coat.

"Cara," a familiar voice said. "It's Helen. I'm at Phoebe's." Besides overseeing Miriam House, Helen worked with homeless women in a variety of roles. Phoebe's Place was a 24 hour shelter for abused women and children.

"Hi."

"Listen, there's a woman here, scared out of her wits. I mean terrified beyond the norm. We talked most of the night. She was almost incoherent. I'm convinced though, from what I heard, she's in serious trouble. I suggested having the police come and she went ballistic. Said she'd leave if I called them."

"What did you hear?"

Silence filled the line for a long moment. "I heard her say 'killed.'" Helen's voice was low. "And 'mob.' I didn't pick up on the segue."

Cara blew out a breath and descended the stairs behind Marcus. "I'll run home and change. Give me an hour, hour and a half?"

"Okay. If I get called away, her name's Jazzie. You can't miss her. She's not what you'd call our typical clientele."

Cara tripped against Marcus, her feet as frozen as her mind. *Jazzie? All That Jazz?*

Laughing, Marcus turned and grabbed her arm before she went sailing. "Fleming, you klutz."

Ignoring him she asked Helen, "Is that short for something?"

"Yes. Jasmine."

She said a quick goodbye into the phone and closed it up. "What's wrong?"

"I think we just found Jasmine Wakefield."

An hour later Marcus parked the car six long, indirect blocks from Phoebe's Place. The area was residential, middle class, big old houses, spacious yards. Though the address was not common knowledge, her partner knew it. Still, they chose not to draw attention to his knowledge by pulling up in front. The sight of an unknown male in the vicinity set off waves of unease.

"Fleming, take this." He bent over, hitched up a pant leg, and unstrapped a small gun holster from his ankle.

"We already had this discussion."

"No, we didn't. We discussed your Glock 22." The big, department-issued gun she'd insisted on leaving at home. "Take this." He held out his personal backup weapon.

"No, Marcus. Helen does not allow any kind of gun inside the house."

"For crying out loud, you're the police!"

"Exactly. If I carry that, I'm the police. If I'm the police, I can't fit in with a group of battered women."

He guffawed. "In that getup you'd fit into all kinds of places, starting with the red light district."

"It's not the getup." She fluffed the black wig's long locks. "Perfect as it is." The coat Marcus objected to was a short white furry thing. Beneath it she wore a black knit dress with long sleeves and straight skirt that almost reached her knees. High black boots with four-inch heels, an authentic-looking diamond, and flashy earrings and bracelets completed the ensemble. Her makeup was worthy of a cosmetic clerk in Saks Fifth Avenue.

"If it's not the getup, what is it?"

"The getup will appeal to Jasmine. She'll think I'm like her, not poverty stricken. I'm my man's trophy. She needs to feel a connection right off, but she won't open up unless what's in my eyes mirrors hers." Cara tapped her temple. "It won't happen if I'm the police."

"What's supposed to be in your eyes?"

"Terror. A victim mentality."

He stared at her. Though he had seen her go undercover in many roles from homeless to prostitute to druggie, the battered wife persona was a first. "I can't picture you a victim, Cucumber."

"You haven't seen me without backup or a gun."

"You want me to hang close by?"

She hesitated at his atypical expression of concern. *Yes, I do.* "No. If this is going to work, I've got to go deep. All the way."

"But you've got the phone?"

They'd argued in her apartment and at last negotiated the terms of her job. The gun stayed at home as well as all forms of identification. He insisted she pack her cell phone and money in an overnight bag with a change of clothes that included a pair of flat shoes and her apartment key. The things were much more than she thought necessary, but he would have kept her there all day if she had not conceded. She never had money when she left Nick. Knowing the bag would not be secure, she tucked the cash in one boot and the phone in the other where, despite its sleek shape, it now chafed against her calf.

"Yes, Marcus, I have the phone, but I am not promising to call any time soon."

"Get out of here," he growled.

"Tell Granny to pray extra, okay?"

His brows shot up. "Cara—"

"Forget I said that." The request, uncharacteristic of her, upset him. She opened the door and stepped out, her legs wobbling on the high heels. "I'm fine."

"You think so?" His crooked grin was spontaneous, and he pointed toward her feet. "Just try not to break an ankle getting there, okay?"

She gave him a thumbs-up, grateful to see his smile did not hide the concern. Despite his professed agnosticism, he would give the message to Rubyann.

~

Jane Waite, aka Jasmine Wakefield, aka Jazzie, was prettier than she had appeared that night in the low-lit restaurant. Au naturel suited her. No makeup spoiled the fine olive tone of her skin. Her bouffant blonde hair was brushed back into a sleek ponytail, and she wore black slacks with a simple lime green sweater. Well, maybe it wasn't all that simple since it looked like cashmere.

Cara walked across the kitchen to where she sat alone at the table. "Hi. Mind if I join you?"

The other woman shook her head, crushed out a cigarette in an ashtray, and blew out a puff of smoke. "Free country."

Cara slid onto a chair. House rules against smoking indoors were bent now and then, especially for newcomers too frightened to step into the backyard.

"You been here long?"

She shook her head and raised a cup to her lips. "There's coffee."

"No thanks." Glancing nervously around the kitchen, Cara refreshed her memory from other visits when she had volunteered to spend a day or night helping out. White cabinets and yellow floral wallpaper produced a warm effect in the large room. The stovetop was on an island in the center with four stools across the counter from it. The table at one end seated eight. In the adjacent dining room twelve could sit at the long table.

Through the pantry there was a sleeping room for two volunteers. Upstairs were five bedrooms with beds to accommodate a dozen. Additional cots were available. Next to the back door a security unit hung on the wall, its red light blinking. The system remained on alert day and night. All in all the house exuded hominess. It was, as well, a safe harbor, a port for many a woman's storm.

Helen had told her privately in the tiny office that only four women and two children had spent the night. She also asked Cara what name she wanted to use.

Though Cara had pieced together a general story about why she sought a shelter for abused women, she hadn't consciously considered a name. At Helen's question, one tripped off her tongue. Hearing it spoken aloud consummated her metamorphosis into a new character.

Cara said it again now by way of introduction to Jasmine. "I'm Cari-Ann."

"I'm Jazzie." She fiddled with a packet of cigarettes. Her eyes were exquisite. Such an odd color. What had Evie the hotel employee said? They were like a tiger's. Bright yellowy flecks against topaz. They looked almost bronze. The platinum-dyed hair offered a harsh contrast, as did the terror within the beautiful eyes.

"Hi." Cara bit her thumbnail.

She had begun the nail chewing while talking with Helen. The action was spontaneous, involuntary, not staged. With the pronouncement of her birth first name and married surname, Cara Fleming in essence reverted to Cari-Ann Davis. She sat in a Seattle shelter for abused women and children. Her left eye felt swollen. Her vision blurred, her head pounded, her heart raced. The kitchen's hominess scarcely registered. Nick was out there somewhere in a drug-induced haze. Cold sober, his cunning would kick into high gear and he would find her. Even this time when she had actually made it to a secure haven. Fear paralyzed her.

A door elsewhere in the house clicked shut.

Cara jumped. She shook her head and blinked. *This is Chicago, not Seattle. I'm on assignment. He can't hurt me.* Her heart still raced. *Lord, help me!*

"I—" She swallowed. "I, uh, just got here."

"Mm."

"That lady said I'll be safe." Her voice quavered. Unintentionally. "I haven't felt safe for so long. I'm not sure I'll recognize it if it happens." She slipped a different finger into her mouth. Unintentionally.

Jazzie stilled her hands and gazed at her. "Don't worry, honey. Safety is not going to happen." Her voice was low and husky, the tone of a woman who had seen it all. "There is no safe place on the face of the earth. I'm thinking maybe Mars would work. Excuse me."

With that she pushed back her chair, gathered the cigarettes and lighter, and left the kitchen.

Her words echoed in Cara's head, bounced around, and finally burrowed themselves into corners. The truth of them seeped into her nerves and she began to shake uncontrollably.

Time and again Nick Davis found her at friends' homes. Time and again she listened to his sweet talk, but it was the memory of his ugly talk that dismantled her fragile attempts at self-acceptance. She was no better than her mother. Worthless. Not pretty. Inept in the kitchen and bedroom. Who else would want her? Who else would put up with her? Time and again she scurried back to him like a cowed dog with its tail between its legs because she feared one thing more than him: homelessness.

As a 12-year-old she had spent two weeks living with her mother in a car. Fourteen days and 13 nights of sheer horror. Nick could do whatever he pleased before she would sign up for a repeat performance of that nightmare. He paid the rent for their tiny trailer, something she'd never be able to afford on her own.

Still, self-preservation had not completely deserted her. When the abuse grew fierce, she called the police. When his drug business grew repulsively lucrative, he threatened to kill her if she called them again. She believed him. The minor fear inched its way into an all-consuming emotion. She discovered homeless shelters and slipped away now and then for a night's sleep. The second-to-the-last beating propelled her to seek the more secure shelter, the place for women and children only, the one with an address not listed in the phone book. The place husbands could not find.

He found her there.

The next time she went to the church. Surely he would respect the church and the priest.

At the sight of Father and Mrs. Palmer lying in the hospital, fear of Nick completely overtook fear of homelessness. She became a street person on the road first, then in other towns, sometimes finding a formal shelter, sometimes not.

And God preserved her, conquering her terror as surely as any knight in shining armor annihilated the foes of his queen and country.

There was, after all, a safe place on earth. She would have to tell Jazzie.

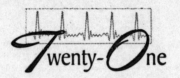

Twenty-One

The night Cara arrived at Phoebe's Place, she lay in bed, glad she'd included her own pajamas when Marcus insisted she pack a change of clothes. Coziness enveloped her as she snuggled in her warm flannel and inhaled the fresh scent of recently laundered sheets. Too late, she understood she'd grown dependent upon *things*. The revelation threw her further off balance. All evening comfort and fear played their game of tag, rendering her useless in the kitchen and in conversation.

Jazzie appeared in a similar condition. Neither of them spoke unless asked a direct question related to the dinner preparation. Before Helen left for the night, she reminded Cara the mute behavior was par for the course for many scared women. Others talked a blue streak. Some walked out the door, not yet ready to travel an unknown road, choosing instead the familiar rut.

Unable to fall asleep, Cara went to the window. Some beds remained empty, therefore she'd been assigned a private room. In the dark she twisted open the blinds, reached behind them and opened the window a few inches. Cold air blew in with a hint of frost and a faint scent of cigarette smoke.

Peering between the slats she saw Jazzie down below, standing alone in the backyard, smoking. Head bowed, she was not looking toward the patch of star-studded sky out-lined by tall trees.

Empathy welled in Cara. What had driven Jazzie to such a point in her life didn't matter. The point was that she stood alone in the dark.

Blinking back tears, Cara returned to the bed. She wanted to talk to someone. "Lord, please?" she whispered. "Am I allowed this time? Someone of flesh and blood? I'm so scared and lonely."

Leaning over, she reached inside one of her boots and pulled out the cell phone and her key chain with its attached penlight. She hit power. Messages were waiting, but they would have to wait. She put her finger on the keypad to speed dial Marcus's number. And then she paused.

She did not want to talk to Marcus. She did not want to talk business. Not that there was any business to talk. Nothing had happened. Jazzie was shut up in her own world...as was Cara in hers. Besides, what she really needed was prayer. Old fears were closing in fast. Up to a point she welcomed them because they transported her to Jazzie's position, enabling her to connect emotionally with the woman. Yet her hesitancy last time going undercover at the hotel warned that fear threatened to disassemble years of training and experience.

She moved her finger to Rubyann's number and paused again.

The woman would be frightened out of her mind hearing Cara's whispered voice at midnight.

Stuart Templeton? The chief of police, one of two people east of the Mississippi who knew her real name? No. Helpful as he'd been, she didn't get the sense he was a praying man.

Lord, please.

Her unconscious, that part of her mind that always held the truth, prodded her attention, and she knew the friend to call. He was the only one who might understand without asking for details, the only one who would seriously pray for her.

But he was fighting his own battles. She didn't have any right to intrude.

Even if he had kissed her.

No. She was on her own.

⁓

Two hours later, her own prayers splattered against the ceiling like paintballs shot randomly skyward with not enough force to penetrate the barrier, Cara picked up her phone and penlight again and huddled under the covers, a pillow over her head. This time, without hesitation, she pressed Bryan's number, memorized because she hadn't wanted to carry it on her person.

He answered on the first ring, his voice not the least bit groggy. "Hi." He must have recognized her number.

"Why aren't you asleep?" she asked softly.

"Are you kidding?" The twinkle in those green eyes was almost audible. "I walked three miles and have eaten nothing but protein and vegetables since yesterday. I'm feeling rather vigorous." His gentle, deep voice mesmerized her. "What are you doing awake?"

"Long story."

"What else do I have to do at two in the morning besides listen to long stories?"

She smiled. "But I can't tell it."

"Then tell another."

"Okay." She thought a moment how to rephrase the dilemma. "Once upon a time there was this undercover cop who thought she was infallible. And then one day she bit off more than she could chew."

Silence filled the space between them.

"The happy ending is that somebody prayed for her and she made it, and lived a long, fruitful life ruled by her newly discovered sense of reasonableness."

"The moral of the story is to tell a friend so he'll know to pray?"

"Exactly. Unless he's got enough on his own plate and shouldn't be bothered at this time."

"A good friend should always be informed. It's never a bother to him."

She closed her eyes. "This same woman thought the worst that could ever happen to her was to be homeless. But she found out it wasn't the worst. Nope. The worst was when her faith died."

"Why did her faith die?"

"This is where the story gets confusing."

"Try me."

"She only thought it died. You know how we can talk ourselves into believing something is true when in fact we've just imagined it? It's totally not real but we totally act like it is?"

"Yes. We easily deceive ourselves. The facts may say something is white, but we're convinced it's black."

"That's what happened. She became homeless, and it was so scary she imagined God had deserted her. But in reality He took care of all her needs. He kept her safe. For a time, though, she couldn't see that. She walked around like a dead person, not feeling a thing." She paused, aware of the ice water flowing through her.

"Until?"

"Until some people loved her." She referred to her friends in Los Angeles. "And then she became a cop and learned how to mingle coldness with God's gift of emotion. Which is what

got her into this thinking she was infallible and could jump
into—" Into what? A shelter for abused women? A vat of
swirling memories that sucked her into its abyss?

"Into?" he prompted.

"A situation. Where she was going all cold again. Because
her faith was getting all eaten up by those memories that
never went away. That never got completely healed."

"But she told her friend, and he prayed, so the story has a
happy ending."

A shudder tore through her. The ending would not arrive
until the journey had been traversed. "Right."

"Right." In one syllable Bryan O'Shaugnessy's tone exuded
conviction. It reminded her of when he stood at the front of
the church, clothed in the vestments symbolic of the Savior he
served, and offered the benediction. *The blessing of God
Almighty, the Father, the Son, and the Holy Spirit, be upon you
and remain with you forever.*

As if hearing the words spoken aloud, she said, "Amen."

"Amen," he echoed. "Call anytime. I mean it."

She knew he did, even in the midst of his doctor-imposed
sabbatical. She thought of his burly self, the bomb ticking
silently within his body. "Are you okay?"

"I am now."

Across northern Illinois tranquil waves of assurance rolled
from west to east. His prayers had begun. They would lull her
to sleep.

⌒

Cara spent the morning curled up on a living room chair
trying to read newsprint that kept wavering in front of her as
scenes of Nick unfolded in her mind's eye. Hours and hours
of reruns held her captive, pumping acid into her stomach.

Jazzie didn't emerge from her bedroom. Normally the volunteer supervisor would have intervened and either cajoled or commanded both of them to get out of their heads for a while. There was housework, laundry, and cooking to do. There was a list of agencies to explore, people who offered assistance in deciding what step they could take next. Helen must have told the woman in charge to give the two newcomers all the space they needed.

At last the house quieted. A volunteer manned the office. Another carted women and children off to a distant park. The kids needed to run. Cara helped herself to chicken salad from the refrigerator and sat at the kitchen table. Food restored some equilibrium.

Jazzie appeared, dressed in the same black slacks and pretty cashmere sweater. "Is the coast clear?"

Cara smiled. "You must not have kids either."

"Good grief, no!" She went to the counter and poured herself a cup of coffee. "What is that you're eating?"

"Chicken salad. There's more in the fridge."

"Is it any good?"

"Well, I can't say that I've noticed. I just thought I should eat."

"You and me both. No sense starving to death over some worthless bozo." She opened the refrigerator and bent her head into it. "You look like a horse that's been rode hard and put away wet."

"I didn't sleep much."

"I didn't sleep a wink my first night here." She shut the door and carried food over to the table. "About three this morning I decided no sense losing my beauty rest over the aforementioned worthless bozo. So I took a sleeping pill. I have plenty if you need one tonight. Assuming you'll be here tonight."

"I don't have anywhere else to go."

"Me neither. Doubt I ever will." She muttered the last phrase to herself as she returned to the counter. "Let me know about the pill."

"Thanks, but I'll pass on that." A different memory erupted. Her mom played a major role in it.

"Not into drugs, huh?"

Cara hadn't seen Jazzie cross the room and sit at the table, but there she was in front of her. The woman must have assumed from Cara's zombie stare that drugs were an issue. "Uh, no, I'm not into drugs. My mom was an addict. Mixed one too many sleeping pills with a bottle of vodka once. Of course something like that only takes once. Scared me off for life."

"My mom was into booze. She actually gave it up about the time I turned twenty-eight. But after twenty-eight years, who cares?" She shrugged and spooned salad onto her dish. "Scared me off too, I tell you." She emphasized the *you*. "The only thing I touch is filtered tobacco. And a sleeping pill, but only after I haven't slept in days. What's your name again?"

"Cari-Ann."

"I'm Jazzie."

"I remembered. It's unusual."

"Short for Jasmine."

"That's pretty."

"Yeah, it is. But Jazzie's kind of...jazzy." She smiled briefly. "Which suits me better." She began eating.

Cara pushed her fork around her plate and tried to gather wits that had scattered the moment she told Helen her name the previous day. They remained elusive, overshadowed by heavy emotions. Since she had become a policewoman and realized both her feet were planted firmly on the ground— probably for the first time in her life—those feelings had disappeared. She thought God scooped them up before they hit and flung them away, as far as the east was from the west. Evidently the image had been false. She knew God had instead collected them in a huge garbage can. She knew that because without a doubt He'd upturned the can and was now dumping it all on her head. Dread, apprehension, regret, self-doubt, vulnerability, hopelessness—

"Yo, Cari-Ann."

"Huh?"

"You're zoning out on me again."

"Sorry."

"No problem. That's how I was yesterday. But, hey, we made it through the night."

Lord God, almighty and everlasting Father, You have brought us in safety to this new day: Preserve us with Your mighty power... Why, oh why, hadn't she packed her *Book of Common Prayer?*

"We're alive to fight yet another day. It's time to gather our wits, Cari-Ann."

Cara stared at her.

"We will not let the worthless bozos rule. And if you think you've got it bad, trust me, my story is way worse than yours." Her chair scraped as she shoved it back and stood. "I haven't baked in years. Want to make some cookies?"

Her mouth watered. "Monster cookies?"

"You know the recipe?"

"No, but I bet it's here." She knew it was; she'd placed the index card in the box herself. "Kids love monster cookies."

"Me too."

Cara stood. "You know whoever fixes dinner doesn't have to clean up."

Jazzie smiled and held up her hand in a high-five gesture. "Well, let's fix dinner too."

Cara lightly slapped the outstretched hand.

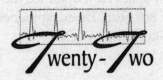

Twenty-Two

Jazzie revealed nothing of her background to Cara while they worked together in the kitchen baking cookies and preparing dinner, but her personality emerged as a smart, practical, sometimes mouthy woman who knew how to laugh at herself. Hard as she tried to take charge and not let the terror of her situation overwhelm her sensibleness, her eyes occasionally lost focus.

Cara knew where Jazzie went. She followed similar rabbit trails. They rocked her to the core. She teetered between hopeless fragility and a complete emotional shutdown—both of which deadened any tendency toward prayer. Her talk with Bryan and the memory of his soothing voice faded into the deep recesses of her mind from which they could not be recalled at will. Scripture, those words that sustained her, evaporated into thin air like fine spray from an aerosol can.

She'd reverted back in time. Cari-Ann Davis was devouring her identity.

After dinner she grabbed one of the winter jackets hanging by the back door. They were all clean and worn, fashions at least a year old, hand-me-downs donated by women who wanted to help, women who came from nice homes.

She followed Jazzie outdoors, adjusting the security system as they went. Punching in codes with every pass through the door was a hassle, but Helen said no one ever complained. Women who stayed at Phoebe's Place welcomed any and all safety measures.

Jazzie's hand shook as she flicked the lighter and unsuccessfully aimed for the cigarette in her mouth. "Coming out here gives me the heebie-jeebies." A few more attempts and the flame steadied on the cigarette.

"The yard looks pretty safe." Cara glanced around from where they stood next to the house. "High privacy fence. Padlocked gates. No trees or bushes for anyone to hide behind. Neighbors on both sides and the back. No dark alley."

Jazzie exhaled. The puff of smoke mingled with her frosted breath in the cold air. "But still..."

"Yeah, I know."

They stood quietly for a few moments.

The cigarette in Jazzie's mouth glowed. She removed it and said, "So what do you think of our housemates?"

Inside three women cleaned up the kitchen with the volunteer supervisor whom Cara was glad she'd never met. It would have been awkward to pull her aside and explain things. Two of the residents were in their twenties; each had a child, two boys ages four and six. The third woman's age was difficult to judge. She was probably younger than her haggard appearance suggested.

Cara shrugged. "They seem nice enough."

"Or scared enough."

"Guess we're all that."

"Mm-hmm. I see you wear a wedding ring. You're married to the worthless bozo?"

"Yes."

"Why don't you take it off?"

Nick's voice echoed in her head. The words were indistinct, but she knew by the tone what he said. "Because when he finds me he'll want to see it there. Or else."

"But he's not going to find you. Is he?"

"Not here. I've never been here. Have you?"

"No. Have you left him before?"

"Yes. But he always found me because I went to a friend's house. Dumb, but he controls the money. No way I could hop on a bus or go to a hotel. Have you left your husband before?"

"We're not married. *He's* married, but not to me." She muttered something under her breath.

"Then it should be easy to leave. No legal mess. You're scot-free."

Jazzie laughed harshly. "You think so? Hon, that is so far from reality, it's not even funny."

"I don't understand."

"Did you ever get a restraining order?"

How many times had she tried the sensible, legal route? How many times had she backed down, not going to court and facing him and requesting a more permanent injunction? "Twice."

"Then you know they're a joke. Doesn't matter if you're married or not. If he wants you, he'll get you. I didn't even try that route. If some cop delivered papers to him, he'd—" She stuck the cigarette in her mouth and puffed.

"Are you saying he stalks you?"

"Oh, we're into something way beyond stalking. His friends are *experts* at finding people who don't want to be found."

"He's got friends who stalk for him? I thought stalkers were like Nick, crazy-obsessed. He'd never want someone else to find me. Why in the world would anyone have friends to— Oh my gosh! That sounds like—"

"Don't even go there. We'll just leave it that I'm in it up to my neck. I give them a week at the most to find me here, which means I gotta leave Wednesday. Thursday at the latest. Helen says she can get me to another place like this one, but then that means she knows where I am. And they can make her tell them."

Cara bit what little was left of a fingernail. "How can they find you?"

She blew out another lungful of smoke. "Cops must know about this place. Those guys know cops. They'll find the right one to bully or bribe. Or some girlfriend of theirs will pose as an abused wife and do exactly what I did. Call the hotline and start the process. Eventually she could end up at Phoebe's Place too."

"Would you go back to him?"

"No way. Ian—the guy was good to me. I thought he loved me. I loved him. Until that Saturday night when I finally woke up and saw the light. Worthless bozo." After one more quick puff she dropped the cigarette on the concrete walkway and crushed it with her toe. "Let me know if you change your mind about a sleeping pill." With that she turned and entered the house.

~

After five minutes of conversing with Marcus on the phone, Cara sensed more of a connection with her icy self than that fragile stranger who'd been dogging her heels at Phoebe's. She began to remember she was a cop.

She spoke softly into the phone, once again in the middle
of the night with the pillow over her head. "Something happened on a Saturday night."

"The yacht incident was a Saturday."

"I think it's when she decided to leave him. Up until that
point, she said she loved him."

"Women." He didn't bother to hide the disgust in his tone.
"How could she love such a lowlife?"

"Oh, there are a lot of reasons. She thinks herself unworthy
of anyone else. He's good-looking. Pays attention to her.
Gives her a home."

"You're defending her?"

"Simply explaining her choices."

"Your voice just went funny."

"I'm whispering under a pillow."

"Are you okay?"

"I'm fine. Anyway, she plans to leave Wednesday or
Thursday."

"You sure you're all right? It's gotta be depressing as heck
there."

Depressing? He had no idea. "It's fine. About her leaving—"

"Where's she going?"

"She doesn't know. I'll invite myself along."

"No, you won't. Just bring her in."

"I don't think she's ready yet. She's like a skittish colt, and
she doesn't trust cops. She figures his men will get information from one of us about this place."

"Then we'll tail her. She sticks out like a sore thumb with
that bleached-blonde hair."

"I know. Which means they have a good chance of spot-
ting her too—"

"And anyone with her."

"I can take care of myself. I can take care of her. Once she realizes she's got nowhere else to go, she'll consider coming in."

"Do you think she has information we could use against him?"

"The two of them were close. If what the housekeeper told me was true, she kept a set of accounts for him. I imagine she knows enough to put him away for a long time. Why else would she believe he'd send his men after her? It's not the case of an obsessed stalker."

"Just try to sell her on police protection before you take off willy-nilly, okay?"

It wouldn't be willy-nilly. Cara had done willy-nilly. No, it would be a series of premeditated steps, probably beginning with dyeing Jazzie's hair. Maybe she could talk her into that—

"Okay?" Marcus sounded irritated.

"Okay! I'll try to at least hide her out at my place. I'm beginning to feel like a sitting duck here."

"Phoebe's Place is the best-kept secret going. Eventually they might find the needle in the haystack, but come on. She hasn't even been there two days."

"How do you think she found the place?"

"Hotline. Different agencies. Like anybody."

"Like anybody. Think outside the box. Why not send a woman?"

He grunted. "It doesn't have to be a man's job, does it?"

"Nope. Okay, on to new business. I forwarded some voice mails to you. A couple need immediate attention. They involve that other—you know—case." She hesitated using proper names or many details about work. To say she and Marcus were cautious of communication by cellular phone was an understatement.

"You don't expect me to hold that witness's hand, do you?"

"I do."

"I'll tell her the soft-touch half of our dynamic duo is unavailable. She'll just have to cope."

"You'll blow it."

He sighed dramatically. "Hurry home, dear. Life is the pits without you."

Nostalgia washed over her as she pressed the power button off. Partnering with Marcus felt as if it had happened a lifetime ago. And the lifetime belonged to someone else.

Wild, vivid dreams haunted Cara throughout the short night, but she awoke unable to recall a single detail. Only a sense of dread lingered, its weight like a ball of iron attached to her lungs.

Quickly she unplugged the cell phone's battery charger and stuffed it deep into a side pocket of her overnight bag. She donned the outfit she'd worn the previous day. It consisted of khaki cargo pants, enough in vogue as to not raise Jazzie's suspicion that she wasn't a with-it Chicagoan. The other advantage was the baggy pocket located on the right side of her thigh. The perfect spot for carrying phone and cash. It even had a button that held the flap closed. A beige fisherman's knit sweater completed her casual look. Not the classic style of cashmere, but then police budgets did not run on the same track as a criminal's. One last glance in the mirror to check the wig and she was ready to go.

The heaviness in her chest interfered with breathing. Her attempts at deep inhalations failed. The pressure remained.

She unbuttoned the pocket and reached for the phone. A thought niggled, something negative, something warning that she was not to use it. Using it was cheating. How could she be Cari-Ann and gain Jazzie's confidence if she cheated? Abused housewives on their last leg did not run off with *backup*.

She struggled for breath. Concerned more that she could not breathe, she grasped instinctively for the instrument as if it were a firefighter's ladder leaning against her bedroom window from which smoke poured. The phone was her lifeline.

She switched it on and found one new message waiting. From a number she had only called once, but one she recognized as easily as the station's.

Bryan's recorded voice filled her ear. Deep and resonant, but pitched at a distinct level of warmth and intimacy.

"Hello. I was just wondering how you are. This sounds trite, but I'll say it anyway: You're constantly in my thoughts and prayers. I suppose you're not at liberty to call? Well, in case you're curious, I'm okay. We have rain here. Ark-building sort of rain. Guess that means another session on the treadmill instead of a round of golf. I finished reading two books and am finding the game of Solitaire not as boring as I thought. Okay." There was a pause. "Take care of yourself. Please."

She pressed the key to save the message, turned off the phone, and gulped enough air to fill her lungs.

⌒

A dream fragment hit her as she rounded the staircase landing. It chased off Bryan's comfort and halted her in her tracks.

Based on real events, the dream placed her in Portland, Oregon, the emotions as real as they were that day 14 years ago. She was tired and hungry, yet hopeful. She had a new job and a bed and shower at a shelter. The hope soon disintegrated. Nick found her. He entered the chain discount store. Working at a store of the same chain she worked at in Seattle had been a dumb move. A willy-nilly decision. But her habit of vigilance, nurtured from childhood, saved her. Ever watchful even as she stocked shelves, she saw him before he saw her.

Later the girls at the service desk asked if that guy had located her. He'd asked them what department she worked in. They thought he was cute. She left Portland that night, using all of her cash to buy a bus ticket to San Francisco.

In the dream he was on the bus with her. In real life, the ride was uneventful.

No. Not quite.

That was the day she realized she'd stopped talking to God.

Cara shook off the memory and continued downstairs. She wasn't alone this time. Bryan cared about her. Marcus cared about her. She hadn't stopped talking to God. Her prayers had simply gone underground, as she herself had.

The little boys were glued to the television. She overheard voices from the direction of the office. They probably belonged to Helen and the middle-aged lady. In the dining room Cara exchanged greetings with the two young moms who were walking through it. No one else was around.

In the kitchen Jazzie looked up from the newspaper she was reading at the table. Her smile wasn't spontaneous enough to erase the pain in her eyes.

"Morning." Cara poured a cup of coffee and refilled Jazzie's. "The paper always makes me feel worse."

She pushed it aside and waved her hand in a gesture of dismissal. "I agree. It's all garbage."

Reading a headline upside down, Cara slid onto a chair. *Street Person Missing*. A small grainy photo of the man accompanied the article. Marcus had told her the story last night. Rossi, the informant who had connected Ian Stafford's name with gunrunning, had not been seen for over two weeks. She caught the subheading. *James Rossi wanted by police for questioning in connection with investigation*.

"Jazzie, why don't you go to the police?"

"I told you. They're in cahoots with the bad guys."

"They can't all be in cahoots. Don't they have— What is it called? Something like witness protection?"

"You think that's any better than a restraining order?"

"It has to be. I mean, it must work. That's how they get people to testify against— You know."

Jazzie shook her head. "How does anybody know? Who ever hears from those people again? They're cut off from their friends and family. Their names are changed. They could be dead for all anybody knows."

"Nah. Not after all the years it's been in place. Someone would have told. I don't know. I think I'd change my name and everything if the choice was either that or...die." She whispered the last word.

"I'd rather disappear on my own."

"Can you do that?"

She didn't reply. Her face crumpled, but no tears fell.

"What is it?"

"No, I can't do that, not without telling first. I've done plenty of wrong things in my life, but that just wouldn't be right." She bit her bottom lip.

"What wouldn't be right?"

"Not telling *somebody!*" Her voice came out a hoarse whisper. "I know where that man is." She pointed at the newspaper.

Cara glanced down at the perfectly manicured red nail that lay on Rossi's photograph. "Where?"

"At the bottom of Lake Michigan! And I saw how he got there!" She clamped a hand over her mouth and bolted from the room.

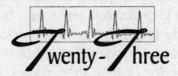

Twenty-Three

Helen's navy blue suit swished and her low-heeled pumps clunked in a businesslike manner against the wood floor. She shut the office door, walked around the desk, and sat. Folding her hands atop the blotter, she waited until Cara sat across from her. Then she asked in a quiet voice, "How's it going?"

"I can't discuss an open investigation."

The eyes of the even-keeled woman suddenly flashed and anger twisted her face. "Don't you dare give me that line in my house!" Her voice nearly hissed and her finger jabbed the air. "I invited you here!"

Cara felt that heaviness pull again on her lungs. While Jazzie stayed in a bedroom behind closed doors, no doubt frozen with terror, she battled anxiety that nearly incapacitated her thought processes. How could she win Jazzie's trust and reveal she was there to help? What if Jazzie ran off while everyone else slept? What if Stafford's henchmen *did* find Phoebe's Place? Realistically, how much time did they have?

Then there were the plights of the other residents. She watched their forlorn faces, their brave attempts at normalcy. Cara Fleming wanted to take them by the hand and walk them to the next step. Meanwhile, the Cari-Ann Davis within her vacillated. Cari-Ann, the meek and mild wife, Cari-Ann, the fierce woman who got away and made something of her life.

On the one hand, she could identify with the others, so strongly she felt their helpless terror as a hollowness in her stomach and their hopeless rage in sporadic flushes of heat. On the other hand, she wanted to get in their face and tell them to get a grip. Change their names, their hair, their clothes, move across the country, go to school, get a job, don't feel anymore, just do it. Welcome the ice.

Helen said, "Cara, you're walking around like a dead person. You haven't got a fingernail left to chew."

Cara blinked and removed her thumb from between her teeth.

"I don't know if I would recognize you at first glance. It's not just the wig. You look like one of them."

At last she found her voice. "I was once."

Helen gazed at her, surprise erasing the frustration.

"My husband abused me, and when I left he stalked me. One time I stayed in a shelter very much like this one. He found me."

"But you've been at Phoebe's many times. You've volunteered, spent the night even!"

"Yeah." She lifted her shoulders in a half shrug. "I had no clue this assignment, this posing, would be any different. But it's...disorienting."

"Well, you look like the real thing. So." She clasped her hands on the desk again and sat up straight as a yardstick. "What are we up against?"

Cara leaned back in the chair. Helen's professional tone worked its charm, drawing out the take-charge detective who'd been overshadowed by Cari-Ann. "Men are out there somewhere. My guess is only two. But they're smarter and more motivated than any husband or boyfriend we've ever come up against. They're mean and well-armed. And they're after Jazzie."

For a long moment the women stared at each other. Understanding dawned in Helen's eyes. "We're all in danger."

She nodded.

"I'll hire some off-duty police to guard the place."

"Like I said, these guys are smarter and more motivated. A cop will not prevent them from getting in. They might even send a woman first. Posing like me. You haven't been told to expect any new arrival this morning?"

"No."

"Good. Don't accept anyone. If you're called, say the place is full. I think we'd all better leave as soon as possible. Can you get the others to a different shelter?"

"Yes. What will you do?"

"Try to convince Jazzie a policewoman is her friend."

"First you'll have to convince her you are one. That faraway look isn't completely gone. Your eyes are focused elsewhere. Your face goes blank."

"The memories won't stop."

"Cara, I've had some of my own that wouldn't stop. The trick is to let them come."

"Let them come? I'd be a babbling idiot if I didn't fight them off."

"God will fight them off for you." Helen's voice mellowed. "He can't unless you're experiencing them again, this time with the knowledge that Christ is right there in the middle. Only He can bind up the wounds and offer the power to forgive. The healing can't begin until then."

"I thought He already healed this stuff. It's from such a long time ago, and He's brought me through so much."

"I'm sure He has, but believe me. I'm fifty-six. It takes a lifetime. The older I get, the more the past catches up. A painful memory will surface, and the process starts all over again."

Cara saw Helen in a new light. "I guess I've never played this role either, as resident counseled by the director. I never appreciated the compassion and wisdom that went on behind the scenes."

"You thought I was just a strict old biddy." She chuckled.

That was a rare sound. Cara smiled at it. "Well, not as much would be accomplished without strict old biddies in charge dotting i's and crossing t's."

"But without faith and prayer, nothing at all would get accomplished. Now go and get us out of this mess."

"Yes, ma'am." At the door she paused and looked back. "Thank you, Helen."

~

Cara knocked on Jazzie's door.

"I'm busy."

"Jazzie, it's me. Cara—Cari-Ann." The back of her neck prickled, an unfailing indicator that time was running out. "We need to talk."

No reply.

After a long moment, she touched the doorknob. "I'm coming in."

Still nothing.

She pushed open the door and entered the bedroom. Dim sunlight filtered through closed blinds. Jazzie lay huddled in a fetal position on one of the beds.

Cara sat beside her on the edge of the bed. "Hey. It's going to be okay."

"What? You got us tickets for the shuttle and we leave at noon for Mars?"

At least she was talking. Cara said, "Next best thing. How about we get out of here on foot?"

"And go where?"

"The streets. I've done this before."

"What do you mean, the streets?"

"We'll be homeless until we figure out what to do. It's a great hiding place."

"Why did you come here then?"

Cara wondered what the difference was between the streets and Phoebe's Place. *Helen.* Of course. "I came here so Helen could convince me not to go back to my husband."

"Yeah, I bet she could do that." Jazzie sat up on the bed. "But you don't know me. I don't know you. Why would you want me with you?"

"Two is better than one."

"But you know what's going on with me."

"We'll be fine once we change our clothes. And I think we should change your hair. That color attracts a lot of attention. We—"

"Why should I trust you?" She scooted backward, to the corner of the bed, against the wall. "Maybe you're one of them."

"Jazzie—"

There was a loud rap on the door and then it was opened. Helen burst in, her face flushed. "We've been compromised!"

"What?" Cara cried. "How do you know?"

"I got a phone call. Let's—"

"Who called?"

"It doesn't matter. We need to—"

"Of course it matters!" Cara stood.

"Look, I've got eyes and ears in the right places. But he's my informant, not anyone else's. I can't expose him. All I can say is he's in a position to know. So let's get moving."

"But what'd he say?"

"The address was given out maybe thirty minutes ago. That's it."

Cara's mind raced. The address was given out. That meant the carefully guarded, the need-to-know basis of a secret was shared with someone who didn't fall into that category. Who gave it? Another agency, a former resident, the police. And who knew it was given? Same choice of answers. Helen's friend was in a position to know.

"Helen, just tell me this guy's connection so we can make an intelligent guess which of the four women is the target. If it's not Jazzie, then we can—"

"I have five women in residence, *Cari-Ann*. Not four."

Cara felt as stunned as if she'd been slapped in the face. She was the target, not one of the other four. Who would know she was at Phoebe's?

The police.

Helen's informant was connected with the department, maybe was a cop himself. He was privy to the knowledge that the address was leaked. By someone who knew she was there, working undercover because Jazzie was there.

Stafford's hired guns didn't even have to search for Jazzie. Somebody had handed him the information in less than 48 hours.

"Helen, you trust this person?"

"Absolutely. How much time do we have?"

"Two minutes. Two days. I think they'll wait until dark."

From the corner of the bed behind Cara came a whimper and then a shout. "Will somebody tell me what is going on?"

Cara looked at her. The pretty olive tone skin had turned the color of her bleached hair. "This place isn't secure anymore. We have to leave immediately."

"It's them!" she screamed. "I knew they'd find me!"

Helen sat on the bed and touched her arm. "Shh, now. We don't know who it is at this point. We all need to just take a deep breath and not fret." Her trademark business tone delivered the compassionate words. "There are things to do and I need your cooperation. All right?"

Jazzie responded by closing her mouth.

"All right. Some unauthorized person knows this address. We have to leave quickly and efficiently. I want you to do exactly what Cari-Ann says. Believe me, you can trust her. I've known her a long time. All right?"

Whimpering and eyes still wide with fright, she nodded.

"Good girl. You'll be all right. You will be." Helen patted her arm. She stood and looked at Cara, brows raised in question.

Their exit already clearly etched in her mind, Cara said, "Dibs on the two dark jackets and size seven Reebocks." She had her own solid military-style, high-top boots; Jazzie's delicate size seven flats needed to be exchanged. "That's it."

Helen nodded curtly and left the room.

Jazzie asked in an alarmed whisper, "It's them."

Cara sat on the bed and faced her. "Probably, but we'll be long gone before they get here. Listen carefully. My name is Cara Fleming, and I'm a detective with the Chicago Police Department."

"What?" she cried. "You're what?"

"I'm here because Helen thought you needed help."

"You're the *police?*" Disbelief and confusion distorted her face. If the windows had been open, neighbors could have heard her two blocks away. "Why did you come? I didn't tell Helen anything!"

"No, you didn't. She only deduced that your situation was a police matter."

"I can't go to the police!"

"You don't have to. I'm already here. Okay?" Enough mollycoddling. She let the adrenaline lower and tighten her voice. "And you've got about thirty seconds to decide whether or not to leave with me." She removed the black wig from her head and laid it on the bed. "Either way, please put this on. You really don't want to walk around in public with that hair color."

Jazzie stared.

"Okay, your thirty seconds are up. Coming?"

A thousand unspoken questions glowed in her tiger eyes. "To where?"

"I told you. The streets. Best hiding place there is." From the mob. And now, from the police.

Jazzie picked the wig up from the bed.

~

Cara scratched the back of her neck beneath her ponytail. They had taken three minutes to adjust the wig over Jazzie's blonde hair, use the bathroom, find thick bobby socks, and exchange terrified goodbye waves with the other women. Now in the kitchen she watched Jazzie, sitting at the table, tie the athletic shoes. The perfectly manicured, bright red fingertips stood out in contrast to the white laces.

"Jazzie, those nails are almost as obvious as your hair. Could you bite them, make them scruffy looking?"

"They're acrylic." Her voiced still sounded unnatural. It remained an octave high, but at least had coalesced into a monotone, giving her the sound of a robot in shock. "They're like cemented on."

"Hmm." Inwardly she cringed. Cemented on? "You look good in the wig."

"Black's my natural color, but Ian— *He* never liked it. I look like a dork in these shoes. Why can't I wear my own shoes and coat?"

"A thin raincoat and slip-ons won't make it."

"Why can't I bring anything besides my wallet?"

"Because I said so. Let's go." She led the way to the back door and lifted the winter jackets from their hooks on the wall. "Green or navy?"

"You think I really care?"

"That's the spunky spirit we need." She handed her the navy one. "Forest green's my color. There's a zippered pocket on the inside. Stick your wallet in that."

Before opening the back door, Cara peered into the yard. Helen was out front, hustling her troops into her minivan. Their departure was synchronized. While the others drove away, Cara and Jazzie would unlock the back gate and walk through the backyard directly behind to the next street over and turn left down that block. At the corner they would turn right, then right again at the next street, in essence back-tracking. Eventually an indirect route would land them at a bus line in a commercial district.

The escape plan was not willy-nilly. Cara had devised it during her first stint as volunteer at Phoebe's. She even walked it once and deciphered the bus routes. If some wacko came after a resident while Cara was on duty, she was prepared to whisk the woman from harm's reach at a moment's notice.

No, the plan was not willy-nilly. Cara would not do things willy-nilly. Not ever again.

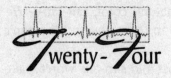

Twenty-Four

Cara sat along the aisle on the bus seat situated just past the rear side-exit door. She watched Jazzie in the window seat pick diligently at her red nail polish. Not much came off, but the action proved she was cooperative. Of course fear could be quite a motivator. Cara sensed the young woman would stay with her only as long as she felt safe. Or until she'd gleaned enough knowledge from her teacher to survive on her own.

"Cari?" Jazzie said, not looking up from her task.

"Cara."

She made a noise of disgust. "I only heard it once!"

"Don't worry about it."

"*Cara*. Now that we're sitting still, will you tell me where we're going?"

The bus slowed to a stop and the front door hissed open. She watched two elderly women board and scanned the sidewalk. She had debated foregoing the next step in her plan, but it would tremendously ease their flight if they took it. "We're going to try to get into my apartment and pick up some things."

"Try?"

"They may be watching it already, but maybe not. There'd be no need if they count on finding us at Phoebe's. My guess

is they'll wait until dark to go there. Which gives us about
four hours' head start."

"Who's 'they?'"

"I think you know."

"We can't stay at your place?"

"No."

"Don't you have a car?"

"I only have the apartment key on me." Besides which,
they probably knew it.

"I have a credit card. We could go to a hotel."

Cara glanced at her.

"Credit card's a no-no?"

"Jazzie, think of 'they' as being either man or woman,
young, old, in-between, skinny, obese, beautiful, creepy,
funny, clumsy, athletic, fashionably dressed, or wearing hand-
me-down jackets and shoes. 'They' fit in anywhere, any job or
street corner. Whoever doesn't work for them can be bribed
or extorted by them." She felt Jazzie's eyes on her and turned.

"Which means they're everywhere?"

"No, but they *can* be anywhere. Just keep your eyes open.
Expect the unexpected."

"How do I know you're not one of them?"

"You don't." *Just like I don't know who sold me out.* "But
I'm not."

"Did your husband stalk you?"

"Yes."

"I think I knew that."

She nodded. "Trust your instincts. I didn't lie about anything except I'm not originally from Chicago. Even the name
Cari-Ann Davis is true. Or was, six years ago."

"You changed it?"

"Yes."

"I changed mine too."

"I was hiding from my husband."

"I was hiding from the stupid girl I was in Milwaukee." Her laugh was a nervous chortle. "Guess I better change it again and hide from the stupid woman I've been in the Windy City."

"I can help."

"That witness protection thing?"

"Yes."

"You know who my boyfriend is."

Cara turned to her. "I'd protect you even if I didn't." She flipped the green hood with its faux fur trim onto her head and tied the string. "Next stop."

Gray clouds scuttled across the late October sky, promising rain if not snowflakes. Jazzie matched Cara's hurried pace along a crowded sidewalk. Cara was glad the woman was in good shape. She must have exercised regularly. In the penthouse? In the Park-Mont's health club?

There were other pluses, a major one being Jazzie was not a whiner. She followed directions without asking for lengthy explanations. Of course, she was still in the early stages of living with panic nipping at her heels.

Cara ran through her mental checklist again. They would walk around the block twice. If no strangers lingered, they would approach the apartment building from the back. Once inside the apartment she would get her large backpack from the bedroom closet and pack essentials: her gun, a different wig, her "homeless" costumes of leggings, baggie skirts and sweaters. Five minutes tops, in and out.

She considered again parking Jazzie in the coffee shop they now approached. Located two blocks from her building, it was one she didn't frequent. Employees in there would not recognize her.

A fire engine siren disrupted her thoughts and jangled her nerves. The truck whizzed by.

What was she doing? Taking to the streets again? This time for her job? Just when she was getting used to feeling settled... to even—in a way—*seeing* someone?

She shook her head. Her trick of compartmentalizing had met its challenge in Bryan.

Slowing her steps, she said, "Jazzie, I want you to wait inside that coffee shop up there on the left. See it?"

"No way. I'm sticking right next to you."

"You'll be safer in there."

"What if you don't come back?"

Cara considered the possibility. She pulled Jazzie over to the storefronts. They stopped beside the brick wall of a floral shop, a few doors from the coffee shop.

"Okay," she said. "Listen carefully. If we get separated, go six blocks east. That's Cedar. There's a bus stop there. Take the Number Eleven to Broadway and Seventieth. Repeat that."

Jazzie glanced around. "Six blocks east. Cedar. Bus stop. Number Eleven. Broadway and Seventieth."

"Perfect. North a block on Broadway is a Salvation Army. They serve supper from five to seven. Look for a black woman. She's about forty-five, very elegant; her hair in a French twist. Her name is Lana."

"She works there?"

"No, she'll be eating there. Tell her you're Detective Fleming's friend and you need help. If I don't show up, she'll keep you safe through the night." Cara glimpsed Jazzie's panic-stricken expression and stopped her perusal of the

street to make eye contact. "Listen to me. Just keep a low profile. You're sharp and you're strong and you know you're not
going back to where you came from. All that puts you ahead
of the game. You can make it with or without me."

She gave half a nod.

"But I will be back." Movement caught her eye. A crowd
exited the coffee shop and joined what seemed to be a general flow of foot traffic. "What's going on?"

A teenager rushing past looked in their direction. He must
have seen her puzzlement. Excitement lit up his face. "There's
a fire!"

Cara touched the back of her neck. The commotion made
her hesitant to leave Jazzie. "Change of plan. Let's walk a little
more."

"Fine with me!"

The smoke came into view when they reached the intersection. Ahead she could see a string of emergency vehicles,
lights flashing, police redirecting traffic.

Away from her street.

"Come on." She grasped Jazzie's arm and began jogging
between people.

At the next corner her apartment building came into view
half a block away. Yellow flames shot out from a third story
double window.

Her window.

"Oh dear God!"

Smoke billowed skyward and found its way into her
throat. The scene was chaos. Firefighters in their helmets and
big coats were everywhere, on the ground and on ladders.
Torrents of water gushed from hoses, their spray falling like
a fine mist.

"Cara, what is it?"

No words came.

"Is that your building?"

She nodded.

"Jeez Louise."

Images of her neighbors came to mind. All were like her, between the ages of 30 and 50, away at work most days, not around much. Pets were not allowed.

Cara glanced to her right and left and hurried across the street to a policeman, a fresh-faced young guy wearing his cap with its black-and-white checkered trim. The short black jacket was tight at the waist, accentuating his shoulders and his hips bulky with holster and baton.

"Ma'am, please stay on the other side—"

"But that's my building! I live there! Is anyone hurt?"

"I'm sorry, ma'am. No, we don't know of anyone hurt. They've searched every unit. Well, except for that top corner one, where it probably started. It's still burning hot, but at least things are contained." He waved at a driver, directing him to make a U-turn. "Last I heard, the super hadn't been contacted yet. Do you know who lives in that top unit?"

Jazzie pinched her arm so hard she cried out. "Ah!"

Jazzie spoke loudly over her exclamation, "Who should we tell?"

"The fire chief." He stretched out an arm. "Over there. See him?"

"Yeah. Do you know how the fire started?"

He shook his head, watching another car approach. "The answer's in that apartment. Excuse me." He walked away.

"Thanks." Jazzie called out, pulling Cara's elbow, steering her back across the street.

Unfeeling, Cara bumbled alongside Jazzie. People and buildings blurred. They crossed more streets. Down and up curbs. A whistle shrilled. Jazzie lowered her fingers from her mouth and brakes screeched. She hustled her into the back of a cab and said something to the driver.

She turned to Cara and whispered, "Okay?"

Cara closed her eyes and put her head back against the seat.

⌒

Only when Cara tripped on the steps leading up to the Art Institute on Michigan Avenue did the numbness begin to dissipate. A wave of nausea pushed it away. She stumbled over to the base of one of the lion sculptures guarding the entrance, leaned against it, and lowered her head.

Jazzie patted her back. "Why don't you loosen your hood?"

She followed her advice. Lessening the pressure on her throat helped. She pushed the hood off and let the cold breeze hit her face.

"Do you want to go inside and use the restroom?" Jazzie asked.

"No." Her new friend stood quietly beside her as she waited for the sick feeling to pass. "Jazzie, I'm so sorry. I totally lost it back there." Stunned afresh with the image of her burning apartment, she choked.

"Are you kidding? Who wouldn't lose control? They just obliterated your home. It was them, wasn't it?"

"I don't know. I can't think. Oh my gosh." She rubbed her forehead where it felt like a hammer had smacked it. "I almost told that cop who I was. Oh my gosh. You got us out of there. Did anyone follow us?"

"What do you mean?"

"Did you see anyone follow us to the cab? Did a car tail us here?" She turned to look at the traffic zipping along Michigan Avenue.

"Hey, all I've learned so far is to keep a low profile. I don't know the first thing about tails."

Whipping her head now in every direction, she noted pedestrians on the sidewalk hurrying along every which way. Some standing still here and there. Watching them? Some waited at the stoplight crosswalk. Two groups clustered on the wide stairway. A few people entered the museum.

"Cara, I'm sorry. All I could think of was to tell the cab driver to take us to some big public place that wasn't too close to—" She clamped her mouth shut momentarily. "To where I used to live."

"You did great, Jazzie. See? I told you you'd do fine without me. Thank you." Tears burned. "What would I have done without you?"

Jazzie laughed, an uninhibited boisterous sound that turned a few heads. "Without me? Cara, without me you wouldn't even be in this situation!"

She smiled crookedly.

"So now what? Look at art or walk to the park?"

"I have to get my bearings. Let's walk."

"Walk, walk, walk." Jazzie dramatically swept her gaze skyward. Then she linked her arm with Cara's. "Have I thanked you yet for these horridly unbecoming athletic shoes?"

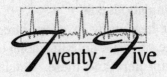

Twenty-Five

Cara and Jazzie sat on one of the long concrete steps which were part of a walkway situated right at the edge of Lake Michigan. Occasional waves lapped up onto the sidewalk itself. A fierce breeze tossed back whitecaps on water the color of pewter, a reflection of the sky's dense cloud cover.

Cara had needed to release the tension that felt like a bedspring wound inside her chest. They had walked for blocks through the expansive Grant Park and eventually crossed Lake Shore Drive to brave the waterfront cold.

While Jazzie wrestled with her cigarette lighter against the wind, Cara struggled to focus. A sense of abandonment kept popping up like steamy kernels of puffed corn that burned within her. What had happened? She was on the street being pursued by an enemy. There was no backup. No Marcus. No Rubyann. No *home*. No God? Where was He?

I can't do this again, Lord. I can't!

The silliness of her complaint struck immediately. She imagined God's reaction. *You think you did it the other time?*

Early one morning many years ago as she stood with her thumb sticking out on Highway 101 south of Salinas, California, she thought she was doing it herself. Late that same night, snuggled in bed in a clean studio apartment above a garage in Los Angeles, she realized she hadn't done a thing. He'd sent Rosa and Guillermo Lopez, a Mexican couple who saw Jesus in everyone they met and, as a result, loved them to pieces. Or wholeness. Yes, they'd loved her to wholeness.

So You'll send someone?

Already have.

His word occasionally came like that. Clear. Solid. Quick as a heartbeat.

But my home, Lord! The one You let me have! My very own!

She took a shaky breath. *Enough about yourself, Fleming. Let it go. Let it go. Don't you hold things loosely? Look around. Think. He will not abandon you.*

From the corner of her eye she peered at Jazzie. *Jazzie?* True, with a prompt decision and nimble-footedness, she'd whisked them out of harm's way, but fear had driven her. And fear, without God's supernatural intervention, would consume both of them. They needed a prayer warrior more than they needed a warm place to—

Bryan. You sent Bryan!

"Thank You."

"You already said that." Jazzie turned. Her cheeks and nose were reddened. She held the hood tightly shut at the neck with her gloved hands and rocked back and forth, puffing frantically on the cigarette. The adrenaline high left over after racing away from the fire scene was clearly fading fast.

"I was talking to God."

"Swell! A Jesus freak *and* a cop."

"There's a priest praying for us."

"How do you know?"

Because he kissed me a few nights ago. "Just one of those things."

Jazzie gazed back out at the water. "Got your bearings now?"

Cara thought a moment. God was with them. Like a match striking a pilot light, the knowledge kindled a flicker of hope, a patch of warmth in a heart that had begun to grow stone-cold.

But the whitecaps whipped about. Rain and snow threatened to descend. Her home was gone. Hired guns were after them. Hired guns who had connections with the police department, which meant they could not go there for protection.

At last she broke her silence. "I can't figure it out."

"That's the easy part. 'They' found out where you live and torched it because you're with me."

"But how did they know we'd left Phoebe's? Was the fire a warning? Did they flush us out of Phoebe's just to get us to the apartment?"

"One too many questions for me, Miss Cop."

Lifting the thigh-length jacket out of the way, Cara unbuttoned the side pocket on her pants and pulled out her phone.

"You've got a cell phone?" Jazzie's voice was leaping upward again. "Isn't *that* a no-no?"

"This is one of those 'yes, but' things. I have to talk to my partner." She pressed a glove-covered finger on the keypad and shivered. Where would they spend the night? None of the shelters she knew were open yet. It wasn't the *season*.

Panic began to thump in her chest.

"Hey." Marcus answered casually.

At the sound of his voice, her throat closed in, choking off words.

He said, "I'm fine, babe." He would know from the number displayed on his phone that the call was from her. "Just on my way out to get some coffee. It's been quite a day."

She closed her eyes. What was he doing imitating a conversation with Renae? Maybe he was in the squad room, moving to a quieter spot.

At last he said, "How you doing?"

"O-okay."

Through the phone she heard footsteps, a shuffling sound. At last he said, "What's wrong?" He would have recognized the anxiety in her voice.

"My..." She chewed a tip of the glove and tried to steady her breathing. "My apartment building is— There was a fire. It started in my apartment."

"What?"

"It's burning. The whole place is full of smoke."

"Whoa. Slow down. What do you mean?"

"Exactly what I said! I saw it!"

"You're not at—"

"No! Somebody called and said the address was leaked."

"What?" he yelled again.

She pulled the gloved finger from her mouth and wiped lint off her lips, gave him time to decipher the news.

"Where are you?"

"It doesn't matter." She knew he would hear the wind in the phone and distant traffic, but her habitual bent toward caution prompted her to hold back. "Just help me figure this out. That's what I need right now. Answers."

"Is she with you?"

"Yes."

"Bring her in."

Cara jumped to her feet and began swiftly pacing along the lake. "You're not hearing me. Someone in the department gives information to the mob."

"You don't know that."

"I do know that." She turned and strode back the other direction. "Whoever called Helen works with the department. That's where he heard Phoebe's address had been leaked. Two plus two equals four. The point is *I* was at Phoebe's. Nobody would have known where Jasmine was except for me— Who knew I was there?"

"The usual. Technically Hampton assigned you." Al Hampton was their lieutenant. "He would have told Jessup." Don, the captain. "Mike and Danny might have heard it from Hampton." Fellow detectives in the special illegal arms unit with them. "Maybe Delaney and Garner." Police officers in the unit. "I don't think anyone else would've needed to know."

"Might have? Maybe? You don't think?"

"Calm down, Fleming."

"Why did anyone need to know?"

"Because we're a team!"

"Well, one of you six— No. One of you *seven*—let's go ahead and count you—team members talked about where I was and what I was doing."

"Thanks for the vote of confidence, partner."

"You try watching your home burn up and then trust people."

"Cara, come on, this is me. We'll get to the bottom of it. Tell me where you are. If you don't want to come in yet, I'll get you to a safe house."

"The last one didn't exactly work, Marcus! You're not hearing me. Somebody is after me. I want answers!"

"Maybe the fire was meant as a warning, to back off from the investigation. But you can't figure it out from the street." His tone shifted subtly, hardened.

She stopped her pacing. Though she was familiar with what she called The Voice, he had never directed it at her.

He went on. "You were sent to gather information, Detective. Not harbor a criminal."

Intuition kicked in full force, making way for the truth to slowly but surely reach her mind. Could she trust Marcus? How could he accuse her of harboring a criminal? How could he not believe the possibility of a leak? Why didn't he just tell her to stay under until he learned more? Why was he arguing with her? Was he tracing the call?

Her entire support system had been knocked out from under her, from the captain on down, from her safe port of an apartment with its wonderful bathtub to the fragile social relationships she'd been forming.

She was on her own. Once again. A distinct chill crept into her veins.

"Criminal?" She watched Jazzie while she talked, leveling her own voice at him as if interrogating a felon. "Are we talking about the same person? The uninvolved bystander who saw Stafford shoot Rossi on the yacht and push him overboard? The one whose choice was to either leave in another boat and keep quiet or be killed herself?" She raised a questioning brow at Jazzie.

The woman gasped and covered the lower half of her face with both hands, but she nodded.

Cara continued, "The one who kept his books—his real set—and made copies?"

Sheer horror filled Jazzie's eyes.

It was all the confirmation Cara needed.

Marcus said, "Have you seen them?"

"No, I haven't seen them! She's one smart cookie. She wouldn't carry them with her."

"What does she say? Can they prove he's dealing in guns?"

"No details until you tell me what's going on. And no way are we coming in until that happens." She resumed her pacing.

"Cara."

She switched the phone to the other ear and rubbed her hand over the one that had heard his whisper. His stab at a kind tone didn't matter. Her home was destroyed and he didn't have a clue what was going on. Or at least was behaving as though he didn't know.

"Trust me," he said.

"No, I don't think I will right now."

"Don't do this by yourself. I'll meet you."

"You're not hearing me, Calloway. *I* don't matter right now. Find out who's behind this."

"I'll call you."

"No, I'll call you from a pay phone after I read about it in the newspaper. 'Detective Calloway Finds Police Snitch.' Until then we're going under. Not even you will be able to find me."

"At least keep your phone on. I'll call in a couple hours."

She laughed in disbelief. "You're kidding, right? We trace these things."

With that she pushed the power button, not slowing the least in her agitated stride. What was wrong with Marcus? Bits of conversations from recent months came to mind. Like puzzle pieces they made no sense individually and were easily dismissed. Now they began falling into a pattern. Her relationship with Marcus hadn't changed dramatically but there were moments when he seemed…not to trust her. Whispered dialogue with a detective here, an officer there. Times he emerged from the chief's office after a closed meeting with nothing to report.

She halted her steps and turned toward the lake. Stretching to her full height, she let the wind enshroud her with its cold. The imaginary ice within her drew strength from it and funneled all the anger and despair into a disciplined energy that clarified her thoughts.

Yes, life appeared hopeless...except for one fact: Bryan was her backup.

With a grim smile she tossed the cell phone into the choppy water, into the 900-plus foot depths of Lake Michigan, and whispered, "Trace that, Calloway."

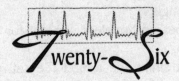

Twenty-Six

"Yo, Padre."

Cell phone against his ear, Bryan smiled at the sound of Ray Abbott's recorded voice. The man had stepped right out of a Dick Tracy comic strip. Bryan imagined he wore a belted raincoat and a fedora pulled low on his forehead. His staccato speech surely was muttered around a cigarette dangling from the corner of his mouth.

"Didn't want to call when there was nothing to report. Needlessly run up your expenses."

Bryan flipped up the recliner's footrest and leaned back, aware that he was still grinning. If the grin weren't proof enough that his hiatus had already worked wonders, he only had to pull the little card from his pocket. On it TJ had written his earlier blood pressure reading; two hours ago a nurse at a nearby clinic had written new numbers, a quizzical expression on her face. Even he grasped the significance of the wide differentiation between them.

Answered prayer? Chicago parish life so distant it had lost the urgency he attached to it? Or Thursday night's kiss?

He gave thanks, but did not want to explore the development too closely yet. With a slight hesitation to break his promise to Meagan to check for messages only twice a day, he turned on his cell phone. His action had something to do with that kiss.

There were no messages from Cara. Not that he really expected any. From the "story" she told during their one conversation, he deduced she was working undercover. That probably meant round the clock. Her voice had been scarcely above a whisper. She wouldn't have opportunity to call.

He understood. That was a cop's life.

Ray's clipped voice continued in his ear. "I talked with a fellow padre. Father Palmer and the Missus are still kicking. Easy enough to find their former church and then a nearby senior citizen complex. You could have done it yourself." He chuckled. "Anyway, they were more than happy to talk to me. Had no problem figuring out who the girl was from the wrong side of the tracks, whose mother died when she was eighteen. Her name's Cari-Ann née Wilson." He spelled the first name with a hyphen. "She married Nick Davis in the church. He put the old couple in the hospital. That was the last they saw or heard from her. No idea yet what happened to him, but I'm on it.

"Oh, by the way, I told them she's doing fine, has a good career. Seemed the least I could do, they were so concerned. They tried to guess what she's up to. Would you believe it? They guessed cop. Well, that or a spy. Said even as a kid she always knew what was going on but kept things to herself. Sounds like you got yourself the perfect woman if she knows how to keep her mouth shut." He chuckled again. "I'll be in touch."

Bryan's grin had faded to a soft smile. He turned off the phone, held it against his chin, and stared out the large picture window. Rain blew like a liquid sheet against it.

Cari-Ann Wilson. A little girl who saw too much, knew too much, bottled it all up inside herself.

244   SALLY JOHN

Cara Fleming. A woman. A policewoman who saw too much, knew too much, bottled it all up inside of herself, letting it out only at the altar rail. Or in the middle of the night on the phone with a long-distant friend who really couldn't do a thing about it.

Except pray.

He turned the phone on again and pressed her number. When he reached her voice mail, he began to speak.

"Hi. I just wanted to... Well, I guess I want to, uh..." He chuckled. "Where's the delete button? The thing is, I'm praying for you. That's it. Well, that's not all of it, but that's the most important. Take care."

He pressed the off button.

That was nowhere near all of it. Nothing else mattered though. His health was fine. In less than four days his blood pressure was low and the exhaustion of recent months vanished. What had driven him to hide out in Galena?

Bryan was in the habit of answering his questions with a single word: God.

Why?

God.

Bringing it all down to a pedestrian level, he admitted TJ's diagnosis was not far off the mark. Maybe it was right on. He enjoyed playing the Messiah, so much so he would catch himself forgetting that the role did not come from his own power. Lately he hadn't bothered to catch himself.

And there was the matter of anger over Vic. Rachel was right. It was still there. He nursed it, used it as a weapon against feeling too deeply. He was not capable of feeling deeply again. The very core of his being had been trampled upon, pummeled to obliteration because the life of his best friend had been hacked like a twig sliced from a branch by a cosmic axe swung in the hand of a God who made no sense.

Overkill, Lord.

"But Your ways are not mine," he whispered and let the tears fall unabated.

Perhaps Cara was the antidote to it all, the only human being who could hold his dead inner self in her warm hands and breathe life into it again.

Perhaps? It was already happening. It started happening that first night he saw her.

Perhaps, then, this unencumbered time was for her. For praying for the infallible woman who had bitten off more than she could chew.

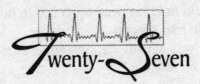

Twenty-Seven

"Why aren't you asking about him?"

Cara looked across the clothes rack and saw Jazzie staring at her. After overhearing the one-sided conversation with Marcus, she would be wondering what Cara had to do with Ian Stafford.

She said, "Because I don't need to know right now. First things first." She resumed her search through a rack of sweaters.

They were shopping at a Salvation Army, three bus transfers from Lake Michigan. It was a large secondhand store, brightly lit and well organized. Several people roamed the aisles.

"What's the first thing?"

Cara sighed to herself. Jazzie was having a difficult time assimilating a street mentality. "Survival. He's way down on the list after things like food. And if we don't look indigent enough, nobody next door will believe we need a free meal."

"What's the second thing?"

"Uh-uh. One thing at a time." Snowflakes had spit on them at the lake, raindrops turned into six-pointed crystals weeks ahead of the average season. The second thing was to check out the bedding aisle and hopefully find a sleeping bag. At the

246

least they needed blankets, heavy enough to survive the night without getting frostbit. First things first and one step at a time. Jazzie wasn't ready to hear that second thing.

Jazzie frowned. "We don't look indigent enough as it is?"

Cara couldn't help but laugh. "Even in a wig and a hand-me-down coat two sizes too big and definitely not your color, no. You do not look indigent enough or at all. Sorry. You're too pretty. It's your eyes. We'll find some shaded glasses to help distract from them. It's probably your teeth too. Try not to smile."

"Ian took care of them." She wasn't smiling. "Braces. Regular checkups and cleaning."

"That'll do it." Studying a thick sweater, she pressed her tongue against the back of her own front teeth and felt the wide spaces between them. At least they were clean nowadays.

"That's why I filched these from the bathroom." Jazzie reached deep into a jacket pocket and withdrew two boxed toothbrushes. "Never leave home without one."

Cara grinned. "Got toothpaste?"

Jazzie produced a tube. "All set. Cara, thank you."

"For what?"

"For saying I'm pretty."

"Well, you are." Unfortunately. She would draw attention. How could they change a flawless complexion, high cheek bones, well-proportioned nose and mouth? The wig was even too nice. They could fix that, though, with a pair of scissors or a box of dye to use on her own blonde hair. The natural features would remain, though. Perhaps after a few nights on the street and some missed meals the haunting look would overshadow them. Cara didn't know how to tell her to fake it. She herself could fake it, but only because of experience.

She glanced across the rack and noticed Jazzie staring off into space. "Jazzie, I need your help. Pretend you want to dress up like a homeless person for Halloween."

She wrinkled her nose in distaste.

"Pretend. Act. Didn't you ever dream about being an actress? A movie star?"

"Yeah. What girl doesn't?"

"Well, now's your chance."

They made their way down the long rack.

"Cara, why can't we buy dinner? I have thirty dollars left. You said you have fifty. Shoot, with these prices we could buy umpteen outfits and not spend half of that."

Her stomach rumbled. She glanced at her watch. It was after six. Her last meal had been breakfast. If they didn't hurry, dinner next door would be over.

"Please? I won't buy any more cigarettes."

Cara smiled.

"I've been meaning to quit. No time like the present. It's gotta be easier without that worthless bozo hanging around stressing me out."

She laughed. Jazzie's attitude just might carry them through the entire ordeal.

∽

They sat in the back corner of a chain restaurant and lingered over hot chocolate. It was cheaper than pie. The place was open 24 hours a day. Cara wondered how long they could postpone their departure. Maybe awhile. Tables remained empty. She and Jazzie didn't look the homeless part yet, so they might not be encouraged to leave when they drained their cups. When they did leave, they would stop in the ladies room and add layers of the used clothing they'd just purchased atop their own.

Jazzie crushed her cigarette butt in the ashtray and blew out a cloud of smoke. "Last one. Good riddance to it and to Ian. Did you know he has a beautiful wife? Two cute kids, a boy and a girl. I always felt bad about him having a family."

"Does she know about you?"

"I'm sure she does. You know, it's just an acceptable form of lifestyle for some people. Wife here, girlfriend there. Sundays for one, Thursdays for the other. I knew my place, and she knew hers. The question of divorce never came up. We each had a role in his life. I used to think he loved both of us, in different ways. But he only loves himself." Though her words were brave, an expression of deep sadness filled her face.

"Did you love him?"

She nodded. "I'm an idiot."

"What is it in us that makes such stupid choices?"

"You loved your stalker?"

"Of course I did. He was cute. Nowhere near as handsome as Ian Stafford, though."

Jazzie's brows went up in surprise.

"And he gave me the attention I needed. Most importantly he kept me off the streets. I thought he loved me."

"Yeah. Same thing with Ian. It's not real love, though, is it?"

"Nope. Only God loves us in the real way."

"I've been thinking a lot about Him today. Will He take care of us?"

Cara bit her lip to hold in the sudden onslaught of emotion. A tidal wave of wild and crazy love burst from her heart...for Him, for people, for life itself...no matter the circumstances, no matter she was on the street again. A rush of gratitude dizzied her head...for their simple meal, the warm room, the two heavy sleeping bags on the seat beside her, for her heart not growing cold. For knowing where to go next.

She whispered, "Yes. He will take care of us." She cleared her throat. "Come on. I want you to meet some friends of mine."

~

Cara and Jazzie walked down the street of a business district closed up for the night. Darkened store fronts reflected streetlamps. Each woman carried a sleeping bag under an arm and wore knit stocking caps pulled low over her ears.

"So where are these friends of yours?" Jazzie asked.

"I'm never exactly sure, but I know one place they might go on a night like this."

"Tell me it's indoors. Please, please tell me it's indoors."

Cara had already explained how the regular shelters, ones they would most likely use, did not open until next month. Evidently hearing that fact had not snuffed out her hope. "Jazzie, this is all my fault. They wouldn't have found you if I hadn't gone to Phoebe's. I am so sorry."

"Hey, no problem. I knew they'd find me sooner or later. Sooner was no worse than later. It was better, really. If you hadn't been at Phoebe's, I would have been out of luck."

"Maybe they wouldn't have gotten there before you left, though. You were planning on leaving."

"Yeah, but my plan was to use my credit card and live in a hotel. And since Ian pays it, he could have gone online and seen its activity and figured out where I was. All of which I didn't know until you told me."

"Why did you go to Phoebe's in the first place?"

"Leaving was a split-second decision. I mean after I saw...you know, the yacht thing...I totally freaked out. I saw it with my own eyes but could not, just could not, believe he did it. I tell you, that put a damper on things. We didn't get along from that moment on. I wanted out. He said no way, not ever. It finally sank in. Duh. Nobody leaves the Outfit. So I faked it the best I could and kept my mouth shut."

"How did you get away?"

"I had a doctor's appointment, and while I was waiting I read a pamphlet about where abused women could go. I thought, well, he doesn't hit me but something ain't right here. So I just got up and left. Went through a back door because my driver was sitting out front. Then I took a cab to the agency listed on the pamphlet. They got me to Phoebe's."

"Good for you."

"Yeah. I guess."

"So why the hotel plan? Why not a bus ticket out of Chicago?"

Jazzie didn't reply.

"It's natural to consider going back to him."

"No, that wasn't it. The thing is... I did his accounting, like you said. I knew he laundered money, and I knew he bought and sold guns illegally. I looked the other way." She glanced at Cara and shrugged. "He paid me a lot. Bought me designer clothes. We didn't just window-shop at Tiffany's."

Cara nodded.

"But cold-blooded murder? Uh-uh." Her voice cracked and she struggled to regain her composure. "Nobody should get away with that. I told you why I didn't go to the police, though. That witness protection thing isn't for me. I don't see me testifying. But I can give them proof about his business dealings."

"You do have copies of things, then?"

"Not in my hands."

"I told Marcus you were a smart cookie."

"I don't feel all that smart since I managed to add my name to somebody's hit list. Anyway, about the copies. I'm not sure how to get them. See, I used my digital camera to take pictures of invoices and stuff. I'm pretty good at photography. I took a class, even. Anyhow, I didn't know if I would actually get away, but I recorded the information just in case. And then I put the memory cards—"

"The little camera thing that holds the photos?"

"Yeah, they're used instead of a roll of film. You don't need negatives."

"How many photos did you take?"

"Five hundred."

Cara took in a sharp breath. *Five hundred?* "And where are the cards?"

"In a gold beaded purse I gave to my housekeeper. Wrapped in a fancy lace hankie and tucked into a little zippered compartment."

A purse to a housekeeper? "Evie!"

"Yeah!" Her incredulous tone escalated. "How in the world do you know that?"

"Well, it's a long story." CliffsNotes or unabridged? They had all night with nothing else to do except stay warm and out of sight of authorities. "It all started when this kid robbed a dear friend of mine named Rubyann."

～

During the telling of the unabridged version, Cara and Jazzie made their way to a deserted warehouse. They sat now on its loading dock, huddled under the sleeping bags and facing south. The northeast wind had diminished significantly. The clouds lost their ominous appearance and served as natural blankets holding in what little warmth the earth had to offer. God was watching over them.

Cara finished her story.

Jazzie said, "So Lathan told you about Rossi and Rossi told you about Ian?"

"Yes, but we already suspected Ian because of the guns we found in his cousin Melanie's place after she died. Rossi helped us move forward a step."

"Okay. So then you pretended to be a housekeeper at the Park-Mont and met Evie and she blabbed all my personal business to you?"

"Well, I encouraged her quite a bit."

"Do you know where she lives?"

"Yes." Evie had provided her last name and number. Finding her address was easy enough after that. "I sent her flowers as an anonymous thank-you gift for the information."

"You are a quandary, Miss Cop. Handcuffs and a heart."

Cara let the remark slide. "I can't remember the street address, but I figured it out once. I can do it again. We'll get the memory cards for you."

"For me? Hey, those pictures are for you."

"Jazzie, that'd be like the biggest, most unbelievable gift ever."

"Well, it's yours. Merry Christmas."

Cara laughed.

"Look!" Jazzie pointed. "Somebody's coming."

Cara looked across the dark parking lot and saw two figures heading their way. One was short and heavyset. The other walked almost sideways, with one shoulder lower than the other, sort of in the way an animal walked after being hit one too many times.

"Don't worry." She grinned. "It's Polly and Ruthie. My friends."

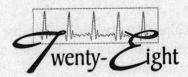

Twenty-Eight

"Polly! Ruthie!" Cara called out. "It's me!"

The women approached. Polly was the slender young one with a timid demeanor and two side teeth missing. She hung behind the older woman and peered around her shoulder.

Ruthie asked gruffly, "Who's me?"

"It's Cara Fleming." She stood and went over to meet them at the short set of stairs.

"Detective Fleming?" Polly asked excitedly and hurried around Ruthie. "What are you doing here?" She sidled up the steps. "I bet you're being undercover!"

Cara grabbed her in a hug. "Nah, I just missed you girls." Polly giggled and held on to her with a fierce embrace.

Cara loosened a hand and waved at Ruthie.

The woman responded with her typical half smile, which some considered a sneer. She dropped a plastic garbage bag onto the floor and tilted her head toward Jazzie. "Who's that?"

Cara said, "That's Janie." She disentangled herself from Polly and ignored Jazzie's questioning stare.

Always fascinated with Cara's work, Polly whispered, "I bet she's being undercover too!"

"Yes, she is. Janie, this is Polly, and that's Ruthie."

They exchanged subdued "hi's," and the newcomers went about preparing their bedding for the night. Like Cara and

Jazzie, they had sleeping bags and wore winter jackets, stocking caps, and gloves. Layers of clothing made them appear thicker than they were.

Polly plopped down beside Jazzie. "Do you have a gun too, Detective Janie?"

"Uh, no."

Ruthie lay down, her bag of possessions held like a teddy bear in the curve of her body, and pulled the sleeping bag about herself. "I hope you're not going to babble all night long. Some of us have to work in the morning."

Cara saw Jazzie's eyes grow wide, obviously not comprehending how that statement could be true. "We'll just talk quietly for a few minutes."

Ruthie made a harrumphing noise.

"'Night," Cara said. "Polly, are you working tomorrow?"

"No, it's my day off." Most days were her days off; the job was very part-time. "We almost got to sleep in a car tonight, but it belonged to Lana's new boyfriend. Her and Ruthie got in a fight, so we had to leave. How many more days before Miriam House opens?"

"Just three, I think. Day after Halloween."

"It's Halloween?"

"Pretty soon. Maybe the stores at the Takoma Mall will pass out free candy."

"Yeah. You and me and Detective Janie can dress up like homeless people." She giggled.

Jazzie coughed as if in disbelief, and then she burst into laughter. "That's a great idea!"

Polly smiled and turned to Cara. "Maybe your partner can come too."

"My partner?"

"That cute one. That hunk. You know."

"The black guy?"

"Yeah! I can't think of his name. He told it to me."

"He did?" Cara's mind was coming up blank.

"Remember that day you said you'd take me to work because my old boyfriend was scaring me again? You drove up when I was walking and Jimmy was there. You jumped out of your car and grabbed him by the collar." She clutched her jacket at the throat in demonstration. "Read him the riot act. I heard your partner laughing his head off in the car, so I looked in the door and said aren't you going to help. He just laughed and laughed. Then I started laughing. We both said she don't need no help!" Polly laughed now at her rendition. "I asked him his name but I can't remember it."

"Calloway."

"That was it! Can he come with us to the mall?"

"No." She remembered the incident Polly described, but she didn't know the part about Marcus meeting the young woman. For certain he would remember *her* name. No doubt he asked her where she worked. He would remember that too.

"Polly, you know I told you about being undercover, about how I can't tell anyone about it?"

She nodded.

"This time even Detective Calloway doesn't know where I am. If he visits you, maybe at work, and asks if you've seen me, can you say you haven't seen me for a while?"

Polly gasped. "That's lying. You want me to lie to a policeman?"

"Well, uh, not exactly. See, we're playing this game, kind of like cat and mouse. And I told him he'd never be able to find me."

Ruthie's bag crackled as she shifted around. "Dumb thing to say to a cop. Like waving a red flag in front of a bull."

Late the next morning Cara and Jazzie sat on a commuter train speeding north, the log-rolled sleeping bags across their laps. Only the rumbling train's rhythmic clickety-clack broke their silent ride. They were tired. Coffee and Danish from a stand hadn't offered the best nutrition. Even after the purchase of items from the Salvation Army, the previous evening's meal, and train tickets, they still had enough money to buy a full breakfast. But neither of them felt hungry after the uncomfortable night spent out in the cold.

Jazzie touched Cara's arm. "I'm sorry we had to leave your friends."

She gave her a small smile and went back to ruminating about how truly dumb her dare to Marcus had been. About the fact that Evie's name and address were written on a file in her locked cabinet next to her desk. About intuitively knowing that Marcus would pick the lock and study her notes like a doctoral candidate working on a dissertation. No possible clue would be overlooked.

After several quiet moments, Jazzie said, "At least you found out your partner knows Polly. What if we'd met up with them after he found out where she hangs out?"

Cara turned again to her. The night had taken its toll. Though they had splashed cold water on their faces in a public restroom and used their toothbrushes, lack of a restful sleep was evident in Jazzie's sallow skin tone. She wore lightly tinted sunglasses that minimized her distinct eyes and the dark, puffy bags beneath them. Gone was the posture of a woman who lived in a penthouse and shopped on Michigan Avenue with a limo driver and someone else's credit card. Jazzie's shoulders had the rounded appearance of one carrying a backpack filled with bricks. There would be no need to remind her not to let loose with one of those dazzling toothy grins. The resolve to stay alive was eclipsing her personality.

Cara teasingly bumped her shoulder against Jazzie's. "Just when I'm about to get truly depressed, you say something positive like that. The timing with Polly was perfect. Thanks for reminding me."

Jazzie's lips formed a tight smile. "Well, I'm diving into a major blue funk here, so don't hold your breath waiting for another uplifting comment from me."

"It's the wig causing you to think that way. Don't worry. Another day or two and you won't even notice that feeling that you're scalp is suffocating and if you don't give it some air soon you'll scream."

Jazzie narrowed her eyes at her.

She chuckled and tapped her coat pocket. "And we'll get to this soon as possible." She referred to the carton of hair dye tucked away. They'd purchased it at a drugstore along with the sunglasses.

"I am so glad you cleared that up, Detective. I was afraid it was nicotine withdrawal." Her tone was characteristically sarcastic, a good sign her descent into the blue funk was not imminent.

Perhaps Jazzie was, after all, a gift from God, a spunky platinum blonde She-Ra princess warrior sent to walk alongside her, swinging a sword to fight off the depths of despair.

⌒

A few blocks from the train station, Jazzie sat on a park bench, her spunkiness wavering on low beam. Cara gave her a thumbs-up and walked away, a tight knot in her own stomach. They didn't have a choice but to separate. Evie was expecting Cara, aka Missy, the temporary Park-Mont Inn housekeeper. Jazzie couldn't come because Evie would recognize her, and then when Marcus visited her—which he would surely do—Evie would have to tell him about the black hair and sunglasses and homeless-type clothing. In order to protect everyone, they separated.

Sunshine warmed the temperatures into the range of an Indian summer day. Cara left her heavy coat, sweaters, sweatshirt, and sleeping bag with Jazzie. She thought she looked fairly normal in slacks and sweater, her hair wound into a makeshift bun with a piece of ponytail elastic.

A block from Evie's apartment building, she slowed and carefully surveyed the street. Evie's name was just one of many in her Stafford files. Still, she was the main connection to Jazzie. Although Cara had shared everything with Marcus about her conversations with Evie, he would now want to have his own with her. She only hoped it wasn't this morning.

When she called Evie from the drugstore, she learned the woman would be at home until noon and no, she was not expecting anyone else. Cara said she really needed to talk to a friend.

Satisfied Marcus's car was not parked on the street and that no one watched the building entrance, Cara made her way inside. On the second floor she found Evie's door and knocked.

Evie opened it, her pouffy blonde hair reminiscent of what lay squashed under Jazzie's wig.

Cara smiled. "Hi."

"Missy? What happened to your hair?"

"Oh, I wear a wig now and then. May I come in?"

"Sure. Wow, you really look different."

With an inward sigh, she entered the apartment.

"Have a seat. Would you like some coffee?"

"No, thanks." Cara glanced around the small, neat living room, and chose an armchair. "I just need to talk for a few minutes."

Evie sat on the couch. "Is it about Tom Cruise?"

"Tom— What?"

Evie giggled. "You know, that story you were telling when those other housekeepers were in the lunch room."

"Oh, that. Well, no. But I have another story to tell. Or rather, the truth. Evie, my name is Cara Fleming, and I'm a detective with the Chicago Police Department. I was working undercover at the hotel."

Evie's eyes grew wide.

"I can't tell you everything. You can probably figure out it has to do with Ian Stafford."

Evie gasped now. "I didn't mean to say anything! I talk too much! I'm always—"

"No, no. You're not in trouble. My goodness, you were such a help to us."

"Really? I was?"

"Yes. It would have taken me ages to figure out Jasmine Wakefield."

"She's still not back at the hotel!"

"I know, but she's safe."

"She is? Oh, I am so glad!"

"Me too. She needs a favor from you."

"Oh, anything! She was so nice to me. What can I do?"

"Well." She held her breath in anticipation. "Do you still have that beaded bag she gave you? The gold one?"

"Sure."

"She wants you to keep it, but she left something in it she needs."

"I didn't find anything except a pretty handkerchief. I left it in there for when I get to use the thing. My boyfriend doesn't like to get dressed up. I'm waiting for my birthday next month. Then he'll do whatever I want. Shall I go get the purse?"

Cara nodded like a bobble-head toy which had just been bumped. "Please."

A few minutes later Cara squeezed four tiny memory cards in her palm, her heart pounding a Sousa march in her chest. "Thank you. Listen, my partner will probably call you. He'll want to ask you some questions too. His name is Marcus Calloway."

"Why, that's the name I just wrote down! He called this morning, right before you got here."

The cymbals clashed and reverberated from her chest into her ears.

Evie went on, "Detective Calloway, right? He wanted to come over now, but I told him I was busy. He asked about my schedule. We finally decided I could meet him on break at the hotel at four."

"Did you tell him what you were busy doing this morning?"

"No. Why would I tell some guy on the phone I've never met what I was doing?"

Why indeed? The cymbals quieted and Cara smiled.

"Since you already talked to me, does he still have to?" Evie's expression resembled a child's wanting to get out of a distasteful chore. "He didn't sound as nice as you."

"Oh yes, I'm afraid he has to talk to you too. He likes to make sure I do things right. He acts kind of gruff, but don't let him bully you. He's really a pussycat. Remember, you haven't done anything wrong. If he bugs you too much, tell him you want a lawyer present." She shrugged. "But really, all you have to do is answer his questions."

Tell him I was here. Tell him Jazzie gave you a purse. Tell him something was in the purse. Tell him I have it. End of Round One. Score: Fleming, one; Calloway, zilch.

~

Cara hurried back to the park. Jazzie still sat on the bench, clutching their pile of jackets and sweaters like a drowning person would a lifesaver. The stunned expression on her face erased the smile from Cara's.

"Jazzie, what is it?"

"We're in trouble. I found this in the trash can." She reached under the clothing and pulled out a newspaper. "Do you believe it? I dug in a trash can to get a paper!"

"Perfectly in character." After one more sweeping glance around the park, she sat beside her and accepted the *Tribune*. "Where— Oh dear Lord."

She stared down at her own photograph.

Black-and-white. One column wide. Metro section. Page three. Above the fold.

"Cara, it doesn't really look like you though, does it?"

The picture showed her smiling, in uniform, no cap, hair pulled back into a bun at the nape of her neck. She yanked the elastic out of her hair and didn't reply.

Jazzie handed her the knit hat she'd removed before going to Evie's and said, "It doesn't. That picture is a totally different person. You keep telling me about changing my whole demeanor. How it's not just in the clothes and the hair. How I have to get into character. Like digging in the trash can. Of course, I did that just so I could read and take my mind off the fact I'm going nuts."

The article accompanying the photo swam before her. She shoved the paper at Jazzie. "What does this say?"

"Shh, not so loud. Come on, Cara. Don't flip out on me here. You were smiling a minute ago. You got the things from Evie, didn't you?"

"Yeah. What does this say?"

"Well, it says too much, but people don't really read that stuff, do they?"

"Jazzie!"

"It says you were working undercover and now you've disappeared. That arson was the cause of the fire which happened to have been started in your apartment. Your neighbors are fine, some smoke damage. Only the one directly beneath your place has to relocate for a long period of time."

Thank God.

"And." Jazzie took a deep breath. "Mr. Anonymous said, *speculated*, that you set the fire to destroy evidence. And that maybe you've had a breakdown of sorts."

"I set it? A breakdown?"

"Shh. Because of the stress. The cases you work on involve high-level people associated with organized crime. They say you're with a platinum blonde woman who is wanted for questioning."

"They can't publicize that stuff!"

"They just did."

"Do they quote anyone by name?"

"Mm, let me see." She skimmed the paper. "Mostly it's just a statement released by the department. Here. Chief Stuart Templeton."

"Templeton?" She nearly shouted the name of the one man in Chicago who knew everything about her background, from

Cari-Ann Wilson Davis in Seattle to her time with the Los Angeles Police Department to shooting at Nick. He had even helped her get her name legally changed. Although she was already a cop, Chicago's department required she attend their training academy. He had ushered her way into that. All because he trusted the word of the LAPD's chief.

She owed him her life. Was he taking it?

Jazzie said, "No, wait. It's somebody *from* the chief's office. A deputy chief. Hugh Acton."

Acton? Not one of her favorite people.

"He says the chief has no comment."

No comment. Really? Then did Templeton even know about the statement? Her knowledge of him said not in a million years would he release such information. Was this all Marcus's doing? How dare he!

Anger and shock totally shut down her ability to think. She wanted to curl up in a ball and cry her eyes out.

"Cara, now what?" A hint of hysteria had crept into Jazzie's voice.

"I don't know." Her tone echoed Jazzie's.

So much for resting on her laurels. Round Two: Fleming, one; Calloway...more than that.

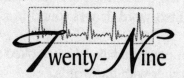

Twenty-Nine

For Bryan, life at the condo settled into a pleasant if somewhat ascetic routine. Keeping his promises to Meagan and TJ, he abstained from coffee, sugar, his pipe, conversation, and the newspaper. He walked vigorously and regularly twice a day, usually outdoors. In between these excursions he immersed himself in worship, prayer, and study.

He worked through caffeine headaches, anxiety over leaving his flock to another's albeit adequate care, and the initial restiveness with the solitude and silence. What he hadn't worked through was a deepening anxiety over Cara. She occupied much of his prayer time.

Wednesday morning, as had become his habit, he stood at the large front picture window drinking herbal tea, watched neighborhood children board a school bus, and said a prayer for them. Suddenly he noticed a miniature ballerina approach the bus, her pink tutu bouncing as she hurried. Behind her came SpongeBob SquarePants. Crossing the street was a four-foot clown holding hands with an astronaut. Bryan deduced it must be Halloween.

In the kitchen he checked the calendar and realized the children would trick-or-treat later. He could either become known as the mean priest who didn't answer his doorbell or the friendly one who gave out big candy bars.

He rerouted the afternoon walk and stopped in the local combination market/gas station to buy the candy, unconcerned with the sugar he was about to handle. They weren't Mrs. G's pies. At the checkout, his eyes strayed as always to the nearest printed word. It was found in a pile of *Chicago Tribunes*.

On the front page a smiling Cara looked up at him.

He didn't bother with the words.

~

Back at the condo, Bryan read the words. He read and reread the article. Evidently there had been a story in the previous day's edition which was causing a lot of flak around town. It had announced Cara was missing and accused her of having some sort of nervous breakdown. A citizens' group, backed by the union, decried the exposure of an undercover policewoman. Another group praised the department's courage to reveal an example of its weakness. The chief of police had been unavailable because he was fishing in Florida. There was even an editorial on the opinion page.

The news article stated Cara was now wanted for questioning along with an unidentified woman who, according to an unidentified source, was suspected as an accessory to a crime. That development placed Cara in a tenuous situation. It was speculated that perhaps no breakdown had occurred. After all, she was last seen with an alleged criminal.

Bryan literally threw his things into his bag. What didn't fit he piled haphazardly in the car's trunk. En route to Chicago he tried Cara's number once, feeling silly performing the pointless gesture. If the police couldn't find her, surely she was not going to answer her cell phone.

He spent the road hours praying for nothing more particular than her safety. He didn't know why he headed home except for a sense that he should be closer to her.

Nearing his neighborhood, he drove slowly through dark streets where a few groups of trick-or-treaters still meandered. At such a late hour, they would be the older kids. He parked in the garage, thinking how he'd left the candy back at the condo. Not that he had a mind to welcome anyone at his front door.

He wasn't sure what he had a mind to do. As if by instinct, he walked across the backyard and, instead of entering the house, went to the church and unlocked the back door nearest the kitchen. His way lit by dim night-lights, he continued through the silent halls, into the church, to the altar, to the railing. He knelt.

What else was there to be done?

⁓

Some time later Bryan became aware of his knees and he rose, shaking out the stiffness. At the back door he fiddled in the dark with the security alarm before opening the door. A movement through the door's window caught his eye.

The church's newer wing stretched like the tall stroke of the letter "L", creating a right angle where both exterior doors were located with not much space between them. Two figures crouched now beside the other door. Trick-or-treaters or kids up to mischief?

Largely due to his size, Bryan hadn't shied away from an iffy situation in 45 years. As a kid, he had also bragged that his dad carried a gun. As a priest, he bragged that God directed his steps, sometimes in the most illogical of ways.

More often than not, Bryan's stock reply was along the lines of *why not?*

He disarmed the system and flung open the door. "You guys need some help—"

Screams drowned out his voice. Feminine screams. The figures jerked to their feet and bumped into each other.

In two quick strides he had grabbed an arm of both before they could disentangle and run away. They struggled against him, flailing their free hands, swatting his arms and chest.

"Hey!" he yelled above their cries. "It's okay!"

"Bryan?"

In the faint light of a distant streetlamp he still could see only the silhouettes of the two people. They wore bulky winter jackets; oversized fur-rimmed hoods covered most of their faces. But he recognized the low voice.

"*Cara?* Ouch!" The other figure kicked him in the shin. "*Cara?*"

"Yes! Jazzie, stop. It's him."

Letting go of their arms, he quickly pulled Cara to himself in a tight embrace. "Oh, thank God! Thank God! Are you all right?"

She nodded against his chest and clutched his shirt, burrowing her face into the flannel.

He heard a muffled sob. His heart felt as if it were about to short-circuit. Sheer elation, exquisite relief, and pure anguish pounded simultaneously within him. "Oh, Cara!"

Holding her snugly with one arm, he pushed the hood from her head. A stocking cap covered most of her hair. He touched her damp cheek, lifted her face, and began kissing the tears from her eyes.

"Oh, Bryan, I'm filthy!" she whispered. "I haven't bathed in four—"

"Shh. You think I love you only when your skin is clean?" He kissed the corner of her mouth. "We're going to have to work on the meaning of unconditional." His lips met hers. And then he remembered they weren't alone.

⁓

Bryan reluctantly cut short the kiss and let go of Cara's face. He held his hand out to the shadowy figure behind her. "I'm Bryan."

"Hi. I'm Jazzie. Or Janie." She let go of his hand and touched Cara's back. "Who am I tonight, Cara?" There was a gentle teasing note in her husky voice.

Cara only sniffed.

"Come inside." He guided them through the open door, one arm still around Cara. She continued to hold onto his shirt, seemingly in no hurry to put distance between them. He locked the door and set the alarm again.

They entered the kitchen and he steered her to one of the stools while Jazzie sat on another across the island from her. The room was lit by a night-light plugged into an outlet above the counter. He didn't turn on the ceiling light. Some old sixth sense flickered to life, the one that sometimes prevented him and Vic from being caught in their unlawful acts as teenagers. He twisted shut the blinds. Though the yard in the L-shaped corner was isolated, he felt an urgent desire to be cautious. No need to advertise the fact that people were inside the church near midnight.

He turned and got his first good look at Cara.

"I'm fine," she said.

His face must have registered the alarm he felt at the sight of her haggard appearance. Even in the shadowy room he saw the dark circles around her eyes, a hollowness in her cheeks, her uncombed strands of hair hanging beneath the stretchy hat.

"We've just been homeless for four days and three nights." Her smile was forced. "But we're not counting."

Jazzie said, "Nope. Living on the street is a piece of cake." She'd pushed back her hood, revealing black hair and a similar stocking cap. Though her eye color was indistinct, they were unusually shaded. At the moment they studied him intensely, like those of a wary animal. "We could have kept going except for that stupid article hitting the front page. And if those guys last night…"

Cara said, "Unnerving. None of it should have— Bryan, what are you doing here, anyway? You're supposed to be on sabbatical."

"I saw the paper this afternoon."

She gazed at him for a long moment, as if weighing her words. She did not ask the obvious question. Perhaps she understood why he had come. Instead she said, "I don't want you here."

The comment wasn't personal. After all, she had kissed him back. "Tough nails." He smiled. "Tell me what you need."

Jazzie cleared her throat. "Cara, I'm a little confused here. This is the priest, right?"

Cara pressed fingertips against her forehead and kneaded. "Right."

Jazzie muttered something about a "kissing lumberjack."

"Bryan, we were just going to borrow your downstairs shelter for the night. I didn't think you would mind since you hope to use it for homeless people anyway. I thought we could give it a trial run."

"With my blessing, but how were you getting in— You were picking the lock."

She nodded.

"There's an alarm."

"I know." She covered her eyes now with both hands, still rubbing her forehead. "I watched you punch in the code once. That Wednesday night we left here together. I'm sorry."

"For what? Reading over my shoulder? Of course you can stay here. Use whatever you need. Let me get you something. Water? Soda? Are you hungry?"

"Excuse me," Jazzie said. "You read that article, right?"

"Yes."

"Shouldn't you be calling the cops right about now instead of waiting on us?"

"She's a cop. One is probably enough, don't you think?" He chuckled. "I guarantee you there's more to the story than that article provided."

Jazzie visibly relaxed, lowering her hunched shoulders and unzipping her coat. "I'll never believe anything I read in the paper again. Cara said we could trust you. She said you're the only person in the whole world she can trust right now. I figured it was because you're a priest, not her boyfriend. Do you mind if I have a glass of water?"

"I'll get it." He took two glasses from a cupboard, filled them with water, and served the women.

"Bryan, seriously, I don't want you here." Cara shrugged off her jacket and tucked it underneath herself. "I don't want you involved or even appearing that you're involved. You could be arrested for harboring us. We'll just drink our water and then we'll go." Her defiant expression lost its punch when her voice warbled mid-sentence.

Jazzie added her two cents with a distinct whimper.

"Ladies, why don't you tell me what's going on and let me decide whether or not to inform the police? The other police. The ones who seem to be chasing you."

Cara bit her lip, clearly on the verge of losing control again. "God will take care of us," she whispered hoarsely.

"Of course He will. He is right now. Who do you think told me to come home?"

Even her shrug was halfhearted.

Bryan slid onto the stool beside hers and wrapped his arms around her. His questions could wait.

Thirty

The warmth so evident in Bryan's eyes and the strength of his arms encircling her was more than Cara could bear. Her tears flowed as freely as they did in her bathtub.

Which made no sense. Why would she lose control while safe within a shelter? The likes of which she had never ever experienced in her entire life?

Perhaps that was the reason itself: She mourned a lifelong absence of security.

And, truth be told, she mourned the future. She would never work again in Chicago, probably nowhere as a cop. She had taken on organized crime as well as law enforcement. Her photo was plastered on a newspaper read by people around the world, including stalkers in Seattle. As soon as Jazzie's situation was resolved, Cara had no choice but to make another exit. Slip away again in the middle of the night. No goodbyes. No forwarding address.

Bryan's voice broke into her hopeless thoughts. His words were undecipherable, but the rumble in his chest soothed.

At the sound of Jazzie talking, Cara took a deep breath that ended in a hiccup. She turned her face sideways in the curve of Bryan's shoulder and heard that her friend was telling him their story.

"We were on the street because she said it was the safest place. My boyfriend—my ex-boyfriend—is connected with the mob. I left him because I saw him kill someone."

Cara felt Bryan stiffen.

Jazzie went on. Her voice grew tight and she rushed her words together. "Now they want to kill me because I had the audacity to tell him it was wrong. I went to a shelter for abused women. Next day Cara shows up, pretending like she was one too. Then we find out some *cop* told Ian's friends Cara was there because I was there, so we had to leave. Obviously we couldn't go to the police since one of them gave her away. Then her apartment blew up and caught on fire."

Bryan shook his head, as if in unbelief.

"Yeah. It happened before we got there, but we saw the fire. Then that night we were with her homeless friends and found out that Polly knows Marcus, so we couldn't hang out with them anymore. We've been on the street since Monday afternoon."

"On the street? Since Monday afternoon?"

"We had enough money to buy food."

Still nestled against Bryan, Cara said, "And we had our toothbrushes and toothpaste. Jazzie made sure we took those with us and used them."

"Our teeth need daily care."

Cara smiled.

Her friend with the perfect teeth returned the smile.

Bryan asked, "Where did you sleep?"

Jazzie replied, "Oh, different places. A loading dock one night. A doorway downtown—"

"Outdoors?" His voice rose. He was clearly becoming agitated.

"Nowhere else to go. We had sleeping bags." Jazzie paused, her breathing audible now, her composure slipping.

Reluctantly Cara straightened, moving away from the safe enclosure of Bryan's arms. "Until last night." The memory of the midnight skirmish still felt as raw as an exposed nerve ending. "My fault."

Jazzie said, "No, it was mine. I wasn't any help. I could have fought harder."

"I shouldn't have taken us there. I knew the area's reputation."

"But we had to go somewhere! We decided it was our only choice."

Bryan exhaled an impatient breath.

Jazzie said, "Three guys jumped us."

He jerked his head toward Cara, his brows far up his forehead again as if in alarm. "Cara!"

"We're fine. Just some pushing and shoving. They only wanted our sleeping bags. So by tonight we were getting a little desperate. The temperature has dropped." She stifled a yawn. Sitting within touching distance of Bryan was too comforting. "Which is why we're here, and why we have to go now. Marcus knows this is my church. He will visit you tomorrow. If you had stayed put over in Galena, you wouldn't have to talk to him and attempt to avoid answering questions such as have you seen Cara Fleming lately?"

Bryan rubbed his chin.

He needed a shave. She'd felt it when he kissed her. She wondered if his beard would grow in as red as his hair. That would be a sight to behold, whether he wore his clerical robes or the jeans and flannel shirt he had on tonight.

"Nobody knows I'm here," he said.

"What?"

"I didn't tell anyone I was coming back. Nobody has seen me. I parked in the garage, which isn't in sight of any neighbor. My friend's condo is available for another week.

For at least another week. The key is in my pocket." He stood. "What are we waiting for?"

Hope stirred within her. She nudged it back down. "For you to realize you could get into a whole passel of trouble."

"A whole passel, huh?" He reached over and touched her cheek. "You never read those juvie files of mine, did you?"

It was his touch, of course, that whipped her hope into such a frenzy she couldn't speak.

He smiled. "We'll come up with a plan. Maybe talk to the federal authorities."

Jazzie said, "She already has a plan."

He laughed. "Why am I not surprised?"

"Well." Cara swallowed. "The details aren't worked out yet."

"Details are my forte."

"Do you have a camcorder?"

"In a closet. It won't be missed. Anything else?"

She shook her head.

"Let's go then."

Jazzie came around the island, thrusting her arms into her coat. "I'm ready. Amazing how little time it takes when you're wearing a wig and don't have any clothes to change into!"

Cara looked up at Bryan. "Are you absolutely sure?"

Jazzie embraced her from behind in a friendly hug. "Hey, you sound like a cop reading him his Miranda rights. This is just what boyfriends do. Huh, Bryan?"

"Yep, Jazzie, this is just what we do."

They slapped a high-five gesture over her head.

Evidently they didn't need her vote.

Beams from the car's headlights created a tunnel on the otherwise pitch-black, two-lane highway. Cara watched, mesmerized by the unbroken corridor they skimmed through. She sat in the passenger seat beside Bryan, who'd insisted he was more awake than she. Soft, rhythmic breathing emanated from the backseat, where Jazzie had slid from view before they'd even turned off Bryan's street.

Cara had dozed fitfully as he drove them in silence along the expressway. The nap took the edge off her exhaustion, leaving her wide awake for the remaining two hours of the four-hour trip. In an effort to keep at bay the nightmares that sat just beyond her consciousness, she turned to prayer.

Thank You, Lord, that she can rest now. Thank You for sending Bryan. Thank You for the safe port he offers. Thank You for his friend who provided the condo.

The litany of gratitude continued mile after mile. It kept her mind off the horror of seeing her home burn...the fear which threatened to swallow her whole...and the undeniable love she felt toward the man beside her.

"Cara." Bryan glanced at her. "You should sleep."

That horror, fear, and love fueled her insomnia, but she didn't want to discuss them with him. "I'm fine. How are you?"

"I'm fine."

They sounded like overly polite people meeting on the street. She peered at him from the corner of her eye and caught his smile. She snickered. "No, seriously, how are you?"

"Well, seriously, I am fine. How could I not be? You're with me, and we're at the start of this mega date."

"Mega date? We're hiding from a bunch of bad guys."

"Yeah, but we're doing it together."

"I was asking about your health."

"It's fine too. The blood pressure has been normal for a number of days. Look, I know you've got a lot on your mind,

but there's nothing to be done tonight. If you're not going to
sleep, I'd rather talk about us."

She thought of what he had said earlier at the church,
something about loving her whether or not her skin was
clean. Turning to face him, she laid her cheek against the seat
back. "Please don't fall in love with me."

"Sorry, darlin'. That one's a done deal. Nothing I can do
about it now. Besides, you kissed me back."

"I can explain that."

"Then you're not denying it?"

She ignored the question. "Did you ever hear about a
phenyl something or other hormone? Terri Schuman
explained it to me. It kicks in when you're in a highly emotional situation, such as being in danger and then getting rescued by someone. It fills you with a rush of ecstatic feelings
that you associate with that someone."

"Purely chemical reaction then?"

"Yes." She didn't bother to add that Terri ended up mar-
rying the guy who shared a highly emotional moment with
her.

Bryan waited a beat. "It doesn't explain the first time."

Well, no, it didn't explain the first time they'd kissed, in her
apartment, that night before he left town. The crux of the
issue was "it" had already happened with her too. She'd loved
him long before he caught her picking his lock, on the verge
of complete despair. Homeless, cold, tired, in physical pain,
and friendless, except for the terrified woman in the backseat.

Not that loving him had any bearing on her future. Nothing
changed the fact that she had to leave town. Permanently and
soon.

But then, he was an easy man to love. She on the other
hand did not exhibit any obviously lovable characteristics.

"Father O'Shaugnessy, you don't know me well enough. You're in love with the idea of being in love."

"I don't think so. I know what goes into being a cop, the dedication, the desire to serve and to right wrongs. I know the faith it must take to maintain that and not lose your original compassion. I've seen your love for God on your face in church. I've seen how you tenderly care for the women at Miriam House, for Rubyann, for Jazzie." He glanced at her. "I know you well enough to love you."

She felt a sudden rush of heat, as if she blushed. His words...that was how he loved her...why she loved him. But... "There's the other me. The one with a crazy husband and an ugly childhood that some days seems more vivid than yesterday."

He reached over and grasped her hand. "That's not the real you. I saw the real you." Abruptly he stopped talking.

"What do you mean, the real me?"

"This is going to sound absurd. I haven't said it out loud to anyone, not even to myself." He squeezed her hand and let go. "You know that night I first saw you, when you were helping out in the church kitchen?"

"Mm-hmm."

"Something happened. I don't know. In less time than it takes to blink, you were surrounded by a bright light. You smiled at me. You were radiant."

Goose bumps pricked her arms.

"It wasn't so much that moment itself, but what followed. I felt— Well, I felt. Period. I *felt*. I hadn't truly felt for years, not since before Vic's death. Then this happened. It was sort of an abstract, undefined mixture of things. I don't know. An ache, a longing, a reawakening." He glanced at her again. "And somehow it was all tied up with you. I haven't been the same since."

Love at first sight? "That is the most absurd thing I have ever heard."

"I know."

"It's even more ludicrous than Terri's hormone." Ridiculous as the goose bumps now erupting from head to toe. They rotated and turned inward, igniting a delightful sensation like a feather lightly tickling her skin inside and out.

He said, "Absurd or not, it's the truth. God is in this, Cara. He brought you into my life for a reason. About all I can do is hang on for the ride."

His faith astounded her. She stared at his profile. The dashboard lights shone bright enough to reveal the slight upward curve of his mouth. It was a private, genuine smile of deep satisfaction, as if God made perfect sense in His unpredictability.

Cara's mind raced, searching for the compartment she already knew did not exist. She found niches for everything, including even the loss of home and possessions. It was how her ten-track mind worked until now. Bryan fit nowhere.

"Bryan, you are wilder than visions and Terri's hormone combined."

He grinned.

On second thought, it wasn't that he fit nowhere. It was that he fit everywhere.

Cara shifted in her seat and went back to gazing through the windshield at the tunnel of light.

Thirty-One

At noon, a mere eight hours since their arrival, Cara stood with Bryan in the living room of his friend's condominium. Though the décor was stylishly modern, it could not mute a permeating hominess. Photos of people were displayed all over the place. Comfortable cushions, pillows, and throw blankets abounded. Books lined a wall of shelves and sat on tables. No doubt about it, a family lived there, if only part-time.

Three stories high, the place offered plentiful room for the odd combination of guests it now housed. A master bedroom and bath filled the top floor. Cara and Jazzie had glanced at it but chose two of the three bedrooms located on the second floor. Bryan's prim-and-proper streak came out of hiding and he offered to go to a motel. They protested, saying they felt safer with him nearby. He moved back into his original room on the ground floor.

Finishing her perusal of the living room, Cara faced Bryan and crossed her arms. "No."

He propped fists on his hips. "I will not lie."

She smiled. Their body language said it all.

"What?" he said.

"We're having our first argument."

282   SALLY JOHN

He ran a hand through his curly hair, which clearly had not
been cut for quite some time. It fell below the top of the crew-
neck of his sweatshirt.

"We'd never make it as a couple," she teased. "You are
way too stubborn."

His green eyes flashed. "I'm too stubborn?"

"Well, I'm not. I'm just looking out for your best interests."
He shook his head.

"Bryan, I know you won't lie. But they probably can't even
figure out the right questions to ask you. Therefore, we will
move this," she tilted her head toward the camcorder attached
to a tripod, "to the kitchen in front of the nondescript refrigerator purchased from Sears like half of them are in America.
That way it will be harder for the cops to pinpoint where
Jazzie was when she taped her story. I don't want her sitting
on that very distinctive couch in front of that original water
color. Nor do I want you in the house when we tape. And I'm
the boss."

"She'd be more comfortable on the couch."

Cara raised an eyebrow.

His face relaxed and he chuckled. "But you're the boss,
who is evidently feeling better?"

Evidently. She was flirting with him. A swift mental kick
took care of that demeanor. "I'll get the camera."

"I'll do it."

She watched him fold up the legs of the tripod. Who
wouldn't feel better after arriving at such a safe port at 4:30
A.M.? Not to mention a shower, an omelet cooked by their
host, five hours of uninterrupted sleep in a gigantic flannel
shirt of his on clean sheets and under warm blankets, lunch
also prepared by their host, freshly laundered clothes—compliments again of him—and the prospect of a long hot bath
in one enormously oversized tub.

He said, "I forgot to mention joy."

"What?"

Lifting the camera equipment he turned to her. "Another lovable characteristic of yours. Obviously it doesn't come from your circumstances." He smiled and walked into the kitchen.

A delightful shiver ran through her. Again.

She hoped the ridiculous sensation wasn't addictive.

⁓

Jazzie sat on a stool, situated with the refrigerator as backdrop, and held up the front page of the *Chicago Tribune*. "I feel like an idiot. And doesn't this make you guys look like kidnappers?"

"Mm-hmm." Cara, bent over, peered through the camera lens. "Or terrorists. Hey, if it works for them…" She looked up at Jazzie. "I'm sorry. It's just a way to prove you did not tape this *before* that date on the newspaper. It helps give credence to the time frame."

"I know." She straightened her shoulders and flipped her long blonde, freshly shampooed and curled hair over a shoulder.

"Okay. Ready?"

Jazzie nodded in a determined way. Except for an underlying gravity, she resembled her old self. She wore the nicest sweater they'd purchased at the Salvation Army as well as makeup. The master bath was a virtual beauty salon complete with cosmetics and hair styling equipment, all of which Bryan said they were welcome to use.

Cara said, "Remember, it's okay to refer to the notes."

They had practiced that morning. Cara wrote down every question she imagined the police and attorneys would ask concerning Jazzie's role in Ian Stafford's life and what she had witnessed, everything from money laundering to murder.

Jazzie gave her a thumbs-up.

Cara encouraged her with a smile. "All right. Go for it, girl." She pressed the record button and sat quietly on a chair beside the tripod.

After a first few halting words, Jasmine Wakefield spoke clearly and succinctly. She confessed guilt, thereby clearing her conscience. At the same time she offered state's evidence which she surely could have used to bargain her way out of being prosecuted for her role as accomplice in a money laundering scheme.

Could have used...if she planned on turning herself in. Something Cara deduced she wasn't about to do. Or could have used...if Cara planned on taking her in. But that too was out of the question. After all, her handcuffs had melted in a fire.

⌒

"Jazzie!" Cara's tone relayed surprise. Facing the mirror, she stood behind her friend in the master bath, a large, fancy powder room which had served nicely as a beauty shop.

Jazzie grinned and fluffed her hair. Gone were the long, platinum blonde tresses. "I told you I'm naturally a brunette."

"Yeah, but you didn't mention how even more beautiful you are this way." The darker shade of hair did not clash with her olive skin tone, and the short layers they had cut complemented her facial structure.

Jazzie's grin softened into a tiny smile. "Really?"

"Really. I'll never figure out why you did not grow up hearing such comments all the time."

She shrugged. "Anyway, now I won't have to worry about dark roots showing or using a curling iron. This style will travel well."

They exchanged a glance in the mirror. An implicit understanding had taken root between them the moment they saw the newspaper article. Cara knew her time with Jazzie would be short. Her eyes misted over at the thought.

Jazzie said, "What I can't figure out is how you can stay so calm, cool, and collected. We watched your home burn up and you couldn't even go back to see if anything was saved!"

The images of things flashed in her mind. Her Bible, her *Book of Common Prayer,* her Winnie the Pooh books. Library books. Letters from grateful citizens. Her driver's license, credit and ATM cards, checkbook. Her Glock 22. The khaki jacket she really liked. She wiped the corner of an eye and reminded herself it was not the worst that could happen.

She said, "Yes, but was that any different than you leaving your home at the Park-Mont? All your beautiful things? Both of our choices were pretty clear."

"But you don't see me calm, cool, and collected, do you?"

"You have moments." She smiled. "Jazzie, I told you God will take care of us. I've been in this position more than once. I've been tired and cold and hungry. Without friends, without possessions. He always sent just what I needed."

"How do you know it wasn't coincidence?"

"Do you think escaping Phoebe's Place was coincidence? Or meeting with Polly? Or that Marcus missing us at Evie's was? Or Bryan being at the church when he shouldn't have been? In the middle of the night?"

"Granted, that's quite a string, but what else can it all be but coincidence?"

"Jesus. He came to earth to prove God is real and to tell us that our real home is with Him. He showed us how to live in the meantime. He said the foxes and birds have homes, but

He, God Himself, did not have a place to lay down his head. Not that He wants us to be homeless or not to fight against the desperate situations of those who are. But He wants us to hold the things of this world loosely. And to trust that the Father, who loves us better than the best daddy in the world, will take care of us no matter what life looks like."

Jazzie blinked. "I don't get it."

"Ask Him to help you 'get it.'"

"You heard what I said on that video. You know what I did! And you know I committed adultery on top of all that. Why would God listen to me?"

"Because He wants to forgive you. Ask Him for that as well. He loves you too much not to give it."

She stared at her in the mirror for another long moment. "That's it?"

"That's where you begin. Jazzie, if you forget everything I've told you about living on the streets, just remember that."

She only continued to gaze at her, unmistakable fear written all over her expression and in her stance, which was something like an upright fetal position.

Cara turned from the mirror and drew her friend into a hug.

⌒

Late that night, Cara took a moment to consciously regard the setting before her and record it as a significant memory. The three of them sat in the family room, an extension of the kitchen. Logs crackled in the fireplace at the far end. Bryan was in an overstuffed armchair. She and Jazzie sat on the cushy sofa by the coffee table. They all held mugs of his herbal tea. Lamplight was on low.

She and Jazzie had treated Bryan by cooking a special dinner. Not wanting to go out in public, she'd sent him to the store but then banished him from the kitchen. By combining their limited culinary talents, she and Jazzie managed to roast chicken, bake potatoes, steam broccoli, and open a bag of pre-washed and trimmed romaine lettuce leaves and its envelope of Caesar dressing. He insisted he would not eat dessert, and so they asked for Chips Ahoy and didn't bother to bake a cake.

As if by unspoken agreement, they had laid aside anxieties and laughed their way through the meal. Bryan was, as she suspected, capable of charming the socks off a snake. Jazzie's personality sparkled, as it surely must have in order to captivate the likes of Ian Stafford.

Jazzie set down her mug of tea and grimaced. "That's disgusting, Bryan."

"No, it's chamomile."

Cara said, "No, it's nasty."

"It's an acquired taste." He smiled.

Cara looked at the laptop computer on the coffee table. It busily hummed away, downloading photographs of invoices and accounts from one of the camera's memory cards onto a disk. She would make a copy for Marcus. The wonder of modern technology always amazed her.

"Bryan, thank you again for buying this computer today."

"You're welcome."

"I'm sure you can return it. They probably said if you're not happy with it, bring it back?"

"I've been wanting one anyway. I think it'll free me up, get me out of my study."

"You could strap it to your Harley and work from anywhere, twenty-four hours a day."

He laughed.

"Not good for the stress level, Father O'Shaugnessy."

"No, I suppose not."

Jazzie said, "I'll pay you for it. I have my checkbook."

Now Cara laughed. "Jazzie, I can't believe all the essentials you managed to stuff into your pockets. I will pay for the computer. Just as soon as I figure out how to get into my account without any form of identification."

"Ladies, I am paying for my own computer."

Jazzie stood. "Well, that settles that. If you'll excuse me, I am so excited about that comfy bed upstairs, I'm going to it before I fall asleep here."

They both told her goodnight as she walked to the doorway.

"Goodnight," she said and stepped into the other room. Half a moment later she reappeared and strode across the room to Bryan. She leaned over and threw her arms around him. "If Ian Stafford were half the man you are, we wouldn't be in this mess!"

Silently he returned the hug.

Without another word she went to Cara, sat down, and gave her a quick hug. The she hurried from the room.

Bryan looked at Cara, concern evident on his face. "She's leaving tomorrow." It was a statement.

"I have no handcuffs." Eyes glued to the computer, she slid to the floor, leaned back against the couch, and tapped in a command on the keyboard. "I'm sure backup from Chicago would never arrive in time."

She heard Bryan stand. Logs thumped into the fireplace. The fire hissed.

She went on with her superficial reasoning. "And the local police force is probably comprised of hicks, you know. Why would I call them?"

She felt his approach, but she still did not look up. His leg touched her shoulder as he sat on the couch directly behind her.

"Bryan, please don't look at this."

"I'm not looking at it. Is it any good?"

She let out the breath caught in her chest since he'd left his chair. "There's enough evidence to put Stafford away even if they can't make the murder rap stick."

"So that's good news." He touched the back of her hair, so lightly it could have been her imagination. "Cara." His voice softened almost to a whisper. "You don't have to be flippant in front of me."

"But it's such a great defense mechanism. No tears involved."

"Nothing wrong with tears."

"True, but I already filled an ocean. It's somebody else's turn." She bit her lip.

"Well, I think I have some to shed for her."

Cara twisted around to look at him. Wrong move.

His eyes glistened, reflecting the firelight. His priestly face mirrored all the angst she herself felt for Jazzie.

She climbed onto the sofa, settled under his outstretched arm, laid her face against his chest, and murmured, "You couldn't have waited until I left the room?"

Thirty-Two

They held each other for a long time sitting together on the couch. The fire's glow dimmed and the room chilled, but neither of them moved to add a log. Light and heat had lost their significance.

Cara let her tears fall quietly and thought how effortlessly Bryan connected with the depths of her heart. Those areas she iced off to the world were as conspicuous to him as if she presented them on a big-screen television. He did not offer judgment, but waited patiently, letting her express them in her own way, in her own time.

Within her mind she prayed for Jazzie, for what lay ahead, for healing of the past, for a hunger to learn about God, for Him to bestow the gift of faith upon her.

And then, after a while, Bryan began to pray aloud. Softly. Naturally. Not in a way that indicated he prayed for a living. No, it was as a son confidently sitting in the lap of his Father.

He echoed Cara's own silent prayers. He expressed those depths of her heart as if they were his own. And then she realized they were.

She thought she had loved the man before that moment. As Rubyann would say, *pshaw*. Such a notion had scarcely been a glimmer of the real thing.

Cara did not want to move. She leaned against Bryan, her head sideways, his heart beating steadily in her ear, and thought she would even give up sleeping again in that luxurious bed in order to remain in his arms.

He murmured against the top of her head. "I didn't know if Jazzie has an ATM card or anything, but I thought if she does, she probably shouldn't use it. So I withdrew five hundred dollars from my account today. Will you give it to her?"

"Of course. Thank you." She had never met such a generous human being. Another wave of warmth flooded through her. The tickling shivers had been ratcheted up a notch. She knew things had soared way beyond the effect of Terri's hormone.

"And I bought a Bible for her."

"You give that to her in the morning. She'll appreciate receiving it from you."

"All right." He paused. "Cara, I have to tell you something." His changed tone zapped the cozy snuggling ambience.

She sat up. "What is it?"

"Well, first off, I love you. As a friend, as a sister in Christ, as a parishioner, and as the woman I'd like to spend the rest of my life with. Therefore—"

"Bryan—"

"Please, let me fin—"

"I love you."

He stared at her.

"But that does not change the situation. My life in Chicago is over, and I'm married. But…I…I wanted you to know." She leaned over and kissed his cheek. "I'm sorry."

SALLY JOHN

"Don't be." A smile spread across his face. "It makes me happier than you can imagine. To be loved by you..." He shrugged.

She whispered, "I'm only going to hurt you."

He smoothed a strand of hair behind her ear, took a hand, and squeezed it. His smile faded. "I'm afraid I've done something to hurt you." He paused. "I hired a private detective to find Nick Davis."

She felt as if she'd been slammed against a wall.

"I hired him before I knew Nick's name, and I did not give him that information after. Ray learned it for himself. He promised not to talk to him. I only want him to find him. Period. Which he hasn't done yet. I talked with him today."

Her breath charged its way back into her body and thrust her voice upward. "And you did this why?"

"Because I love you."

"Bryan! That's not a reason!"

"It's all the reason I needed. You're still trapped in this web of fear—"

"The man wants to kill me!" She pulled her hand from his, scooted back, and huddled against the sofa arm like a cornered rabbit. Her lungs and throat ached from the sudden intake of air.

"Cara, I trust this guy. He has no reason to lie to me, but if somehow Nick got wind of him...I'm thinking of your apartment, the fire. Would he...?"

She shook her head. No. Nick was an in-her-face kind of guy. He wouldn't bother with destroying her property.

His chest rose and fell, as if in relief. "When did you see him last?"

The memory flung itself onto center stage in her mind, in vivid color and with full surround sound. Glock 22 shells blasting.

"Cara?"

"Six and a half years ago. It seems too long, I know. But before that, it was seven years. I thought I was safe that time. I won't make the same mistake again."

"You can't keep running the rest of your life."

"Do I have a choice? Between your detective snooping around and my picture in the newspaper, I'd say it's pretty obvious I can't stay."

"I want to find him, learn about him. Maybe he's changed."

"And maybe the dinosaurs are coming back."

"Oh, Cara, darling, we can face this together." He leaned toward her, his arm along the back of the couch, his tone assertive. "He can't harm you anymore, I promise. I won't let him."

She would have laughed at his naïve declaration—if he hadn't said *darling*. The word took hold, wound its way through her mind, into her heart, pushed the memory back into the distant past. It fought the old terror like a knight on a galloping white steed, his lance knocking her foe senseless. It soothed and calmed. Her breathing became normal again.

And then she waited for the ice to come. The ice would keep her cool and collected, able to cope.

It didn't show up. But another rush of warmth did.

She wrapped her arms around her drawn-up knees, rested her chin atop them, and looked at Bryan. "Where's your shining armor, O knight?"

He smiled. "Sorry, all I've got is a special collar."

"Maybe it's the same thing."

"Maybe."

"Do you know what's so ironic? That I avoided church all these years because that's how he found me. He totally missed my going to college and the police academy or serving as a cop for five years. But two months after I started attending church, he showed up at my apartment." She shook her head. "Now in Chicago I start going to your church and look what happens."

"Do you understand why I couldn't let it go? Why if there was even a ghost of a chance to rectify the situation, I would pursue it?"

"Not really."

He whispered, "It's what boyfriends do."

"I see." She straightened. "Well, it's all moot at this point. Whoever gave my picture to the *Tribune* took care of that. I'm a sitting duck for him and the others."

"The others?"

"The ones after Jazzie."

"But if she's gone, then what?"

Uh-oh. She didn't want to travel this road of reasoning with him. "I'm no longer a threat."

He opened his mouth and closed it.

"Bryan, please don't ask about our plans. The less you know, the better."

"But I want to help."

"Your prayers are everything."

He nodded. "How about another hands-on project?"

That was an easy one. *Hold me through the night and make the world go away.* She stood abruptly before her heart decided to vocalize the unthinkable. "Would you mind taking us over to Dubuque tomorrow?" The city was in Iowa, about 30 miles from the condo. Larger than the touristy town of Galena, it offered better escape routes for Jazzie and added distance from Bryan.

"Of course not." He rose from the couch. "I'd take you anywhere." He wrapped his arms gently around her shoulders. "It's what boyfriends do. And..." He inclined his face. "They also give goodnight kisses."

Long, lingering ones, as it turned out.

"He loves you, doesn't he?" Jazzie snapped the jacket collar tight at her neck, a small Bible clutched in her hand.

Cara stood near her in the parking lot of a large chain discount store and watched Bryan drive away. The lump in her throat grew as his brake lights went off and the car pulled out onto the busy highway. She thought he raised his arm in goodbye, but it was probably her imagination. He was too far away and the wind had made her eyes water.

"And you love him too, don't you?"

She turned to Jazzie. Her dark lenses reflected the sunlight shining from a cold blue sky. "Yes." Her voice was a whisper.

"He's not picking you up later, is he?"

She shook her head. Her throat rattled as she coughed away the lump. "No. I don't want him involved any more than he is."

They had left the condo in the Galena Territories after a late breakfast. The ride into Galena had been quiet except for Jazzie's occasional comments about expansive vistas and pretty historical homes. Her attitude never ceased to impress Cara. It strengthened her hope that Jazzie would be all right.

During the 20-minute stretch from the town to the Mississippi, Bryan drove with one hand, holding tightly onto Cara's with his other. As they crossed the bridge, Jazzie oohed and aahed about the mighty river while Cara estimated the penalty for transporting a fugitive from the law over state lines. They reached Iowa, and she read the Dubuque directions she'd copied from the Internet that morning. In a few minutes they reached a busy, sprawling shopping district.

Now Jazzie giggled. "Well, from the looks of his goodbye, I'd say he wants to be about as involved as he can get. That was some kiss. Woo-ee! There he was in public, wearing his *priest* clothes, all black with that white collar, holding your face in those big lumberjack hands. No question about it, you weren't going anywhere until he was done! I tell you, I never would have guessed priests knew how to kiss like that. If he weren't so whipped over you, I'd go after the man myself."

She laughed. "Jazzie, I am going to miss you."

Her friend attempted a smile, but a haunted expression chased it away.

"Hey, you will be fine."

"Can we go over the details again?"

"Sure." She reached into her pocket and withdrew an envelope. "But first, this is from Bryan. He wanted to give it discreetly."

Jazzie stared at it for a moment, and then she dug into her own pocket. "I've got one for you."

"He didn't." They exchanged envelopes, each with their name printed neatly on the front. Cara peeked inside hers. "Oh my gosh. It's the same as yours. Five hundred dollars!"

"Five hundred?" Jazzie squealed.

"Oh, Bryan." She whispered his name tenderly. His generosity had opened up a host of options. She wouldn't have to hitchhike back to Chicago. She wouldn't even have to skip a meal. Jazzie could stay in motels until she found a job. The immediate future brightened considerably, all because a faithful man was God's instrument of provision.

"See, Jazzie? God takes care of us. He really does."

Thirty-Three

Bryan entered the condominium. Its silence resounded in his head, thunderous as a brass band playing in the front room.

With a heavy heart he walked through the emptiness. Cara had spent hardly more than 24 hours in the place, but the impact of her personality must have rearranged its very atoms. Her laughter. That little smile when she teased him. The compassion for Jazzie which she wore like a huge flowing robe. They all rustled the air.

The home was not the same home he had moved into the previous week. Though abstract and indefinable, the contrast was real.

He could think of no reason to stay.

Unless she came back.

He should stay then.

But she wasn't coming back. She would have asked for a ride. He assumed she would return to Chicago, but would not want him involved further.

But—

"Lord, have mercy. I sound psychotic."

He'd better sit down and get a grip. Surely love wasn't meant to destroy a man's equilibrium?

With determined strides he turned down the hall to the first-floor bedroom he'd been using. A quick glance told him his *Book of Common Prayer* was not in its usual place.

"That's right. Cara borrowed it this morning. She said she left it...in her room."

He hurried up the stairs. Which room had she used? He'd had no reason to be on the second floor since he first arrived and looked over the place.

Even before he saw his book on the bed, he knew the room was hers. It was the smaller, humbler in décor. Its window faced east. She would like that, the morning sun.

An envelope stuck out at the top of the book. He removed it and saw his name written in a feminine cursive. Remembering how he'd left a similar envelope for her, he smiled. Some of his heaviness lifted.

He sat on the bed and removed a letter from the envelope.

"Dear Bryan, thank you again for everything. You have made all the difference in our friend's life—and mine, but that's a different story. We found clean sheets and changed the beds. The others are in the dryer."

He smiled again. Her pragmatic bent ran true to form.

"About what comes next. Marcus will get my phone records and find your number listed. You can tell him I will contact him tomorrow. If you can avoid telling him—at least for the time being—that we've been here, I would appreciate it. I plan to turn in the evidence along with my resignation. What I said about me not being a threat to the bad guys? True enough, but I didn't mention their custom of administering revenge. As I said, sitting duck.

"About your PI. I understand. But..."

The ink had smudged, as if it had gotten wet.

"I have to leave Chicago, Bryan. There is no other choice."

The writing became almost illegible.

"I trust that boyfriends forgive? I love you. Cara."

Darkness had fallen long before Bryan moved from the bed. Tears had given way to burning anger. It ran the gamut, directed first at Cara, then Marcus Calloway, Nick Davis, the entire Chicago Police Department, the world in general, God specifically, and finally himself.

He went downstairs, clenching the letter in his hand.

"Lord, have mercy." His tone reduced the prayer to nothing more than a challenge, but he didn't stop ranting words heavenward. "You gave her to me. Don't take her away. You can't take her away now!"

He would call Ray back from Seattle, send him after Cara. She had to listen to him. She couldn't just leave! She couldn't just take off!

But she could. She knew how. She'd done it before. She'd fallen off the face of the earth.

"Lord! Don't let that happen!"

He would call Calloway. Talk some sense into him. They couldn't just let her hang out there, a forgotten piece of laundry flapping in the breeze!

But cops did that sort of thing, didn't they? They offered sacrificial lambs when it suited them.

He turned on his phone and saw two unanswered calls. He punched his way into voice mail, heard Meagan's chirpy hello, and skipped over her message. The next voice was the one he wanted.

"Reverend O'Shaugnessy, this is Detective Marcus Calloway. I have some questions to ask you regarding my partner, Cara Fleming. Please give me a call as soon as possible." He said his phone number.

Bryan didn't catch it, but heard the friendly automated voice explain how to return the call. He pressed that key. After a series of beeping tones and a long silence, he heard a ring.

"Calloway."

"Detective, this is Bryan O'Shaughnessy."

In reply came a noisily exhaled breath. "Where is she?"

"I don't know."

"Of course not! You wouldn't be calling me if you did!"

The man's abruptness permitted Bryan to answer in like manner. No reason trying to establish a rapport. "She gave me a message for you. She said she will contact you tomorrow."

The cursing that followed was muffled. Calloway must have covered his phone.

Bryan ran his hand through his hair. He identified with the effect of Cara on her partner.

Marcus offered one more choice word and said, "What else did she say?"

"Nothing else." At least not for him to hear. "But I have some questions, like—"

"Reverend—"

"Like why was her picture put in the paper, her cover exposed?" Too late, Bryan realized he was bellowing.

The line remained silent.

He looked at his phone to see if the connection had been lost. It hadn't. He returned the cell to his ear. "It's a simple question!"

At last, in a stony voice, Marcus said, "Reverend, I can't talk about it."

"Her life is endangered because of some idiotic decision to tell the newspaper and you can't talk about it?"

"No, I can't."

"Is anything being done to protect her now?"

"I can't talk about it."

"Well, then maybe I can talk about it! I'm sure the *Tribune* would like to hear more. There's got to be a tale of dirty cops in here somewhere."

"Is that a threat?"

"Interpret it however you want, Detective. At this point, I really don't care." He pressed the power button off.

His loud sigh filled the house. "Oh, Lord! What am I supposed to do?"

Turmoil nearly overwhelmed him. He stomped back and forth between the kitchen and family room like a propelled marble ricocheting its way through a pinball game.

At last gravity intervened. The marble ran out of steam and Bryan sank to his knees. He placed his elbows on the armchair. It wasn't low enough to convey the anguish of wanting to empty himself of himself.

What was he supposed to do? Who did he think he was? *He* couldn't do anything in his own power.

He bent over until his head lay on the carpet.

And then he begged for the mercy that had never failed him yet.

Thirty-Four

Cara walked across the nearly deserted Greyhound bus station to a row of molded-plastic, rock-hard, iron-blue chairs. She sat down beside Jazzie. "Here."

"What?" Jazzie looked up from filing her unpainted fingernails.

Cara held out the money envelope. "Take this."

"It's yours."

"I bought my bus ticket. I don't need any more."

"You bought our lunch. You bought this backpack and everything in it. Underwear, jeans, sweatshirt, toiletries. Keep your money."

"I'm going back to Chicago and a bank account."

"I can't take any more from you."

"Jazzie." She pulled out her friend's hand and planted the envelope in it. "Yes, you can."

Tears pooled in her eyes. "Thank you."

"You are so welcome." She took a deep breath and released it.

Jazzie's departure time neared. Her first stop would be Davenport, Iowa. After that, Cara did not know. Omaha to California? St. Louis to Florida? Indianapolis to New York?

They sat in silence.

Cara ran through a mental checklist, wondering if she'd forgotten anything. She didn't think so. During the past six days she had told Jazzie her own story, from leaving Seattle to hitchhiking to living in shelters to working odd jobs to finding Christian friends to going to college to starting all over in Chicago, complete with legal name change. Jazzie had learned firsthand how to survive on the street. Cara also had freely shared her faith, holding back nothing from the message of Jesus.

They had discussed how Jazzie could try using her ATM and credit cards en route to her final destination. If Ian hadn't canceled them yet, she could max them out on cash withdrawals and quickly leave town, thereby hiding her trail. With that money added to Bryan's gift, she could be across the country, staying in a motel, and landing some menial job within a few days. She might not have to seek refuge in a shelter or on the streets.

And she was smart. She had already played the scene before: Go to a new city and start a new life. She would be fine.

"Cara, why can't I contact you?"

"It's for your own safety. Worst-case scenario, Stafford gets out of jail and threatens to kill me if I don't tell him where you are. In such a situation, he's probably going to kill me anyway, but at least he won't force your location out of me. I'll die happy knowing you're safe."

"Cara!"

"It won't happen, hon. There's too much evidence against him, and I don't think his friends like him so much right now. It'll be a race between the authorities and the mob as to who gets to him first." *Besides, I won't even be in Chicago.* She didn't want to tell Jazzie. Her friend would blame herself for causing the trouble that led to Cara's photo being in the newspaper.

Jazzie smiled. "Someday I might write to Bryan."

"Someday."

"And you'd better be with him."

An announcement crackled on the PA system. The bus for Davenport was boarding.

They exchanged a brief look of panic which ended in nervous laughter. Standing, they embraced in a fierce hug.

"Cara, thank you for saving my life."

"It's a good one to save. Take care of it. I'll never forget you, Jazzie. God be with you."

Parting, they grasped hands in one last touch, each blinking back tears.

Jazzie whispered, "Let him love you." With that she turned and walked away.

Cara followed slowly, her eyes on Jazzie until she disappeared into the bus. A moment later a window slid open and her friend waved a hand through it. Cara waved back until the bus lumbered off.

Let him love you. She doubted Jazzie referred to God.

The last of Cara's coins plunked their way through the slot in the pay phone. Exhaustion blurred her vision as she slowly pressed the keypad numbers. A phone at the other end began to ring.

The bus ride from Dubuque had taken six long hours. Behind her the post-midnight street of the Chicago neighborhood was deserted, but she turned and scanned it, her eyes darting from shadow to shadow. A lifetime of watchfulness did not set with the sun. Neither did it grow deaf in the midst of applause after a battle won. Fatigue only energized it.

The bus ride from Iowa had offered hours of reflection. Gratitude filled her heart. Rightly or wrongly, she celebrated Jazzie's departure. She could not blame her for distrusting the system. She herself had been there. And she pondered all that had led to her own predicament. Though the threads of Stafford and the fire and the department's lack of support might remain forever tangled, one clear choice stood out: She would hand over the evidence to Chief Templeton along with her resignation.

What she didn't contemplate was Bryan. The memory was too fresh, too raw and biting. Perhaps in time its sweetness would overpower the sharpness.

The phone stopped ringing. "Miriam House." The voice was groggy but recognizable.

Thank You, Lord. "Helen? It's Cara. I'm down the block."

~

"Cara, finish that toast," Helen whispered as she set a cup of tea on the nightstand. "You'll sleep better with something in your stomach."

"I've never witnessed your mother hen imitation. It's cute." Cara, sitting cross-legged on the cot's thin mattress, smiled at the woman's frown and nibbled at the perfectly buttered toast.

Helen removed her blue terrycloth robe, gathered the long flannel nightgown about her, and sat down on the other cot. "Cute," she scoffed. "It's my job."

Their hushed conversation took place behind the kitchen in a small bedroom reserved for volunteer staff sleeping at the newly opened Miriam House shelter. On the opposite side of the kitchen a dozen women slept, hopefully oblivious to the breaking of rules. At least they would have no one to complain to since the director herself had unlocked the door in the middle of the night.

Another safe port. Cara, clothed in flannel pajamas, let the first of her defenses crumble. It was all right to let go now, at least for a few hours.

"Helen, you're like a one-woman social service. What *are* you doing here tonight?"

"Obviously I'm here so I could let you in." She smiled, as rare an occurrence as had been the hug for Cara when she let her inside. "Saturday night. My volunteers bailed out at the last minute. Times like this I begin to understand why I'm single. No man would put up with my lifestyle."

"I hear you. The last we saw each other, I was heading out the back door with a mob doll, and you were driving off with a van full of women and children hiding from abusive husbands. Are they all safe and sound?"

"Yes. Cara, just eat. We'll talk tomorrow."

"Did Marcus question you?"

"Yes, but we will talk tomorrow. I'm serious. You're on the edge, about ready to collapse."

"I tell my body when it can and cannot collapse. I've got a good ten minutes left."

"You always were a smart mouth who didn't need a mother hen."

Cara ignored the comment. "What did you tell Marcus?"

"Nothing except that I did not know where you were. But really, what could I tell him? He had all the facts I had: You were at Phoebe's and then you weren't."

"Did he drop it?"

She nodded.

"Good. You saw my picture in the paper?"

"How could I not? That business about you setting fire to your own apartment was especially rich."

Gratitude flowed through her. "Thank you for letting me in."

"It's my job to let in the homeless."

Cara chuckled. "Is Polly here? And Ruthie?"

"Yes, and a few others you know. It's a full house." She yawned. "Now finish that toast and have some tea."

She popped the last bite into her mouth and mumbled, "I want to visit with them and then I promise, I'll leave."

"You'll sleep and then we'll decide what you're doing."

"Helen, it's not safe to be around me. You've already seen proof of that."

"My source at the police department will tell me when it's not safe to be around you. Tea." She pointed at the cup.

"Please tell me who he is."

She lifted her covers and slid under them. "Goodnight."

"'Night." Cara took the cup and turned off the light. "Thank you."

"Mm-hmm."

As she put the cup to her lips, a familiar scent rose. Chamomile. "Helen, you've gone herbal on me."

No reply came except the sound of a soft snore.

In the dark Cara returned the cup to the nightstand. Snuggling under the covers, she gave up and let the memory chase away all other thought. A cozy family room, a crackling fire, chamomile tea, soft laughter, strong arms warding off despair.

The sweetness of it lulled her to sleep.

The sense of Bryan's shield dissipated early that afternoon.
After almost 12 hours of undisturbed sleep, Cara awoke, confused at the time she read on the radio alarm clock. Was it two
o'clock A.M. or P.M.? Daylight seeping through the blinds gave
her the answer.

She had slept through the hubbub of a dozen women
going through their morning routine of breakfast and prepa-
rations to be gone for the day. Against all rules and regulations, Helen allowed Cara to remain in the shelter, which was
officially closed until 7 P.M.

A note caught her eye on the nightstand.

"Stay put. Will see you tonight. I'm on duty again. H." A
twenty-dollar bill was clipped to it.

Cara rolled onto her back, gazed at the ceiling, and tried
to remember what day it was. Sunday. She had said she
would contact Marcus. His cell phone was never turned off.
She should walk out into the kitchen and call him. No, she
wasn't sure about Marcus. She was going to call the chief first.
Meet with him. The money would pay for a cab.

A tear slid from the corner of an eye.

She wanted to call Bryan.

Her body's craving for rest shut off further thought, and
she fell asleep before the saltwater dried on her temple.

～

That evening a dozen women filled Miriam House. They
took turns showering. Some shared the laundry facilities.
Others watched a sitcom on the television in a corner. Helen
was in the kitchen; one of the women helped her pack
tomorrow's lunch bags.

The atmosphere was that of a family at home, complete with disagreements, jealousies, unresolved issues, die-hard devotion to one another and, on occasion, warm fuzzies.

More than ever Cara felt one with the women. Although Helen had canceled that night's volunteers, thereby ensuring a bed for Cara, she didn't feel like one of the helpers. She was, except for that group, without a support system. The thought of leaving it cast a shadow over the time of camaraderie.

"Detective Cara." Polly grinned across the table and scooped a handful of popcorn from a large bowl in its center. "You make the best popcorn."

"Thanks." She forced a smile in return.

Polly said, "Did he find you?"

Her mind went blank.

"Detective Cal-Cal. Cal what?"

"Calloway. No, he didn't find me. Did he talk to you?"

Her head bobbed and her grin widened, revealing the gap along the side of her upper teeth. "He said did I see Detective Fleming, and I just said real loud 'I want my lawyer!'"

Cara burst into laughter. Skinny Polly's rendition of an irate thug dissipated the cloud hanging over her. "Then what happened?"

"He went like this." She cocked her head, scrunched her lips to one side, and drew her brows together. "And walked off."

Cara tapped a finger to her head. "You know he probably thinks no one is home."

"Ask me if I care." Polly laughed and reached over to slap a high five.

"You're perfect. Thank you."

Polly blushed. "You're welcome. Are you still doing undercover?"

"No, we're all done with that."

Ruthie, sitting beside her, joined the conversation. "Good. Then you can tend to this moron for me. If I take the shortcut to work, he's there bullying for right-of-way payment. Gave him five dollars last week."

"Oh, Ruthie. You draw them like ants to a picnic."

One of her infrequent smiles erased ten years from her face. "It's my beauty."

Cara nodded. "It's got to be."

Later that night an old nightmare crept into her sleep, snuffing out the comfort of the women and the memory of Bryan. Details, as always, remained elusive, but she awoke in a sweat. Her ears had the feel of deafness in them, like they did after a shooting.

Like after that time she had emptied her gun into her apartment wall where mere seconds before Nick had been standing.

She trembled in the darkness and thanked God yet once more that behind the wall were mortared bricks and not another apartment in which people lived. Try as she might, she could not thank Him for Nick's escape.

The next morning she helped Helen cook breakfast. The woman's mother hen demeanor still surprised her. Cara only caught glimpses of what she had always thought of as her executive personality, the one which tolerated no nonsense or a bending of regulations. It emerged the previous evening when two women fussed over lockers and again when she smelled alcohol.

"Helen, do you mind if I spend one more night?"

"Spend as many as you want. Goodness, you could live here full-time. You're a natural with the women. They feel safe with you because you're a policewoman, and on top of that you make even Ruthie smile."

"Thanks." She cracked eggs into a bowl and stirred them. "But one more night will do it."

"Cara, your apartment was gutted. Where else do you have to go?"

"It's not a question of where, but of the fact that I can't *not* go." She added milk to the eggs. "I'm toxic, Helen, like I was at Phoebe's Place, only worse. Not only are Jazzie's ex-friends upset with me, the department's none too happy either."

"Isn't there someone you can go to? Someone you trust?"

"Bryan." The name flowed right off her tongue, completely missing the juncture where she decided whether or not to say something.

"Bryan?"

Too late, she kept her mouth shut and focused on her chore. She tipped the bowl over an iron skillet of foaming butter. The yellowy cream sizzled.

"Who's Bryan? Cara Fleming, you've never mentioned a man's name."

"Marcus."

"He's your partner, not a man."

She pushed a spatula through the eggs. "Bryan's my priest, not a man."

"The guy you brought to our meeting? The big redhead?"

"Mm-hmm."

"He's not Roman Catholic, is he?"

She glanced up and saw Helen's smirk. "You're an expert on types of clergymen?"

"My dad was a pastor. He wanted me and my sisters to avoid dating certain denominations. Back to Bryan. He may be your priest, but he's also a man. And I know that because you're flustered."

Cara just kept on attending to the eggs.

"You're never flustered, Detective."

No, she wasn't. Nor did she feel delicious tickles inside herself. Nor did she long for sweet kisses and strong arms to hold the world at bay.

She had her own personal phenomenon of global warming. Slowly but surely Bryan O'Shaugnessy was melting the ice.

Thirty-Five

Cara spread her arms. "That's it, Chief. End of story."

The man on the other side of the broad desk did not say a word. His intelligent blue eyes and stoic expression revealed nothing. Chief Stuart Templeton's clean-shaven jowls were tan from his trip to Florida. Although there were rumors of his retiring and he had begun to fish more often than the police commissioner and mayor liked, he still exhibited the committed freshness of a rookie on the street eager to defend the helpless and enforce justice.

Cara felt as comfortable with him as the day he'd welcomed to Chicago Cari-Ann Davis, a woman running from her past who needed a new identity and who wanted to join the force.

She added, "End of story except—I let her get away."

He squinched briefly, a hint of the struggle going on behind the cold demeanor. "I'm not arresting you. At first glance I'd say Jasmine Wakefield wasn't aware of what she was involved in until recently. She would have gotten off. As for your role, that suspicious fire and the *Trib* nonsense forced you into a corner." His voice rumbled now, his anger at a low boil. "We should have been there for you. Now we can't even figure out who leaked the information. The bonehead reporter left town suddenly and is unavailable. But the buck stops here. I apologize."

She had suspected as much, but felt relief at the admission. He hadn't sold her out.

He narrowed his eyes and fingered a camera memory card which held Jazzie's accounting evidence. Beneath them lay Cara's makeshift report which she'd written at the shelter.

He said, "We'll get the ball rolling for witness protection."

"I told you, she doesn't want that. All I ask is that you drop the charges. Bury them so she can use her Jane Waite social security number again without being hunted down. We owe her that much. She's given us Stafford."

"I'll take care of it. You go ahead and place your coded ad in the *Wall Street Journal* or whatever. Let her know she's got the go-ahead to get on with her life."

"Thanks." She smiled. He was like that, knowing almost exactly what she was planning. She had told Jazzie to keep checking the Sunday *New York Times* personals for one that read "Janie, clear sailing forecast. Go for it."

He winked. "We would have made a good team if only you'd been born thirty years earlier." He paused then, the subtle animation of his face gone as quickly as it had appeared. "Cara, I was talking about you for witness protection."

His words filtered through her almost in slow motion. A program for her?

"Relocation, new identity, money, the whole shebang. Maybe a job in a private security organization. I don't think we could swing another police department. You're too much of a standout. You made detective here much too fast for some envious coworkers."

"I-I don't know. On the surface it sounds inviting, but…" She visualized again her photo on the front page and heard Marcus's unsupportive response the last time they'd talked.

Templeton tapped the videotape he'd watched with her. "But you're like Jasmine Wakefield. You refuse to trust a soul. You'd rather do it yourself. Look, I'm trying not to overreact here. Your work won't knock them out of the saddle, but it is going to be a significant bust. Stafford's not happy, but he'll be in custody today. That's going to set off a chain reaction and some people…Fleming, you know—" He pressed his lips together, cutting off his rising voice.

She nodded. "I know. They won't let me go. I have to disappear."

"Completely. We're not talking a nutty husband. Cara, take the pressure off yourself. Let the government help this time. It owes you too."

Uncertain, she shrugged. She had never considered the possibility. "Can we just start with a photo ID today? Everything was lost in the fire."

"Of course. But think about the other for as long as you need. We'll put you up in a safe house."

Jail by a different name, a jail insiders would know about. The hair on the back of her neck prickled. Something inside her backed away. "I'm fine."

"Where are you staying?"

"With friends." She patted her backpack. "And I've got a wig."

He clenched his jaw. "I'm assigning a cop to you round the clock."

A cop. An insider. Templeton was missing the point. "Chief, the bad guys aren't my main worry. I've studied them for years. What really concerns me is the mole inside your department. The one who leaked I was at Phoebe's Place and then talked to the reporter."

He stared at her for a long moment. Again his face closed up. "It's being looked into."

Well, that wasn't good enough. She pulled an envelope from her bag, laid it on his desk, and stood. "Sorry it's not typed, but it reads the same. I'll have my desk cleaned out in five minutes." She smiled. "Or less. No apartment, no place to put things. I might take a pen or two, if you don't mind." She stood, stretching her arm out toward him.

He rose and clasped her hand. "This isn't right."

She gave him a half nod. "It happens."

He pursed his lips, continuing to hold her hand, his eyes almost boring into hers. "Cara, you're the best."

She figured that was about as close to a warm fuzzy as anyone would ever get from him. It helped keep her tears at bay. "Thank you."

"We will get to the bottom of this. You just take care of yourself. And please, think about the program. Talk to me in a couple days."

Her smile was noncommittal as she extracted her hand. "Thank you for everything, Stu."

He nodded. "I'll have a guy meet you at your desk. Do me a favor and let him play bodyguard."

She waved a silent goodbye and left. Backup would have been nice *last* week.

~

Cara entered the detectives' room with trepidation. To reach her desk she had to walk past others, four of them now occupied by male investigators. One averted his eyes.

Another, on the phone, turned his back as she neared. The third, also on the phone, stopped talking and simply stared at her.

The fourth was Marcus. He smiled. It wasn't his nice smile. And they all thought she was the icy one.

She dropped her backpack on the floor beside her desk and sank onto her chair, annoyed to feel her legs trembling, and looked over at Marcus.

He linked his hands behind his head, elbows akimbo. "The fugitive returns."

"I got a 'get out of jail free' card."

"Good for you. Must have been some rip-roaring evidence."

"It was. How's Granny?"

"Upset. Crazy with worry."

"Tell her I'm okay?"

He nodded. "Renae went to church with her."

"Really?" The news took her by surprise. His girlfriend, sweet and giving as she was, had all the answers, a condition which left little room for the mysteries of God.

"Really. She figures there must be something to it because Gran hasn't cut me out of the will yet for not finding you."

She pulled open a drawer and rummaged through miscellaneous desk junk. All meaningless. Stuff she would leave behind. "If I had a will, I'd cut you out." She snapped her fingers. "Like that."

A short silence ensued while she continued opening and shutting drawers.

Marcus said, "Want to go down the street, get some coffee?"

She coughed a noise of disbelief and looked across the desks at him. Anger blurred her vision. "You don't see it? The bull's-eye on my forehead?"

"You helped paint it there yourself."

Cara's hand was on a small notepad. She threw it at him. It bounced off his shoulder. He bent over to retrieve it from the floor.

She slammed the drawers shut. There was nothing she needed from them. Someone else could clean away six years' worth of accumulated paraphernalia. She gathered desktop items. The few personal things—a mug, a ceramic pencil holder, a tube of hand cream, a basket of chocolate drops— had lost their appeal. Why not just scoop them into the large bottom drawer? Or the trash can? Yes, the trash can.

Marcus brushed against her arm. He was kneeling, shoving the notepad into her backpack on the floor. "Looks like Cucumber's on vacation. You're going to have to get her back here, you know. Calm, cool, and collected keeps you safe on the street."

Ignoring that comment, she said, "What was I supposed to have done?"

"Trusted me," he whispered, now gazing at her, his face millimeters from her nose.

Footsteps shuffled behind her. "Excuse me."

She turned to see a skinny young man in baggy jeans and a black leather jacket. He needed a shave, and his blond hair was pulled back into a ponytail.

"Detective Fleming?" he said. "I'm Officer Evan Vogel. Your escort."

Marcus stood. "How old are you, anyway?"

Cara grabbed her bag and rose, nudging Marcus aside. "Don't mind him, Officer."

"He'd better mind me. Look, Vogel, my name is Calloway, and if anything happens to her, you'll be in a world of hurt."

"Yes, sir. Shall we go, ma'am?"

"Call me Cara." She took a step in front of Marcus and paused. Behind his trademark sneer she caught sight of his grandmother's maple syrup brown eyes. The smart remark on the tip of her tongue fizzled. "Give my love to Granny."

He blinked in reply and she walked away.

Officer Vogel fell in behind her. She was grateful for the screen he provided to the stares she knew her fellow detectives directed at her back.

Ex-fellow detectives.

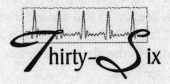

Thirty-Six

Before leaving the police station, Cara pulled her newly appointed bodyguard into an interrogation room and shut the door. "Let's go over the ground rules, Evan. May I call you Evan?"

"Sure."

"What's your plan?"

"Stick next to you."

She shook her head. "That makes us both obvious. They know me. They don't know you."

"Excuse me. Who are 'they'?"

She raised her fist and flipped out one finger at a time as she enumerated the three entities he might as well know about. "Organized crime goons. Some unknown cops whose loyalty is with them and not us. My stalking husband."

"I see." He smiled, undaunted.

"I want you to tail me inconspicuously. If we can make eye contact, you're too close. Can you handle that?"

"You don't want a bodyguard."

"You're quick. No, I don't. By myself I can disappear."

"Chief says I'm your bodyguard."

"How about a compromise? You drive me around, stay with me while I make some stops." She listed the courthouse, her bank, and the DMV. "Then we'll go into Water Tower

Place." A popular, multistoried shopping mall on Michigan Avenue. "When I lose you, that's the signal your shift is over. Okay?"

"When you lose me?" His tone mocked.

She gave him a frosty smile.

"Okay then." His greenish eyes twinkled now; she imagined because of the adrenaline pumping through him. "But the chief says you're supposed to lay low until they arrest the dude."

"I don't have time to lay low. I have to..." She hoisted the backpack onto a shoulder and thought of what she had to do: leave Chicago as soon as possible, preferably with money and identification. A complicated process after a fire. "Evan, they're probably arresting him this very minute. Let's go."

As they walked down the corridor, she thought about the chief's offer. Maybe she should accept it. Let the government take care of the details. Give up control. Give up the vague hope of contacting Bryan somehow, somewhere, in the distant future. That hope, of course, was worse than vague. It was impossible. She had never reached backward and touched base with Father and Mrs. Palmer or Guillermo and Rosa Lopez. Fear for them as well as for herself was too great.

But Bryan... Bryan's love and courage nearly engulfed that fear. For the first time in her life she wondered if things could change. No matter how dim the hope to see him again, it fed her own courage, enabling her to take the next step. Which was to get out of Chicago in one piece.

A heaviness in her chest had been steadily building. Now it threatened to cut off her air supply. What was wrong? She knew how to exit. To leave Seattle, Los Angeles, and various cities in between had each been easy decisions to make, an easy task to accomplish. In imminent danger from Nick, with birth certificate and money in her pocket, she skedaddled.

The only exceptionally dear friends she left behind were the Palmers and the Lopezes, couples who sent her on her way with their blessings because they'd experienced firsthand the horrendous reality of Nick.

Chicago was different because in Chicago there lived Rubyann, Polly, Ruthie, so many others like them, Helen, Renae. Though she didn't know what was up with Marcus, that didn't erase their years together. And there lived...Bryan.

Bryan.

In spite of her apartment going up in smoke, what she had in Chicago was *home*. And home, she now understood, made all the difference in the world. Too bad she hadn't known that before it was time to leave it.

~

Cara studied her reflection in the full-length mirror of a Lord and Taylor dressing room and blew out a breath of satisfaction. "Mission accomplished."

Gone was the ragtag appearance of an indigent woman. It had served to hide her on the streets. It had also walked with her into the police station and her bank. She needed a new persona.

She murmured, "Move over, Helen." She was certain the woman owned a similar black suit jacket and straight skirt like the one now hanging just so on herself.

Black pumps and a white silk blouse completed Cara's outfit. A black all-weather coat hung under plastic on one of the room's hooks. She had placed receipts, cash, sunglasses, and cosmetics in a large black leather shoulder bag. Her face glowed with newly applied foundation, subtle blush, eyeshadow, and mascara. Her cinnabar-colored lips shimmered.

She even smelled good. Exotic. Jazzie would be impressed. Her short, dull nails didn't pass muster, but leather gloves on a cool autumn afternoon were not out of place. Like millions of other big-city women, her image announced "power." She would blend in.

Cara stuffed the clothing she'd lived in for the past week into a shopping bag. In went her military-style boots, khaki cargo pants, sweater, and hooded jacket. She would stash them with the backpack behind a nearby door marked "Employees Only" through which she'd glimpsed a large cluttered area. Hopefully the used clothes would go unnoticed until she was out of the store and eventually make their way to a needy woman.

She reached into the backpack for the wig. Jazzie had styled it for her and wrapped it in tissue paper.

Her hand fell on something hard. Not her toothbrush. What else had she put in—

It was a gun!

She pulled it out. It was Marcus's pistol, the small one he carried in a holster on his leg.

She stared at it in her palm, thinking how he had knelt beside her desk and placed the notepad in the backpack. That must have been when he...

"Oh, Marcus," she whispered and sank onto the single padded chair.

Tears spilled from her eyes. He'd been posing the whole time. All that tough-guy routine. In character for him and yet so out of character when directed toward her. A cover-up. For what?

Oh, Lord! What is going on? All I want is to be with Bryan! Instead, here I am! Spending half a paycheck on one outfit so I can run away from him and sitting in a fancy dressing room, crying over a stupid gun!

❧

Cara repaired her makeup, arranged the wig over her hair, and donned the sunglasses and long coat. She strode through the ladies department, a touch of disdain in her expression as if she saw its paltry offerings as a personal affront to her exquisite taste. Shoulders back and head held high, she was an important executive on her way to meet an important client to discuss important business over cocktails.

Riding the escalator down to the ground floor, she scanned the customers. Evan was nowhere in sight. The last time she had seen him was on the sixth floor in the middle of a crush bottlenecked at the elevator doors. A cute girl bumped into him. He turned, she assumed in order to apologize. And that was that.

He was young.

Cara went through the revolving doors and out into the late afternoon. Her attention was drawn immediately to a commotion on her left. Strobe lights flashed from an ambulance and fire engine parked at the curb. The vehicles were partially hidden behind a crowd of bystanders.

Two women rushed past her, visibly upset. "In broad daylight!" one of them said. "In Marshall Field's!"

The back of Cara's neck prickled.

Instantly, intuitively she understood two things. One, whatever had happened in broad daylight in Marshall Field's had happened to Evan Vogel. And two, she should walk away.

But if the first were true, she could not obey the second. The old Cara Fleming could have, the one nicknamed Cucumber. Nothing to be done for him now. Don't jeopardize the mission, even if that mission is only self-preservation.

But Cucumber was gone. The Ice Lady had melted right out of existence onto the floor of a Lord and Taylor dressing room. God used Bryan and Jazzie and Helen and Marcus to finally answer her prayer: *Dear Lord, melt the ice water in these veins. Soften my heart.*

She turned left and wove her way around the soaring colonnade and people leaving the scene. Skirting the crowd of onlookers, she edged along plate glass windows and marble façade until only a policeman stood between her and the unfolding horror.

As he ordered people to stand back, paramedics and fire-fighters emerged from a door not ten feet from her. They wheeled a stretcher, slowed to maneuver their equipment, parted slightly. Between them she glimpsed a slender figure covered in a white sheet, strapped down, blond-haired, an oxygen mask over his face. A firefighter walked by carrying a black leather jacket.

Cara put a shoulder against the wall and leaned into it, her arm pressed against her midsection.

"Shame, isn't it?" A male voice came from behind her. "Shot in public in broad daylight. What is this world coming to?"

Fighting a wave of nausea, she felt the man move nearer.

"There was quite a bit of blood, but he was conscious." His breath was on her cheek now, the voice low and hushed. "That's always a good sign. He even talked. Said his name. I think it was something like Kevin. Or maybe it was..." A pause. "*Evan*. Are you all right, Detective?"

That he addressed her by title came as no surprise. His words were already there in her mind with the other knowl-edge, that intuitive perception lying just out of reach. To hear it spoken aloud gave the whole scene a sense of déjà vu. She knew, had always known, that if she had turned right instead of left, they would not have spotted her.

"Or is it *former* Detective? The wig is a nice touch, by the way."

The cluster surrounding the stretcher reached the back of the ambulance. *Get him inside! Hurry! Go! Lord, don't let him die!*

"Look to the left." His lips brushed at her ear. "Do you see the young woman? The very pregnant one?"

She refocused from the ambulance and saw her.

"She'll be next. That's my friend behind her, the one in the baseball cap. He has a silencer, but he's rather fond of his knife."

Doors slammed. The ambulance? Or her brain shutting down?

"Come now." He looped his arm through hers and his voice rose to a normal pitch. "Buck up, dear. You know you shouldn't watch these things. They're much too distressing. The car's this way."

For one brief moment clarity returned. Sirens wailed to life. She felt the minuscule weight of Marcus's gun in her coat pocket. Intuitively her muscles tensed for offensive action. A kick, an elbow jab, the gun at his head, his arm twisted up his back. *Freeze!* A shout to the policeman two yards away for assistance.

An image of the young woman sprawled on the sidewalk dammed the flow of adrenaline, and Cara became like a walking dead person.

$\mathcal{T}$hirty-$\mathcal{S}$even

Late Monday afternoon Bryan stood in the formal dining room of the rectory, hands at his hips, and gazed through the tall mullioned windows. Their old thick glass distorted the view of the backyard, giving the leafless tree a wavy appearance. Beyond it a faint light glowed through the window of his church study to the other side of the yard.

Meagan was in there, organizing his paperwork in order of urgency. She had banned him from returning to active duty until his full two weeks were up. Despite TJ's visit that morning and his declaration Bryan was fit as a fiddle, she would not reconsider. Thankfully no parishioner had died in his absence; she would have put the funeral on hold indefinitely.

Not that he wasn't composing his own requiem. The death of a relationship deserved recognition. Like any life, its existence should be celebrated after death. True, the thing had never gotten off the ground, but that didn't lessen its reality.

He had waited for Cara at the condominium just in case she returned. He waited through Saturday night and half of Sunday, funneling his anger and frustration into the treadmill. The cell phone never left his hand. Whenever fear for her safety attacked him, he prayed it away. When hopelessness struck, he drove home and searched the church basement.

Anger, frustration, fear, and hopelessness. Some requiem material those were.

She was gone. He didn't have a say in the matter. If he called the newspapers, raised a hue and cry against the police department, that would not bring her back. It would only serve to satisfy his own sick desire for personal revenge.

Vengeance is mine, saith the Lord.

Her written words flashed in his head. *I didn't mention their custom of administering revenge.*

At that precise moment a cloud swallowed the sun, and a shadow filled the room. It grew. He felt it seep into his mind, a thick blackness consuming all light. A horrifying thought arose: All was lost.

Dear God! No!

At his cry, the darkness fled.

And he knew he could not let her go. If God was in it, as Bryan had confidently told her, then there was a point. He refused to believe the point was to abandon her or his own mind. Which was exactly how he'd spent the past 48 hours.

She must be in the city by now. She had things to settle. Things that would take time.

Where would she stay? With Rubyann? No, not with Marcus's grandmother. Did she have trustworthy friends? Friends who wouldn't believe the newspaper article? Friends who would welcome her into their home in spite of her trouble? Or would she go back to the streets—

Of course.

Miriam House.

Bryan sat astride his motorcycle parked directly in front of Miriam House while waiting for the night shelter to open. He watched customers come and go at a liquor store. A grocer locked his door. The metal gate rattled into place, covering the shop front.

He was on the bike because his car had needed gas, and he was not in the mindset to dally with necessary chores like stopping at a station or going back inside the house to retrieve his helmet. The pair of clear glasses left on the bike were enough to shield his eyes. He was out on the street in 60 seconds flat.

Noise and wind flung suppressed energy from him as if he himself roared instead of the engine. His hand twisted the throttle. His fingers flicked at levers, working clutch and brakes. His feet pressed the pedals like a choreographed dance. His body tilted the heavy machine, leaned into turns. The process provided him with the feel of control and power. Delusional control and power were better than none.

A woman approached now, her face hidden in the early evening shadows. She stopped at the door tucked unobtrusively between the liquor store and the market and inserted a key.

"Helen?" Bryan guessed. If the woman weren't Helen, she might at least know the director.

She turned. "Yes?"

Relief filled him. He swung his leg over the motorcycle and went forward. "I'm Bryan O'Shaugnessy. I don't know if you remember me. Cara Fleming introduced us."

She smiled. "Yes. The redheaded priest. I remember you."

"I'm looking for her."

She chuckled and pushed open the door. "I knew you would be. She said she'd be back tonight. You're welcome to wait inside."

Relief flooded through him now, weakening his knees. "Thank you. I'd like that."

"I may put you to work though. Just shut the door. Thanks." She climbed the steps; he followed. "It has been one full day of haggling over funds. I'm not up for refereeing the ladies tonight." She glanced over her shoulder at him. "Priests make good referees, don't they?"

He smiled.

They entered the main room of Miriam House, and she flipped on ceiling lights. He noticed that beds were neatly lined up now along the two side walls, barracks-style, a wide aisle between the rows. The table where they had eaten tacos during their meeting had been replaced with a long picnic table with attached benches. A television was in the far corner. Chairs and a couch sat on a braided rug in front of it.

"Father, you can put your jacket on the coat tree here." Helen unbuttoned her long winter coat and shrugged out of it. Underneath she wore a business suit which, as Bryan recalled, complemented her demeanor.

"Please, call me Bryan."

"Well, Bryan, would you like some coffee? I only have the real stuff."

Hang the diet. "That'll be great, thank you." He followed her through a door into a kitchen. "What did you mean you knew I'd be looking for her?"

She went about preparing the coffee. "Your name came up in conversation this morning."

"You saw her this morning?"

"Yes. She left early, to walk Ruthie to work and then take care of some things." She looked at him. "I don't know how much you know..."

"Probably more than you. She's in major trouble."

Helen nodded and turned back to the coffeemaker. "I asked her if there was someone she could trust. She said your name."

"I was wondering whom she could trust and Miriam House came to mind."

She smiled. "So here you are. I'm very glad. Though she'd never admit it, she needs you. Have a seat."

~

Like schoolgirls not wanting to be tardy, the women filed upstairs immediately after Helen unlocked the door at 7 P.M. Bryan tried to make himself inconspicuous and hid out in the kitchen. Polly, whom he had met that time with Cara, became his shadow. He didn't mind. She endeared herself to him with her life's story and questions about God.

They sat in the kitchen on stools that had seen better days and watched Helen clean up. She had just packed a dozen sack lunches. A large clock on the wall above the cabinets ticked away the seconds, each one heightening the anxiety he and Helen relayed in exchanged glances. She was certain Cara would be there long before lights out at 10:30. She had said the night would be her last at the shelter. Helen knew how Cara enjoyed her time with the women; she would not come only to sleep.

The time neared ten o'clock.

Polly winked at him now, behind the director's back. "Helen, men are against the rules." Her voice was a loud whine.

Helen whirled around. "Honestly, Polly! I told you—"

The young woman burst into laughter. "He's a priest! He's allowed! Ha! I got you, Helen! I got you!" Her caramel eyes danced with humor.

Helen shook her head. "Yes, you sure got me, Polly. You're gonna drive me crazy one of these days."

Polly threw her arms around the taller woman. "Cara says you're like those French rolls she buys me at the coffee shop: hard on the outside, soft and doughy on the inside."

Helen hugged her back. "Oh you! Go get ready for bed."

"Yes, ma'am." She waved shyly at Bryan and left the kitchen.

Helen leaned against the counter. "Ordinarily I don't worry about Cara. She's a cop. She works late at night. Through the night. Something probably came up." The tears in her eyes belied the matter-of-fact tone.

"Police business." He nodded, looking at the window that opened out onto the fire escape. His arms itched to swing his stool and smash it against the large pane. Physical action would take his mind off the elephant in the room, the one reminding them Cara could not possibly still be employed by the department. Police business had not detained her.

The phone rang, breaking their silence. Helen went to it. "Hello...No...Last night...Now?...All right." She hung up the phone, all color drained from her face. "Marcus Calloway is coming."

"Does he know something?"

"I don't think he would come unless he did."

"She doesn't trust him."

"I know, but I do." She resumed her stance against the counter and crossed her arms. "Is talking to you confidential, like with a doctor?"

"Yes."

"All right. I think you should know, so you can trust him too." Her eyes focused somewhere behind him. "A long time ago, when I worked with the Department of Children and Family Services, I hired a social worker, a young college graduate. Her fiancé was Marcus, a rookie fresh out of the academy. She had a passion for abused women because her mother was one. She started volunteering at the homes. One night a berserk husband found the place. He killed her."

Bryan winced.

Helen looked at him. "I doubt Cara has heard any of that. He doesn't talk about it. Later, when his rage cooled, he began to keep his ear to the ground. He learns things, like when word leaks about where a private shelter is located."

"And he tells you?"

She nodded. "Cara knows I have a source in the department, but she doesn't know it's Marcus. He wants to remain anonymous. And he doesn't ask for information in return. He's just paying a debt to a woman he loved."

Satisfied with the explanation, Bryan stood. "I'll go let him in."

~

While the women settled in for the night in the main living area of Miriam House, Bryan sat on a cot in a tiny room off the kitchen. Helen stood in a corner, her arms crossed over her chest, more of a huddled posture than an unreceptive one.

Marcus finished his search of Cara's side of the room. He touched the empty shelf, the empty bed, the empty space beneath it, each three times.

Bryan wondered if the man thought himself psychic.

"Marcus," Helen said, "she came with nothing but the clothes on her back and a backpack. She left with the same. Sit down and talk to us, please. We're about to lose our minds." She glanced at Bryan, who did not contradict her last statement.

The detective did as he was told. He sat heavily on the cot, his face haggard, and rubbed his eyes. "It doesn't look good." Propping his elbows on his knees, he leaned forward. "When she left the station this morning, the chief sent a bodyguard along with her."

Thank God, Bryan thought.

"Late this afternoon he was shot in Marshall Field's at Water Tower Place." He patted the space on the cot next to him. "Helen, sit down here before you fall down."

Trembling uncontrollably, she plopped onto the bed. Bryan unfolded the blanket at the foot of the one he sat on and handed it to her.

"Officer Vogel is going to be all right. I talked to him briefly when he came to after surgery. He said Cara dodged him at the mall. I told him the approximate time it was when he was shot. He figured he probably hadn't seen her for an hour and a half before that." Marcus curled his hands into fists and cursed under his breath. "She thinks it's all a game."

A long moment passed. Bryan hoped he wouldn't lose control before Marcus got his back. They'd never get anywhere with the two of them emotional wrecks.

Marcus said, "Up until the point she slipped away, he said they went a number of places. She had identification, cash, an ATM card. He saw her purchase a black leather shoulder bag, black low-heeled shoes, and cosmetics. Said she spent a bundle. And she looked at business suits."

Helen, blanket clasped about her shoulders, said, "None of that sounds like Cara."

"No, it doesn't. It's a new disguise. She mentioned to the chief she had a wig in her backpack. I saw her wear a black one recently when she was undercover."

Bryan thought of Jazzie's hair when they first met, of how real the black looked, more real than the blonde revealed later.

"Heeled shoes and business suits," Marcus said. "Cara was trying to disappear."

Bryan said, "Maybe she did."

"Do you know who we're dealing with?"

"Organized crime."

"She won't make it on her own."

"The police department wasn't much help." Bryan didn't tamp down his anger.

Marcus studied him before responding. His face grew deadpan again, as if he'd reigned in his own feelings. "I know. We didn't. There's someone on the inside. Someone connected to them. Information is flowing like water through a sieve." He glanced at Helen and then gazed again at Bryan. "I got word to Phoebe's Place. My partner knows how to take care of herself. I had to keep an eye on the guy who told me something was going down there. That's all I can say about it."

"Did you arrest Ian Stafford?"

His brows shot up.

Bryan merely shrugged a shoulder. He felt his jaw clench and his eyes narrow. *Make me tell you how I know that.*

Marcus ignored the challenge. "No. We can't find him."

"Probably that same someone alerted him."

"I think I know who the someone is, but I can't prove it. And I haven't figured out who he's talking to."

At a brisk knock on the door, they all jumped.

Polly stepped partially into the room and shook her forefinger in reprimand. "Helen! No men!"

Helen only stared at the young woman, all the heart gone from her personality.

Polly smiled. "Just kidding. Priest and cops are okay! 'Night!" With that she backed out and shut the door.

Priests and cops. Cops and priests. No difference. A familiar sentiment.

Flynn.

No dame detective's gonna pull a number on my brother. Just tell her to back off.

His brother's warning to Cara.

Back off from what? Just how much had Flynn known about Cara's investigations? Had he been privy to details leaked by someone who knew, someone close to Cara?

Bryan long suspected Flynn's path crossed in more than one way with those outside the law. Why would he care about her work unless it directly affected his *friends?*

"Detective, do you happen to know Officer Flynn O'Shaugnessy?"

Thirty-Eight

Mindless of the posted speed limit, Bryan charged through the nearly deserted streets on his motorcycle. Turning onto the expressway, he opened up the bike and wove between cars as if they were at a standstill. An unmarked police car followed at close range, its driver never falling more than a car length behind.

He led Marcus to his brother's house. Twenty minutes of blasting wind and roaring noise expelled pent-up energy but reduced his prayer life to *Lord, keep her safe. Lord, keep her safe.*

They parked in the driveway. There were no lights showing through the house windows. He watched Marcus walk over to him from his car.

"Hey, Evel Knievel. What do you for an encore? Jump the Chicago River?"

Bryan smiled grimly, and they went to the front door.

"You and your brother close?"

"No." He pressed the doorbell, holding it in long enough to wake one sleeping off a 12-pack.

"Oh. I see."

He had told Marcus about Flynn's suspect behavior, but hadn't revealed any personal family history.

The porch light went on. The door opened and his sister-in-law, Ellen, peered around it, clutching a robe at her neck. She pushed open the storm door, sleep clearly still in her half-mast eyes. Her short salt-and-pepper hair was matted down.

"Bryan? What's wrong?"

"We need to talk to Flynn."

"I'll wake him up. Come inside. Have a seat."

Bryan entered and shut the door behind Marcus. Instead of sitting, they shuffled their feet, runners anxious to continue the race.

Marcus whispered, "Good cop's wife. Doesn't ask questions."

Bryan nodded. In his opinion Ellen had always been more the community's servant than her husband.

He heard noise from the back of the house, footsteps, doors opening, closing, water running. At last his brother emerged from the hallway, his eyes puffy and complexion noticeably florid even in the low light. He wore blue jeans and an unbuttoned flannel shirt.

Without preamble, Bryan said, "This is Marcus Calloway."

Marcus held out his hand.

After a second's hesitation, Flynn shook it. "Detective." Evidently he recognized the name.

Marcus nodded. "Officer."

"What's up?" Flynn sat heavily in a recliner.

Bryan said, "Cara Fleming is what's up. Where is she?"

"Huh?"

Marcus sat on the couch. "They picked her up this afternoon after shooting an officer assigned to be her bodyguard."

"Who's they?"

"I think you know."

Flynn glanced at Bryan.

Marcus went on. "I'm curious about the relay team. Does the information go from Hugh Acton to you to the big guys, or are there some intermediaries in between? Say a detective or somebody like Ian Stafford?"

Flynn glared now at Bryan. "Some brother you are."

"Look!" He pointed a finger at him. "You're the one who told me to warn Cara to back off. I did, but she didn't, and now they've got her. You knew what was going on!"

"The broad got to you, didn't she? I'm surprised, you being a man of the cloth and all." He shrugged. "Sorry to be the bearer of bad news, but if they've got her, you might as well start searching car trunks. That's usually their favorite spot for stuffing dead—"

Bryan lunged at his brother. The recliner tipped and they fell onto the floor. A lamp crashed as they wrestled. They rolled, each struggling to pin the other. Ellen shouted. A hand stronger than hers grabbed Bryan's arm.

Marcus hauled him off of Flynn.

Ellen yelled, "Good grief! Still behaving like kids. Aren't you two ever going to get over it? Bryan, what's with you? You're the sane one I count on."

Her words filtered through the roar in his head and he stopped straining against Marcus, who held his shoulders from behind. "I'm sorry, Ellen. I'm sorry."

Flynn raised himself on an elbow and scooted back against the fallen recliner. "He thinks he's in love, El."

"Bryan?" She turned to him. "You are?"

Instead of answering he got to his feet, moved over to the couch, and sat.

Marcus said, "He's in love with my partner, the woman we're talking about. We have to find her. Flynn can point us in the right direction."

Ellen knelt beside her husband. "Flynn, help them!"

"She's a cop. What's he want with a cop?"

"Don't ask me. I've only loved one for thirty years."

He exhaled a heavy breath. "Do you know what you're asking?"

There was a long moment of silence as they stared at each other. Some unspoken communication passed between them.

Ellen touched her husband's arm. "You owe him, Flynn."

He gave her a half nod and turned. "Calloway stays here."

⌇

Bryan flew again through the night on his bike, this time behind his brother's shiny new Lexus. He didn't want to think about the money used to purchase such a vehicle.

Marcus hadn't been happy about his role as second fiddle. Flynn refused to budge until the detective agreed to stay put and wait for Bryan to call him. Helping them find Cara did not mean Flynn would incriminate his mob connection in front of a Chicago police detective. A priest in love was a different matter.

The man's house lay hidden behind a stone wall. Flynn had called ahead; security guards waved them through.

Inside the mansion, Bryan met the boss himself, a face he wanted to forget along with the address and ensuing conversation. He feared for his brother, knowing that he asked a favor which probably numbered his days as a reliable source of police information. It meant a loss of income. Bryan prayed it did not mean a loss of anything else for Flynn.

The meeting was brief and succinct. Ian Stafford had fallen out of favor some time ago. His so-called employees answered to this boss. This boss would make some phone calls. He left the room.

Within minutes he returned, whispered something to
Flynn, and raised a hand in farewell to Bryan. "Light a candle
for me, Father."

He nodded, and then they were ushered out the door.

"Flynn?" he said as they hurried across the wide driveway.

"Warehouse. Twenty minutes from here."

Bryan inhaled a lungful of cold clean air and breathed out
a prayer of thanks. *Lord, let her be safe.* He pulled his cell
phone from a pocket.

"Bry, forget Calloway."

"But we said—"

"Stafford's there with her now."

Lord, have mercy!

"And Calloway's just around the corner. Partners don't give
up that easy." Flynn slapped his shoulder. "Let's go."

Thirty-Nine

Ian Stafford loomed over Cara. Rage distorted his handsome features, twisting his full mouth and bulging his blue eyes. His neck veins were pronounced. Even his thick brown hair was affected, its waves hanging limp and stringy.

The scene of uncontrolled fury blurred as tears of pain filled Cara's eyes, a response to the backhand he had just swung across her face. She tasted blood in her mouth. Her cheek stung where the diamond ring on his little finger had cut.

As if unseen hands cupped her ears, his shriek of obscenities grew muffled.

Cara felt a sense of detachment, almost comfortable in its familiarity. She had been here before, helpless at the hands of an animal in human form.

She fought the desire to escape, to sink into that known oblivion. To do so was to give up. It was to agree with her accuser that yes, she deserved such treatment because she was, after all, only scum.

No! She knew better.

The scene was *not* the same as that one of so many years ago. She did not sit huddled and whimpering in acceptance. No. On the contrary, her surroundings were unknown. The bare, windowless room was bright with fluorescent ceiling lights. She sat on the sole piece of furniture, an old-fashioned wooden desk chair. Her wrists were bound to its arms with rope, her ankles tied together, her mouth taped shut. She wore a stylish black suit skirt and silk blouse. She stared at the barrel of a gun wielded mere inches from her face by a madman.

No, not the same scene at all.

And yet it was the same. The very same.

Jesus!

Suddenly the room felt crowded. Crowded with memories. There was Nick shouting, pummeling. There was her mother, self-absorbed in a drunken stupor. There was the nameless, faceless dad, walking away, as always his back toward her.

Forgive them. The thought was not hers.

I have.

Forgive them.

I have!

Forgive them.

I can't! I can't! I won't!

She wouldn't? How dare she. But how could she?

To forgive meant…recognize their sins committed against her…name the horror, without excuse for the people responsible…accept Christ's power to release them from the debt they owed her…and then look to Him to fill the hole in her heart. For there would be a hole once she relinquished her dependence on that fear which had always guided her decisions.

She had never truly forgiven those who should have loved her. She clung to their neglect and abuse, those things which instilled and fueled the fear. Did she want to die still harboring such ugliness?

She couldn't forgive them. But she could take the first step.

Lord, I forgive them. Give me the grace to forgive them. To release them to You. My mother, my father, my husband. Ian Stafford.

Stafford ripped the tape from her mouth, jerking her back into the present moment.

"Where is she?" he screamed.

"I don't know."

"How can you not know?" A fine spray of saliva glimmered in the bright light.

What can mere man do to me? Cara felt a corner of her mouth lift. The smile was not prompted by conscious thought. Something greater than herself was flowing into that hole, bringing with it a glorious sense of peace. What could mere man do?

"Face it, Ian. Jazzie wins, you lose."

He spun on his heel, shouting a tirade against womankind, and marched to the open doorway. There he yelled at the top of his lungs, "Hayes! Richter! Get in here!"

Hayes and Richter could have been the men who had picked her up at Water Tower Place and brought her to what appeared to be a warehouse. The size of the room she sat in suggested it had once been an office.

Stafford paused to take a breath.

In the brief interval she said in a clear voice, "Jesus loves you."

He cursed at her and yelled once more for his cohorts. There was no reply.

"He does."

Stafford stomped back across the room toward her. "I killed Rossi. I can kill you."

"And Jesus loves you."

"If you and Jazzie hadn't— I was a made man with them!"

She knew what he meant. His committing a murder was an initiation rite, allowing him into the inner circles of organized crime.

He whirled away from her. "Hayes! Richter!"

She heard the desperation in his voice. Her and Jazzie's actions had probably "unmade" him. The two women had signed the man's death warrant.

And that thought filled Cara with desperation. "Ian! He loves you!"

He spun around to face her. "Shut up!"

"That's why He came to earth."

Stafford raised the gun and pointed it at her. "I said shut up!"

"He died on the cross because He loves Ian Stafford."

A thunderous boom rocked the building.

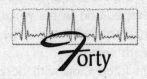

Forty

For one horrific eternal moment the warehouse hallway shuddered violently as one blast after another deafened Bryan.

He lay sprawled on the floor where Marcus had shoved him aside. He struggled to an upright position now in the agonizing slow motion of a nightmare. His legs felt mired in quicksand. Fifteen feet ahead, Marcus and Flynn disappeared inside the room from which they'd heard Cara's voice. Hers and that other one...that one from the pit of hell.

Lord, have mercy.

The acrid scent of fired gunpowder met him at the doorway. He took in the scene with a glance.

A black wig lay on the floor.

Near that, Flynn bent over a writhing, groaning figure. "Aw, can it, Stafford. You ain't begun to feel real pain yet."

To the right of them Marcus bent over a chair, hugging the person who sat in it.

Cara!

A faint voice reached his eardrums, still dulled by the gunshot blasts.

"I'm fine."

Cara! A living, breathing Cara!

Bryan touched Marcus's shoulder.

He turned, unshed tears shimmering. "She's fine."

"Move."

With a half smile and a quiet sniff, he did just that.

And then her eyes met his.

"Bryan?" Surprise widened her eyes and raised her voice.

"Cara, darling." He knelt beside her, wrapped his arms around her shoulders, and kissed her forehead.

"Bryan?"

His throat closed up, cutting off speech. Tears fell freely down his cheeks. *Thank You, Lord.*

"Bryan? Is it really you?"

Marcus said, "Her hands are turning blue. Here." He nudged Bryan's arm. "Cut that one loose while I get her feet."

Bryan took a pocket knife from him and sawed at the thin rope wrapped tightly around her wrist.

"Bryan." She touched his face.

"I'm here." He rubbed her other hand, the one he'd just freed. The area around her mouth was red. A jagged cut marred her cheek. A bruise was swelling. "It's really me."

"I saw an angel." Abruptly her eyes closed and she slumped over.

He caught her before she slid from the chair. "Cara!"

Marcus said, "I think she fainted." Chuckling, he helped Bryan ease her to the floor. "I never thought I'd see the day Cucumber Fleming wore designer clothes, but watching her faint sure beats all."

Bryan thanked God the man had seen such a day.

Forty-One

Cara sat on a gurney in a hallway, her back propped against its raised end, her legs stretched out before her. Bryan stood alongside. Feeling had returned to her hands, and she clutched his like one would a life preserver.

She felt herself fade in and out of awareness, almost as if she drifted between two distinct worlds. Though she was certain the men had drugged her, she did not think it explained what had happened as a frenetic Ian Stafford ranted and raved. During his tirade, she had stumbled into another place, one full of unspeakable brightness and peace. She didn't want to leave it.

Except when she looked at Bryan and saw his clear green eyes directed toward her, love unabashedly pouring from them. She wanted to stay wherever he was, even if that meant the shadowy land where paramedics hovered over her, cops milled about, and the echo of gunshots resounded in her head along with disjointed thoughts of the past 12 hours.

"Bryan, is Stafford okay?" Her voice sounded raspy.

He leaned over and kissed her cheek, the one that didn't sting. "Yes, he'll be fine. The other ambulance just took him away."

"Marcus shot him?"

"And Flynn did too." He glanced toward the end of the gurney. "In the arm. Superficial wounds."

She turned and saw Marcus standing just beyond those leather pumps still on her feet. "His arm?" she asked him in disbelief. "The guy has a gun to my head and you take the time to aim for his arm?"

He grinned. "Nice to have you back among the living, Cucumber. That's the third time you asked Bryan about Stafford but the first time you chewed me out."

The third time?

Marcus said, "Hey, you know we couldn't waste him. You, on the other hand, are expendable, but we need him to name names. He kept yelling for Hayes and Richter, but there was no one else in the building when we arrived. I think his boss warned them we were coming. Stafford has been left out in the cold. He'll be begging to talk to us." He patted her ankle where the stocking was mangled from the rope. "By the way, you're welcome. It was no trouble at all saving your life. Glad to do it."

His hint sank in. "Thank you."

"Flynn here found you and helped put Stafford out of commission."

She looked beyond Marcus and saw a shorter, older version of Bryan, at least physically in his build and red hair. Unlike Bryan though, he glowered. A darkness emanated from him. She didn't let her gaze linger. "Thank you."

"Anything for my brother." He walked away.

"Ma'am."

She turned toward the voice. It belonged to a paramedic, a young guy fussing at her other side with a blood pressure cuff.

"Can you tell me your name?"

"Cara Fleming."

"And where are you, Cara?"

"On a gurney in a building I've never been in before." She eyed his watch. "And it's about one-fifty in the morning."

Another medic, standing behind her, dabbed at her cheek with something that smelled of antiseptic. After a moment the cut's sting lessened. A cold pack was pressed against her cheekbone.

The first guy wasn't finished with his list of questions. "How did you get here?"

Inwardly she sighed, wishing they could skip the formalities. She thought of her friend Terri, who once told her cops made some of the worst patients. They always had a better idea. "Do you know Terri Schuman?"

"No."

"She's a paramedic too. Oh, her last name is Andrews now. She's a newlywed. Married a firefighter."

Bryan said, "Cara."

She turned her head. Such concern on his face and in his hushed voice. And it was all for her.

"How did you get here, darling?"

And that! That word of endearment. She'd never been called— "Ouch!" She swiveled her head to the medic again. A needle was in her arm, and he was attaching an IV tube to it. "I only *almost* got shot. I'm fine."

"You're dehydrated, Cara. Now." He laid his gloved hand on her arm and looked straight into her eyes. "How did you get here?"

Bryan squeezed her hand.

Marcus rubbed her ankle.

There was no avoiding an answer.

"I don't know," she whispered.

She sensed exchanged glances, murmured words, a shuffling of positions. Someone slipped off her shoes. A blanket was placed over her. A needle stuck her other arm. They would be taking blood now. Through it all Bryan's hand remained firm around hers.

She sought his face and found him slightly farther down the gurney, still focused on her. He would be praying.

Marcus spoke. "Cara, what do you remember?"

She turned. He had replaced the first medic at her side. "Water Tower Place. They shot Evan." Her voice caught.

"He's going to be fine." Marcus caught the tear seeping from the corner of her eye with his little finger.

She remembered her partner hugging her. Waking the man's emotional side had taken extreme measures. She hoped it would stick around long enough for Renae to witness.

He went on. "I talked to him after his surgery. He was madder than a hornet at you, but pretty impressed you ditched him." He paused. "How did they find you?"

She tried to explain what happened, how she had been drawn inexplicably to the scene, how her presence caught their attention, how they threatened her. "I had no choice but to get into the car."

He nodded.

"Then...they must have given me something. I don't remember the ride or arriving here."

The pressure in her left arm stopped. Bryan moved nearer again and smoothed her hair from her forehead.

Marcus said, "What do you think?"

"Rohypnol." A sedative ten times stronger than Valium.

He nodded in agreement. "It would wipe out your short-term memory."

"I do remember becoming aware. If this is still Monday, or rather Tuesday morning, I don't think they gave me much. It would have been just for the ride here, to keep me coop-erative. Anyway, I came to in another room, not the one

where…" Where Ian screamed and she forgave Nick and her
parents and felt, at long last, peace. Where Marcus hugged her
and Bryan arrived, the sight of him very nearly as glorious as
that of the angel.

"Did they hurt you?"

"No. I mean there was no evidence." She touched the collar
of her silk blouse. "My nice new suit wasn't even wrinkled. By
the way, where's the jacket?"

Marcus smiled and straightened the IV tube as she lowered
her arm. "Close by. What was the other room like?"

"There was a couch, a lamp, and a washroom. I was comfortable enough, I guess, considering the circumstances. I
found my raincoat. I'd put your gun in its pocket. Thank you
for that."

He nodded. "I thought it might come in handy."

"It didn't, but it made all the difference, Marcus. It said
you hadn't deserted me."

"I've been investigating people on the inside." His voice
had grown husky. "I'm sorry. I couldn't let on I trusted you."
He blinked a few times. "I suppose the gun was gone?"

"And the door locked. It was about midnight. I must have
dozed. Then those two guys came in some time later."

"Hayes and Richter?"

"That's my guess."

"Can you describe them?"

She hesitated. "Yes."

Understanding flickered in her partner's eyes. The fact they
had allowed her to see them meant she hadn't been expected
to walk out of the building alive.

"They said Stafford wanted to talk to me. They took me to
the other room and…and tied me in the chair." The horror of
the moment sent a chill down her spine.

Marcus made a noise of disgust. "What a chicken! He had a gun and two thugs and couldn't handle one unarmed woman." His quirky humor defused the memory, and gratitude for his friendship chased off her fear.

"Oh," she said with nonchalance, "I just figured my reputation must have preceded me."

Marcus and Bryan laughed.

She smiled. "And then you guys arrived. My knights. End of story. Now I want to go home."

The medic said over Bryan's shoulder, "Excuse me, ma'am, but we want to transport you to the hospital."

"I'm fine. You know that drug flushes right out of your system in no time. After twelve hours or so, I'm sure it's gone."

"There are possible side effects that linger."

"I'm just tired. I promise not to do anything but sleep."

Marcus touched her shoulder. "Go to the hospital. Let them check you over thoroughly."

"I'm fine."

"Fleming!" Frustration laced his voice. "Why don't you simply cooperate? Besides, where is home for you these days anyway, huh? Galena? Dubuque? Miriam House? The priest told me what you've been up to."

She turned to Bryan and found the smile she knew would be there for her. Grinning back at him she said, "Don't worry about it, Calloway. Everything is under control."

～

Outside the warehouse, Cara walked through the parking lot leaning heavily on Bryan's arm. The crisp 4 A.M. air heightened the giddiness she began to notice after he called her "darling." She didn't think it was the drug. Why should she feel giddy? She was alive and Bryan O'Shaugnessy loved her.

In any case she wasn't about to tell the medics she felt as though she were zipping around on a carousel. She had convinced them she was all rehydrated and well enough to go home. Terri would throw a fit when she heard.

Bryan's motorcycle came into view, and she laughed. "This is your white steed?"

"Afraid so." He chuckled.

"Fleming!" Marcus called from behind. "No way! Uh-uh! You are not riding that thing. Not with him! He's a wild man on two wheels!"

Bryan lowered his face to hers. "Your partner's getting a little overprotective, wouldn't you say?"

"Definitely. Can you lose him?"

"Probably not."

"I can. Let me drive."

"I don't think so."

"I know how."

"I'm sure you do. However, there are two things I'm extra particular about."

"Your bike and...?"

"Pie. The crust has to be made from scratch." He kissed her forehead. "Maybe you should ride with him."

"No way. I'll hold on tight."

"I'll go slow."

"Cara!" Marcus had caught up to them. "I'll take you. You'll be more comfortable, not to mention you'll get there in one piece. Wherever there is. Hey, buster." He stepped between Bryan and the cycle. "Where do you get off thinking you're in charge? I'm her partner."

Bryan moved closer and drew himself to his full height, forcing Marcus to lift his chin in order to look him in the face.

"You're her *ex*-partner and I'm her boyfriend."

Marcus brushed past him. "Cara, please."

"Oh, turn around, Calloway." She gathered the long coat about her and hiked up her skirt as Bryan mounted the bike.

Marcus groaned, but spun on his heel. "You know what my worst nightmare is, don't you? Telling Granny you've been hurt."

Laughing, she propped her foot on the runner, steadied herself against Bryan's shoulder, and swung her leg up and across the seat. He started the engine. Its roar drowned out Marcus's protests.

She slipped her arms around Bryan's waist.

He looked back at her, a pair of clear wire-rimmed glasses in place. "All set?"

"All set."

With the ease of an experienced cyclist at the helm, the bike zipped smoothly across the parking lot. Cara squealed in delight at the sudden onrush of cold air and the flittering sensation in her stomach. Total freedom seemed within her grasp as it had when, as a child, she twirled on a merry-go-round or soared on a swing.

At the street, he braked and waited for Marcus to catch up. She buried her face in Bryan's back.

Lord, let this ride last forever.

*F*orty-*T*wo

The hour neared dawn. Though less than 30 miles separated her from the warehouse, Cara felt transported as far away as Pluto. She sat on a large comfortable bed in the rectory, Bryan's home. Like some fairy tale princess, she wore a frilly high-necked flannel nightgown. A puffy down comforter and stack of pillows surrounded her.

She drained a glass of milk, the last of a breakfast of scrambled eggs and toast, and smiled at Mrs. G, who sat on a chair across the room. "Thank you. I didn't think I was hungry."

"You're welcome." She returned the smile, concern still evident in her vigilant gaze.

Bryan had cooked the meal, but Mrs. G arrived in time to serve it to her on a tray in the master bedroom. She had also provided the nightie and a robe, welcome apparel after Cara's long soak in the bathtub. The woman's TLC added to the royal ambience.

Cara glanced around the sizeable room. It held a double chest of drawers as well as two armchairs and lamp table. Curtains were drawn across three sets of windows. Bryan had told her he didn't use the room. "Mrs. G, why doesn't he use his own master bedroom and bath?"

She shook her head. Despite the early hour, she wore a neatly pressed long-sleeved denim dress; her gray hair was

356

pinned in its tight bun. "You've probably noticed Father is conservative to the core. He says what would he need with all this space when he's got two studies and an entire church building? He thinks it serves best as a guest room."

"It's wonderful, complete with bubble bath and shampoo." She winked. "You do take excellent care of him and his guests. I can't believe he called you at four-thirty in the morning."

"Well, he does try to do most everything by himself, but when it comes to matters that need a woman's touch, he knows to call me. Else I nag him worse than his own mother." She walked to the bed and lifted the tray from Cara's lap. "You should sleep. I need to talk your partner into using another guest room instead of the living room. He looks as dead on his feet as you and Father."

Marcus had insisted on staying in the house. His uncharacteristic display of concern hadn't abated; he declared himself The Bodyguard until further notice. Not that she minded. Feeling atypically vulnerable, she welcomed his presence almost as much as Bryan's.

"Mrs. G, would you ask Bryan to come up?"

The woman hesitated in the doorway and balanced the tray on her hip.

"I know you must think it's inappropriate, but..." She bit her lip and blinked back tears. *But I can't help it. I need him like a drug addict needs a fix.*

"Cara, I'm not the one who thinks it inappropriate. Father told me you almost got killed tonight. In my opinion what you need is for him to crawl right in there with you and hold you in his big strong arms until that memory is long gone."

Cara's eyes widened in surprise. And she had thought Mrs. G stern!

"No, I'm not the prude in this house."

Cara remembered Bryan offering at the Galena condominium to go to a motel. Except for the night he kissed her, he had kept his distance, even in the kitchen. And he hadn't set foot upstairs where their rooms were.

"But," Mrs. G continued, "I suppose if word ever got out that he was holding you in the bed, some parishioners would be appalled, even though they know he has been above reproach all these years and would do nothing to disgrace his position anyway. I'll send him up, hon."

"Just to talk. You don't need to tell him your opinion."

Mrs. G smiled. "I might though. The man could do with some loosening up. Sleep well."

~

Once inside the rectory, Cara had felt her exhilaration take a nosedive. Adrenaline had run its course, allowing reality to set in. She knew enough about posttraumatic stress disorder to realize her life would never be the same. It would always be colored with the night's events. Time would be referred to as before or after "it" happened. Odd things would occur, such as needing desperately to see the man who loved her. Exhausted as she was, sleep would not come without Bryan O'Shaugnessy in plain sight. Her Bryan fix. She hoped the condition was temporary.

He knocked on the open door and walked inside. "Hi."

She feasted her eyes on him: his wild paprika red curls; his lumberjack arms and shoulders covered in the humble black shirt of his life's calling; the big, lightly freckled hands. "Hi. Breakfast was great. Thank you."

"Mm-hmm. You okay?"

"No."

He smiled. "Stupid question. What can I do for you, darling?"

The word melted her hesitancy. "I really truly hate feeling vulnerable."

"I think I knew that." His smile widened. "But under the circumstances, it's a totally acceptable emotion."

"Then." She took a deep breath. "Will you stay with me?"

"I'm not going anywhere."

"I mean right here next to me in this room. Until I'm ready to sleep? I still feel kind of wound up."

"Of course." He gazed at her. "Where did my rough-and-tumble cop friend go?"

"I left her in a dressing room at Lord and Taylor. I think I'll leave her there."

"Well, her courage is still in place." He carried one of the armchairs over to the bed.

"Courage? I'm shaking like a leaf and can't go to sleep without somebody standing guard. Make that two somebodies, one upstairs and one down."

He sat on the chair and hunched forward.

To within arm's reach. She held her hand out to him, and he clasped it. His touch sent a tidal wave of warmth through her, filling the cold, empty spaces.

"Well," he said, "what would you call telling the man about to kill you that Jesus loves him if not courage?"

"That was forgiveness talking. You know how they say your life flashes before your eyes? What flashed before mine was unfinished business. Things like forgiving my parents and Nick. Oh, Bryan, I finally asked God to forgive them and to help me to forgive them. I added Ian Stafford to the list too. How could I not at that point?"

He smiled, leaned over, and kissed her cheek. "Amen."

"That's when I saw the angel."

A startled expression crossed his face.

"Hey, you had your strange moment when you saw me all bright while I was serving mashed potatoes. I can have mine."

He laughed. "But they drugged you."

"Not with an hallucinogen!"

"Okay." He pressed his lips together and his eyes crinkled shut.

"Bryan, please listen. There's no one else I can tell."

Her words must have hit him as they did herself because he sobered and a silence engulfed the room, a silence full of meaning. They had each other and no one else in quite the same way. Nothing in the world could change those facts.

He said, "And what did this angel look like?" There was no mockery in his tone.

"He was huge. Enormous. I couldn't even see his face. He filled the room and above. I didn't hear him, but it was like he gave me the words to say to Ian."

"Jesus loves you."

"Yes."

"You're incredible."

She shook her head and began to wonder if she could fall asleep with him nearby. He unnerved her with a glance. That said nothing of the effect of his unflinching attention.

"Actually, Bryan, I was just setting the stage for you. Some man needs to visit Ian and tell him again and explain it all."

"Hmm. I'd have to forgive him before I do that."

"Yeah. Right." She smiled. "That's a given."

"I'm not quite ready."

"Father O'Shaugnessy! I am sorely disappointed."

"You'll get over it." His tone was serious.

"You're not teasing."

He touched his chest. "Beneath the clothes I am just a man who nearly lost the woman he loves because of that criminal. Ask me tomorrow."

She realized then how disturbed he was. "What exactly happened tonight? How did you find me?"

"Ask me that tomorrow too. It's a long story, and you need to sleep." He stood, leaned over, and placed a finger under her chin. "I do love you, Cara." He kissed her softly. "Sweet dreams. I'll be right here."

As he sat back down, she slid under the covers, her being saturated with a sense of completeness for which there were no words.

A life-threatening experience. An angel. A knight in shining armor disguised as a priest. What else was there?

One thing.

She turned on her side and slid a hand out from under the blanket, palm up on the sheet. Bryan placed his over it.

She closed her eyes.

Forty-Three

Bryan settled back in the chair, close enough to the bed to comfortably hold Cara's hand. Her arm was the only part of her—except for her face—not covered with the big comforter. Once she'd turned sideways to face him, she had fallen asleep within seconds.

Dawn brightened the curtains. He should get up and turn off the lamp at the other end of the room, but he didn't want to chance disrupting her sleep. Earlier he had shared a pot of coffee with Marcus; he would be awake for a while. He was concerned she would have nightmares or wake up, see no one, and panic. He didn't want to let that happen.

Nor did he want to let go of the week's events just yet. They all pointed him to one thing: He wanted to marry her. If he had asked her now, before she fell asleep, he suspected she would have said yes, answering from a place of great vulnerability. It would not have been fair of him. But if he waited until she returned to her independent self, what then? He fought down his own panic.

And he reminded himself he could not add a single cubit to his life's span by worrying, let alone change a woman's mind.

Lord, have mercy.

As if in silent agreement that Cara should not be left alone, everyone took a turn to sit in her bedroom. Once convinced she was in a deep sleep, Bryan handed the reins over to Mrs. G and slipped away to sleep the remainder of the morning in his own room. His sister Meagan relieved her; Rubyann Calloway spent the evening beside her "granddaughter."

While Bryan felt time hung in suspension, the women rallied to bring normalcy to the situation. To their chagrin, Marcus dozed in the living room, his gun holster clearly visible as he sprawled in the recliner. They covered him with an afghan. Rubyann and Mrs. G joined forces and cooked up a storm in the kitchen. Meagan left for a while, returning with a bagful of new personal items and a car packed with a secondhand wardrobe donated by her friends, all for the homeless detective asleep in his guest room.

The police chief, Stuart Templeton, overrode Mrs. G's objections and looked in on Cara. Evidently satisfied with what he saw, he held a private meeting with Marcus in his car out of earshot. Bryan ate a plateful of food Rubyann set before him and did not ask questions. The less he knew about police affairs, the better.

Except for his brother's. He would call him later. After Cara woke up.

At 11 P.M. he sent Mrs. G off to bed and took up the vigil again, wondering at how deep Cara's exhaustion must have been to cause her to sleep for so long.

He drifted off to sleep in the chair and awoke some time later when Marcus entered the room.

The detective handed him the cordless phone he hadn't heard ring. "Says his name's Ray." He left the room.

"Hello." Bryan spoke softly. "Ray?"

"Hey, Padre. Sorry for the late hour."

He glanced at the bedside clock and saw it was near midnight.

"But I just found him. Thought you'd want to know ASAP."

A surge of adrenaline hit his senses—the north wind rattled a windowpane, the room felt cool, a faint scent of fabric softener rose from his sweatshirt, a small night-light cast a halo around itself, the acid taste of fear coated his tongue—but his mind shut down. "Found...him?"

"Hello-o. I found Nick Davis."

Christ, have mercy.

Twenty-four hours after she had fallen asleep, Cara said, "Bryan?"

He put his coffee mug on the nightstand and leaned toward her. In the predawn grayness he saw that her eyes weren't open. As he watched they fluttered until she was looking at him through slits. He said, "Morning, darling."

She smiled. "It wasn't a dream. You really are there." She yawned. "Calling me darling."

"No, it's not a dream."

"I suppose that means nothing else is either?" Her eyes were fully wide now, the smile diminished.

"Afraid not, but it's a brand-new day. Would you like some coffee before you face it?"

"I'd love some coffee. Meet you in the kitchen?"

He nodded and left to brew a fresh pot. The rest of the household slept. Rubyann and Mrs. G had both stayed overnight, occupying the other two spare bedrooms. Marcus had made a bold move from the chair to the couch.

A short time later Cara entered the kitchen as the last of the coffee dripped into the carafe. The first ray of dawn flashed through the window and glowed on her, highlighting a rosy, just-scrubbed face. The cut on her cheek was less pronounced, the purple bruise above it a shade darker. Her hair was brushed back into a ponytail. She wore blue jeans, a red sweatshirt, and a shy smile.

Bryan thought his heart would break at the sight. How had this woman come into his life? Did he dare hope she would stay?

She said, "Did I just pass Marcus snoring on the couch?"

He laughed and handed her a mug. "He's your new self-appointed bodyguard."

"I'll have to dock his pay." She gestured at her clothes. "Where did all this come from? And the personal stuff in the bath? It looks like a group of elves have been at work."

"Just Meagan. A few of her friends donated the clothes. She's quite a bit shorter than you."

"I haven't even met your sister." Her eyes watered. "When did she— Goodness, how long have I been asleep?"

"A day and a night. Twenty-four hours."

"Really? I wondered why it was getting lighter instead of darker. It's morning! And you were still in my room?"

"Not the entire time. I tried, but Mrs. G and Meagan and Rubyann kicked me out."

"They're all here? And Marcus?"

"Mm-hmm. You had some visitors too. I asked TJ, my doctor friend, to come. I wanted another opinion on that drug. Helen stopped in."

"Helen Rafferty? How did she know—"

"That story will have to wait. Your chief came first thing."

"Templeton?" Surprise kept her voice pitched high.

"Yes. Mrs. G almost didn't allow him in, but he insisted he needed to see you with his own eyes to make sure you were all right. She gave him ten seconds. And I met Renae; she brought some things for Marcus and took a turn with the other women keeping you company through the day. I had the night shift."

She wiped the corner of her eye. "Wow. All those people." She put the mug to her mouth. And promptly burst into tears.

Bryan caught the wobbling cup and set it on the countertop while pulling her into his arms.

He had wondered how long before she would let everything go. Even as her sobs wrenched at his heart, he thanked God for the timing. Pure selfishness or whatever it was called, he had wanted to be the one to comfort her. Perhaps it was just what boyfriends did.

Lord, have mercy.

Forty-Four

Kindness, of course, was the straw that broke the camel's back. Kindness the Ice Lady would have refused if awake.

Cara figured the tears represented 38 years' worth of sadness. They soaked Bryan's sweatshirt and scraped her throat raw. She didn't struggle against them. To contain them would mean burying the pain again and waiting for a candlelit bath to let a few tears seep. The practice had worked like a valve releasing just enough steam to keep her from popping. For a time it had been enough. Until Bryan...

At last she raised her head. Bryan was a blur, but she saw tracks of his own tears...and a smile. He reached for a box of tissues on the counter and handed her one.

"Thanks."

"Mm-hmm." He sniffed and pressed a tissue to his own eyes. "You are an interesting woman, Cara Fleming. An hour after almost getting killed, you laugh and shout like a banshee on the back of my motorcycle. Now you hear about people showing concern and you fall apart."

"I've never..." She shrugged and took a deep breath. "Had anyone watch over me. No one." *As in my mother.* "Not ever." *As in when I was little.* "Or show such care. I don't expect it. I don't think I've ever truly trusted anyone."

"That's a natural response. You've been so wounded, you had to keep running away from people, afraid to trust and let them love you. God will take all those places that used to be filled with pain and fill them up with Himself. He'll use others to help."

She wadded the tissue in her fist. "How do you know?"

"I've been there."

She saw, then, the careworn signs on the gentle face bristly with unshaven whiskers. Crows' feet and creases in his cheeks spoke of battles fought. The ever-present green sparkle declared them won.

He grinned. "I guess God just needed to get you into my life so I could be the one to show you a more excellent way."

She heard his teasing tone. "I see. And why exactly were you the chosen one for this work?"

"Because He knew *I* needed *you*. I've been a little deaf myself." Bryan smoothed hair back from her damp cheek. "Are you hungry? I'll fix breakfast."

She smiled at how he kept her off balance by changing subjects. Still enthralled with his touch on her face and his gentle counsel, she felt no need whatsoever, even for food.

He said, "Rubyann made cinnamon rolls yesterday. I'm surprised that smell alone didn't wake you. She put some aside before Marcus polished off the batch. And I saw Mrs. G's famous egg-and-spinach casserole in the fridge."

She knew Rubyann's rolls. She had sampled Mrs. G's cooking. On second thought... "Let's eat."

❧

They sat at the kitchen table and ate breakfast. Much as Cara longed to hug Rubyann and thank everyone else, she

Moment of Truth369

was in no hurry to shorten her exclusive time with Bryan. The future was a black shadow, the past two weeks a tangled mess, both undecipherable. Only the present moment made sense.

He reached across the table and touched her wrist. "How are you?"

"Stronger. The food helps. Granny and Mrs. G have got to be two of the best cooks in the world."

Her answer didn't erase the worry on his face. "You're kind of fading in and out on me."

"I was just thinking of all the unanswered questions. And how I'd rather not think of them."

"You don't have to think about them yet. There's no need to rush yourself. When you're ready, I'm here as well as Marcus to help answer them."

"It's not like me to play ostrich."

"I'm sure that's a temporary condition."

Smiling, she shrugged and cut another bite of the egg casserole with her fork.

"What?"

"I almost hope it's not temporary."

The sparkle returned to his eyes. "Aw, but I'd miss my rough-and-tumble cop friend."

"What if a rough-and-tumble social worker friend took her place?"

He grinned. "Would she miss chasing the bad guys?"

"Not a chance."

"No problem then." He picked up his coffee mug. "Did the ostrich just pull her head out of the sand?"

She squished a piece of egg casserole with her fork, fighting back the memory.

"Cara, we can save this. We can talk another time."

We. His choice of pronoun created an instant hedge around her, insulating her as securely as that hole in the sand. She was safe.

"No." She looked at him. "I should probably let the memories come when they're ready, not when I think I'm ready. Oh, Bryan! Are you sure you want to be part of this?"

"Of what?"

"Of me. My baggage."

"We all have baggage. The real you is not baggage." He stretched his hand across the table. "Yes, I'm sure I want to be part of this."

She laid her hand in his. No need to ask him why. He wore love like a neon sign. "Okay."

"Okay."

With his fingers wrapped around her hand, she dove into the jumbled past 72 hours and found the moment that made sense. "It happened at the Water Tower Place. The split second I sensed something dreadful happened to Evan Vogel, I knew I was done being a cop. Just like that, blink of an eye."

"Do you know why?"

She shook her head. "All I know is the ice is gone. I don't think it's coming back, else I would have used Marcus's gun or tried to talk Stafford out of shooting me. I would not have sat there and given him the gospel. I'm done. My heart is at Phoebe's Place and Miriam House and your St. James's shelter-to-be. It's with Polly and Ruthie and others like them."

"This is a major decision."

"The real major decision is it means I want to stay in Chicago."

His eyes closed briefly and his shoulders sagged.

An old familiar fear stabbed her. "But—"

Bryan squeezed her hand. "But nothing."

"I was leaving. I had my new disguise and money. I was on my way to the train station. I was going to Florida." She rushed her words together, trying in her own power to run from that fear biting at her heels like a rabid dog. "I didn't want to. I don't want to. But I don't see how I can stay—"

"Cara! He's dead."

"What?"

"He's dead. Nick is dead."

She felt as though her mind hit a time warp. Bryan's words jumped from the future into the past, skipping the present. They made no sense.

"You don't have to run anymore. You don't have to be afraid anymore. Ray tracked him down. Ray, the private investigator. He called last night. It's okay, darling. It's over." Bryan went around the table and moved her chair so she faced him. He knelt and took both her hands in his. "It's all over."

The initial shock filtered away. A mixture of relief and sadness pushed breath back into her lungs. "When?"

Bryan kissed her hands. "Six months ago. In Denver."

She stiffened. He had been moving east, following her trail—

"Cara." Bryan squeezed her hands. "It's over."

She stared at him, at the tenderness on his wide face, at the halo of red curls, the promise of peace that shone through his clear green eyes.

Yes, it was indeed over.

⌒

Try as she might, Cara was unable to connect again with the ostrich. The news about Nick and the unfolding day required all her attention.

Hugs were exchanged, even with Marcus and Mrs. G, two of the most reserved people she'd ever met. Meagan, a delightful spitfire version of Bryan, hugged her before being introduced. Cara whispered to Rubyann what happened to Nick; the little woman somberly squeezed her for a long time. The three women spent the morning showering her with attention, complete with an endless list of ideas of where she could live. They all offered her a room and schedules for apartment hunting.

She was grateful when Chief Stuart Templeton appeared; he insisted on speaking to her alone.

Bryan ushered them into his study. Twenty minutes later the chief broke all pattern of character and gave her a bear hug. He left with a nod, a smile of satisfaction on his face.

She sank back onto the couch, folded her legs beneath herself, and tucked an afghan tightly around them, chilled to the bone. Her head spun with all the information she hadn't begun to even guess at earlier.

The chief had checked with the Denver police and corroborated Ray's story. Bryan's private investigator learned that Nick Davis had been beaten to death. Identifying the body took months. No one was arrested for the crime.

Evidence indicated that Hugh Acton, an assistant to the chief, was the culprit in leaking the story about her to the newspaper. His nephew Danny Delaney, an officer who sometimes worked with Cara and Marcus, was the missing link in a flow of information streaming out to Flynn O'Shaugnessy and others. Stu said "the priest" would explain that connection.

And the fire at her apartment? Delaney. Her Glock 22 was found in his home. The search warrant was issued after he bragged to Marcus how he broke into her apartment and planted an incendiary which he set off remotely.

He bragged to *Marcus?*

Her partner had suspected Acton. He spent weeks talking behind her back, getting close to him. Delaney as well as Acton assumed Marcus sided with them against her and what they called her "antics." Acton even hinted Cara would be exposed. That was when Marcus called to warn Helen. Not until after the fire did her partner learn of Delaney's role. By then she had disappeared.

That explained Marcus's changed behavior toward her on the phone and in the office. He was keeping up an appearance.

What did the others have against her? Stu said it was pure jealousy.

He invited her back on the force. Considering how she had gained "hands-off" status with the underworld, he could find a place for her. He wouldn't push her luck though; he'd move her from organized crime into a different area.

She searched her heart for a long moment. No ice. No way. She politely declined his offer.

Bryan and Marcus joined Cara in the study, a comfortable room with two walls of old-fashioned paneling and two of bookshelves. It was full of rich wood and leather scents. Still huddled on the couch in an afghan, she listened as they described the events leading up to their appearance at the warehouse two nights ago.

Her partner stretched out on a worn leather armchair, his head back, his legs across the matching ottoman. Atypically he wore blue jeans and a rumpled sweater. Renae must have delivered those clothes. Cara could hear her admonition through them, "Chill out!" He always carried his electric razor with him so his jaw was smooth though decidedly haggard. He looked as if he'd been up for at least 48 hours which, as far as she knew, was close to the truth.

Bryan too had shaved. Changed into his black clothes and white collar, he appeared fresh and energized at the opposite end of the couch from her.

At last their story caught up with what she knew. "So you left Miriam House, leaving poor Helen alone. But she knows we're okay, right? You said she came over yesterday."

Bryan nodded. "I called her from the warehouse. I had some time on my hands when the paramedics shoved me out of the way so they could get at you. Which reminds me, somebody else shoved me out of the way that night." He looked pointedly at Marcus. "Shoved me flat out on the floor."

Marcus shrugged. "Couldn't have the religious help getting shot. Who'd give the last rites? Which reminds *me*, you wouldn't have been in the way if you'd called like you promised instead of charging on ahead and arriving before I did."

"That you'll have to take up with my brother."

His brother, Cara thought. The unlikely key to their success in tracking her down. The story Stu had not completed.

She interrupted their bantering. "Bryan, why did he do it?"

He turned to her, his smile fading. "What?"

"Why did Flynn..." The enormity of what he'd done struck her. "He took you to the big guy's house?"

"Yes."

"And simply asked him where I was?"

"Yes."

"And this head honcho gave Flynn the go-ahead to save a *cop?*"

"Yes. As you suspected earlier, Stafford was quickly losing status with his employers. He wasn't very smart about his activities. Jazzie's information sealed his fate."

"But Flynn— My gosh! They don't let people do that sort of thing. If he's a source for them, how can they trust him now? I can testify against Stafford. I can identify Mutt and Jeff."

"Hayes and Richter," Marcus corrected. "You know those two are halfway to Timbuktu by now. They'll just relocate for a while. Stafford, nobody cares about. And yes, Flynn took a risk exposing himself to them and to us." He paused, flitting his eyes toward Bryan. "He gave Templeton his resignation yesterday. With you safe and sound and Stafford in custody, charges may not be filed against him."

Speechless, Cara widened her eyes in disbelief at what yet another stranger had done for her. "But what about the other guys?"

Bryan said, "Flynn told me he'll be all right. They owed him a favor. Now they're even. Who knows? Maybe he'll try honest work for a change."

"But why?" she asked. "Why would he do it?"

Her partner laughed. "Fleming, they're brothers. Why wouldn't he? Good grief. Anyone paying any attention can figure out Bryan has the hots for you. Pardon my French. How could Flynn turn his back and allow you to die?"

She saw Bryan shift uncomfortably, enough to confirm her hunch. "Because," she said, "I have the feeling they don't exactly get along. And Flynn's not too crazy about female cops. If they get in trouble, it's their own stinking fault; they should pay the consequences."

Bryan met her gaze. "Sometimes life revolves around favors."

"He owed you?"

He nodded.

She closed her mouth before asking why. It really was none of her business. Except for the fact her life had been saved because of it. "Do you mind talking about it? I mean, the guy risked his life and saved mine. I'm a little curious."

He looked at Marcus. "It won't leave this room?"

Marcus shook his head.

Bryan did not continue immediately. His eyes seemed inwardly focused. At last he said, "You may have noticed we look alike. As kids we were often mistaken for twins. He's a few years older. I was still in high school when he went to a community college. He needed his associate's degree in order to enter the police academy. One night, on a lark, he committed armed robbery." He held out a hand and dropped it in his lap, a gesture of incomprehension. "The cops showed up at our house. It was the only time I saw Flynn truly afraid. We both knew it would kill our dad if he didn't get into the academy. But first Dad would kill Flynn." He shook his head. "I loved my big brother. I was the one always in trouble. Not for armed robbery, but Dad suspected I'd work my way up to that. No big deal. I took the rap and saved the family. With Dad's connections, I spent only a few months in a home. Flynn became a cop. And we never spoke of it again."

Marcus said, "Until two nights ago."

"Right."

Cara said, "The juvie files you told me about."

He nodded. "I've held it against him all these years."

She tossed aside the afghan, scooted on her knees to the cushion beside him, and put her arms on his shoulders. "Oh, Bryan. God does work all things out for our good."

He cocked his head, questioning, and slipped his hands around her waist.

"You sacrificed your life for your brother's. If you hadn't, I might not be here today."

"I suppose now you think I should forgive him as well as Stafford?"

She smiled.

Behind her Marcus cleared his throat. "Are you two about done?"

Bryan replied, "No, we're not, Marcus. Why don't you find something else to do? Preferably somewhere else. And shut the door, please."

Her partner moved noisily out of his chair and grumbled. "All I've got to say is it's a good thing you didn't have a boyfriend before, Fleming. We never would have accomplished a dadburn thing."

She heard the door open and shut.

His eyes at half-mast, his lips centimeters from hers, Bryan murmured, "It's Grand Central Station out there."

"I noticed."

"We've got exactly three minutes before someone comes in to check on our damsel in distress. I'd rather not use those three minutes talking."

"Hmm. What did you have in mind?"

His lips against hers sent those shivers of delight racing again. The earlier chill melted in their heat.

He pulled back. "Florida? Why were you going to Florida?"

She grinned. "You told me your parents live there. I planned to find them, move into the neighborhood, and wait for you to visit."

Bryan wasted their entire three minutes laughing.

Forty-Five

Two weeks later, the day after Thanksgiving, Cara placed a butter dish on the dining table, which had been set for 16 by Mrs. G. It was an elegant picture, worthy of a magazine cover. The white bone china with silver trim and Waterford goblets were the dishes Bryan shied away from using. Silverware glistened atop the white linen tablecloth and napkins. Tall silver candlesticks graced each side of an autumn floral arrangement Marcus and Renae had brought with them.

She circled the table slowly, reading the names printed neatly on tiny cards at each place setting. Most of the guests had pitched in the previous day, serving a turkey dinner at a community soup kitchen. Now they had come together to celebrate the holiday. Marcus, Renae, Rubyann, Terri, Gabe, Flynn, Ellen, Helen, Meagan, her husband and two children, Mrs. G, and Roger the custodian. Only Jazzie was missing.

As she did at least once a day, she breathed a prayer for her friend. The coded personal ad had been running in the *New York Times* for two Sundays now. She hoped Jazzie had seen it.

Where was her own place card? She reached the other end of the table.

No, she thought. Not there. Not on an end, opposite the head where Bryan would sit. Mrs. G deserved that place of honor.

She went out into the entryway and saw Bryan in the living room where he stood between Gabe and Marcus. Everyone was dressed up for the occasion. Bryan wore a black jacket over his black shirt. He looked more handsome and healthier than when they had first met. Convinced it wasn't only love that kept his blood pressure down, he still followed his new diet, delegated some parish matters to others, and played racquetball regularly.

She motioned to him. As he excused himself, she smiled. The intimacy they shared which allowed her to crook a finger and fully expect his response was almost too delicious. Did love hit harder the older one was, after so many empty years?

He smiled at her. "What?"

She tilted her head and, of course, he followed. In the dining room she whispered, "I need to switch. Mrs. G has me at the end here. It should be her position. She's the hostess. Okay with you? I don't want to ruin her order or anything."

In a normal pitch he said, "It was my idea. I wanted you to try it out. Here." He pulled the chair away from the table. "Sit down. See what you think."

She sat. His suggestion was like that crooking of her finger. "But, Bryan, I don't—"

"Shh." He went to the other end and sat down. "Just sit for a moment."

They looked at one another down the length of the long formal table.

She held out her hands in a hopeless gesture. "It's not right."

He sighed rather dramatically and pushed back his chair. "Wait. I have something that may help." He strode to her end of the table.

And then he knelt before her on one knee.

And pulled something from his jacket pocket.

She felt her eyes widen. "We just met!"

"I told you, I'm forty-five and life is short. Will you marry me, Cara?"

"This isn't fair. I haven't got my feet back on the ground yet. I'm—" She rotated her hand in the air, searching for words. "I'm in...in transition. You can't ask me this now!"

He smiled. "I know. I thought of all that. However, our joining forces is probably just what you need. First of all, you don't have a place to live."

True. She was living with Rubyann, sleeping on the hide-a-bed in her front room.

"I have this whole house. Secondly, you have no means of income."

True. She had plenty of time for volunteering though. "I have my savings, the fire insurance. My car."

"I have a monthly check that nicely feeds and clothes two."

"Bryan, I'm still not normal. I haven't left this neighborhood in two weeks. I still have nightmares. "

"I'm used to being called out in the middle of the night."

"You don't want me. I'm not ready."

His smile stretched into a grin. "I know what I want, and what I want is you. Up close. Personal. For my wife."

Her breath caught.

"I love you, Cara. Will you marry me, please? Soon?"

"Soon? Oh no! You're pushing me now— How soon is soon?"

"The church is absolutely breathtakingly beautiful at Christmastime."

"Christmas!"

"Like I said, I'm forty-five. I may turn forty-six by the time you answer me."

"Bryan." She heard love and disbelief and wonder and indecision in her tone.

"Hold on, darling. My knee is giving out." He switched his legs around in order to kneel on the other one. "Want to see the ring?"

As so often happened, he threw her off guard. She couldn't imagine trying to interrogate the man. "The ring?"

He held out a tiny box.

Had he really gone and bought a ring? "Okay. I'll look at it."

"Sorry." He snatched it out of her reach. "Not until you answer. I can't have you saying yes or no based on what you think of the ring."

"I know what you're doing. You think I'm so curious to see it I'll— I can't believe you really bought a ring. All by yourself?"

"Yes, all by myself. Call me old-fashioned, but this ring is symbolic of my undying love and my promise to cherish you forever. Not to mention an announcement to the world that you're spoken for."

She tried not to encourage him with a smile, but she could not help it. She loved that old-fashioned air hanging about him and his home. She loved the timelessness of his work. "My goodness, I suppose if I had parents, you would have asked them for my hand, even at my age."

"Well, actually I did that too."

"What?"

"Rubyann."

Of course. She bit her lip now to hold in the bubbly sensation threatening to spill out in laughter. "And she said?"

"Yes, that was fine with her. Mrs. G agreed. As did Marcus. Renae and Meagan cried. Flynn waffled a bit, but Ellen said he had no room to talk since she's married to a cop—"

"Bryan! They all know what you're doing?"

"How do you think I got them to put a turkey dinner on hold? I'm turning forty-six and the bird is drying out—"

"Yes!" She laughed. "Yes, I will marry you!"

His face turned somber. "Really?"

"Really. I love you, Bryan. I don't want to live my life without you." She leaned over and kissed him. "But think about it. I don't sing or play the organ or teach Sunday School or bake all that well. I won't easily fit in."

He smiled. "Just run my shelter for me?"

She stroked his face. "I would love to run your shelter. But it'll cost you."

"Anything."

"How about what you're holding in your hand?"

He laughed and opened the ring box.

Cara wasn't sure what she expected, but the diamond was perfect. A round solitaire on a simple gold band glinted in the chandelier's light. It was neither tiny nor large.

Perfect. Just like Bryan O'Shaugnessy.

The church was indeed absolutely breathtakingly beautiful at Christmastime.

On a December evening, Cara stood at the back entry clutching Marcus's black tuxedo sleeve. A glorious Telemann suite poured forth from strings and a flute, the instrumentalists all parishioners. What a find! The music soothed her nerves.

She peered over the shoulders of Terri and Renae, who stood before her in forest green satin. Her sweeping glance registered dimmed lights, glowing candles, gold embroidered tapestries, evergreen garlands, and wreaths. White poinsettias filled every nook and cranny. She focused on the Advent wreath near the pulpit, the lone purple and three pink candles lit in anticipation of the Christ child's birth.

A promise fulfilled and recalled year after year after year.

In a few minutes, she and Bryan would promise to love each other. *Lord, give us years to recall it together in honor of You.*

The place was packed. When she agreed to a December date, she hadn't counted on it being a big deal, but then she hadn't known the bishop would marry them. His presence always created somewhat of a big deal by adding extra formality. If she had comprehended the situation months in advance, she easily could have balked. Yes, Bryan knew what he was doing.

Neither of them wanted the attention of hundreds of people, but—as she was learning—a priest drew attention like a honeycomb did bees. His hundreds of congregants got wind of their engagement and before she realized what was happening, a full-fledged pre-Christmas wedding was in the works. An early Thanksgiving date allowed three weeks of preparation, plenty of time in which a legion of motivated women could perform. Cara wondered exactly how many surrogate mothers watched over Bryan.

Wanda Koski declared a buffet dinner in order and went about organizing one with some long-distance help from Bryan's mother. Talented donors came out of the woodwork and provided floral arrangements, cake, and music. No need for official invitations. They placed an announcement in the bulletin and newsletter; Gabe Andrews posted flyers at the fire stations, Helen spread the word in her domain. The only thing required of Cara was to shop for a dress and show up at the appointed time.

She dragged Renae and Terri along. Terri dragged Rachel Koski over from Iowa. They went to a suburban mall. Cara wasn't up for downtown shopping; the others understood. Rachel expertly steered them through the process and found a gown for herself for her February wedding.

Cara glanced down now at her dress. *Gown*, she corrected. If anyone expected frilly white and a puffy veil, they would be disappointed. But she wasn't, and she didn't think Bryan would be. Ivory in color, the straight, long-sleeved gown's only distinctions were a dropped waist, pouffy shoulders, and a zillion satin-covered buttons down the back. She wore her hair in a low bun, a circle of silk flowers around it, a short veil attached beneath it. Delicate teardrop pearl earrings dangled from her ears.

The music changed, the organ taking over with a Bach fugue. In the distance Bryan came into view. Her heart pounded a furious double-time beat, and she did not let her gaze linger. Behind him came his brother and TJ.

Terri turned slightly and smiled at her; then she proceeded to walk into the church, followed by Renae. Their gowns were simple, knee-length, fitted at the waist and long-sleeved. They carried single, long-stemmed red roses.

Cara watched the people turn. Rubyann was seated up front, in the mother-of-the bride's honored spot. Across the aisle from her sat Bryan's parents. Deirdre was warm and charming, a gentle spirit like her son. Flynn Sr. would take some work.

Cara saw Gabe, a proud smile on his face. The children beside him, his daughter and son, grinned unabashedly. Cara had met them. They loved Terri and knew the qualms she endured wearing a dress and walking in front of all those people.

Near them sat Rachel and her fiancé, Phil. Cara felt a rush of gratitude for the widow of Bryan's best friend, not only for her practical help but for her genuine acceptance of the new woman in Bryan's life. Though he told her there was nothing between them beyond that special connection in Vic and through his death, Cara had wondered if that sentiment was only his side of the story. Getting to know Rachel convinced her it was both sides of the story.

Cara found Helen. Seated in her row were Polly, Ruthie, and other homeless women she knew. She felt another overwhelming sense of gratitude, not only for their loyal friendship, but for the fact she had a home, one she could share because it was large and right next door to it was a forthcoming shelter of which she had already named herself director.

She glanced at other faces, some of them already familiar because she had seen them week after week in the services. There was Chief Templeton and his wife. She counted three pews of firefighters in dress uniform. She knew Bryan had counseled many of them.

Again she felt the absence of Jazzie, but at least she had a memento from her now. She kept the postcard in the *Book of Common Prayer* Bryan had given her as an engagement gift to replace the one lost in the fire. The card arrived in an envelope addressed to Dr. TJ Carlton at his Galena Territories condominium address. It was the type dentists sent out for appointment reminders with Garfield the comic strip cat holding a toothbrush, his grin nearly wider than his face. On the back she had written "No clouds on the horizon. The beach is great. God does take care of us. Love, Janie."

From the reference to clear weather Cara assumed Jazzie had seen the newspaper message. Although the postmark was from Atlanta, Cara guessed she had settled near a beach, on a coast. And she was finding God faithful.

Amen.

Marcus squeezed the hand she clutched around his elbow and whispered, "It's time."

She noticed then people rising to their feet and heard the change in music. Behind her Meagan—who, as it turned out, knew a thing or two about coordinating weddings—echoed his words in her other ear.

Marcus tilted his head to make eye contact. "Ready?"

She had asked Marcus to escort her down the aisle because she did not want to do it alone. She was finished with going at life alone. As her friend and partner, Marcus was the one to accompany her and present her to her best friend and new partner.

But he wasn't going to do it with that face.

"Calloway, try not to scare people away."

His expression softened with a smile. "You're going to ruin me, Fleming."

"I hope so." She winked. "Did you get it?"

"A whole carat. It's under the Christmas tree." He leaned over and planted a swift kiss on her cheek.

"Come on, Cucumber. Let's get this show on the road."

"Cara, will you have this man to be your husband…"

She smiled up at "this man" and saw a love she did not know until a few short weeks ago could possibly exist for her on earth.

"I will."

"Bryan, will you have this woman to be your wife…"

The look in his eyes said he was not disappointed in her choice of gown or hair arrangement.

But then, Bryan viewed life differently from most. She suspected a moth-eaten sweater or baggie muumuu would have elicited the same response.

"I will."

He was his most complete, handsome self wearing a black suit. The usual black shirt had been replaced with a distinctly dressier one. In place was the telltale collar, the symbol which elicited so many contradictory responses. Gone was her illusion that he could not find in her a suitable helpmate.

"Now that Cara and Bryan have given themselves to each other by solemn vows...I pronounce that they are husband and wife...Make their life together a sign of Christ's love to this sinful and broken world, that unity may overcome estrangement, forgiveness heal guilt, and joy conquer despair."

The beauty of their first communion together as husband and wife nearly broke her heart. That God would so liberally pour out His love and forgiveness upon her was more than it could contain. Grappling with the fact He had placed her beside Bryan, to be loved by those hundreds of parishioners behind her and to, in turn, love them sent tears down her cheeks.

Terri was right. Love did strange things to the hormones. Cara wondered again what she was signing up for.

And then Bryan smiled at her, reached over and gently pressed a handkerchief to her face.

"O God...Grant that by Your Holy Spirit, Cara and Bryan, now joined in Holy Matrimony, may become one in heart and soul..."

Amen.

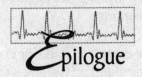

Epilogue

In the absolute middle of nowhere in Iowa, a light southerly breeze wafted across the deck, delivering the sweet scent of clover from some distant field. Under a cloudless July sky, Cara O'Shaugnessy, Terri Andrews, and Rachel Rockwell sat in white wicker chairs padded with yellow-and-green floral print cushions. Large orange tumblers of iced tea sat on a round, glass-topped table between them.

Rachel's granddaughter Victoria, aged two and a half, sat on Terri's lap. Her dark brown pigtails bounced as she eagerly chatted with Terri about golden retrievers.

Cara stood and stretched, rotating in a small circle. With few interruptions, cornfields rolled to the horizon in every direction. Behind the ground-level deck was the back of the Rockwells' two-story white farmhouse. Off to one side were red barns and outbuildings. In one of them now Phil was showing his new combine to Bryan and Gabe. Nearby a patch of willow trees ringed the edge of a pond. A bullfrog croaked, and a faint wind rustled the knee-high corn plants.

"Rachel, this country is amazing. I can't imagine living surrounded by all this quiet."

"I don't suppose Chicago church life is very quiet."

"No, not exactly." She chuckled. "And now with the shelter in full swing, our hands are full. But we're learning to pace each other. Mrs. G fusses at us if we get overdone."

"It's obvious being a rector's wife agrees with you."

"It does. The work fits me like a glove, and Bryan is..." smiling, she held our her arms and let them drop at her sides, "beyond description."

"I've never seen him happier. His Jesus vibes are stronger than ever. I'm so glad he found you."

She smiled. "Thanks. And how is the farmer's wife doing?"

"You mean besides gaining weight and throwing up every morning?"

Cara laughed. The pregnancy had been a welcome surprise to Rachel and Phil. "Yes, besides that."

"I love it. It's a change, of course, but it suits me like your new work suits you. God is good."

"He is that."

Rachel opened her mouth, closed it, and then reopened it. "How are you doing, Cara?"

Terri said, "Rache, you can ask her straight. You're wondering if she's still a basket case."

Rachel glanced skyward. "I don't know what happened to your bedside manner."

Terri laughed. "Hormones! Blew them to bits! Isn't that right, Victoria?" She nuzzled the little girl's neck and was rewarded with a squeal of delight.

"Speaking of hormones, Miss Uncomfortable with Kids." Rachel's grin was sly. "Maybe they're changing your attitude?"

Terri made a noise of disbelief. "In your dreams, Grandma."

Rachel ignored her. "Cara, I wouldn't word my question quite like that."

"I know." She smiled. "Terri tries her utmost *not* to molly-coddle me. Which is a good thing. Bryan does too much of it. Anyway, I don't mind you asking. The nightmares come less often now. Bryan has taken me to Water Tower Place three times, and I have lived to tell about it. By the time Ian Stafford's trial takes place, I should be in good shape to testify." She still didn't know why the man hadn't been killed by his former associates even while he waited in jail. Perhaps her husband's visits to him left Jesus vibes palpitating around the man, warding off evil.

Terri said, "Hey, Cara, you're making me nervous pacing around like that. Isn't this the start of your belated honeymoon? You're supposed to relax. Why don't you sit down?"

"Because my groom has been out of sight for thirty minutes. Excuse me."

Terri and Rachel's laughter trailed behind her as she bounded off the low deck and strode through the yard. As if on cue, Bryan exited the barn and walked toward her. She grinned. Perhaps a month on the road driving cross-country would cure them of the mutual, incessant desire to be together.

They were going to visit Father and Mrs. Palmer in Seattle, the Lopezes in Los Angeles, and, in San Diego, her long-lost sister located by Ray, the private investigator. Cara had called each one; their eagerness for a reunion heartened her own.

She would always hold things loosely, but never again relationships. If home consisted of the ones she loved, then the time had come to rebuild bridges and to link them with her husband.

She ran to him now.

Grinning from ear to ear, Bryan scooped her into his arms and twirled around.

She knew she was home to stay.

Dear Reader,

I hope you've enjoyed our journeys with Rachel, Terri, and Cara, and that your time away in fiction was a rewarding respite from the world. I hope too that it fed your soul with the truth of Christ's love for us.

I always enjoy hearing how the stories touched you. Please feel free to contact me at:

sallyjohnbook@aol.com

or

www.sally-john.com

or

c/o Harvest House Publishers
990 Owen Loop North
Eugene, OR 97402-9173

Current plans call for the beginning of a new series. Lord willing, we can meet next in San Diego, California, in The Beach House series. For you Midwestern fans, I apologize in advance for the lack of snowstorms.

Peace be with you,

Sally John

Discussion Questions

Cara's story is one of homelessness, both the internal and external aspects of it. She identifies with those who live on the streets because she feels she herself is without a home, a place she belongs, where she is loved and accepted, where her soul can rest.

She believes the longing for home is built into hearts and that God will fulfill it after we leave this earthly life. Not until near the end of the story, though, does she overcome her fears and begin to allow herself to believe He would grant her a taste of home in the here and now.

1. How do you define home?

2. Why does Cara resist remaining in Chicago? How is her mind changed?

3. Does something from your past dictate today's decisions?

4. Besides the fear factor, Cara does not feel worthy enough to receive love and earthly comforts. Why is this?

5. Does something prevent you from accepting another's love?

6. How does Cara guard against becoming too unfeeling? Obviously in her police work she must temper compassion with the necessity for lawbreakers to pay consequences. Is there an area in your life where such a balance is necessary? How do you handle it?

7. So often forgiveness is the key to unlock the gate to change. How does this happen in Cara's life? Have you experienced it yourself?

8. What is your attitude toward the homeless and indigent?

9. What does your community or church do for people in these situations? Do you help in any way or have a desire to do so?

10. And then there's Bryan. What did you think of him?

Books by Sally John

THE OTHER WAY HOME SERIES

A Journey by Chance
After All These Years
Just to See You Smile
The Winding Road Home

IN A HEARTBEAT SERIES

In a Heartbeat
Flash Point
Moment of Truth

Sally John is a former teacher and the author of several books, including the popular books of The Other Way Home series and the In a Heartbeat series. Sally and her husband, Tim, live in the country surrounded by woods and cornfields. The Johns have two grown children, a daughter-in-law, and a granddaughter.